W9-API-342

J. Johnson
Trlr. 2
4325 Lenville Rd.
Moscow, ID 83843-7844

PARADISE
LOST

Books by J. A. Jance

Joanna Brady Mysteries

DESERT HEAT
TOMBSTONE COURAGE
SHOOT/DON'T SHOOT
DEAD TO RIGHTS
SKELETON CANYON
RATTLESNAKE CROSSING
OUTLAW MOUNTAIN
DEVIL'S CLAW
PARADISE LOST

J. P. Beaumont Mysteries

UNTIL PROVEN GUILTY
INJUSTICE FOR ALL
TRIAL BY FURY
TAKING THE FIFTH
IMPROBABLE CAUSE
A MORE PERFECT UNION
DISMISSED WITH PREJUDICE
MINOR IN POSSESSION
PAYMENT IN KIND
WITHOUT DUE PROCESS
FAILURE TO APPEAR
LYING IN WAIT
NAME WITHHELD
BREACH OF DUTY
BIRDS OF PREY

and

HOUR OF THE HUNTER
KISS OF THE BEES

PARADISE LOST

J. A. JANCE

KINDRED NURSING & REHABILITATION
ASPEN PARK HEALTHCARE
420 ROWE ST
MOSCOW, ID 83843

wm

WILLIAM MORROW
75 YEARS OF PUBLISHING
An Imprint of HarperCollins*Publishers*

2001

PARADISE LOST. Copyright © 2001 by J. A. Jance. All rights reserved. Printed in the United States of America. No part of this book may be used or reproduced in any manner whatsoever without written permission except in the case of brief quotations embodied in critical articles and reviews. For information address HarperCollins Publishers Inc., 10 East 53rd Street, New York, NY 10022.

HarperCollins books may be purchased for educational, business, or sales promotional use. For information please write: Special Markets Department, HarperCollins Publishers Inc., 10 East 53rd Street, New York, NY 10022.

Designed by Sarah Maya Gubkin

ISBN 0-380-97729-X

For LaVerne Williams
and in memory of Rose and Lyn Bennett
in thanks for their years of devotion to Scouting

PARADISE
LOST

PROLOGUE

C onnie Haskell had just stepped out of the shower when she heard the phone ringing. Hoping desperately to hear Ron's voice on the phone, she grabbed a towel and raced through the house, leaving a trail of wet footprints on the worn carpeting of the bedroom and hallway. For two weeks she had carried the cordless phone with her wherever she went, but when she had gone to the bathroom to shower that morning, she had forgotten somehow and left the phone sitting beside her empty coffee cup on the kitchen table.

By the time she reached the kitchen, the machine had already picked up the call. "Hello, Mrs. Haskell. This is Ken Wilson at First Bank." The disembodied voice of Connie's private banker echoed eerily across the Saltillo tile in an otherwise silent kitchen. As soon as she heard the caller's voice and knew it wasn't her husband's, Connie didn't bother to pick up the receiver. It was the same thing she had done with all the other calls that had come in during this awful time. She had sat, a virtual prisoner in her own home, waiting for the other shoe to drop. But this call from her banker probably wasn't it.

"I'm calling about your checking account," Ken Wilson continued. "As of this morning, it's seriously overdrawn. I've paid the two outstanding checks that showed up today as well as one from yesterday, but I need you to come in as soon as possible and make a deposit. If you're out of town, please call me so we can make some other arrangement to cover the overdraft. I believe you have my number, but in case you don't, here it is."

As Ken Wilson recited his direct phone number, Connie slipped unhearing onto a nearby kitchen stool. In all the years she had handled her parents' affairs—paying bills and writing checks after her father had been incapacitated by that first crippling stroke and then for her mother after

Stephen Richardson's death—in all that time, Connie had never once bounced a check. She had written the checks and balanced the checkbooks each month under Stephen's watchful and highly critical eye. Because of stroke-induced aphasia, her father had been able to do nothing but shake his head, roll his eyes, and spit out an occasional "Stupid." But Connie had persevered. She had done the task month after month for years. After her marriage to Ron, when he had volunteered to take over the bill-paying, she had been only too happy to relinquish that onerous duty. And why not? Ron was an accountant, wasn't he? Dealing with numbers was what CPAs did.

Except Ron had been gone for two weeks now—AWOL. For two long, agonizing weeks there had been no word to Connie. No telephone call. No letter. She hadn't reported him missing because she was ashamed and afraid. Ashamed because other people had been right about him and she'd been wrong, and afraid she might learn that there was another woman involved. The woman was bound to be far younger and far better-looking than Constance Marie Richardson Haskell. She was unable to delude herself into thinking there was a chance of foul play. No, Connie had made a point of checking Ron's carefully organized side of the closet. Her missing husband had simply packed one of his roll-aboard suitcases with a selection of slacks and custom-made, monogrammed shirts, and left.

The main reason Connie had kept silent about his absence was that she didn't want to have to face up to all those people who had told her so. And they *had* told her so—in spades. Any number of friends and relations had tried, both subtly and not so subtly, to explain that they thought Connie was making a mistake in marrying so soon after her mother's death. Connie's older sister, Maggie—someone who never suffered from a need to keep her opinions to herself—had been by far the most outspoken.

"If you ask me, Ron Haskell's nothing but a gold-digging no-account," Maggie MacFerson had said. "He worked for Peabody and Peabody for six months before Mother died. He knew everything about Mother's financial affairs, and now he knows everything about yours. He also knows how naive you are, and he's taking you for a ride. For him, you're nothing but a meal ticket."

"We fell in love," Connie had declared hotly, as if that one fact alone should resolve all her older sister's concerns. "Besides, Ron's resigning from the firm, so there can't be any question of conflict of interest."

In response, Maggie MacFerson had blown an exasperated plume of smoke in the air. She shook her head and rolled her eyes. When she did that, she looked so much like Stephen Richardson that Connie had expected to hear her father's familiar pronouncement of "Stupid!"

"We all have to make our own mistakes, I suppose," Maggie said with a resigned sigh. "At least do yourself a favor and get a pre-nup agreement."

That was the one and only time the two sisters had discussed Ron Haskell. Naturally, Connie hadn't followed Maggie's advice. She hadn't wanted to ask for a prenuptial agreement because she was afraid if she mentioned it, Ron might think she didn't trust him, which she did—absolutely and with all the lovesick fervor of a forty-two-year-old woman who had never fallen in love before, not even once.

But now, sitting alone in the house on Southeast Encanto Drive—a house that had once belonged to Stephen and Claudia Richardson but that now belonged to Connie and Ron Haskell—she suddenly felt sick to her stomach. What if Maggie had been right about Ron? What if his disappearance had nothing to do with another woman and everything to do with money? What if, in the end, that was all Ron had wanted from Connie—her money?

As soon as the thought surfaced, Connie shook her still-dripping hair and pushed that whole demeaning notion aside. Surely that couldn't be. And whatever was going on at the bank was all a simple mistake of some kind. Maybe there had been a computer glitch, a virus or something. Those happened, didn't they? Or else maybe Ron had merely forgotten to transfer money from one of the investment accounts into the household bill-paying account.

By then, the answering machine had clicked off, leaving the light blinking to say there was a message, which Connie had already heard and had no need to hear again. The solution was perfectly simple. All Connie had to do was call Ken Wilson back and tell him to make the necessary transfer. Once she did that, everything would be fine. Connie could return to her lonely vigil of waiting for Ron himself to call or for some police officer somewhere to call and say that Ron was dead and ask her to come and identify the body.

Taking a deep breath, Connie grabbed the phone. She punched in *69 and let the phone redial Ken Wilson's number. He answered on the second ring. "Ken Wilson here."

"Ken, it's Connie," she said, keeping her tone brisk and businesslike. "Connie Haskell. Sorry I missed your call. I was in the shower. By the time I found the phone, your call had already gone to the machine. I can't imagine what's going on with the checking account. Ron is out of town at the moment. He must have forgotten to make a transfer. I'd really appreciate it if you could just handle that for us—the transfer, I mean. I'm not sure what checks are outstanding, so I don't know exactly how much is needed."

"Which account do you want to use to transfer funds?" Ken asked.

Connie didn't like the guarded way he said that. It sounded wary and ominous. "You know," she said. "We always transfer out of that one investment account. I can't remember the number exactly. I think it's nine-four-something."

"That would be account number nine-four, three-three-three, two-six-two. Is that right?"

Connie could barely contain her relief. "That's right," she breathed. "I'm sure that's the one."

"But that account was closed two months ago," Ken Wilson returned.

Suddenly Connie felt her pulse pounding in her throat. "Closed?" she stammered. "It was?"

"Why, yes. I thought you knew that. Mr. Haskell came in and closed all your accounts except for the checking. He said that you had decided to go with another banking institution, but since you had all the automatic withdrawals scheduled from that account, he'd leave just that one as is for the time being. He closed all the investment accounts, as well as taking all the CDs. I advised against it, of course, especially the CDs, but . . ."

"He closed them all?" Connie asked incredulously.

"Yes. After all the years I'd been looking after your family's accounts, I was personally very disappointed. I thought we'd done a good job of handling things for you and your parents both, but I didn't feel it was my place to argue with your husband."

The kitchen seemed to swirl around her. Connie closed her eyes in an effort to stop the spinning. "Which checks?" she asked woodenly.

"I beg your pardon?"

"Which checks are overdrawn?" she asked. Connie knew that she hadn't written any checks since Ron had disappeared. Unless he had the checkbook with him and was still writing checks, the overdrafts most likely had come from some of those automatic deductions.

"One to Blue Cross, one to Regency Auto Lease, and the third is to Prudential," Ken told her.

Connie nodded. Their health insurance premium, the lease on Ron's car—his new BMW 740i—and their long-term care. After years of being the unpaid maid-of-all-work for her ailing and eventually bedridden parents, Connie Haskell had been determined to have the wherewithal to pay for long-term care for both herself and her husband should they ever reach a point where their own declining health required it. It was the one purchase she had insisted she and Ron make as soon as they returned from their honeymoon.

"How much?" she asked.

"The total outstanding?" Ken returned.

Connie nodded wordlessly, although her private banker couldn't see that.

"Let's see," he said. "That's eighteen hundred forty-six dollars and seventy-two cents, including the service charges. Under most circumstances I'd be happy to waive the service charges, but since we no longer have any of your other business . . ."

He let the rest of the sentence hang in the air. Meanwhile Connie, grappling with finding a way to fix the problem, wrote down the amount he had mentioned.

"What about my credit card?" she asked. "Can we transfer the money in from my VISA?"

Ken Wilson cleared his throat. "There's a problem there, too, Connie," he said apologetically. "Your VISA account is over the limit right now, and the payment was due yesterday. That's another seventeen hundred sixty dollars and forty-three cents. That would just bring the balance down to where you wouldn't be over your limit."

As Ken Wilson spoke, Connie was remembering how Ron had encouraged her to sign application forms for several other credit cards—ones that evidently weren't with First Bank. "Even if we never touch them," Ron had told her, "we're better off having them available." And indeed, if any of those applications had been approved, the resulting credit cards had never made it into her hands or purse. And if her VISA at First Bank was maxed out, what about balances on the other cards—ones Connie had no record of and no way to check?

I won't think about that right now, Connie told herself firmly as she wrote down the second figure. After adding that one together with the first, she arrived at a total of $3,607.15. Swallowing hard, Connie drew a circle around it.

"Your office is still on Central, isn't it?" she asked.

"That's right," Ken Wilson replied. "Central and Camelback."

"And how long will you be there?"

"I have an appointment out of the office this afternoon, but that won't be until one o'clock. I'll need to leave here around twelve-thirty."

"All I have to do is dry my hair and throw on some clothes," Connie told him. "I should be there with the money within forty-five minutes."

She heard Ken Wilson's sigh of relief. "Good," he said. "I'll be looking forward to seeing you."

Connie hung up the phone. Then, with her whole body quaking and unmindful of her still-dripping hair, she walked back through the house. She went to the room which had once been her mother's study—the green-walled cozy room which had, after her mother's death, become

Connie's study as well. With trembling hands she opened the bottom drawer of the dainty rosewood desk and pulled out her mother's frayed, leather-bound Bible. One by one she began to remove the old-fashioned but still crisp hundred-dollar bills that had been concealed between many of the thin pages. Claudia Armstrong Richardson had told her daughter the story so many times that even now Connie could have repeated it verbatim.

Claudia had often related how, as an eleven-year-old, her idyllic life had been shattered when she awoke that fateful morning in October of 1929 to learn that her once affluent family was affluent no longer. Her father had lost everything in the stock market crash. There had been a single payment of three hundred dollars due on the family home in Columbus, Ohio, but without sufficient cash to make that one payment, the bank had foreclosed. Months later, the day they were scheduled to move out of the house, Claudia's father had gone back inside—to make sure the back door was locked, he had told his wife and daughter. Instead, with Claudia and her mother waiting in a cab outside, Roger Armstrong had gone back into the empty room that had once been his book-lined library and put a bullet through his head.

"So you see, Constance," Claudia had cautioned her daughter over and over, "you must keep some money set aside, and not just in banks, either, because many of the banks were forced to close back then, too. The only people who were all right were the ones who had cold, hard cash put away under their mattresses or hidden in a sock. You have to keep the money someplace where you can get your hands on it when you need it."

Over the years, long after Claudia had married Stephen Richardson and long after there was no longer any valid need for her to be concerned about such things, Claudia Armstrong Richardson had continued to put money in the Bible, right up until her death, insisting that Connie put the money there for her once Claudia herself was no longer able to do so.

There were times Connie had argued with her mother about it. "Wouldn't it be safer in a bank?" she had asked.

"No!" Claudia had declared heatedly. "Absolutely not."

"What if the house burns down?"

"Then I'll get a new Bible and start over," Claudia had retorted.

After her mother's death, Connie had left Claudia's Bible as it was and where it was—in the bottom drawer of the desk. It had seemed disrespectful to her mother's memory to do anything else. Now, as Connie counted some of those carefully hoarded bills into a neat pile, she was glad she had abided by her mother's wishes. She had told no one of her mother's private stash—not her father, not her sister, and not even her new husband.

When Connie had counted out enough money to cover her debt, she started to put the Bible back in the drawer. Then, thinking better of it, she took it with her. In the kitchen, she stuffed the Bible into her capacious purse. After hurriedly drying her hair and slathering on some makeup, she dressed and headed off for her meeting with Ken Wilson. Twenty minutes later she was standing in the foyer of the private banking offices of First Bank of the Southwest. At that point, Connie had her involuntary quaking pretty well under control.

Ken Wilson himself came out to greet her and take her back to his private office. "I hope this hasn't troubled you too much, Connie," he said kindly.

She gave her banker what she hoped passed as a supremely confident smile as he showed her to a chair. "Oh, no," she said, willing her face not to reveal the depth of her humiliation. "It's no trouble at all. I'm sure this is nothing more than an oversight on Ron's part. He was called out of town on business and ended up being gone longer than either of us intended. I expect to speak to him later on today, and we'll get this whole thing straightened out. In the meantime, I brought along enough cash to dig us out of the hole."

Carefully she counted out thirty-seven hundred-dollar bills. As she pushed them across the smooth surface of Ken's desk, the banker cleared his throat. "I took the liberty of looking at your account again," he said. "There's another four hundred dollars' worth of life insurance premiums that will be deducted within the next two days. Do you want to deposit enough to cover those as well?"

Grateful she had brought along the Bible, Connie extracted four more bills and shoved them over to Ken Wilson. "Good," he said. "Very good." He stood up. "If you'll wait just a moment, I'll be right back with your change and a receipt."

Connie nodded and then sat staring out the window at traffic rushing by until he returned. He handed her the receipt and carefully counted out the change.

"If you'll forgive my saying so," he said hesitantly, "it sounded as though you had no idea these monies were being transferred from First Bank. I trust there isn't some kind of problem. I mean, your family—you and your parents—have been good customers for a very long time—since long before First Bank became First Bank, as a matter of fact. I'd hate to think we had allowed something untoward to happen, although, since the accounts were all joint accounts—"

"Oh no," Connie interrupted, answering too quickly and too brightly. She wanted to ask where the funds had gone, but she fought that one down. She didn't want to admit to Ken Wilson that she had been kept totally in the dark. She didn't want to admit to being that irresponsibly stupid. "If Ron decided to move the funds, I'm sure he must have had a good reason," she continued. "As soon as I talk to him, we'll have the whole thing ironed out."

"Good, then," Ken Wilson said. "I'm glad to hear it."

Connie grabbed her purse and fled Ken Wilson's office. She dashed through the marble-floored bank lobby and sank gratefully into the overheated leather of her mother's oversized Lincoln Town Car. Although it was not yet the end of May, the Valley of the Sun had been sweltering in triple-digit temperatures for almost two weeks. Even so, Connie felt chilled. When she switched on the engine, she quickly turned off the air conditioner and opened the window, letting in a blast of broiling outside air.

Joint accounts! she chided herself. She had done that on purpose, too. In a fit of defiance, Connie had put Ron on as a signatory to all her accounts just to spite people like her sister Maggie and the other naysayers who had told her Ron was only after her money. Had she listened? Had she paid any of them the slightest bit of heed? No. Her father had been right after all. She *was* stupid—unbelievably stupid. She had taken everything Ron Haskell told her as gospel, and he had betrayed her. Other women might have railed and cried and blamed their betrayers. Driving back home, her eyes dry and gritty with unshed tears, Constance Marie Richardson Haskell blamed only herself.

Once in the house, Connie saw the blinking light on the answering machine as soon as she put her car keys and purse down on the kitchen counter. Hurrying to the machine, she punched the play button. First came Ken Wilson's message, which she had already heard but had failed to erase. She fast-forwarded through that one. Then, after a click, she heard Ron's voice, and her heart leaped in her throat.

"Connie," he said. "It's Ron. I don't know if you're there or not. If you are, please pick up." There was a pause, then he continued. "I guess you're not. I don't know where to start, Connie, honey. I'm so sorry. About everything. I'm at a place called Pathway to Paradise. I thought these people could help me, and they are—helping me, that is. It's going to take time, and I want to talk to you about it, Connie. I want to explain. Maybe you'll be able to forgive me, or maybe not. I don't know.

"I can't leave here, because I've made a commitment to stay for the full two months, but it would mean so much to me if you would come here to see me. That way I can be the one to tell you what happened instead of your having to hear it from somebody else. Please come, Connie. Please, preferably this evening. Pathway to Paradise is at the far end of the Chiricahua Mountains, just outside Portal on the road to Paradise. It's north of town on the right-hand side of the road. You'll see the sign. Wait for me along the road, sometime between nine and ten, and—"

At that point an operator's voice cut in on Ron's. "If you wish to speak longer you'll have to deposit an additional one dollar and sixty-five cents."

"Please," Ron added.

And then the answering machine clicked off. For almost a minute afterward, Connie stood staring blankly at the machine, then she began to quake once more.

Connie Richardson Haskell was a woman who had always prided herself on keeping her emotions under control. Her father had expected it of her. After all those years under her father's tutelage, Connie had come to expect it of herself. The whole time she had cared for her aging and at times entirely unreasonable parents, she had never once allowed herself to become angry.

But now anger roared through her system with a ferocity that left her shaken. It filled her whole being like an avalanche plunging down the throat of some narrow, rock-lined gorge. *How dare he! After disappearing for two weeks without a word, after taking my money without permission, now he calls and expects me to come running the moment he crooks his finger and says he's sorry?*

Finally she nodded. "I'll be happy to join you in Paradise, you son of a bitch," she muttered grimly. "But I'm going to bring along a little surprise."

With that, she turned and walked into the bedroom. There, behind one of her mother's vivid watercolors, was Stephen Richardson's hidden wall safe. Inside the safe was her father's well-oiled .357 Magnum. Connie didn't need to check to see if the gun was loaded. Stephen Richardson had always maintained that having an unloaded weapon in the house was as useless as having a plumber's helper with no handle.

Not taking the time to shut the safe or rehang the painting, Connie walked back to the kitchen, where she stuffed the pistol into her purse right next to her mother's Bible. Then, without a backward glance and without bothering to lock up the house, turn on the alarm, or even make sure the door was firmly closed, Connie went back out to Claudia's Town Car. Her father had always insisted on keeping a Rand McNally *Road Atlas* in the pocket behind the seat. Connie pulled out the atlas and studied the map of Arizona until she located the tiny dots that indicated Portal and Paradise. After charting a route, she put the atlas back in its spot and climbed into the driver's seat.

This time, when she switched on the engine, she turned on the air conditioner as well. Until that moment, Connie Richardson Haskell had thought the term "heat of anger" was only a figure of speech.

Now she knew better.

Slamming the big car into reverse, she tore out of the garage and headed for Pathway to Paradise to find her husband. As she drove down the citrus- and palm-tree-lined street and away from the house that had been her home her whole life, Connie didn't bother to look back, and she didn't notice that the garage door had failed to close. There was no reason to look back. It was almost as though she knew she was finished with the house and the neighborhood, and they were finished with her. No matter what happened, Connie Richardson Haskell wouldn't be returning. Ever.

1

At one o'clock Friday morning, Sheriff Joanna Brady let herself back into the two-room suite at the Marriott Hotel in Page, Arizona. Butch Dixon, her husband of a month and a little bit, lay sound asleep on the bed with his laptop computer sitting open in front of him. The laptop was evidently sleeping every bit as soundly as Butch.

Joanna kicked off her high heels and then stood still, gratefully wiggling her cramped toes in the plush carpet. Butch had the room's air conditioner turned down as low as it could go, and the room was pleasantly cool. Joanna took off her jacket and sniffed it. Wrinkling her nose in distaste, she tossed it over the back of the desk chair. It reeked so of cigar and cigarette smoke that she'd need to dry-clean the suit before she could wear it again. But, after an evening spent playing cutthroat poker with fellow members of the Arizona Sheriffs' Association, what else could she expect?

Peeling off her skirt and blouse, she draped those over the chair as well, hoping that hanging out in the air-conditioned room overnight would remove at least some of the stale-smelling smoke. Then, going over to the dresser, she peered at herself in the mirror. There was an impish gleam in her green eyes that even the lateness of the hour failed to dim. Reaching into her bra, she plucked a wad of bills, along with some change, from one of the cups. After counting the money, she found the total amounted to a little over two hundred dollars. Those were her winnings culled from all but one of her poker-playing opponents and fellow Arizona sheriffs. Leaving that money on the dresser, she removed a much larger wad from the other cup of her bra. That was the money she had won from one poker player in particular, Pima County Sheriff William Forsythe.

That sum came to just under five hundred dollars, $488.50, to be exact. Over the course of the evening, the other players had dropped out one by one until finally it had been just the two of them, Joanna Brady and Bill Forsythe, squaring off. It had done Joanna's heart good to clean the man's clock.

For the first two years of her administration, Joanna had kept a low profile in the Arizona Sheriffs' Association. She had come to the annual meetings, but she had stayed away from the camaraderie of the association's traditional poker party. This year, though, fresh from yet another slight at the hands of the obnoxious Sheriff Forsythe and his department, she had gone to the meeting intent on duking it out with the man over beer, cards, and poker chips.

Joanna Lathrop Brady had learned to play poker at her father's knee. Cochise County Sheriff D. H. "Big Hank" Lathrop had been a skilled player. Lacking a son with whom to share his poker-playing knowledge, he had decided to pass that legacy on to his daughter. To begin with, Joanna hadn't been all that interested. Once her mother, Eleanor, began voicing strenuous objections, however, Joanna had become far more enthusiastic. She had, in fact, turned into an apt pupil and an avid devotee. Now, years after Big Hank's death, his patiently taught lessons were still paying off.

Quietly easing the door shut behind her, Joanna hurried into the bathroom, stripped off the remainder of her clothing, and then stepped into a steaming shower. When she returned from the bathroom with a towel wrapped around her head and clad in one of the hotel's terry-cloth robes, Butch had closed the laptop, stripped off his own clothes, and was back in bed.

"Sorry," she said. "I didn't mean to wake you."

"That's all right," he said. "I wasn't really asleep. So how's my red-headed dynamo, and what time is it?"

"Your redhead is great, thank you," she told him crisply. "And the time is just past one."

"How'd you do?"

Smiling smugly, Joanna walked over to the dresser and retrieved both wads of money. She handed Butch the smaller of the two, giving him a brief peck on his clean-shaven head in the process. "Whoa," he said, thumbing through the money. "There must be two hundred bucks here."

"Two hundred eleven and some change," Joanna replied with a grin.

"Not bad for a girl." Butch Dixon smiled back at her. He had been only too aware of the grudge-match status behind his wife's determination to join the poker game. "How much of this used to belong to Sheriff Forsythe?" Butch added.

"Some of *that,*" Joanna told him triumphantly. "But *all* of this." She plunked the other chunk of money down on Butch's chest. Then she went around to her side of the bed, peeled off the robe, and crawled in. Sitting with her pillow propped against the headboard, she began toweling her hair dry.

On his side of the bed, Butch started counting the money and then gave up. "How much?" he asked.

"Four eighty-eight."

Butch whistled. "And all of this is his?"

Joanna dropped the towel. Naked and still damp, she lowered her pillow and snuggled up against Butch's side. "He deserved it, too," she said. "Bill Forsythe was drunk. He was showing off and making stupid bets. Eventually everybody but the two of us dropped out, but they all hung around to watch the fireworks. The drunker Bill got, the worse he played. I wound up wiping the floor with him."

"Beating the pants off Sheriff Forsythe isn't going to do much for interdepartmental relations, is it?" Butch asked.

Joanna giggled. "He never was a fan of mine to begin with. This isn't likely to make things any worse. They were already in the toilet anyway."

"You just added salt to the wound."

"He shouldn't have said I was hysterical," Joanna said, referring to an incident that had occurred a good two months earlier.

"And some people shouldn't pack grudges," Butch replied. "So now that you've won all this cash, what are you going to do with it? It's almost seven hundred dollars."

"I was thinking about that while I was in the shower," Joanna said. "I think I'll do something Bill Forsythe wouldn't be caught dead doing. I think I'll donate the whole amount to the Girl Scouts. Jenny's troop is trying to raise enough money for a trip to Disneyland at the end of the summer, just before school starts. Seven hundred dollars that they weren't expecting would give them a big leg up."

"Speaking of Scouts, Eva Lou called."

Eva Lou and Jim Bob Brady, Joanna's former in-laws and her daughter's paternal grandparents, were staying out at High Lonesome Ranch to look after the house and the animals during Joanna's and Butch's absence at the Sheriffs' Association conference and for the remainder of the weekend as well.

Joanna raised herself up on one elbow. "Is something the matter with Jenny?" she asked, as a note of alarm crept into her voice. Being away from her daughter for extended periods of time still made her nervous.

"Nothing's the matter," Butch reassured her. "Nothing to worry about, anyway. It's just that because of the severe drought conditions, the

Forest Service has posted a statewide no-campfire restriction. They're closing the public campgrounds. No fires of any kind will be permitted."

"Great," Joanna said glumly. "I suppose that means the end of Jenny's camp-out. She was really looking forward to it. She said she thought she'd be able to finish up the requirements on two separate badges."

"Surely you can give Faye Lambert more credit than that."

Faye Lambert, wife of the newly appointed pastor of Bisbee's First Presbyterian Church, had stepped into the vacuum left by two departing leaders. After recruiting one of the mothers to be assistant leader, she had succeeded in infusing new life into Jenny's floundering Girl Scout troop.

"According to what Eva Lou said, the camp-out is still on. They just won't be cooking outdoors, and they won't be staying in regular camp-grounds, either. Faye has managed to borrow somebody's RV. They'll camp out on private land over near Apache Pass. The girls will be doing their cooking in the motor home, and they'll have indoor bathroom facilities to boot. All they'll be missing is the joy of eating food that's been incinerated over open coals. No s'mores, I guess," he added.

"Oh," Joanna said. "That's a relief then."

"And Eva Lou said something else," Butch added. "She said to tell you she managed to find Jenny's sit-upon. What the hell is a sit-upon?"

"Jenny will kill me," Joanna said at once. "The girls made them years ago when they were still in Brownies. Jenny wanted me to throw hers away the minute she brought it home, but I insisted on keeping it. Because it was up on the top shelf of Jenny's closet, it didn't get wrecked along with everything else when Reba Singleton did her job on the house."

Days before Joanna and Butch's wedding, a distraught woman who blamed Joanna for her father's death had broken into the house on High Lonesome Ranch, leaving a trail of vandalism and destruction in her wake. Although Reba had wrecked everything she could lay hands on in the rest of the house, she had left Jenny's bedroom entirely untouched—including, as it turned out, Jenny's much despised sit-upon.

"You still haven't told me what a sit-upon is," Butch grumbled.

"The girls made them—as part of an arts-and-crafts project—by sewing together two twelve-by-twelve-inch squares of vinyl. Jenny's happens to be fire-engine red, but there were several other colors as well. The girls used white yarn to whipstitch the two pieces of vinyl together. Once three sides were sewn together, the square was stuffed with cotton batting. Then they closed the square by stitching up the last side. And, *voilà!* The next time the girls go out into the woods, they have a sit-upon to sit upon."

"I see," Butch said. "So what's the matter with Jenny's? Why did she want you to get rid of hers?"

"You know Jenny, how impatient she is—always in a rush. She did fine with the stitches on the first side. They're really even and neat. On the second side the stitches get a little longer and a little more ragged. By the third side it's even worse. On the last side, there were barely enough stitches to hold the batting inside."

"In other words, it's pug-ugly."

"Right. That's why she wanted me to throw it away. But I maintain that if I'm going to keep mementos for her, I should keep both good stuff and bad. It's what Eleanor did for me. I knew Faye Lambert had put sit-upons on the list of required equipment for the camp-out. Knowing Jenny's feelings on the matter, I had planned to just ignore it, but Eva Lou isn't the kind to ignore something if it happens to be on an official list of required equipment."

"That's right," Butch agreed with a laugh. "Eva Lou Brady's not the ignoring type."

He wrapped an arm around Joanna's shoulder and pulled her five-foot-four frame close to him. "The poker game was obviously an unqualified success. How did the rest of your day go?"

Joanna sighed. "I spent the whole afternoon in a terminally boring meeting run by a nerdy little guy who's never been in law enforcement in his life. His job—as an overpaid 'outside' consultant from someplace back East—Massachusetts, I think—is to get us to sign up our departments for what his company has to offer."

"Which is?"

"They do what he calls 'team building' workshops. For some exorbitant amount of money, everyone in the department is cycled through a 'rigorous outdoor experience' where they learn to 'count' on each other. What the hell does he think we do out there day after day, sell lollipops? And what makes him think I can afford to pay my people to go off camping in the boonies instead of patrolling the county? He claims the experience 'creates an atmosphere of trust and team spirit.' I felt like telling him that I'm a sheriff, not a cheerleader, but some of the other guys were really gung-ho about it."

"Bill Forsythe's such a cool macho dude," Butch offered. "That program sounds like it would be right up his alley."

"You're on the money there," Joanna said. "He and a couple of the other guys are ready to write the program into their budgets the minute they get back home. Maybe their budgets can handle it. Mine can't. I've got my hands and budget full trying to deal with the ten thousand Undocumented Aliens who come through Cochise County every month. What about you?"

Butch grinned. "Personally speaking, I don't have a UDA problem."

Joanna whacked him on the chest. "You know what I mean. What did you do today?"

She glanced at the clock. In anticipation of the late-night poker session, she had drunk several cups of coffee during dinner. Now, at almost two in the morning, that dose of late-in-the-day caffeine showed no signs of wearing off.

"Nothing much," Butch replied.

"You mean you didn't go antiquing with the wives?"

Butch shook his head. "Nope. You know me and antiques. I opted out of that one."

"Golfing, then? I heard somebody raving about the golf course here." Butch shook his head. "No golfing," he said.

"Did you go someplace then?" Joanna asked.

"We drove up to Page in a county-owned vehicle," Butch reminded her. "That makes it a vehicle I'm not allowed to drive, remember?"

Joanna winced. "Sorry," she said. "I forgot. So what did you do?"

"I finished."

"Finished what?"

"The manuscript."

For over a year Butch had been working on his first novel, banging away at it on his Toshiba laptop whenever he could find time to spare. He had even taken the computer along on their honeymoon trip to Paris the previous month. He had spent the early-morning hours working while Joanna had reveled in the incredible luxury of sleeping in. Shy about showing a work in progress, Butch had refused to allow anyone to read the text while he was working on it, and that had included Joanna. Over the months she had come to regard his work on the computer as one of those things Butch *did*. In the process, she had lost track of the idea that eventually his book might be *done* and that she might actually be allowed to read it.

Joanna sat up in bed. "You finished? You mean the book is really finished? That's wonderful."

"The first draft is done," Butch cautioned. "But that doesn't mean the book is finished. I doubt it's what an agent or editor would call finished. I'm sure there's a lot of work still to do."

Joanna's green eyes sparkled with excitement. "When do I get to read it?"

Butch shrugged. "I'm not sure. I'd rather you read a printed copy.

That way, if you have any comments or suggestions, you can make note of them in the margins on the hard copy."

Joanna brimmed with enthusiasm. "But I want to read it now. Right away."

"When we get home," Butch said, "I'll hook up the computer and run you off a copy."

"But we won't be home until Monday," Joanna objected.

With Jenny off on a three-night camp-out with her Girl Scout troop, Joanna and Butch had some time to themselves, and they were prepared to take full advantage of it. They were scheduled to stay over in Page until Saturday morning. Leaving there, they would drive back only as far as Phoenix, where Butch was scheduled to be a member of the wedding of one of his former employees, a waitress from the now-leveled Round-house Bar and Grill up in Peoria. Drafted to stand up for the bride, Butch had been appointed man of honor, as opposed to the groom's best man. The rehearsal dinner was set for Saturday evening, while the wedding itself would be held on Sunday afternoon.

"I want to read it now," Joanna wailed, doing a credible imitation of a disgruntled three-year-old's temper tantrum. "Isn't there some way to have it printed before Monday? I'm off work the whole weekend, Butch. You'll be busy with the wedding and man-of-honor duties tomorrow and Sunday both. While you're doing that, I can lie around and do nothing but read. I haven't done something that decadent in years."

"You're quite the salesman," Butch said, laughing. "No wonder Milo Davis had you out hawking insurance before you got elected sheriff. But maybe we could find a place in Phoenix that could run off a copy from my disk, although I'm sure it would be a lot cheaper to do it on our printer at home."

"But I won't have a weekend off when we get home," Joanna pointed out. "As soon as we cross into Cochise County, I'll be back in the soup at home and at work both, and you'll be tied up working on plans for the new house. We won't even have time to sit down and talk about it."

Between Joanna's job and Butch's project of herding their proposed house design through the planning and permit stage, the newlyweds didn't have much time to spend together.

"All right, all right," Butch agreed with a chuckle. "I know when I'm licked. Now look. It's almost two o'clock in the morning. What time is your first meeting?"

"Eight," she said.

"Don't you think we ought to turn off the light and try to get some sleep?"

"I'm not sleepy. Too much coffee."

"Turn over then and let me rub your back. That might help."

She lay down and turned over on her stomach. "You say you'll rub my back, but you really mean you'll do something else."

He nuzzled the back of her neck. "That, too," he said. "I have it on good authority that works almost as well as a sleeping pill."

"Maybe you're the one who should have been selling insurance," she told him.

It turned out he was right. Before long, caffeine or not, Joanna was sound asleep. When the alarm went off at six-thirty, she reached over and flicked it off. She was still in bed and dozing when a room service attendant knocked on their door at seven-fifteen, bringing with him the breakfast Butch had ordered the night before by hanging a form on the outside of their door.

While Joanna scrambled into her clothing and makeup, Butch settled down at the table with a cup of coffee and *USA Today*.

"I really like this man-of-leisure stuff," he said, when she came out of the bathroom and stood shoving her feet into a pair of heels. Like everything else in Joanna Brady's wardrobe, the shoes were new—purchased as replacements for ones destroyed by Reba Singleton's rampage through Joanna's house. The shoes looked nice, but they were still a long way from being comfortable.

"Don't rub it in," she grumbled. "If you're not writing, what are you planning to do while I'm in meetings?"

"Today the wives are scheduled to take a trip out to the Navajo Reservation," Butch answered. "Since I'm done writing, I thought I'd tag along with them on that. I'm especially interested in Indian-made turquoise and silver jewelry."

"In other words, while I'm stuck listening to one more dreary speaker, you'll be spending the day on a bus loaded with a dozen or so women I don't know."

Butch lowered the paper and looked at her. "You're not jealous, are you?"

Joanna shrugged. "Maybe a little," she admitted.

"Have you *seen* any of those other women?" he asked. "They're all a lot older than you are, Joey, and not nearly as good-looking. In addition, I'm short and bald. That doesn't make me what you'd call the sexy leading-man type."

"Yul Brynner and Telly Savalas were both bald," Joanna countered. "And so is Andre Agassi. Nobody says any of them aren't sexy."

She sat down at the table and took a tentative sip of her coffee. He reached across the table and touched her hand. "But I'm in love with you, Joey," he said. "And you're in love with me, so don't go around worrying about the competition. There isn't any."

She smiled back at him. "Okay," she said.

Just then Joanna's cell phone rang. She retrieved it from the bedside table where she'd left it overnight, recharging. The display said the call was coming from High Lonesome Ranch.

"Good morning, Jenny," she said. "How are things?"

"Do I *have* to go on the camping trip?" Jennifer Ann Brady whined.

Joanna felt a stab of worry. Maybe Jenny was sick. "Are you feeling all right? You're not running a fever, are you?" she asked.

"I'm not sick," Jenny answered. "I just don't want to go is all. Mrs. Lambert told us last night at the troop meeting that we won't be able to cook over a campfire because we can't have any fires. Some dork at the Forest Service decided it's too dry for campfires. Without cooking, I probably won't be able to earn any of the badges I thought I was going to earn. I'd rather stay home."

"You know that's not an option, Jenny," Joanna said firmly. "You said you were going when you signed up. Now you have to keep your word."

"But I hate it. I don't even want to be a Girl Scout anymore. It's dorky."

The word "dork" is certainly getting a workout this morning, Joanna thought. But the idea of Jenny wanting to quit Girl Scouts was news to Joanna. From the moment her daughter had been old enough to join Daisies, Girl Scouting was something Jenny had loved.

"Since when?" Joanna asked. "Is it because you have a new leader? Is that it?"

"No. Mrs. Lambert is nice and so is the new assistant leader. I like them both, but it's still dorky."

"I'm a little tired of things being dorky at the moment," Joanna said. "Could you maybe think of some other word to use? As for the subject of quitting, if that's what you decide to do, fine, but only *after* we have a chance to discuss it as a family. Right now, you've made a commitment to go on a camp-out, and you need to keep that commitment. Mrs. Lambert has made arrangements for food and transportation and all those other details. It wouldn't be fair for you to back out now. You need to live up to your word, Jenny. Besides, Grandma and Grandpa Brady agreed to look after the ranch for the weekend. They didn't agree to look after the ranch and you as well."

"That's another thing," Jenny said crossly. "Grandma Brady found my stupid sit-upon. She says I have to take it along because it was on the list Mrs. Lambert gave us. You know, the sit-upon I made back when I was in Brownies? I always thought you threw it away. I *asked* you to throw it away. It's so ugly. When the other girls see it, they're going to laugh at me."

"No, they won't," Joanna countered. "You girls were all in Brownies when you made those. I think there's a good chance that some of theirs are every bit as ugly as yours is. Remember, Mrs. Lambert said you're going to be listening to lectures from those young interns from the history department at the University of Arizona. You'll need something to sit on during those lectures, and a sit-upon is just the thing. Would you rather come home with sandburs in your butt?"

"That means I have to take it?"

"Yes."

"It's not fair," Jenny said. "You're all just being mean to me. I don't even want to talk to you anymore. Good-bye." With that she hung up.

Joanna turned to Butch. "I don't believe it," she said. "My daughter just hung up on me."

Butch didn't seem overly dismayed. "Get used to it," he said. "Jenny's twelve, going on twenty. She's about to turn into a teenager on you, Joey. It goes with the adolescent territory."

"Since when do you know so much about adolescents?"

"I was one once."

"And now she wants to drop out of Girl Scouts," Joanna continued.

"So I gathered, and maybe she should," Butch said, from behind his newspaper. "If that's what she really wants to do. Just because you stayed in Scouting as long as you did doesn't mean your daughter has to."

"You're going to take her side in all this?" Joanna demanded.

"I'm not taking sides," Butch said reasonably. "But if Jenny really wants to drop out of Girl Scouts, I think we should let her do what she wants to do."

"What if she wanted to drop out of school?" Joanna returned. "Would you let her do that, too, just because it was what she wanted?"

Butch looked exasperated. "Joanna, what's gotten into you?"

"I don't know," she said with a shrug. "I seem to be having a bad morning." With that, she grabbed her purse, stuffed her phone into it, and then stomped out of the room, slamming the door shut behind her. The loud bang from the closing door reverberated up and down the hallway. Two doors away, Pima County Sheriff Bill Forsythe turned and glanced back over his shoulder.

"My, my," he murmured, clicking his tongue. "Sounds like a lovers' spat to me."

Before Joanna could reply, her phone rang again. Considering the fact that she was about to tell Bill Forsythe to mind his own damned business, the ringing phone was probably a lifesaver. There were two more rooster-like squawks before she managed to retrieve the distinctively crowing cell phone from the bottom of her purse. As soon as she picked it up, Joanna saw her chief deputy's number on the phone's digital readout.

"Good morning, Frank," she said, walking briskly past Bill Forsythe as she did so.

Frank Montoya hailed from Willcox, Arizona, in northeastern Cochise County. He came from a family of former migrant workers and was the first member of his family to finish both high school and college. Years earlier he had been one of Joanna's two opponents running for the office of Cochise County sheriff. After she won and was sworn into office, she had hired him to be one of her two chief deputies. Now Frank Montoya was her sole chief deputy. He was also the person Joanna had left in charge of the department during her absence.

"How's it going?" she asked.

"Are you all right?" Frank asked. "Your voice sounds a little strained."

"I'm *fine!*" she told him. "Just not having a smooth-running morning today. Now what's up? I'm on my way to the meeting. Anything happening that I should know about?"

"We had another carjacking on I-10 yesterday afternoon, over near Bowie."

Joanna sighed. This was the sixth carjacking along the Cochise County stretch of the interstate in as many weeks. "Not again," she said. "What happened?"

"A guy named Ted Waters, an elderly gentleman in his eighties, had pulled over on the shoulder to rest because he was feeling a little woozy. Some other guy came walking up to the car and knocked on the window. Waters rolled it down. As soon as he did, the young punk reached inside, opened the door, and pulled Waters out of the car. He threw Waters down on the side of the road and drove off. Border Patrol stopped Waters's vehicle this morning at their checkpoint north of Elfrida. It's a late-model Saturn sedan. At the time it was pulled over, it was loaded with seven UDAs. My guess is that the people in the car this morning had no idea it was stolen."

"Coyotes again?" Joanna asked.

People who bring drugs and other contraband across the border are called mules. For a price, coyotes smuggle people. Since vehicles involved in smuggling of any kind are subject to immediate confiscation and impoundment, it had suddenly become fashionable for coyotes to use stolen cars for transporting their human cargo. That way, when the vehicles were impounded, the coyotes were out nothing. They had already been paid their exorbitant smuggling fees, and someone else's car wound up in the impound lot.

"What time did all this happen?" Joanna asked.

"The carjacking? Four in the afternoon."

"Good grief!" Joanna exclaimed. "The carjackers have started doing it in broad daylight now?"

"That's the way it looks," Frank said.

"How's the victim doing? What's his name again?"

"Waters, Ted Waters. He's from El Paso. He was on his way to visit his daughter who lives up in Tucson. He was banged up a little, but not that much. Had some cuts and bruises is all. He was treated at the scene and released. We called his daughter. She took him home with her."

"Was Mr. Waters able to describe his assailant?"

"Not really. The first thing the guy did was knock off the old man's glasses, so he couldn't see a thing. Waters said he thought he was young, though. And Anglo."

"The border bandits are hiring Anglo operatives these days?"

"It doesn't sound too likely," Frank replied. "But I suppose it could be. We're asking Border Patrol to bring the car to our impound yard instead of theirs, so Casey can go over it for prints later this morning."

Casey Ledford was the Cochise Sheriff's Department's latent fingerprint expert. She also ran the county's newly installed equipment loaded with the AFIS (Automated Fingerprint Identification System) software.

"Let me know if she comes up with something," Joanna said. "I'll put the phone on buzz instead of ring. That way, if you call during a meeting, I'll go outside to answer or, if necessary, I'll call you back. What's DPS doing about all this?"

"After the first couple of carjackings, the Department of Public Safety said they were beefing up patrols on that sector, but so far as I know, that still hasn't happened," Frank told her. "We're the ones who took the 911 call on this latest incident, and our guys were the first ones on the scene. By the time the first DPS car got there, it was all over."

"Who is it at DPS who's in charge of that sector?" Joanna asked.

"New guy," Frank answered. "Name's Hamilton, Captain Richard Hamilton. He's based up in Tucson."

"Do you have his number?"

"No, but I can look it up," Frank offered.

"I'll do it," Joanna told him. "But I won't have time to call him until later on this morning, when we take our break. Anything else going on down there that I should know about?"

"Just the usual," Frank said. "A couple domestic violence cases, three DWIs, and another whole slew of UDAs, but that's about it. The carjacking was the one thing I thought you should be aware of. Everything else is under control."

"Right," Joanna told him with a sigh. "Sounds like business as usual."

2

It was late on a hot and sunny Friday afternoon as the four-vehicle caravan turned off Highway 186 and took the dirt road that led to Apache Pass. In the lead was a small blue Isuzu Tracker, followed by two dusty minivans. A lumbering thirty-five-foot Winnebago Adventurer brought up the rear.

Sitting at the right rear window in the second of the two minivans, twelve-year-old Jennifer Ann Brady was sulking. As far as she was concerned, if you had to bring a motor home complete with a traveling bathroom along on a camping trip, you weren't really camping. When she and her father, Andrew Roy Brady, had gone camping those few times before he died, they had taken bedrolls and backpacks and hiked into the wilderness. On those occasions, she and her dad had pitched their tent and put down bedrolls more than a mile from where they had left his truck. Andy Brady had taught his daughter the finer points of digging a trench for bathroom purposes. Jenny's new Scout leader, Mrs. Lambert, didn't seem like the type who would be caught dead digging a trench, much less using one.

The Tracker was occupied by the two women Mrs. Lambert had introduced as council-paid interns, both of them former Girl Scouts and now history majors at the University of Arizona. Because the assistant leader, Mrs. Loper, was unavailable, they were to help Mrs. Lambert with chaperone duties. In addition, they would be delivering informal lectures on the lifestyle of the Chiricahua Apache, as well as on the history and aftermath of Apache wars in Arizona.

History wasn't something Jenny Brady particularly liked, and she wondered how much the interns actually knew. What she had noticed about them was that they both wore short shorts, and they looked more like high school than college girls. But then, she reasoned, since they were former Girl Scouts, maybe they weren't all bad.

Behind the little blue Tracker rolled two jam-packed minivans driven by harried mothers and loaded to the gills with girls and their gear—bedrolls, backpacks, and the sack lunches that would be that evening's meal. Once the mothers finished discharging their rowdy passengers, both they and their empty minivans would return to Bisbee. They were due back Monday at noon to retrieve a grubby set of campers after their weekend in the wilderness.

Behind the minivans, Mrs. Lambert and one of her twelve charges lumbered along in the clumsy-looking Winnebago. The motor home belonged to a man named Emmet Foxworth, one of Faye Lambert's husband's most prominent parishioners. Upon hearing that the U.S. Forest Service had closed all Arizona campgrounds due to extreme fire danger, most youth-group leaders had canceled their scheduled camp-outs. Faye Lambert wasn't to be deterred. She simply made alternate arrangements. First she had borrowed the motor home and then, since public lands were closed to camping, she petitioned a local rancher to allow her girls to use his private rangeland.

Even Faye Lambert had to admit that borrowing the motor home had been nothing short of inspired. She might have taken on the challenge of being a Girl Scout leader, but she had never slept on the ground in her life. Having the motor home there meant she could keep her indoor sleeping record unblemished. Also, since the ranch obviously lacked camping facilities, the motor home would provide both rest-room and cooking facilities in addition to the luxury of running water.

Cassie Parks, seated in the middle row of the second minivan, turned around and looked questioningly at Jenny through thick red-framed glasses. "Who's your partner?" Cassie asked.

Cassie was a quiet girl with long dark hair in two thick braids. Her home, out near Double Adobe, was even farther from town than the Bradys' place on High Lonesome Ranch. Cassie's parents, relative newcomers who hailed from Kansas, had bought what had once been a nationally owned campground that had been allowed to drift into a state of ruin. After a year's worth of back-breaking labor, Cassie's parents had completely refurbished the place, turning it into an independent, moderately priced RV park.

When school had started the previous fall, Cassie had been the new girl in Jenny's sixth-grade class at Lowell School. Now, with school just out, the two girls had a history that included nine months of riding the school bus together. Much of that time they had been on the bus by themselves as they traveled to and from their outlying Sulphur Springs Valley homes. They also belonged to the same Scout troop. In the course of that year, the two girls had become good friends.

If Jenny had been able to choose her own pup-tent partner for the Memorial Day Weekend camp-out, Cassie would have been it. But Mrs. Lambert, who didn't like cliques or pairing off, had decided to mix things up. She had shown up in the church parking lot with a sock filled with six pairs of buttons in six different colors. While the twelve girls had been loading their gear into the minivans, Mrs. Lambert had instructed each one to pull out a single button. To prevent trading around, as soon as a button was drawn, Mrs. Lambert wrote the color down on a clipboard next to each girl's name. Jenny had already drawn her yellow button when she saw Cassie draw a blue one.

The last girl to arrive in the parking lot and the last to draw her button was Dora Matthews. Glimpsing the yellow button in Dora's fingers, Jenny's heart sank. Of all the girls in the troop, Dora Matthews was the one Jenny liked least.

For one thing, Dora's hair was dirty, and she smelled bad. She was also loud, rude, and obnoxious. She couldn't have been very smart because she was thirteen years old and was still in a sixth-grade classroom where everybody else was twelve. Mrs. Lambert usually brought Dora to troop meetings and was always nice to her, even though Dora wasn't nice back. Two months before school was out, Dora and her mother had returned to Bisbee and moved into the house that had once belonged to Dora's deceased maternal grandmother, Dolly Pommer. All their lives, the elder Pommers had been movers and shakers in the Presbyterian Church. Out of respect for them, Faye Lambert had done what she could for their newly arrived daughter and granddaughter. That also explained why Dora Matthews was now the newest member in Jenny's Girl Scout troop.

Not that Dora was even remotely interested in Girl Scouts—she was far too mature for that. She was into cigarettes. And boys. She bragged that before she and her mother had moved back to Bisbee, she'd had a boyfriend who had "done it" with her and who had wanted to marry her. Dora claimed that was why her mother had left Tucson—to get her daughter away from the boyfriend, but Jenny didn't think that was the truth. What boy in his right mind would ever want to marry someone like Dora?

"Guess," Jenny muttered dolefully in answer to Cassie's question.

Behind her thick glasses, Cassie Parks's brown eyes widened in horror. "Not Dora," she said, wrinkling her nose.

"You've got it," Jenny replied and then lapsed into miserable silence. She hadn't wanted to come on the camping trip to begin with. It was bad enough that Grandma Brady had insisted she bring her stupid sit-upon, but

having to spend the weekend with Dora Matthews was far worse than anything Jenny could have imagined. After three whole nights in a pup tent
with stinky Dora Matthews, Jenny would be lucky if she didn't stink, too.

Slowly the four vehicles wound up the dusty road that was little more
than a rutted track. On either side of the road, the parched desert was
spiked with spindly foot-high blades of stiff yellowed grass. Heat shim-
mered ahead and behind them, covering the road with visible rivers of
mirage-fed water. At last the Tracker pulled off the narrow roadway and
into a shallow, scrub-oak-dotted basin. Kelly Martindale and Amber Summers leaped out of the Tracker and motioned the other vehicles to pull in
behind them. By the time the motor home had maneuvered into place, all
the girls had piled out of the minivans and were busy unloading. Dora,
who had been accorded the honor of riding along with Mrs. Lambert in
the motor home, was the last to arrive. She hung back, letting the other
girls do the work of unpacking.

"All right, ladies," Mrs. Lambert announced as soon as the minivans
drove away. "You all know who your partner is. Take tents from the luggage compartment under the motor home. Then choose your spots. We
want all the tents up and organized well before dark. Let's get going."

Each pair of girls was required to erect its own tent. Of all the girls in
the troop, Jenny had the most experience in that regard. While Mrs. Lambert and the two interns supervised the other girls, Jenny set about
instructing Dora Matthews on how to help set up theirs.

When it came time to choose a place for the tent, Dora selected a spot
that was some distance from the others. Rather than argue about it, Jenny
simply shrugged in agreement. "Fine," she muttered. Without much help
from Dora, Jenny managed to lay the tent out properly, but when she asked
Dora to hold the center support pole in place, Dora proved totally inept.

"Don't you know how to do anything right?" Jenny demanded impatiently. "Here, hold it like *this*!"

Instead of holding the pole, Dora grabbed it away from Jenny and
threw it as far as she could heave it. The pole landed in the dirt and stuck
up at an angle like a spear.

"If you're so smart, Jennifer Brady, you can do it yourself." With that,
Dora stalked away.

"Wait a minute," Mrs. Lambert said, picking up the pole and walking
toward the still unraised tent. "What seems to be the problem, girls?"

"Miss Know-It-All here thinks I'm stupid," Dora complained. "And
she keeps telling me what to do. That's all right. If she's so smart, she can
have the stupid tent all to herself. I'll sleep outside."

"Calm down, Dora," Mrs. Lambert said reasonably. "These aren't called two-man tents just because they hold two people. It also takes two people working together to put them up. Now come over here and help."

Dora crossed her arms and shook her head. "No," she said.

"Look here, Dora," Mrs. Lambert cajoled. "The only reason Jenny knows so much more about this than you do is that she and her dad used to go camping together sometimes. Isn't that right, Jenny?"

Jenny thought about her father often, but hearing other people talk about him always brought the hurt of his death back with an intensity that made her throat ache. Jenny bit her lower lip. She nodded but said nothing.

"So come over here and help, Dora," Mrs. Lambert continued. "That way, the next time, you'll know what to do."

"I don't want to know how to pitch a tent," Dora stormed. "Why should I? Who needs to learn how to pitch tents anyway? These days people live in houses, not tents."

Rather than waste any more time in useless discussion, Mrs. Lambert turned to Jenny. "Never mind. Here, Jenny. Let me help. We'll have this up in no time. Besides, we're due at the evening campfire in twenty minutes."

"Campfire!" Jenny exclaimed. "It's too hot for a campfire. And it isn't even dark."

"In this case, campfire is only a figure of speech. With the desert so dry, it's far too dangerous to have one even if there aren't any official restrictions here. We won't be having a fire at all. I brought along a battery-powered lantern to use instead. When it comes time for after-dinner storytelling, we can sit around that."

"Storytelling is for little kids," Dora grumbled. "Who needs it?"

Mrs. Lambert didn't respond, but Jenny heard her sigh. For the first time it occurred to her that maybe her troop leader didn't like Dora Matthews any more than the girls did.

It was almost dark before all the tents were up and bedrolls and packs had been properly distributed. As the girls reassembled around their makeshift "campfire," Jenny welcomed the deepening twilight. Not only was it noticeably cooler, but also, in the dim evening light, no one noticed the mess she had made of her sit-upon.

Once all the girls were gathered, Mrs. Lambert distributed the sack lunches followed by bags of freshly popped microwave popcorn and a selection of ice-cold sodas, plucked from the motor home's generator-powered refrigerator. Taking a refreshing swig of her chilled soft drink and munching on hot popcorn, Jenny decided that maybe bringing a motor home along on a camping trip wasn't such a bad idea after all.

"First some announcements," Mrs. Lambert told them. "As you can probably guess, Mr. Foxworth's motor home has a limited water-storage capacity for both fresh water and waste water. For that reason, we'll be using the rest room as a number-two facility only. For number one, you can go in the bushes. Is that understood?"

Around the circle of lantern light, the girls nodded in unison.

Jenny raised her hand. "What about showers?" she asked.

"No showers," Mrs. Lambert said with a smile. "When the Apaches lived here years ago, they didn't get to take showers every day. In fact, they hardly took showers at all, and you won't either. Unless it rains, and that doesn't appear to be very likely. The reason, of course, is that since we don't have enough water along for showers for everybody, no one will shower. That way, when we go home, we'll all be equally grubby.

"As for meal preparation and cleanup, we're going to split into six teams of two girls each. Because of limited work space in the motor home, two girls are all that will fit in the kitchen area at any given time. Tomorrow and Sunday, each tent will do preparation for one meal and cleanup for another. On Monday, for our last breakfast together, Kelly, Amber, and I will do the cooking and cleanup honors. Does that sound fair?"

"What if we don't know how to cook?" Dora objected. She had positioned herself outside the circle. Off by herself, she sat with her back against the trunk of a scrub oak tree.

"That's one of the reasons you're here," Mrs. Lambert told her. "To learn how to do things you may not already know how to do. Now," she continued, "it's time for us to hear from one of our interns. We're really lucky to have Kelly and Amber along. Not only are they both former Girl Scouts themselves, they also are well-versed in the history of this particular area.

"When I first came to town two years ago, one of the things I offered to do was serve on the textbook advisory committee for the school board in Bisbee. In my opinion, the classroom materials give short shrift to the indigenous peoples in this country, including the ones who lived here before the Anglos came, the Chiricahua Apache. It occurred to me that there had to be a better way to make those people come alive for us, and that's why I've invited Kelly and Amber to join us on this trip. Kelly, I believe we should start with you."

Kelly Martindale stood up. She had changed out of her shorts into a pair of tight-fitting jeans and a plaid long-sleeved shirt. Her dark hair was pulled back into a long ponytail.

"First off," she said, "I want you to close your eyes and think about where you live. I want you to think about your house, your room, your yard, the neighbors who live on your street. Would you do that for me?"

Jenny Brady closed her eyes and imagined the fenced yard of High Lonesome Ranch. In her mind's eye, she saw a frame house surrounded by a patch of yellowing grass and tall shady cottonwoods and shorter fruit-bearing trees. This was the place Jenny had called home for as long as she could remember. Penned inside the yard were Jenny's two dogs, Sadie, a long-legged bluetick hound, and Tigger, a comical-looking mutt who was half golden retriever and half pit bull. Tied to the outside of the fence next to the gate, equipped with Jenny's new saddle and bridle and ready to go for a ride, was Kiddo, Jenny's sorrel gelding quarter horse.

Kelly Martindale's voice imposed itself on Jenny's mental images of home. "Now, just suppose," she said, "that one morning someone showed up at your house and said that what you had always thought of as yours wasn't yours at all. Supposing they said you couldn't live there anymore because someone else wanted to live there instead. Supposing they said you'd have to pack up and go live somewhere else. What would you think then?"

In times past, Jenny would have been the first to raise her hand, the first to answer. But she had found that being the sheriff's daughter came with a downside. Other kids had begun to tease her, telling her she thought she was smart and a show-off, all because her mother was sheriff. Now, in hopes of fitting in and going unnoticed, she tended to wait to be called on rather than volunteering. Cassie Parks suffered no such qualms.

"It sounds like what the Germans did to the Jews," she said with a shudder.

Kelly nodded. "It does, doesn't it? But it's also what the United States government did to Indian tribes all over this country. And the reason I know about it is that very thing happened to my great-great-grandmother when she was just a little girl—about your age. Her people—the Apaches—had lived here for generations—right here in the Chiricahuas, the Dos Cabezas Mountains, and in the surrounding valleys. When the whites came and the Apaches tried to defend their lands, there was a war. The Apaches lost that war and they were shipped off to a place called Fort Sill, Oklahoma. My great-great-grandmother was sent there, too. Although she and her family were prisoners, she somehow fell in love with one of the soldiers guarding the camp. They got married, and she went to live with him in Arkansas. But that's why I'm here in Arizona. It's also why I'm a history major. I'm trying to find out more about my people—about who they were, where they came from, and what happened to them.

"For example, this place." Kelly raised her hand and swept it around the tree-dotted basin where they were camped. "During the Apache Wars, this place was the site of a good deal of fighting, mostly because up there—in that canyon—there's a spring. Wagon trains came through here for that very reason—because of the availability of water. In the 1850s, Nachi, Cochise's father, attacked one of those trains. Thirty people were killed and/or mutilated. Two of the women were sold down in Mexico. But you have to remember, as far as the Apaches were concerned, they were defending their homeland from unwelcome invaders.

"In later years, the dirt road we followed coming up here from the highway was the route for the Butterfield Stage Line. There were several fierce battles waged around the Apache Pass Stage Stop. During one of those battles, Mangas Coloradas, another Apache chief whose name in English means Red Sleeves, was shot and seriously wounded. In the next few days, as we explore this area, I want you to remember that, to some of us, Apache Pass is just as much a sacred battlefield as places like Gettysburg in Pennsylvania or the Normandy beaches in France are to other people."

"Will we find arrowheads?" Dawn Gaxiola asked.

"Possibly," Kelly replied. "But arrowheads won't necessarily be from the time of the Apache Wars. By then, bows and arrows were pretty much passé. The U.S. soldiers had access to guns and gunpowder, and so did the Indians."

"What about scalping?" Dora Matthews asked. For the first time she seemed somewhat interested in what was being said. "Did the Indians do a lot of that?"

"There was cruelty and mutilation on both sides," Kelly answered. "A few minutes ago, I mentioned Mangas Coloradas. When Red Sleeves was finally captured, the soldiers who were supposedly guarding him tortured him and then shot him in cold blood. Mangas was big—six foot six. After he was dead, the soldiers scalped him, cut off his head, and then boiled it so they could send his skull to a phrenologist back east, who claimed his head was bigger than Daniel Webster's."

"Yuck!" Dawn said with a shudder. "And what about that other thing you said—a friendologist or something. What's that?"

"Phrenologist, not friend," Kelly corrected. "Phrenology was a supposed science that's now considered bogus. During the eighteen hundreds, phrenologists believed they could tell how people would behave by studying the size and shape of their heads.

"But getting back to the Apaches, you have to remember that history books are usually written by the winners. That's why Indians always end up being the bad guys while the U.S. soldiers who turned the various tribes out of their native lands are regarded as heroes or martyrs."

"You mean like General Custer?" Cassie asked.

Kelly smiled. "Exactly," she said. "Now, tomorrow Amber and I will be leading a hike up to the ruins of Fort Bowie. But wherever you go tomorrow or later on, when you visit places like the Wonderland of Rocks or Cochise Stronghold, I want you to bear in mind that Anglos weren't the first people here. I'd like you to look at the land around here and try to see it through some of those other people's points of view."

Abruptly, Kelly Martindale sat down. After that, Mrs. Lambert saw to it that the evening turned into the usual kind of campfire high jinks. There were games and songs and even an impromptu skit. Finally, a little after ten, she told the girls it was time for lightsout and sent them off to their tents.

"It's too early to go to bed," Dora muttered, as she and Jenny approached their tent. "I never go to bed at ten o'clock. I'm going for a walk."

"You can't do that," Jenny said. "You'll get in trouble."

"Who's going to tell?" Dora demanded. "You? Besides, I need a cigarette. If I smoke it here, Mrs. Lambert or those two snooty college girls who think they're so rad might smell the smoke and make me put it out because I might start a fire or something. You wanna come along?"

Jenny was torn. On the one hand, she didn't want to get in trouble. On the other hand, she wasn't ready to go to sleep yet, either. Not only that, their tent seemed to be far enough away from the others that it was possible no one would notice if they crept out for a little while.

"I'll go," she said after a moment's hesitation. "But first we'd better climb into our bedrolls and pretend like we're going to sleep."

"Why?"

"Because I'll bet Mrs. Lambert will come around to check on us, that's why."

"Okay," Dora grumbled. "We'll do it your way."

It turned out Jenny was right. Ten minutes after they lay down on their bedrolls, they heard the stealthy rustle of shoe leather approaching through dry grass. Moments later, the light from a flashlight flickered on the outside of the tent.

"Everybody tucked in?" Faye Lambert asked.

"Tucked in," Jenny returned. With the tent flap closed, the stench of Dora's body odor was almost more than Jenny could bear. She could hardly wait for their leader to go away so they could slip back out into the open air.

"Well, good night then," Mrs. Lambert said. "I've made out the duty roster. The two of you will be cleaning up after breakfast. Is that all right?"

"It's fine," Dora told her. "I'm better at cleaning up than I am at cooking."

The flashlight disappeared. Jenny listened to the sound of Mrs. Lambert's retreating footsteps and then to the slight squeak as the door to the motor home opened and closed. Kelly Martindale and Amber Summers were sleeping in their own two-man tent. Mrs. Lambert would spend the night in the motor home.

"Shall we go then?" Dora demanded.

"Wait a few minutes longer," Jenny cautioned.

Ten minutes later, the two girls stealthily raised the flap on their tent and let themselves out. Walking as silently as possible, they slipped off through the scrub oak. While waiting in the tent, their eyes had adjusted to the lack of light. Once outside, they found the moonlight overhead surprisingly bright. Walking in the moon's silvery glow, they easily worked their way over the near edge of the basin. Within minutes they were totally out of sight of the other campers. At that point, Dora sank down on a rock and pulled two cigarettes out of the pocket of her denim jacket.

"Want one?" she asked.

Jenny shook her head. "I don't think so," she said.

"Come on," Dora urged. "What are you, chicken? Afraid your mom will find out and put you in jail?"

For the second time that evening, Jenny was aware of the burden of being the sheriff's daughter. She wanted nothing more than to be accepted as a regular kid. This dare, made by someone she couldn't stand, was more than Jennifer Ann Brady could resist. "Okay," she said impulsively. "Give me one. Where do you get them?" she asked, as Dora pulled out a lighter. She lit her own cigarette first, then she lit Jenny's.

"I steal them from my mother's purse," Dora admitted, inhaling deeply. "She smokes so much that she never misses them as long as I only take a few at a time."

Jenny took a few tentative puffs, holding the smoke in her mouth and then blowing it out again. Even that was enough to make her eyes water.

"That's not how you do it," Dora explained. "You're supposed to inhale—breathe the smoke into your lungs—like this."

She sucked a drag of smoke into her lungs, held it there, and then blew it out in a graceful plume. Jenny's game effort at imitation worked, but only up to a point. Moments later she found herself bent over, choking and gagging.

"You're not going to barf, are you?" Dora Matthews demanded.

"I think so," Jenny managed.

"Well, give me your cigarette, then. Don't let it go to waste."

Jenny handed over the burning cigarette. Embarrassed, she stumbled away from where Dora sat, heaving as she went. Twenty yards farther on, she bent over a bush and let go. In the process she lost the contents of her sack lunch along with the popcorn and Orange Crush from the campfire. Finally, when there was nothing left in her system, Jenny lurched over to a nearby tree and stood there, leaning against the trunk, gasping and shivering and wishing she had some water so she could get the awful taste out of her mouth.

"Are you all right?" Dora asked from behind her. She was still smoking one of the two cigarettes. The smell of the smoke was enough to make Jenny heave again, but she managed to stave off the urge.

"I'm all right," she said shakily.

"You'll be okay," Dora told her. "The same thing happened to me the first time I tried it. You want an Altoid? I always keep some around so my mom can't smell the smoke on my breath."

With shaking hands, Jenny gratefully accepted the proffered breath mint. "Thanks," she said and meant it.

The two girls stood there together for some time, while Jenny sucked on the breath mint and Dora finished smoking the rest of the remaining cigarette. When it was gone, Dora carefully ground out the butt with the sole of her shoe. "I wouldn't want to start a fire," she said with a laugh. "Somebody might notice. Then we would be in trouble."

They were quiet for a time. The only sound was the distant yip of a coyote, answered by another from even farther away. Then, for the first time that evening, a slight breeze stirred around them, blowing up into their faces from the valley floor below. As the small gust blew away the last of the dissipating cigarette smoke, Jenny noticed that another odor had taken its place.

"There's something dead out there," she announced.

"Dead," Dora repeated. "How do you know?"

Jennifer Ann Brady had lived on a ranch all her life. She recognized the distinctively ugly odor of carrion.

"Because I can smell it, that's how," Jenny returned.

The slight softening in Dora's voice when she had offered the Altoid disappeared at once. "You're just saying that to scare me, Jennifer Brady!" Dora declared. "You think that because they were saying all that stuff about Apaches killing people and all, that you can spook me or something."

"No, I'm not," Jenny insisted. "Don't you smell it?"

"Smell what?" Dora shot back. "I don't smell anything."

Jennifer Brady had seen enough animal carcasses along the road and out on the ranch that she wasn't the least bit scared of them, but she could tell from Dora's voice that the other girl was. It was a way of evening the score for the cigarettes—a way of reclaiming a little of her own lost dignity.

"Come on," Jenny said. "I'll show you."

Without waiting to see whether or not Dora would follow, Jenny set off. The breeze was still blowing uphill, and Jenny walked directly into it. After watching for a moment or two, Dora Matthews reluctantly followed. With each step, the odor grew stronger and stronger.

"Ugh," Dora protested at last. "Now I smell it, too. It's awful."

Their path had taken them up and over the ridge that formed one side of the basin where the troop had set up camp. Now the girls walked downhill until they were almost back at the road that had brought them up into the basin. And there, visible in the moonlight and at the bottom of the embankment that fell down from the graded road, lay the body of a naked woman.

"Oh, my God," Dora groaned. "Is she dead?"

Jenny's neck prickled as the hair on the back of it stood on end. "Of course she's dead," she said, wheeling around. "Now come on. We have to go tell Mrs. Lambert."

"We can't do that," Dora wailed. "What if she finds out about the cigarettes? We'll both be in trouble then."

Jenny was worried about the same thing, but the threat of getting in trouble wasn't enough to stop her. Neither was Dora Matthews.

"Too bad," Jenny called over her shoulder. "I'm going to tell anyway. Somebody's going to have to call my mom."

3

It was after eleven when the vibrating of Dr. George Winfield's tiny pager jarred him awake. Next to him in bed his wife, Eleanor, let loose a very unladylike snore. The Cochise County Medical Examiner tiptoed across the room and silently pulled the door shut behind him before he switched on the light and checked the number on the digital readout. He was used to being rousted out of bed by middle-of-the-night calls from various law enforcement agencies, but the number showing on the screen wasn't one he instantly recognized.

To make sure the sound of conversation wouldn't awaken Eleanor, he went all the way to the kitchen and used that phone to return the call. "Chief Deputy Montoya," a voice answered after less than half a ring. "Doc Winfield?"

"That's right," George answered, rubbing his eyes. He hadn't been asleep for long, but his eyes were gritty, and he was having a hard time pulling himself out of the fog. "What've you got, Frank?"

"A problem," Frank replied.

"Someone's dead, I assume," George said, tuning up with a hint of sarcasm. "If that weren't the case, you wouldn't be calling me. What's the deal?"

"White female," Frank Montoya answered. "A Jane Doe. From the looks of her, I'd say she's been dead for a day or two. On the other hand, it's been so hot lately that maybe it's less than that."

"Where was she found?"

"On the road to Apache Pass. Looks like someone threw her out of a vehicle and let her roll down an embankment. She's naked. No identification that we've been able to find so far, but we'll have wait until morning to do a more thorough search."

Something about Apache Pass niggled in the back of George Winfield's consciousness, but right then he couldn't quite sort it out. Still, there was no denying the underlying urgency in Frank Montoya's voice. Even half asleep, George noticed that and assumed Frank had found something deeply disturbing about the condition of the body. Maybe the woman had been mutilated in some unusually gruesome way.

"I'll get dressed and be there as soon as I can," George Winfield said. He was relatively new to the area, a transplant from Minnesota, so his grasp of southeastern Arizona geography was still somewhat hazy, forcing him to make copious use of his detailed topo guide to get wherever he needed to go. "How far is Apache Pass from here and where is it exactly?"

"Off Highway 186. From Bisbee it's about an hour's drive," Frank answered, his native-son knowledge apparent in the casual ease of his answer. "Depending on how fast you drive, of course." Deputies around the Cochise County Sheriff's Department didn't call the new county medical examiner "Doc Lead Foot" for nothing.

"Good," George replied. "I'll be there as close to that as I can manage. See you then . . ."

"Wait," Frank interrupted. "Before you come, there's something else you should know. Jennifer Brady is the one who found the body—she and one of her friends, a girl named Dora Matthews."

By virtue of having married Eleanor Lathrop, Dr. George Winfield was stepfather to Sheriff Joanna Brady and stepgrandfather to Joanna's daughter, Jenny. It came to him then that the something that had been niggling at the back of his mind throughout his conversation with Frank Montoya was something Eleanor had mentioned in passing: Jenny and her Girl Scout troop would be camping on a ranch in the Apache Pass area over Memorial Day Weekend.

"How did they manage that?" he asked.

"According to Jenny, after lights out, she and Dora took off on an unauthorized hike. They were going off by themselves to have a cigarette—"

"Jenny was smoking cigarettes?" a disbelieving George Winfield demanded. "She's twelve years old, for cripes' sake! How the hell did she get hold of cigarettes?"

"Beats me," Frank answered. "I'm just passing along what Faye Lambert, the troop leader, told me. Faye's royally pissed at the two girls, and I don't blame her. I would be, too. She wants to send them home."

Concerned that Eleanor might have awakened and stolen out of the bedroom, George glanced over his shoulder before resuming his conversation. "What about Joanna?" George asked, lowering his voice. "Have you called her?"

"Not yet," Frank admitted. "I'm about to, but first I wanted to have some game plan in place for getting those two girls back to town. It's already after eleven, and Page is six hundred miles from here. It doesn't make sense having Joanna drive hell-bent-for-leather from one end of the state to the other in the middle of the night so they could come pick them up."

"What about the other girl's mother?" George Winfield asked. "Couldn't she come get them?"

"Negative on that. I tried calling Dora Matthews's house up in Tombstone Canyon. There's no answer."

"You're not asking me to bring them home, are you?" George Winfield asked warily. "They can't very well ride home in my minivan along with a bagged-up body."

"You're right," Frank agreed. "It's totally out of the question, but I am asking for suggestions."

"Why can't you do it?"

"Because Jenny's the sheriff's daughter," Frank said. "It'll look like she's being given special treatment. Assuming Joanna decides to stand for election to a second term, you can imagine how that would play if it fell into the hands of her opponent."

"I suppose you're right about that," George Winfield agreed. "What about calling Jim Bob and Eva Lou Brady?" he asked after a short pause. "As I understand it, they're staying out at High Lonesome Ranch to look after things while Joanna and Butch are out of town. When it comes to Jenny, I'm sure they'll do whatever needs doing."

"Good idea," Frank Montoya replied, sounding relieved. "So who's going to call them, you or I?"

"I'll make you a deal," George said. "Since you're the one who's going to have to deal with Joanna, I'll be happy to call Jim Bob and Eva Lou."

"Thanks," Frank said. "That'll be a big help."

"Are you going to tell her about the cigarettes?" George asked.

"Not if I don't have to," Frank said. "I'd as soon leave that chore to someone else—like Faye Lambert, for instance. The murder investigation is my responsibility. The cigarettes aren't."

"Good luck," George said with a laugh.

Once Frank was off the line, George located the speed-dial number for High Lonesome Ranch that Eleanor had coded into their phone. Jim Bob Brady answered on the third ring.

"Hey, Jim Bob, it's George."

"I figured that out by looking at the caller ID."

"Hope I didn't wake you."

"Naw," Jim Bob said. "Eva Lou's in the bedroom getting ready for bed. I'm sitting here watching Jay Leno. Why? What's going on?"

In as few words as possible, George Winfield outlined the problem. "Whoa!" Jim Bob exclaimed once he'd heard the whole story. "Joanna's going to pitch a fit."

"I don't doubt that," George agreed.

"Does she know yet?"

"Frank will be calling her in a few minutes, but he's waiting to make sure you'll go out to Apache Pass and bring Jenny and the other girl home. Otherwise, he's afraid Joanna will light out of Page and drive all night to get here."

"Give me Frank's number," Jim Bob said. "As soon as I give him a call, Eva Lou and I will head right out to go get them."

"You don't think Eva Lou will mind?"

"Good grief, no! When it comes to handling ornery kids, there's nobody better than Eva Lou."

"I'm sure that's true," George Winfield agreed. Much as he loved his own wife, he had no doubt that in this kind of crisis Eleanor Lathrop Winfield would be far less help than Jenny's other grandmother. "See you there," he added.

"Will do," Jim Bob said. "Drive carefully."

George put down the phone. Barely breathing, he crept back into the bedroom and retrieved his clothing, wallet, and keys. Despite his caution, the clatter of lifting his keys from the glass-topped dresser was enough to waken his wife.

"George?" Eleanor asked. "Is that you?"

"Yes," he returned. "I've been called out on a case. Go back to sleep."

"Will you be long?"

"You know how it goes," he said. Leaning down, he kissed her lightly on the top of her forehead. "If I'm not home by breakfast, save me a place."

"Will do," she said sleepily. Then she rolled over, sighed, and immediately resumed snoring.

George stood there feeling that he had somehow dodged a bullet. Only for the time being, of course. Once Eleanor found out about Jenny and the body and the cigarettes and once Eleanor figured out that George had known about the situation without immediately telling her, then there would be hell to pay, but George was used to that. He and his first wife had hardly ever quarreled. In this new life and in his second marriage, he was learning to enjoy his almost daily sparring matches with the perpetually volatile Eleanor. George got a kick out of the daily skirmishes and even more enjoyment out of making up again afterward.

Makes life more interesting, George thought to himself as he once again let himself out of the bedroom and silently pulled the door shut behind him. *It helps keep us young—or at least not as old as we would be otherwise.*

Joanna Brady was asleep and dreaming that she was driving her Blazer across a bone-dry wash bed. Halfway through the wash, the engine stalled. Time and again, Joanna twisted the key in the ignition, but the engine refused to turn over. Hearing a rumbling sound coming from outside, Joanna looked up in time to see a wall of flash-flood-swollen water bearing down on her. She was reaching for the door handle when the phone rang. She grabbed up the receiver of the hotel phone, but still the persistent racket continued. On the second try she located her cell phone.

"Hello?" she said, without even bothering to check the caller-ID readout as she did so.

Beside her, Butch rolled over and groaned. "What now?" he muttered.

"Morning, Boss," Frank Montoya said. "Sorry to wake you."

"What time is it?" Joanna asked.

"Almost midnight."

"What's up?"

"A homicide," Frank replied. "Out in Apache Pass. Jenny and one of her friends, Dora Matthews, discovered the body."

Joanna sat straight up in bed. "Jenny?" she demanded. "Is she all right? Is she in any danger?"

"No," Frank said. "I'm sure she's fine, although I haven't actually seen her myself. I'm still at the crime scene. She and the other girl are back at camp. Faye Lambert is here with me. We'll be going up there as soon as Ernie Carpenter and Doc Winfield show up to take charge of the crime scene."

Holding the phone with one hand, Joanna scrabbled out of bed and began gathering clothing. "It'll take some time to get checked out," she said. "But if we leave within the next half hour, we can probably be there by eight-thirty or so."

"Slow down, Boss," Frank was saying. "I don't think that's necessary."

"What do you mean, it isn't necessary?" Joanna returned. "If my daughter is involved in a homicide—"

"I didn't say she was involved," Frank corrected. "I said she found a body. From the looks of it, the woman's been dead for a while, so it isn't as though Jenny actually witnessed a crime in progress. Not only that, I just now got off the phone with Jim Bob Brady. He and Eva Lou are on their way out to Apache Pass to bring Jenny and the other girl, Dora Matthews, back into town."

"I still think we should get dressed and head out just as soon as—"

"Why?" Frank interrupted. "What difference is it going to make if you get here at eight o'clock in the morning or at two o'clock in the afternoon? Jenny's fine, and she'll be in good hands with the Bradys taking care of her. As for the homicide investigation, we have that under control. Ernie Carpenter and Doc Winfield are both on their way and should be here in a matter of minutes. As soon as one of them shows up, I'll go check on Jenny, but from what Faye Lambert said, I think she's fine. Jenny and her friend found the body, and they reported it to Mrs. Lambert right away."

"But where was it, right there where they're camping?"

"Not exactly," Frank said. "It seems that after lights-out, Jenny and the other girl, Dora Matthews, snuck off by themselves to smoke a cigarette—"

"They did what?"

"Went to smoke a cigarette. Jenny evidently got sick to her stomach and barfed her guts out. It was sometime after that they found the body. I'm at the crime scene now. I'd say it's a good half mile from where the girls are camping."

"What's going on?" Butch asked in the background. "Has something happened to Jenny?"

"Cigarettes!" Joanna exclaimed, waving aside Butch's question. "Jenny was smoking *cigarettes*? I'll kill her. Put her on the phone."

"I can't. I already told you, she isn't here right now," Frank said. "She's back at camp and that's a good half a mile from the crime scene. Faye left the girls in a motor home back at the campsite and gave them strict orders not to budge until we get there, which shouldn't be all that long now."

"As soon as I can get dressed and out of here, we'll be on our way," Joanna said.

"Come on, Boss," Frank returned. "Page is at least an eight-hour drive from here, even the way *you* drive. It's also the middle of the night. The last thing we need is for you to take off at midnight to drive home. You'll end up in a wreck somewhere between here and there. I've got things under control as far as the investigation is concerned, and your in-laws are coming to take care of Jenny. I suggest that you try to get a decent night's sleep right where you are and then drive home in the morning."

Joanna had been pacing back and forth across the room with the phone in one hand and a fistful of clothing in the other. Now she stopped pacing and took a deep breath. Even in her agitated state she could see there would be plenty of time for her to deal with Jenny and her experimentation with cigarettes. The real point of Frank's middle-of-the-night phone call was the homicide in Joanna's jurisdiction. That meant she needed to switch off her motherly outrage and put on her sheriff persona.

"You'd better tell me what you know about the victim," she said. "Any idea who she is?"

"No," Frank answered. "She's naked. No ID, nothing."

"And no vehicle?"

"Not that we've been able to find so far. I'd say she was killed somewhere else and then dumped here. Of course, Doc Winfield will be able to tell us more about that."

"You'll cast for tire tracks?" Joanna asked.

"Yes, but depending on how long ago she was brought here, I doubt if tire casts will do us any good."

By then, Butch had switched on his lamp and was sitting up on his side of the bed. "Do I get dressed or don't I?" he asked.

Joanna knew Frank Montoya was right. Driving through the night on less than two hours' sleep made no sense. "No," she said to Butch. "Not yet."

"Not yet what?" Frank asked.

"I was talking to Butch. You're right. We probably shouldn't leave until morning, but I'd like to talk to Jim Bob and Eva Lou before I make a final decision. And to Jenny," she added.

"All right," Frank said. "Since I've got a decent cell-phone signal here, it'll probably work at the camp, too. As soon as we're all in one place, I'll give you a call back."

"Thanks," Joanna said. "Sounds good."

She ended the call and then crawled back into bed.

"So what's the deal?" Butch asked.

"Jenny and Dora Matthews snuck out of camp after lights-out to smoke cigarettes," she answered. "While they were doing that, they stumbled upon a homicide victim. Jim Bob and Eva Lou are coming to pick the girls up and take them home to Bisbee."

"But the girls are both all right?"

"Fine," Joanna answered testily. "At least they will be until I catch up with them. I can't believe it. Jenny smoking! What do you suppose got into her?"

"She's twelve," Butch said, stifling a yawn. "She's growing up, trying her wings. Don't make a federal case out of it."

Joanna turned on him, mouth agape. "What do you mean by that?"

"I mean stay cool," he said. "It's only cigarettes. The more you overreact, the worse it'll be. Think about you and your mother. What about all the things Eleanor used to tell *you* not to do?"

"I couldn't wait to go out and try them," Joanna conceded. "Every single one of Eleanor's thou-shalt-nots, right down the line, turned into one of my must-dos."

Butch reached over and wrapped an arm around Joanna's shoulder, pulling her toward him. "There you are," he said with a grin. "I rest my case. Now tell me all about our daughter finding a body. Cigarettes be damned, it sounds to me as though Jenny's trying her damnedest to follow in her mother's footsteps."

Jennifer Ann Brady sat miserably on the leather couch of Mr. Foxworth's surprisingly spacious motor home and waited to see what would happen. Jenny's mother got angry sometimes, but when she did, her voice was really quiet—a whisper almost. When Mrs. Lambert was angry, she yelled, loud enough for everyone in camp to hear every word. She had yelled about what an incredibly irresponsible thing it had been for Jenny and Dora to run off like that. And how unacceptable it was for them to smoke cigarettes! Furthermore, Mrs. Lambert said, since Jenny and Dora had proved themselves to be untrustworthy, she was in the process of notifying their parents to come get them. They wouldn't be allowed to stay in camp for the remainder of the weekend.

For Jenny, who wasn't used to being in trouble, Mrs. Lambert's red-faced tirade was uncharted territory. Because Jenny knew she deserved it, she had taken the dressing-down with her own flushed face bowed in aching embarrassment.

Dora, on the other hand, had casually shrugged off the whole thing. As soon as Mrs. Lambert finished yelling at them, grabbed her cell phone, and marched outside, Dora had stuck her tongue out at Mrs. Lambert's retreating back as the door closed.

"What does she know?" Dora demanded. "The hell with her! I'm going to go take a shower."

"A shower!" Jenny yelped. "You can't do that. You heard what Mrs. Lambert said. No showers. There isn't enough water. If you use too much, the other girls may run out of water before the weekend is over."

"So what?" Dora asked with a shrug. "What do I care? She's going to send us home anyway."

"But we'll get in even more trouble."

"So what?" Dora repeated with another shrug. "Who cares? At least I'll be clean for a change." With that, she flounced into the bathroom and locked the door behind her.

Jenny, alone in the living room, was left wondering. She had always thought Dora was dirty because she liked being dirty and that her body odor was a result of not knowing any better. Now, as Jenny listened to the shower running for what seemed like endless minutes, she wasn't so sure.

There was a knock on the door. Jenny jumped. She started to get up to answer it, but then thought better of it. "Who is it?" she asked. Since the shower was still running, she prayed whoever was outside wouldn't be Mrs. Lambert, and her wish was granted.

"It's Frank Montoya, Jenny," the chief deputy said. "I need to talk to you."

Relieved to hear a familiar voice, Jenny raced to the door and flung it open. Then, embarrassed, she stepped away. "Hello," she said in a subdued voice.

"Are you all right?" he asked.

She nodded. "I guess so," she said. "Did you call my mom?"

"Yes."

"Is she coming home?"

"Not tonight. She'll be home tomorrow."

Jennifer Brady heaved a sigh of relief. She wasn't yet ready to face her mother.

"Your grandparents are coming to get you," Frank Montoya continued.

Jenny's stomach did a flip-flop. "Which ones?" she asked.

"Mr. and Mrs. Brady. They'll be here soon."

Jenny swallowed hard and offered Frank Montoya a tentative smile. Grandpa and Grandma Brady would be far easier to deal with than Grandma Lathrop Winfield would be. Her mother's mother had a way of always making things seem far worse than they were, although, in this case, having things get worse hardly seemed possible.

"What about Dora's mother?" Jenny asked. "Is she coming, too?"

"So far we haven't been able to contact Mrs. Matthews," Frank Montoya explained. "We may have to ask your grandparents to take Dora into town as well. If Mrs. Matthews still isn't home by the time you arrive, maybe your grandparents can look after Dora until we're able to notify her mother."

"No," Dora said, emerging barefoot from the bathroom. She was wearing the same dirty clothing she'd worn before, but her clean wet hair was wrapped in a towel. "I can go home even if my mom isn't there. Just have them drop me off at our house. I'll be fine."

"I'm sorry, Dora. We can't do that. Your mother expects you to be on the camp-out until Monday morning. She also expects you to be properly supervised. We can't drop you off at home without an adult there to look after you. Mrs. Lambert would have a liability problem if we did that, and so would the sheriff's department."

"I don't know why," Dora said. "I stay alone by myself a lot. It's no big deal."

"You're sure you don't know where your mother is?"

Dora shrugged. "She has a boyfriend," she said offhandedly. "They probably just went off someplace. You know, for sex and stuff. I'm sure that's why she was so set on my going on the campout—so she could be rid of me for a while."

Taken aback by Dora's matter-of-fact manner, Frank looked at her and frowned. "Does your mother do that often, leave you alone?"

"I can take care of myself," Dora retorted. "It's not like I'm going to starve to death or anything. There's plenty of food in the house. I can make sandwiches and stuff."

Frank's radio crackled, announcing Dr. Winfield's arrival at the crime scene. "Before you head back to town, I need to ask you a few questions," Deputy Montoya said. "You girls didn't see anyone around when you found the body, did you?"

Both girls shook their heads in unison.

"Or see anything that seemed odd?"

"No," Jenny answered.

"What about picking something up or moving it?"

"I know enough not to mess with evidence," Jenny put in. "As soon as we saw the body, we came running straight back here and told Mrs. Lambert."

"But the body's a long way from camp, almost half a mile. What made you go so far?"

"As soon as we put out the cigarettes, I could smell it—the body, I mean. I told Dora something was dead, but she thought I was just making it up, so I had to show her. I thought we'd find a dead deer or a cow or a coyote, not a woman. Not a person. Do you know who she is?"

"Not yet," Frank replied. "We'll figure it out eventually."

Before Frank had a chance to back out of the motor home, there was another knock from outside. As soon as Frank opened the door, Eva Lou Brady darted inside. She wrapped both arms around Jenny and pulled her granddaughter into a smothering bear hug. "Are you all right?" she demanded.

Trapped between Eva Lou Brady's ample breasts, all Jenny could do was nod.

Her grandmother loosened her grip on Jenny and turned to Dora. "And you must be Sally Pommer's little girl. I knew your grandmother," Eva Lou added kindly. "Dolly and I used to volunteer together out at Meals on Wheels. I understand someone brought your backpacks and bedrolls up from your tent. Jim Bob's loading them into the car right now. Are you ready to go?"

Dora unwrapped the towel and dropped it on the floor. "I am," she said. Jenny was surprised to see that Dora's usually dingy brown hair was shining in the glow cast by the motor home's generator-powered fluorescent light fixture.

Eva Lou bent over, picked up the wet towel, and handed it back to Dora. "I'm sure you didn't mean to leave this lying on the floor. As soon as you hang it up, we'll be going."

For a moment Jenny thought Dora was going to say something smart. Instead, without a word, she stomped back into the bathroom and jammed the wet towel onto a wooden towel bar. "If that's okay, maybe we can go now."

"Yes," said Eva Lou, guiding Jenny and Dora past Frank Montoya, who still stood in the open doorway. "I'm sure that will be just fine."

The girls and their gear were both in the back of the Bradys' Honda when Frank Montoya handed his phone to Grandma Brady. With a sinking feeling, Jenny knew at once that the person on the phone had to be her mother. Sliding down in the car seat, Jenny closed her eyes and wished she were somewhere else. A minute or so later, Eva Lou tapped on the window and motioned for Jenny to get out of the car.

"It's for you," Grandma Brady said. "Your mother wants to speak to you."

Reluctantly, Jenny scrambled out of the car and took the phone, but she walked around to the far side of the motor home before she answered it. There were flashlights flickering in the other tents. Jenny knew that in the stillness, all the other girls in the troop were watching the excitement and straining to hear every word.

"Hello, Mom," Jenny said.

"Are you all right?" Joanna demanded.

Hot tears stung Jenny's eyes. "I guess so," she muttered.

If Joanna had been ready to light into Jenny about her misbehavior, the faltering, uncertain sound of her daughter's subdued voice was enough to change her mind and melt her heart. "What happened?" she asked.

Jenny's tears boiled over. "I got into trouble, Mom," she sobbed. "I didn't mean to do it . . . trying the cigarette, I mean. It was like an accident, or something. Dora asked me and I said yes, even though I knew I shouldn't have. I'm sorry, Mom. Really I am."

"Of course you're sorry, Jenny," Joanna said. "Grandma and Grandpa are there now to take you home, right?"

"Yes," Jenny murmured uncertainly with a stifled sob, her tears still very close to the surface.

"We'll talk about this tomorrow," Joanna said. "But in the meantime, I want you to know I love you."

"Thank you."

"Grandma told me that you reported finding the body even though you knew you'd probably get in trouble. That was brave of you, Jenny. Brave and responsible. I'm really proud of you for doing that."

"Thanks," Jenny managed.

"You go with the Gs now. I'll see you tomorrow when I get home. Okay?"

"'kay, Mom."

"Bye-bye."

"Bye."

"I love you."

Jenny switched off the phone and then blundered back toward Grandma and Grandpa's Honda. At the far end of the state, Sheriff Joanna Brady turned to her new husband.

"How'd I do?" she asked.

"Cool," he said. "Understated elegance. Now come back to bed and let's try to get some sleep. I have a feeling we're going to need it."

4

It was only a little past seven when Joanna and Butch, packed and break-
fasted, left the Marriott in Page for the five-hour drive to Phoenix.
After the flurry of late-night phone calls, Joanna had had difficulty in
falling asleep. She had lain awake for a long time, wondering if the dead
woman in Apache Pass might be connected to the epidemic of carjackings
that had invaded Cochise County. True, the previous crimes hadn't been
that vicious. None of the other victims had been badly hurt, but that
didn't mean whoever was doing it hadn't decided to do the crime of carjacking one better.

Leaving Page, Joanna was still thinking about the dead woman and
whether or not finding the body would leave any lingering emotional
scars on either Jenny or Dora. Lost in her deliberations, Joanna hardly
noticed the miles that passed in total silence.

Butch was the one who spoke first. "No matter how long I live in
Arizona," he said, "I'll never get over how beautiful the desert is."

For the first time, Joanna allowed herself to notice the scenery. On
either side of the endless ribbon of two-lane blacktop, the surrounding
desert seemed empty of human habitation—empty and forbidding. Early-
morning sunlight and shadows slanted across the red and lavender rock
formations, setting them in vivid relief against an azure sky. High off
against a cloudless horizon, a solitary buzzard drifted effortlessly, floating in
graceful, perfectly drawn circles. Just inside a barbed-wire fence a herd of
sheep, their wool stained pink by the dust raised by their dainty hooves,
scrabbled for bits of life-giving sustenance. Joanna drove past a meager
trading post and a line of run-down makeshift clapboard sales stands where
Native American tradesmen were starting to lay out their jewelry, baskets,
and rugs in hopes of selling them to passing tourists.

As a lifelong desert dweller, it was difficult for Joanna to see the stark landscape through the eyes of a Chicago area transplant. What Butch saw as wonderfully weird and exotic struck her as simply humdrum.

"I keep thinking Cochise County is sparsely populated," Joanna said with a laugh. "I suppose that compared to this, it's a metropolis."

Butch reached over and took her hand. "Speaking of Cochise County," he said, "have you made up your mind about whether or not you're going to run again?"

Joanna heaved a sigh. With the wedding and everything else going on, Joanna had kept sidestepping the issue. But now, three years into her term of office, she was going to have to decide soon.

"I can't quite see myself going back to selling insurance for Milo Davis," she said with a rueful laugh.

"No," Butch agreed. "I can't see that either."

"But I lived with my dad when he was running for office," Joanna continued. "It was hell. When it was time for an election campaign, we hardly ever saw him—he was either at work or out politicking. What do you think?"

"I can't imagine seeing you less than I do now," Butch replied, "but I also know better than to get into this. It's totally up to you, Joey. Since I'm currently a kept man, I don't think I should actually have a vote. If I say, 'Go for it!' people might think I was just interested in your paycheck. If I say, 'Give it up,' they'd say I was bossing you around and stifling you—not letting you live up to your full potential."

"You're not a kept man," Joanna objected. "The income that comes in each month from the sale of the Roundhouse isn't to be sneezed at. You're serving as the general contractor on the construction of our new house and you just finished writing a book. You also cook and look after Jenny. How does that make you a kept man?"

"Maybe not in your eyes," he said. "But I doubt the rest of the world gives me the same kind of break. Still, when it comes to running for office, I'm serious when I say I'm leaving that up to you. I'll back you either way, but you're going to have to decide for yourself. You like being sheriff, don't you?"

"Yes," Joanna admitted.

"And you're doing a good job."

"As far as I know, although the final decision on that score will have to be up to the voters."

"Is there anything you'd want to do more than what you're doing now?"

"Nothing that I can think of," she answered.

"Well, then," Butch said with a shrug, "as far as I'm concerned, it really is up to you. Have you discussed it with Marianne?"

The Reverend Marianne Maculyea had been Joanna's best friend since junior high. She was also pastor of the Tombstone Canyon United Methodist Church, where Joanna was a faithful member. Marianne and her stay-at-home husband, Jeff, were in much the same position Joanna and Butch were—with Marianne being the primary breadwinner while Jeff took care of their two small children and worked on the side refurbishing old cars. In the old days, Joanna had asked Marianne for advice on almost everything.

"With the new baby and going back to work, she hardly ever has time to talk anymore," Joanna said.

"What about Jenny?" Butch asked. "Have you talked to her about it?"

Joanna shook her head. "Not really."

"Maybe you should ask her opinion," Butch persisted. "Your decision is going to have a lot bigger impact on her than it will on anyone else."

"Even you?" she asked.

"I'm a big boy," Butch said.

In the silence that followed, Joanna thought about what had been said. She couldn't remember her father ever asking for her opinion about whether or not he should run for office. Fathers did what they did. Discussion from outsiders was neither solicited nor accepted. Joanna had always idolized her father and been slightly embarrassed that her mother had never "worked outside the home" or had what Joanna would have considered a "real" job. Instead of being grateful for having a stay-at-home mother, Joanna had chafed under Eleanor's ever-vigilant attention.

"I'll ask her," Joanna agreed finally.

The miles flew by on the almost deserted roadway. As they neared Flagstaff, flat desert gave way to mountains and forest. As soon as they were within range of a signal, Joanna's cell phone began to squawk. Butch plucked it off the seat.

"Who is it?" she asked.

Butch examined the caller ID. "It says Winfield," he answered, "so it's either George or your mother."

"I'm voting for George," Joanna said, as she took the phone, but it wasn't.

"Has your phone been turned off, or what?" Eleanor Lathrop Winfield demanded when she heard her daughter's voice. "I've been trying to reach you for over an hour."

"We're between Page and Flagstaff, Mother," Joanna replied. "The signal's just now strong enough for the call to come through. What's up?"

"What in the world were Jim Bob and Eva Lou thinking! For all they knew, Dora Matthews is a juvenile delinquent who could have stabbed them to death while they slept."

"Dora spent the night?" Joanna asked.

"You mean you haven't talked to them yet?"

"We're driving, and we left the hotel bright and early. If anyone's been trying to call me, they've had the same luck you have. The last I heard, Jim Bob and Eva Lou were taking Dora home because no one could locate her mother."

"And they still haven't!" Eleanor huffed. "The woman went off without telling anyone where she was going or when she'd be back, so Jim Bob and Eva Lou kept Dora overnight, which I think was completely unnecessary—and at *your* house, too," Eleanor pointed out. "That's why this county has foster homes, you know—licensed foster homes—to care for just *those* kinds of children. And what kind of influence do you suppose that little hooligan is exerting on Jenny? Cigarettes! Why, of all things!"

"Mother," Joanna managed, "Jenny and Dora found a *body*. Someone had been murdered. When you think of what might have happened to them, trying a cigarette loses some of its impact, don't you think?"

"I don't think anything of the kind," Eleanor returned. "And I don't care if Dora's grandparents were pillars of the Presbyterian Church up in Old Bisbee. The daughter and granddaughter are totally out of control. A child like that shouldn't be associating with our sweet little Jenny and leading her astray. You don't put a good apple in with a bunch of bad ones in order to make the bad ones better, now do you? Life doesn't work that way."

As Eleanor continued to rail about the cigarettes, Joanna's own temper began to rise. "Mother," she said, trying to sound unflappable. "There's no use trying to blame the whole thing on Dora Matthews. Jenny has some culpability in this situation, too. Dora didn't exactly force Jenny to take that cigarette. Dora offered it, and Jenny *took* it of her own volition. She told me that herself."

"But the point is, Dora should never have had cigarettes at a Girl Scout camp-out in the first place," Eleanor continued. "That isn't the way Girl Scouts worked when I used to be involved. What kind of a soft-headed leader is Faye Lambert anyway?"

"She happens to be the only person who stepped up and volunteered for the job," Joanna returned. "She's the one person in town who was willing to say she'd take over the troop when it was about to be dissolved for lack of a leader, remember? She's also someone who's volunteering because she thinks Girl Scouting is important and not because she happens to have a girl of her own in the troop."

"That's my point exactly," Eleanor said. "Faye Lambert doesn't have a daughter. As a matter of fact, she doesn't have any children at all. How much can she possibly know about girls Jenny's age? What makes her think she's qualified?"

As usual when dealing with Eleanor, Joanna felt her temper rising. On occasions like this it seemed as though Eleanor never heard a word Joanna said.

"Mother," Joanna countered, "if you're talking about parenting skills here, let's put the blame where it really belongs—on me. I'm where you should be pointing the finger. If Jenny and Dora are out of line, haul me on the carpet, and Dora's mother, too. But it's not Faye Lambert's fault that our children misbehaved any more than it's yours or Eva Lou's."

"I should hope not!" Eleanor sniffed. "Faye Lambert isn't the only one I'm ticked off at either," she continued. "I'm disgusted with George, too. He knew all about this last night—knew that Jenny was in some kind of trouble. He should have told me about it at the time and had me go along out to pick those girls up instead of calling on Jim Bob and Eva Lou. I can tell you for sure, if I'd been the one in charge, a girl like Dora Matthews would never have spent the night at High Lonesome Ranch!"

Luckily for her you weren't in charge, Joanna thought. "How did you find out about it then?" Joanna asked mildly.

"Jenny called a few minutes ago," Eleanor said. "I'm sure Eva Lou made her call. Otherwise I wouldn't have known a thing about it. All I can say is, I certainly hope you're coming home today to get this mess straightened out."

That, of course, had been Joanna's intention—to drop Butch off in Peoria and head for Bisbee, but now, with her mother issuing orders, Joanna's first instinct was to balk. "Now that the phone is working, I'll be talking to the department and to both Jenny and Eva Lou before I make any decisions," Joanna said.

Across the car, Butch Dixon smiled tolerantly to himself and shook his head. He was growing accustomed to the ongoing battles waged between his new wife and her overbearing mother.

"Aren't you even *concerned* about this?" Eleanor continued. "It doesn't sound like it. Here's your own daughter spending time with the wrong kinds of friends and most likely headed for trouble, but you're totally blasé. I don't think you're even worried about it."

"Of course I'm worried," Joanna began. "It's just . . ." Then, as though she'd been blindsided, Joanna had an inkling of what was going on with her daughter. When Jenny had agreed to sneak away after lights-out and when she'd tried that fateful cigarette, she had simply been trying to fit in—to be one of the regular kids. The same thing had happened to

Joanna when she herself had been Jenny's age and when Joanna's own father, former copper miner and deputy sheriff, D. H. Lathrop, had been elected sheriff of Cochise County.

In the tight-knit and socially stratified community of Bisbee, where what your father did dictated your social milieu, Big Hank Lathrop's change of job and elevation to the office of sheriff had dropped Joanna out of her old familiar social context and into another—one in which she hadn't been especially welcome. Her former friends felt she was too stuck-up to play with them, while kids with white-collar parents didn't think she was good enough to be included in their activities and cliques. Some of her discipline troubles at school—like the fierce fistfight that had cemented her lifelong friendship with Marianne Maculyea—grew out of Joanna's efforts to fit in, of trying to find a place where she would be accepted.

Before Eleanor could say anything more, the phone beeped in her hand. "Look, Mom," Joanna said, knowing Homicide Detective Ernie Carpenter was on the line. "One of my detectives is trying to reach me. I have to hang up now."

"Tell me one thing," Eleanor demanded. "Are you coming home today or not?"

"I'll have to call you back on that," Joanna replied, ending the call. After dealing with Eleanor, getting on board a homicide investigation sounded like a relief.

"Good morning, Ernie," Joanna said. "What's up?"

"I'm working the Jane Doe from Apache Pass."

"What about her?"

"Doc Winfield says it looks like she's been dead for a day or two. He thinks what killed her is blunt-force trauma. He'll know more about that when he does the autopsy this morning. But believe me, Sheriff Brady, there's a lot more to it than just being whacked over the head. The woman was tortured before she died. It was ugly—really ugly."

Joanna closed her eyes and wondered how much of that Jenny and Dora Matthews had seen and how much of it they would carry with them, waking and sleeping, for the rest of their lives.

Meanwhile, Ernie continued. "We've had a crime scene team out there since first light this morning, and that's why I'm calling you. They may have found something important. It's one of those medical ID warning bracelets that says no penicillin and no morphine. It gives a name and address in Phoenix. One of the links was broken, so there's no way to tell for certain whether or not it belonged to our victim, but I think the odds are good that it did because it doesn't look like it's been out baking in the weather for very long. Frank tells me you're going to be in Phoenix today.

I was wondering if you'd be interested in trying to track down this address and see if you can find someone named Constance Marie Haskell. Otherwise, either Jaime or I will have to do it."

Joanna's homicide detective division consisted of two officers—Ernie Carpenter and Detective Jaime Carbajal. It was silly for one or the other of them to make a seven-hour round-trip drive to and from Phoenix in order to do something Joanna could handle without having to go more than a few miles out of her way.

"Do you have an address and phone number?" she asked. Motioning to the notepad on her dashboard, Joanna pantomimed to Butch that she needed him to write something down. Ernie read off the name from the bracelet as well as the phone number and an address on Southeast Encanto Drive. Joanna repeated the information for Butch's benefit so he could jot it down.

"Anything else I should know about this?" Joanna asked when they finished.

"Not that I'm aware of," Ernie said. "Just what I said a minute ago. The bracelet could belong to our victim, but we don't know that for sure."

"In other words, you don't want me bouncing up to the front door and saying, 'Does Constance Marie Haskell live here and, if so, would you mind letting me talk to her because I need to find out whether she's alive or dead'? I should be able to come up with something a little more appropriate than that."

"But if you'd like me to ask someone from Phoenix PD to handle it . . ." Ernie began.

"No, no," Joanna told him. "It's no trouble. What's Frank up to this morning? I haven't heard from him yet."

"I'm not surprised. He was out at the crime scene most of the night. He's most likely home grabbing some shut-eye."

"Probably a good idea," Joanna said. "But I'm curious about something. Did you two discuss the possibility that this latest homicide might be related to our carjacker?"

Ernie Carpenter gave a hearty chuckle. "You sure you didn't already talk about this with Chief Deputy Montoya or Doc Winfield?"

"No," Joanna said. "I never discussed it with either one of them."

"Well, then it's a case of great minds thinking alike. The three of us were talking it over last night out at the scene. The problem is, there haven't been any fatalities before this, but our guy could be turning up the heat. My understanding was that Frank was alerting all deputies and Border Patrol agents to be on the lookout for another stolen car. But we have no idea what kind of car we're looking for. That's where checking out that address up in Phoenix comes into play."

It made Joanna feel good to realize that the theory she had dreamed up on her own during a relatively sleepless night was the one her investigators had come up with as well.

"What's the scoop on Dora Matthews? My mother just told me that she's still out at the ranch."

"You know who she is, don't you?" Ernie asked.

"Eva Lou told me last night. Her mother used to be Sally Pommer. I know of her, but not all that much. She was a couple of years ahead of me in school. You still haven't found her?"

"That's right. We sent a deputy up to the house last night and again this morning, but there's still no sign of her."

"That's not so surprising," Joanna said. "If Sally Matthews thought Dora would be out camping the whole weekend, maybe she decided to do something on her own—go on a trip up to Tucson or Phoenix, for example. Single mothers are allowed a little time to themselves on occasion."

"That may well be," Ernie agreed, "but something Dora told Frank last night has been weighing on my mind. Let me ask you this. You and Butch don't go off and leave Jenny by herself, do you?"

"No. Of course not. Why?"

"From the way Dora talked, she expected someone to just drop her off at home whether or not we could locate her mother. It sounds like she's been left alone a lot. She claimed it was no big deal, and maybe it isn't. All the same, Frank says we should keep trying until we reach Sally. In the meantime, as long as Jim Bob and Eva Lou don't mind looking after Dora, we're planning on leaving her there. Have you spoken to either one of them about it?"

"Not yet, but I will," Joanna assured him. "Now, is there anything else?"

"Not that I can think of."

"Good enough, Ernie," she answered. "I'd say you guys have things pretty well under control. Keep me posted."

After ending the call and putting the phone down, she glanced in Butch's direction. He was studying her from across the Crown Victoria's broad front seat. "I guess you're working today," he said glumly.

"It won't take long," she assured him. "Ernie thinks he's got a line on identifying the homicide victim from Apache Pass. He wants me to try locating her next of kin. With that phone number and address, it shouldn't take any time at all."

"What about going to Bisbee?" he asked.

With a sigh, Joanna picked her phone back up and punched in the memory-dial number for High Lonesome Ranch. Jenny answered after only one ring. "Hello, Mom," she said.

"How are things this morning?" Joanna asked, forcing herself to sound cheerful.

"Okay."

"I hear you talked to Grandma Lathrop," Joanna said.

"I didn't want to, but Grandma Brady made me," Jenny replied. "She said Grandma Lathrop needed to hear it from me instead of from someone else."

"That seems fair," Joanna said without mentioning that she was relieved that she herself had been spared being the bearer of the bad news. "What did she say?"

"You know. That I was a disappointment to her. That people judge me by the kind of company I keep. All that stuff. Why does Grandma Lathrop have to be that way, Mom?" Jenny asked. "Why does she have to make me feel like I can't do anything right?"

Good question, Joanna thought. *She makes me feel the same way.* She resisted the temptation to ask how Jenny *really* was. Jenny sounded fine. If she had achieved some kind of emotional even keel, Joanna was reluctant to make any mention of the body the girls had discovered in Apache Pass. Instead, she contented herself with asking about Dora.

"She's fine, too," Jenny said. "Grandma has her helping with the dishes right now. Do you want to talk to her?"

"No," Joanna replied. "If you don't mind, put Grandma on the phone."

As Eva Lou came on the line, Joanna could almost see her drying her hands on her ever-present apron. "How are things?" Joanna asked.

"We're all doing just fine," Eva Lou reported briskly. "I told that nice Frank Montoya that Dora is welcome to stay as long as she needs to. I'm sure her mother will turn up later on today. When she does, we'll take Dora home where she belongs. In the meantime, I have Dora and Jenny doing some little chores around here—vacuuming, dusting, and so forth. As a penance, if you will. Nothing like using a little elbow grease to help you contemplate your sins."

"I was thinking about dropping Butch off in Phoenix and then coming home . . ."

"Don't you do anything of the kind," Eva Lou said. "Isn't Butch supposed to be in a wedding or something tonight?"

"Yes, tonight and tomorrow, but I thought—"

"Think nothing," Eva Lou declared. "If you have to come home because of something related to work, that's fine, but don't do it because of the girls. Jim Bob and I are more than happy to look after them. It isn't as though the two of us don't have some experience in dealing with kids," she added. "You maybe didn't know Andy back when he was twelve and thirteen, but I can tell you he was a handful at that age—a handful, but still not smart enough to put much over on us, either. You just go to your wedding, have fun, and don't worry."

"All right," Joanna said. "I'll think about it."

"Good. Do you want to talk to Jenny again?"

"No," Joanna said. "That's probably not necessary."

She put down the phone and was amazed to realize they were almost in Flagstaff.

"Well?" Butch asked.

"Typical," Joanna said. "My own mother gives me hell. Eva Lou tells me everything is fine and not to worry."

"Should I call now and tell them that you'll probably miss the rehearsal dinner?"

Bolstered by her back-to-back conversations with Ernie and High Lonesome Ranch, Joanna Brady shook her head. "You'll do no such thing," she said. "I've made up my mind. Things sound like they're under control at home. There's no need for me to go racing back there. I'll do the next-of-kin interview and be back in plenty of time for the rehearsal dinner."

"Good enough," Butch replied, with a dubious shake of his head. "If you say so. Are you going to call Eleanor and let her know?"

Joanna shook her head. "I think I'll let sleeping dogs lie," she said.

They stopped for gas in Flagstaff. After leaving Flag, Butch leaned over against the passenger-side door and fell sound asleep. For a change, the cell phone remained blissfully silent, leaving Joanna some time alone to mull over her thoughts.

If Jenny was suffering any ill effects from her experience on Friday night, it certainly wasn't apparent in anything she had said just then on the phone. So, even though Joanna was relieved on that score, she still wondered about how much having a mother who was a sheriff had contributed to Jenny's walk on the wild side. That immediately brought Joanna back to the discussion she and Butch had been having about whether or not Joanna should run for reelection.

Three years earlier, when she had agreed to stand for election the first time, it had been in the stunned and awful aftermath of Andy's death. A Cochise County deputy at the time as well as a candidate for sheriff in his own right, Andrew Roy Brady had been murdered by a drug dealer's hit man. Refusing to accept the officially proffered theory that Andy had taken his own life, Joanna had forged ahead with an investigation of her own that had eventually revealed a network of corruption in the previous sheriff's administration.

Joanna's key role in bringing that corruption to light had eventually resulted in her being encouraged to run for office in Andy's stead. When she won, Joanna had taken her election to mean that the voters of Cochise County had given her a mandate to go into the sheriff's department and clean house. Which was exactly what she had done. But that departmental housecleaning had come at a steep personal price, one that had been paid by Joanna and by Jenny and now, to a smaller extent, was being paid by Butch Dixon as well.

At the moment Butch was fine about it, but Joanna wondered how he would feel months from now if she was still doing the job of sheriff and running for reelection at the same time. Would their marriage withstand that kind of pressure? What if Butch decided he wanted a family of his own? He loved Jenny, and he was good with her, and he had said that as far as the two of them having children together went, he was content to abide by Joanna's wishes. Maybe that was fine for the short term, but what if he changed his mind later on?

Joanna's thoughts strayed once again back to what Jenny had said the previous night. She claimed she had taken the cigarette by accident, that she had done it without really intending to. Joanna was struck by the similarity between Jenny's misadventure with Dora's cigarette and the way in which Joanna herself had become sheriff. It had happened almost by accident. But now she was up against decision time—the same place Jenny would be if ever she was offered another cigarette. Joanna was at the point where, as Big Hank Lathrop would have said, it was time to fish or cut bait.

Which meant it was time to ask herself what she, Joanna Brady, really wanted. If she wasn't sheriff, what would she do instead? She was an indifferent cook and had never been much of a housekeeper. In that regard, Butch made a far better stay-at-home spouse than she did. Did she want to go back to managing an insurance agency for Milo Davis? No. That no longer spoke to her, no longer challenged her the way it once had. Joanna had to admit that she liked being sheriff; liked working the good-guy side of the bad-guy street. She liked the challenge of managing people and she felt that she was doing a good job of it. But the election was a stumbling block. She might feel she was doing a good job, but what about the voters? Did they feel the same way? And what if she stood for reelection and lost? What then?

Eventually the Civvie—as she preferred to call the Crown Victoria emerged from the cool pine forests and dropped off the Mogollon Rim into a parched desert landscape where the in-dash digital display reported a temperature of 118 degrees.

There's too much on my plate for me to even think about this right now, Joanna told herself. *When the time's right, I guess I'll know.*

5

A little after two that afternoon, Joanna drove into the shaded porte cochere of the new Conquistador Hotel in downtown Peoria. A doorman in white shirt and tie approached the driver's door and opened it, letting Joanna out of air-conditioned comfort into a stifling and breath-robbing heat even though overhead mist ejectors were futilely trying to provide evaporative cooling. Looking at the doorman, Joanna was grateful that he was the one wearing a tie while she was dressed in the relative comfort of a T-shirt and shorts.

"Checking in today?" the doorman asked.

Joanna nodded. As she and Butch stepped out of the car, Butch looked around and whistled in amazement. It had taken less than a year for a fully landscaped, twelve-story resort hotel to sprout on the property that had once contained Butch's Roundhouse Bar and Grill, along with any number of other small mom-and-pop-style businesses. The gentrification process had left behind no trace of the old working-class neighborhood's funk or charm.

"There goes the neighborhood," Butch said with a grin. "It's so upscale now, I'm not sure they'll let us in."

"Will you need help with your luggage?" the doorman asked. Joanna nodded. "And we have valet parking," he added. "Just leave your keys in the car."

He handed Joanna a ticket. Once a bellman had loaded their luggage onto a cart, a valet attendant started to drive the Crown Victoria away. Joanna stopped him.

"I'll just be a couple of minutes," she said. "I have an errand to run. If you don't mind leaving the car here . . ."

"Sure," he replied, stepping back out. "But we'll have to keep the keys."

Butch glanced at his watch. "It's two now. The dinner starts at six. Why don't you leave from here? I can handle getting us checked in. That way you'll be finished that much sooner."

Joanna looked down at the wrinkled shorts and T-shirt that had already done five hard hours in the car. "I have to change," she told him. "I can't very well do a next-of-kin notification dressed like this."

Butch nodded. "You're right about that," he said. "But I'm betting you won't make it back in time for dinner."

"I will, too," Joanna declared.

While Butch followed the luggage inside, Joanna used her cell phone to contact the department in Bisbee where, despite its being Saturday, Frank Montoya was nonetheless hard at work. "How are things?" she asked.

"Doc Winfield completed the Jane Doe autopsy. According to him, the woman was beaten to a pulp, tortured, raped, and had her head bashed in—not necessarily in that order."

Joanna cringed at the litany of violence. "Sounds like the carjacker is out of the picture."

"I'd have to agree there," Frank said. "This perp is a whole other breed of cat. Or, if he is the carjacker, the rules of engagement just changed for the worse."

"Even if the Apache Pass murder isn't connected to the carjackings, both incidents have happened at almost the same time, and they pose a serious threat to public safety. Can we schedule extra patrols along I-10?" Joanna asked.

"I don't know," Frank said. "Our resources are already stretched pretty thin."

"What about moving units away from the southern sector and putting them up north?"

"Considering the situation along the border, is that wise?" Frank asked.

Joanna knew what he meant. For months now, Cochise County's eighty miles of international border had been deluged with an unprecedented flood of illegal immigrants. Increased INS enforcement in Texas and California had led to an influx of illegals throughout Joanna's jurisdiction. Even with additional help from the U.S. Border Patrol and INS, things along the border were still out of control. All the extra enforcement made her county resemble an armed camp.

"What about the guys who were picked up driving the Saturn?"

"UDAs again. The guy driving it was an illegal with no license and no insurance. He may have known the vehicle was stolen, but I doubt it. Lots of fingerprints, but so far, Casey Ledford's found nothing useful."

"Tell you what, Frank," she said. "Let's beef up patrols in the northern sector of the county and along our portion of I-10. Since the feds have brought in all those extra Border Patrol agents, we'll let them take up some of our slack for a change. God knows we've been doing plenty of *their* work."

Moments later, Frank was giving Joanna computer-generated driving directions that would take her from the Conquistador Hotel in Peoria to Southeast Encanto Drive near downtown Phoenix. By the time she finished up with her phone call, Butch was coming back across the driveway carrying a pair of room keys, one of which he handed to her.

"We're in room twelve fourteen," he said. Looking at her closely, he frowned. "You're upset. What's wrong?"

"The autopsy's in on the Apache Pass victim," Joanna said. "It's pretty bad."

"Does that mean you want to head home and go to work on it?" Butch asked. "If that's the case, I can rent a car to do what I need to do here."

"No," Joanna assured him. "As they told us in one of the sessions up in Page, we sheriffs need to learn to delegate. From what Frank and Ernie have both told me, I think they have things under control. Besides, I have a part of the job that needs doing right here in Phoenix, remember?"

Up in the room, Joanna changed into a skirt, blouse, and lightweight microfiber jacket. At home in Bisbee and in order to save wear and tear on her own newly re-created wardrobe, she had often taken to wearing a uniform to work. For the Sheriffs' Association Conference, she had brought along mostly business attire, and for next-of-kin notifications, that was the kind of clothing she preferred. Out of respect for the victim, she always felt she needed to show up for those heart-rending occasions wearing her Sunday best—along with her small-of-back holster.

"Be careful," Butch told her, giving her a good-bye hug. "And, in case you're interested, I think changing clothes was the right thing to do."

Even though the car had been parked in the shade, the Crown Victoria felt like an oven. The route Frank had outlined took her down the Black Canyon Freeway as far as the exit at Thomas. On Thomas she drove east past Encanto Municipal Golf Course to Seventh Avenue. There she turned south. Southeast Encanto Drive wasn't a through street, but as soon as Joanna turned off Seventh onto Monte Vista, she knew she was in one of the old-money neighborhoods in Phoenix. The houses were set back from the street on generously sized lots. Around the homes were the kinds of manicured lawns and tall, stately trees that thrived in the desert only with careful attention from a professional gardener and plenty of irrigation-style watering.

The address turned out to be an ivy-covered two-story red brick house with peaked-roof architecture that revealed its pre–World War II origins. Joanna pulled into the driveway and parked the Crown Victoria behind a bright-red Toyota 4-Runner. Turning off the ignition and dropping the car keys into the pocket of her blazer, Joanna felt the same kind of misgiving she always experienced when faced with having to deliver the kind of awful news no family ever wants to hear.

Just do it, Joanna, she told herself firmly. *It's your job.*

Letting herself out of the car, she walked up the well-groomed sidewalk. Here in the center of Phoenix, surrounded by grass and shaded by trees, it didn't seem nearly as hot as it had on the shiny new blacktop that graced the driveway at the Conquistador Hotel.

Reaching for the doorbell, Joanna was startled to see that the door was slightly ajar. A steady stream of air-conditioned air spilled from inside out. She hesitated, with her finger reaching toward the bell. Then, changing her mind, she pushed the door open a few inches.

"Hello?" she called. "Anybody home?"

There was no answer, but deep within the house she heard the sound of murmuring voices. "Hello," she called again. "May I come in?"

Again no one answered, but Joanna let herself in anyway. Inside, the house was cool. Drawn curtains made it almost gloomy. The furniture was old and threadbare, but comfortably so—as though whoever lived there preferred the familiarity of top-of-the-line pieces from a bygone era to newer and sleeker steel-and-glass replacements. The voices seemed to emanate from the back of the house. Following them, Joanna made her way through an elegantly furnished dining room. Only when she reached a swinging door that evidently opened into the kitchen did she finally realize that the voices came from a radio program. On the other side of the door a loud boisterous talk-show host was discussing whether or not it might be possible for this year's Phoenix Cardinals to have a winning season.

Joanna eased open the swinging door. On the far side of the kitchen, a woman sat at a cloth-covered kitchen table, her head cradled in her arms. The woman was so still that for a moment Joanna thought she might be dead. On the table beside her, arranged in a careful row, were three separate items: a half-empty bottle of Johnnie Walker Red Label, a completely empty tumbler-sized crystal glass, and a handgun—a small but potentially lethal Saturday-night special.

Holding her breath, Joanna waited until a slight movement told her the woman was alive. The droning voices of the talk-show host and his call-in guests had drowned out the sound of Joanna's own entrance. Standing there, Joanna battled a storm of indecision. If she spoke again, this near at hand, what were the chances that the startled woman would react by reaching for her gun? Wakened out of a sound sleep and probably drunk besides, she might shoot first and ask questions later. It was then, with her heart in her throat, that Joanna Brady came face-to-face with the realization that she had come on this supposed mission of mercy without one of the Kevlar vests she insisted her officers wear whenever they were on duty.

Joanna hesitated, but not for long. Still using the noisy radio program for cover, she tiptoed across the room and retrieved the handgun. She slipped it into the pocket of her blazer along with her keys and phone. As she did so, the woman issued a small snort that sent Joanna skittering back across the room and safely out of reach. Only when she had regained the relative safety of the doorway did she turn around. The woman had merely changed her position slightly, but she was still asleep. Joanna allowed herself a single gasp of relief. At least the still-sleeping woman was no longer armed.

Once Joanna had regained control of her jangled nerves, she tried speaking again. "Hello," she said, in a more conversational voice. "Are you all right?"

This time the woman stirred. She sat up and stared uncomprehendingly around the room. Once her bleary eyes settled on Joanna, the woman groped for her missing gun. The fact that it was no longer there made tingles of needles and pins explode in Joanna's hands.

"Who are you?" the woman demanded. "What are you doing here? Who let you in?"

"I'm Sheriff Joanna Brady from Cochise County. Who are you?"

"Maggie," the woman said flatly. "Maggie MacFerson."

"Do you live here?" Joanna asked.

Maggie MacFerson glared belligerently at Joanna from across the room, but before she answered, she reached for the bottle and poured a slug of Scotch into the glass. "Used to," Maggie said after downing a mouthful of it. "Live here, that is. Don't anymore."

"Who does?"

"My sister and that worthless shit of a husband of hers. He's the one I'm waiting for—that no-account bastard. One way or another he's going to tell me what he's done with Connie's money."

"Connie?" Joanna asked. "That would be Constance Marie Haskell?"

Maggie nodded. "She never should have changed her name. I told her not to. You'd think she'd be able to learn from somebody else's mistake. I did," she added bitterly. "Took old Gary MacFerson's last name, that is. Look what it got me."

"Where's your sister now?" Joanna asked.

"Beats me. Probably dead in a ditch somewhere if the message on the machine is any indication. 'Meet me in paradise,' the son of a bitch says to her on the phone. Meet me in paradise, indeed! I'm here to tell you that if that SOB has killed my sister, I'm going to plug him full of holes. Where's my gun, by the way? Give it back. I've got a license to carry, if that's what you're worried about. It's right over there on the counter in my purse. Check it out for yourself if you don't believe me."

"You're saying you think your sister's dead?" Joanna asked. "Why's that?"

"The neighbors called me because Connie took off sometime on Thursday. They noticed she left the garage door open. When it was still open . . . What day is it?"

"Saturday," Joanna answered.

"When it was still open on Friday, they were worried enough to call, and I came to check things out after work. That's when I heard the message on the machine. You can listen to it too, if you want to."

An answering machine sat on the kitchen counter next to a large black satchel-style purse. Joanna pressed the message button. "You have no new messages," a recorded voice told her.

"Damn," Maggie MacFerson muttered, taking another swig from her glass. "Must have punched 'erase' without meaning to. But that's what he said. 'Meet me in paradise.' The dumb broad was so completely enthralled, so totally besotted with the weasely little shit that if he had said 'Jump in the lake,' Connie would have done it in a minute even though she can't swim a stroke. There's no fool like an old fool."

"You said something about her money. What about that?"

"There was another message on the machine as well—from Ken Wilson. He's Connie's personal banker, but he's also mine. He was our parents' private banker before that. I heard that message, too. He said Connie had bounced a check. Which wouldn't happen—never in a million years. Connie never bounced a check in her life—unlike some other people I could mention."

Maggie grinned ironically and took another mouthful of Johnnie Walker. "I, on the other hand, have never balanced a checkbook in my life, and I'm still here to tell the tale. But I did call Ken Wilson. I nailed his feet to the ground and made him tell me what the hell was going on. That bastard Ron Haskell has cleaned Connie out, lock, stock, and barrel, just like I said he would. Except it doesn't feel all that good to say I told you so. It's gonna break Connie's heart, as if she hasn't had enough heartbreak already."

Standing at the counter, Joanna glanced into the purse. A small wallet lay at the top. "Your license to carry is in this?" she asked, lifting the wallet.

Maggie MacFerson glanced away from pouring herself another drink. "It's there," she said. "Help yourself."

Joanna opened the wallet and thumbed through the plastic card holders. One of the first things she saw was a press credential that identified Maggie MacFerson as a reporter for Phoenix's major metropolitan newspaper, the *Arizona Reporter*. As soon as the woman had mentioned her name, it had sounded familiar. Only now did Joanna understand why.

That Maggie MacFerson, Joanna thought. *The investigative reporter.*

Behind the press credentials was indeed an embossed concealed-weapon license. Joanna put down the wallet and then reached into her pocket to remove the weapon. "Is this thing loaded?" she asked.

"Sure is," Maggie replied. "My father used to say that having an unloaded weapon in the house was about as useful as having one of those plumber's whaddaya-call-its without a handle. I can't think of the name for the damned thing now. You know what I mean, one of those plunger things."

"You mean a plumber's helper?" Joanna offered.

"Right," Maggie agreed. "A plumber's helper without a handle. Dad wasn't big on telling jokes. That's about as good as his ever got. And that's gone, too, by the way."

"What's gone?"

"Dad's gun. From the bedroom. The safe is open and the gun is gone. I'll bet the jerk took that, too."

Gingerly Joanna opened Maggie MacFerson's gun and removed the rounds from the cylinder. If Maggie wasn't *still* drunk, then she was well on her way to being drunk again. Joanna had already heard the woman threaten to shoot her hapless brother-in-law. Under those circumstances, handing Maggie a loaded weapon would be outright madness. Joanna dropped the nine bullets into her blazer pocket before placing the gun in Maggie's purse.

"So what are you doing here anyway?" Maggie asked, peering at Joanna over the rim of her raised glass. "What'd you say your name was again?"

"Joanna. Joanna Brady. I'm the sheriff in Cochise County."

"Tha's right; tha's right," Maggie said, nodding. "I 'member you. I came down to cover the story when you got elected. So whaddaya want?" With every word spoken, Maggie's slurred speech grew worse.

"I'm here because a body was found last night in Apache Pass down in the Chiricahuas," Joanna said quietly. "A medical identification bracelet was found nearby with your sister's name on it. We need someone to come to Bisbee and identify the body."

Maggie slammed her empty glass onto the table with so much force that it shattered, sending shards of glass showering in all directions.

"Goddamn that son of a bitch!" she swore. "I really *am* going to kill him. Just let me get my hands on him. Where is he?"

She sat there with her eyes wide and staring and with the palms of both hands resting in a spray of broken glass. From across the room, Joanna saw blood from Maggie MacFerson's lacerated hands spreading across the otherwise snow-white tablecloth. Maggie didn't seem to notice.

"Come on," Joanna said calmly. "Come away from the broken glass. You've cut your hands."

"Where's the body?" Maggie demanded, not moving. "Just tell me where Connie's body is. I'll go right now. I'll drive wherever it is. Just tell me."

Watching the blood soak unheeded into the tablecloth, Joanna knew Maggie MacFerson was in no condition to drive herself anywhere. Walking over to the table, Joanna gently raised Maggie's bleeding hands out of the glass.

"I'll take you there," she said quietly. "Just as soon as we finish cleaning and bandaging your hands."

Several hours later, after opening the car door and fastening Connie MacFerson's seat belt, Joanna finally headed out of Phoenix for the three-and-a-half-hour drive to Bisbee while Maggie slept in the Civvie's spacious front seat. Once out of heavy city traffic, Joanna reached for her phone and asked information for the Conquistador Hotel. Rather than speaking to Butch, she found herself dealing with an impersonal voice-mail system.

"There's been a slight delay," she told him in her message. "I'm on my way to Bisbee to do a positive ID. I'm just now passing the Warner Road Exit going southbound, which means you're right. I *am* going to miss that rehearsal dinner. I'm so sorry, Butch. I'll call later and let you know what time I'll be back at the hotel. Give me a call on the cell phone when you can."

What she didn't say in her message was that she had spent the better part of two hours in the ER at St. Joseph's Hospital while emergency room doctors and nurses removed dozens of tiny pieces of crystal from Maggie MacFerson's glass-shredded hands and put stitches in some of the longer jagged cuts. Both hands, bandaged into useless clubs, now lay in Maggie's lap. Even had the woman been stone-sober—which she wasn't—Joanna knew Maggie wasn't capable of driving herself the two hundred miles to Bisbee to make the identification—not with her hands in that condition.

Joanna settled in for the trip. She generally welcomed long stretches of desert driving because they provided her rare opportunities for concentrated, uninterrupted thinking. With Maggie MacFerson temporarily silenced, Joanna allowed herself to do just exactly that—think.

Weeks earlier, as Joanna sat in her mother's living room, she had thumbed through George Winfield's current copy of *Scientific American*. There she had stumbled upon a column called "Connections." The interesting content had tumbled back and forth across the centuries showing how one scientific discovery was linked to another and from there bounded on to something else. At the time, Joanna had recognized that the solutions to homicide investigations often happened in much the same way, through seemingly meaningless but nonetheless critical connections.

Was the death of Constance Marie Haskell linked to the outbreak of carjackings that had plagued Cochise County? If Maggie MacFerson's version of events was to be believed, Connie Haskell had an absent, most likely estranged, and quite possibly dishonest, husband. Once Ron Haskell was located, he would no doubt be the first person Joanna's detectives would want to interview. Still, rape, torture, and a savage beating were more in keeping with a random, opportunistic killer than they were with a cheating spouse. And so, although Ron Haskell might well turn into the prime suspect, Joanna wasn't ready to dismiss the idea of a crazed carjacker who, upon finding a lone woman driving on a freeway late at night, might have veered away from simple carjacking into something far worse.

Picking up her cell phone, Joanna dialed Frank Montoya's number. "What are you doing calling me?" he asked. "You're supposed to be at a wedding rehearsal and dinner."

"Think again," she told him. "I'm on my way to Bisbee bringing with me a lady named Maggie MacFerson. We have reason to believe she's the sister of Constance Marie Haskell, the Jane Doe from Apache Pass. I'm bringing her down to George's office so she can ID the body."

"On your weekend off?" Frank objected. "What's the matter? Doesn't Maggie know how to drive?"

"Knows how but can't," Joanna replied. "She hurt her hands."

She discreetly left out the part about probable blood alcohol count in case Maggie MacFerson wasn't sleeping as soundly as she appeared to be.

"How about calling Doc Winfield and having him meet us at his office uptown," Joanna continued. "It should be between eight-thirty and nine, barring some unforeseen traffic problem."

"Wait a minute," Frank said. "I'm the one who's supposed to tell your mother her husband has to go in to work on Saturday night? Is that so you don't have to do it?"

"That's right," Joanna returned evenly. "You're not Eleanor Lathrop Winfield's daughter. She can't push your buttons the way she does mine."

"Okay, Boss," Frank said. "But I'm putting in for hazardous-duty pay."

Joanna smiled sadly. It hurt to know that Eleanor Lathrop Winfield's reputation for riding roughshod over everybody was common knowledge around the department.

"What else?" Frank asked.

"According to Maggie MacFerson, Connie's husband, Ron Haskell, emptied his wife's bank accounts before he took off for parts unknown. He left a message on his wife's answering machine Thursday sometime. Ms. MacFerson inadvertently erased it, so I don't know exactly what it said. Something about seeing Connie in paradise, which Ms. MacFerson seems to have concluded was a death threat."

"You want me to trace the call?"

"You read my mind."

"Okay. Got it."

Frank, an inveterate note-taker, may have balked at having to deal with Eleanor Lathrop Winfield, but he had no concern about tackling telephone-company bureaucracy. As far as Joanna was concerned, that left Eleanor in a league of her own.

"Next?" Frank prodded through the momentary silence.

"Did you get a list from the DMV on vehicles registered to that Encanto Drive address?"

"Yes, ma'am. I have it here somewhere. A Lincoln and a BMW, if I remember correctly."

Joanna listened as he shuffled through loose papers. "Once you find them," she said, "I want those vehicle descriptions posted with all of our patrol units and with the folks from Border Patrol as well."

"So you're still thinking this might be just another carjacking?" Frank asked.

"Until we know otherwise, I'm not dismissing any possibilities," she replied. "A single woman traveling alone at night might be easier pickings for a carjacker than that little old guy in his Saturn."

"We don't know for sure Connie Haskell was coming to Cochise County," Frank objected.

"We sure as hell know that's where she ended up!" Joanna responded. "And since she didn't fly from Phoenix to Apache Pass, that means she must have driven."

"I see your point," Frank conceded. "I have that DMV info. It was buried on my desk. I'll have Dispatch put it out to the cars right away."

"Good, but before you do, let's go back to that carjacked Saturn," Joanna added. "You said it was picked up at a Border Patrol checkpoint. How many other stolen or carjacked vehicles have ended up in Border Patrol impound lots? Has anybody ever mentioned that particular statistic to you?"

"Not that I remember," Frank said. "But I can try to find out."

"Okay. Now, what's happening on the Dora Matthews front?"

"Not much," Frank said. "As far as I know, she's still out at the High Lonesome, and there hasn't been a peep out of Sally. The last time I checked, the note we left for her was still pinned to the screen door on her house up Tombstone Canyon."

Joanna groaned inwardly. "When I asked The Gs to look after the place while Butch and I were gone, they were supposed to look after the animals. Now they're having to deal with two adolescent kids as well."

"I'm sure they can handle it," Frank returned.

"I'm sure they can, too," Joanna said. "But they shouldn't have to."

"Where are you now?" Frank asked.

"I just passed the first Casa Grande turnoff, so I'm making progress," Joanna said.

"I should probably get on the horn to Doc Winfield and let him know you're on your way. Do you want me to meet you at the ME's office?"

"No," Joanna said. "Don't bother. It's Saturday night. You're a good-looking single guy, Frank. Don't you have anything better to do on a Saturday night besides work?"

"Not so as you'd notice," Frank told her.

They signed off after that, and Joanna continued to drive. Still accustomed to the time the trip had taken under the old fifty-five-miles-per-hour speed limit, Joanna was amazed at how fast the miles sped by. At last Maggie MacFerson groaned and stirred.

"Where am I?" she demanded. Using one of her clubbed fists, she brushed her lank brown hair out of her face. "What happened to my hands, and who the hell are you?"

Joanna looked at her passenger in surprise. "I'm Joanna Brady," she said. "I'm the sheriff in Cochise County. Don't you remember my coming to the house?"

"I've never seen you before in my life," Maggie answered. "And if you're a cop, am I under arrest, or what? I demand to talk to my lawyer." She squinted at an approaching overhead freeway sign. "Cortaro Road!"

she exclaimed. "That's in Tucson, for God's sake. Where the hell are you taking me? Let me out of this car!"

She reached for the door handle. With the car speeding down the road at seventy-five, it was fortunate that the door was locked. As Maggie struggled to unlock it with her clumsy, bandaged hands, Joanna switched on her emergency lights, pulled over to the shoulder, and slowed to a stop.

"Ms. MacFerson, please," she said reassuringly. "You're not under arrest. Don't you remember anything?"

"I remember going to Connie's house and waiting for that son of a bitch of a brother-in-law of mine. I listened to the messages, talked to Ken Wilson, and after that . . . nothing." She stopped struggling with the door and turned to look at Joanna. "Wait a minute. Is this about Connie?"

Joanna's mind reeled. She had gone through Constance Haskell's next-of-kin notification once, but it evidently hadn't taken. Maggie MacFerson remembered none of it. Joanna had heard of alcoholic blackouts, but this was the first time she had ever dealt with someone who had been functioning in one. Maggie MacFerson may have been able to walk and talk. She had seemed aware of what was going on around her, but apparently her brain had been switched off. For all she remembered, Maggie might as well have been asleep.

Joanna took a deep breath. "I'm afraid I have some bad news for you," she said. "A woman's body was found in Apache Pass last night. This morning my officers found a broken medical identification bracelet nearby, a bracelet with your sister's name and address on it. I came by your sister's house this afternoon and found you there. I told you what had happened, and you agreed to come with me to identify your sister's body. That's what we're doing now. We're on our way to Bisbee."

Maggie turned and stared at Joanna, who waited for an outburst that never came.

"Then what are we doing sitting here talking about it?" Maggie demanded at last. "Let's get this show on the road."

Joanna nodded. Checking in the mirror for a break in traffic, she eased the idling Crown Victoria back onto the roadway. Once they reached highway speed, she switched off the flashing lights.

"You still haven't told me what happened to my hands," Maggie said. "Did I get in a fight and punch somebody's lights out?"

"You broke a glass," Joanna told her. "A crystal glass. The ER folks at Saint Joe's took out as much glass as they could find and stitched up the worst of the cuts. You're supposed to go see your own doctor next week to have the bandages and stitches removed. The doctor also said there's a good chance he may have missed some of the glass. The pieces were small and difficult to see." Joanna paused. "How are you feeling?" she added.

"Hungover as hell," Maggie admitted. "But I've had worse. I'm thirsty. My mouth tastes like the bottom of a birdcage. Can't we stop and get something to drink?"

"As in a soda?" Joanna asked. "Or as in something stronger?"

"A Coke will be fine," Maggie MacFerson said. "Hell, I'd even drink straight water if I had to." And then, after all that, she started to cry.

6

After stopping at a Burger King long enough to get a pair of Cokes, Joanna once again headed down the freeway. By then Maggie MacFerson had stopped weeping. She sat up straight and wiped her nose on the back of one of her bandaged hands and sipped her soda through a straw.

"I'm sure you told me all of this before," she said, stifling a hiccup, "but I don't remember any of it. Tell me again, please. From the beginning."

Joanna did. When she finished, Maggie continued to stare out through the windshield in utter silence. "You said earlier you thought your brother-in-law was responsible," Joanna added at last. "Any particular reason?"

"Connie met Ron Haskell during our mother's final illness," Maggie answered quietly. "He was a CPA working for the accounting firm that handled our parents' affairs, Peabody and Peabody. Connie had Mother's power of attorney so she could handle finances, pay bills and all that. Ron Haskell knew everything about Mother's affairs, right down to the last penny. I think he saw that my sister was a vulnerable old maid who would eventually be well-to-do. He set out on a single-minded quest to grab Connie's half of our mother's estate. I don't know what the hell Ron did with the money, but according to Ken Wilson, it's gone. Ron closed all the accounts and then disappeared. If Connie's dead, it's probably a good thing. Finding out that Ron had stolen the money would have killed her. For her, being dead is probably preferable to being betrayed, cast off, and dirt-poor besides, or, even worse, having to come crawling to me for help."

"At the house, you said something about a message from your sister's husband, one that was on the machine. Something about him wanting to meet your sister in paradise."

Maggie nodded. "Right," she said. "Something like that. I was off work. I'm afraid I'd already had a couple of drinks before I got there. Ron said, 'Meet me in paradise. Join me in paradise.' Something like that. I don't remember exactly, but it sounded to me like he meant for her to be dead. Maybe he was planning one of those homicide/suicide stunts. Connie was so stuck on the guy that she would have done whatever he asked, even if it killed her."

After that, it was painfully quiet in the car. The sun had set completely. Once they exited the freeway at Benson, traffic grew sparse. "I wish I still smoked," Maggie said. "I could sure use a cigarette about now, and something a whole lot stronger than soda."

"Sorry about that," Joanna said. "Cop cars aren't meant to be cocktail lounges."

"I suppose not," Maggie said.

When they came through the tunnel at the top of the Divide, Joanna was surprised to see the flashing glow of emergency lights just to the right of the highway. They danced and flickered off the steep mountainsides, making the whole canyon look as if it had caught fire. From the number of lights visible, there were clearly lots of emergency vehicles at the scene. Something big had happened at the top end of Old Bisbee. Joanna reached over and switched on her radio.

"Hey, Tica," she said, when Tica Romero, the night-shift dispatcher, came on the air. "Any idea what's happening at the upper end of Tombstone Canyon?"

"That would be the Department of Public Safety's Haz-Mat team," Tica advised her. "Bisbee PD called DPS in to clean up a meth lab they found in a house just above the highway. Since it's inside the city limits and not our jurisdiction, I didn't bother with all the details. Want me to find out for you?"

"No, never mind," Joanna told her. "I have a possible relative of the presumed Apache Pass victim with me. We're meeting with Doc Winfield for an ID. When we finish with that, I'll most likely go back to Phoenix."

"So Chief Deputy Montoya is still in charge?" Tica asked.

"That's right. Ever since Dick Voland left, Frank's been itching to run an investigation. Looks to me like he's doing a good job of it."

Minutes later, Joanna wheeled the Civvie in under the portico of the office of the Cochise County Medical Examiner. The building, a former grocery store turned mortuary turned morgue, still bore a strong resemblance to its short-lived and unsuccessful mortuary incarnation, a connection Maggie recognized at once.

"They've already sent Connie to a funeral home?" she asked. "You told me we were going to the morgue."

"This *is* the morgue. It used to be a funeral home," Joanna explained, pulling in and parking under the covered driveway. "A company called Dearest Departures went out of business several years ago. Some bright-eyed county bureaucrat, intent on saving the local taxpayers a bundle of money, bought the building out of bankruptcy and remodeled it into a new facility for our incoming medical examiner. His name is George Winfield, by the way," she added. "Dr. George Winfield."

Joanna got out of the car. Then, remembering Maggie's bandaged hands wouldn't allow her to operate the door handle, Joanna hurried around the Crown Victoria to let her passenger out. Once on her feet, Maggie leaned briefly against the side of the car, as if she wasn't quite capable of standing on her own. Concerned, Joanna reached out and offered to take Maggie's arm. "Are you all right, Ms. MacFerson?" she asked.

Maggie bit her lip. "Maybe it won't be her after all," she said, as tears welled in her eyes. "Connie's only forty-three, for God's sake. She turned forty-three in March. That's too young."

"You're right," Joanna said gently. "It's far too young. Will you be all right with this?"

As she watched, Maggie MacFerson nodded, straightened her shoulders, and drew away from both the car and Joanna's proffered assistance. "I'm a reporter," she said determinedly. "This isn't the first dead body I've ever seen, and it won't be the last."

Joanna led the way to the door. Because George Winfield's Dodge Caravan was parked in its designated spot, she knew her stepfather was already there. She also knew that after hours, when George worked alone, he usually kept the outside door locked, buzzing visitors in only after they rang the bell and identified themselves over an intercom.

Joanna did so. George Winfield came to the door looking capable and handsome in his white lab coat. "Good evening, Sheriff Brady," he said.

By mutual agreement, when meeting in a work setting, Joanna and her stepfather addressed each other by their formal titles. Maintaining a strictly business approach made it simpler for all concerned.

Joanna nodded in return. "This is Maggie MacFerson," she said. "And this is Cochise County's medical examiner, Dr. George Winfield."

George held out his hand in a solicitous, gentlemanly fashion, then, noticing the bandages on Maggie's hands, he withdrew it at once. "Connie is . . . was my sister." She faltered.

"I'm so sorry—" George began, but Maggie pulled herself together and cut him off in mid-sentence.

"Don't," she said, holding up one hand in protest. "Let's get this over with."

"Of course," he said. "This way, please."

He led the two women into a side room that must have once served as a small chapel. George had had a window installed along one wall. Opening a curtain on that allowed grieving family members to view their loved ones without having to venture into the brightly lit, sterile chill of the morgue itself. Joanna and Maggie MacFerson waited for several minutes in a silence softened only by the muted whisper of an air-conditioning fan.

Eventually George pulled the curtain open, revealing the loaded gurney that he had rolled up beside the window. Winfield reappeared on the other side of the window after he had pulled aside the curtain. Maggie stood up and leaned against the double-paned window. Slowly George Winfield drew back a corner of the sheet, revealing a stark-white face.

Standing next to Maggie, Joanna felt the woman's body stiffen and heard her sharp intake of breath. "It's her," she whispered. "It's Connie."

With that, Maggie turned and fled the room. Joanna stayed long enough to nod in George's direction, then she followed Maggie out into the reception area, where she had dropped into a chair.

"Are you all right?" Joanna asked.

"What on earth did he do to her? Dying's too good for the son of a bitch!" Maggie growled. "Now take me someplace where I can have a drink."

Joanna understood at once that this time a Burger King soda would hardly suffice. "Really, Ms. MacFerson," Joanna began. "Don't you think—"

"I think I need a drink," Maggie interrupted. "If you won't take me to get one, then I'll find one myself." With that, she got up and marched out the door. George Winfield entered the reception room just in time to hear the last of that exchange.

"What was that all about?" he asked.

"Maggie wants a drink," Joanna explained. "Which, if you ask me, is the last thing she needs about now. She was so drunk earlier this afternoon that she didn't remember my telling her that her sister was dead, and she didn't remember cutting her hands with pieces from a broken glass, either."

"She was functioning in a blackout?" George asked.

"Must have been," Joanna replied. "That's the only thing I can figure."

"How long has it been since she's had a drink?"

"A couple of hours," Joanna replied with a shrug. "Several, actually."

"If I were you, then," George said, "I'd get her the drink she wants right away. If she's enough of a problem drinker that she's suffering black-outs, I'd advise not cutting off her supply of alcohol. She could go into DTs and die on you."

Joanna was stunned. "Are you serious?"

"Absolutely. Her body is most likely accustomed to functioning with a certain level of booze in it. If you take the alcohol away suddenly, without her being under a doctor's care, you risk triggering a case of DTs that could possibly kill her."

"In that case," Joanna said, "I'd best go buy the lady a drink. I'll have Maggie call you later to give you all the relevant information, date of birth and all that. Before I go, I have to ask. Frank gave me the high points on your autopsy results—that Connie Haskell was beaten, raped, and tortured. Anything else?"

George Winfield shook his head. "Isn't that enough? Whoever did this is a real psycho."

"DNA evidence?" Joanna asked.

"Plenty of that. Either the guy didn't think he'd get caught or else he didn't care. Whichever the case, he sure as hell didn't use a condom. And you'd better catch up with him soon," George added. "If you don't, I'm guessing he'll do it again."

On that grim note, Joanna started to leave. Before she made it to the door, George stopped her. "There's something else I need to tell you," he said. "Not about this," he added hurriedly. "It's another matter entirely."

"Something about Mother?" Joanna asked.

"Well, yes," he said, avoiding her eyes. "In a manner of speaking."

"Look, George," Joanna said. "I'm in a bit of a hurry here. Could you stop beating around the bush and tell me what's going on?"

"Eleanor called CPS early this afternoon."

"She did what?"

"Ellie called Child Protective Services. She was concerned about Dora being out at the ranch, so she called CPS. An investigator went to Sally Matthews's house up in Tombstone Canyon. No one was home, but she went nosing around in the backyard, where she saw enough telltale debris to make her suspicious. She tracked down a judge. This evening she came back with a search warrant and reinforcements." George paused.

In her mind's eye, Joanna once again saw the pulsing emergency lights flashing off the sides of the canyon as she drove through the Bisbee end of the Mule Mountain Tunnel. "Don't tell me Sally Matthews is dead, too," Joanna breathed.

"No, I don't suppose so," George said. "Nothing like that. At least not as far as we know."

Joanna wanted to shake the man to stop his hemming and hawing. "What do we know?" she demanded.

"It looks like Sally Matthews has been running a meth lab in her house, the old Pommer place up Tombstone Canyon. The Department of Public Safety Haz-Mat guys are up there right now, trying to clean it up."

"What about Dora?" Joanna asked.

"That's the part I didn't want to tell you." George Winfield shook his head sadly. "Jim Bob called me a few minutes ago. That same CPS case-worker just showed up out at the ranch and demanded that Jim Bob and Eva Lou hand Dora over to her. Which Jim Bob and Eva Lou did, of course—hand her over, that is. The caseworker told them they didn't have a choice in the matter. Dora's headed for a foster home out in Sierra Vista. I guess both Dora and Jenny were pretty upset."

"I should think so," Joanna said. "Wouldn't you be?"

"Yes," George Winfield admitted. "I'm afraid I would."

Joanna turned on her heel and started away. Then she stopped and turned back. "There are times when that wife of yours is a meddlesome—" She bit off the rest of the sentence.

George Winfield sighed. "I know," he said. "Believe me, I know."

Coming out of George Winfield's office, Joanna sat in her Civvie for a moment, calming herself and catching her breath. The anger she felt toward her interfering mother left her drained and shaken. She wanted to grab her telephone, call Eleanor up, and rail at her for not minding her own business, but yelling at her mother wouldn't change a thing. Farther up the canyon, emergency lights still flashed and pulsed off the steep hill-sides. Somehow, seeing those lights and knowing that the Haz-Mat team was still at work and probably would be for hours propelled her out of her anger-induced paralysis. It was time to focus on a course of action.

There was no question about what had to be done. Not only had Jenny found a body, she had also been traumatized by seeing one of her friends—someone who had done no wrong—taken into what must have seemed like police custody. Joanna had to go to Jenny, the sooner the better. If the choice was between comforting her daughter and attending a wedding with Butch, there was no contest.

But what about Maggie MacFerson? Joanna was the person who had brought Maggie to town, and it was her responsibility to take the woman—drunk or sober—back to Phoenix. The thought of Maggie wandering through a strange town on her own was enough to make Joanna start the engine and put the Crown Victoria in gear.

She caught sight of Maggie several blocks away, trudging deter-minedly downhill. The white bandages on her hands caught in the beams of passing headlights and glowed like moving, iridescent balloons. Joanna pulled up beside the walking woman and rolled down her window. "Where are you headed?" she asked.

Maggie MacFerson stopped walking and turned to glare at Joanna through the open window. "I didn't see any watering holes as we came into town. I figure if I go downhill far enough, I'm bound to run into something."

"Get in," Joanna urged. "I'll give you a lift."

"No lectures?"

"No lectures."

Joanna got out, went around the car, and let Maggie in. Then she fastened her seat belt.

"Thanks," Maggie said grudgingly. "That was a bitch!"

Joanna knew Maggie didn't mean getting in and out of the car. She was talking about the ordeal of identifying a murdered loved one. "Yes," Joanna said. "I know."

"Do you?" Maggie asked sharply.

Joanna nodded. "You interviewed me when I was elected, after my first husband was shot and killed, remember?"

"Oh, that's right," Maggie said as the anger drained from her voice. "I forgot. Sorry." She fell silent then as Joanna struggled to ignore her own rampaging emotions while she drove the narrow winding thoroughfare called Tombstone Canyon. That one exchange had been enough to catapult Joanna back into the unimaginable pain she had lived with immediately after Andy's murder. She knew too well how much that kind of violent death hurt and the kind of impact it had on the people left behind. Andy's murder was now three years in the past, but Joanna doubted the pain of it would ever go away entirely.

Maggie ducked her head to look up at the glowing lights from houses perched on the steep hillsides on either side of the street. "The people who live in those places must be half mountain goat," she said.

Grateful for Maggie's attempt to defuse the stricken silence, Joanna responded in kind. "If I were you," she said, "I wouldn't bother challenging any of them to a stair-climbing contest."

Coming into the downtown area, Joanna drove straight to the Copper Queen Hotel and pulled up into the loading zone out front. Once again, she went around the car and opened both the door and the seat belt to let Maggie out.

"The bar's right over there," Joanna said, nodding her head toward the outside entrance to the hotel's lounge. "Why don't you go on inside. I need to check on something."

While Maggie headed toward the bar, Joanna hurried to the desk. "Do you have any vacancies tonight?" she asked the young woman behind the counter.

"We sure do. What kind of a room?"

"Single. Nonsmoking."

"For just one night?"

Joanna nodded. The clerk pushed a registration form across the counter. Joanna filled it out with Maggie's name, and paid for the room with her own credit card. Once she had the key in her hand she went into the bar, where Maggie was sitting in front of a glass filled with amber liquid. Out of deference to her bandaged hands, the bartender had put a long straw in the cocktail glass.

"Something's happened at home," Joanna said, settling on the stool next to Maggie. "I'm going to have to spend some time with my daughter. I hope you don't mind, but I've booked a room for you here at the Copper Queen, courtesy of the Cochise County Sheriff's Department. Here's the key. Tomorrow morning, first thing, I'll take you back to Phoenix. I hope that's all right."

"Can't you put me on a bus?"

"There isn't a bus."

"A taxi, then?"

"There isn't one that'll take you as far as Phoenix."

"Well, then, I guess it'll have to be all right, won't it?" Maggie replied after slurping a long swallow through the straw. "Was it something I said, or are you just opposed to riding around with drunks in your car?"

Joanna ignored the gibe. "Here's my home phone number," she added. Next to the key on the counter, Joanna placed a business card on which she had scribbled her number at High Lonesome Ranch. Maggie peered at the card but made no effort to collect it or the key. When Maggie said nothing more, Joanna left the lounge, stopping back by the front desk on her way out.

"Maggie MacFerson, the guest in room nineteen, is in the bar," she told the desk clerk. "You'll recognize her right away. She's got bandages on both hands and probably won't be able to manage a key. It's probably not going to take much Scotch to put her back under, either. Would you please be sure she makes it to her room safely?"

"Sure thing, Sheriff Brady," the desk clerk said. "I'll be glad to. Does she need help with her luggage?"

Joanna didn't recognize the young woman, but by now she was accustomed to the idea that there were lots of people in Cochise County who knew the sheriff by sight—or maybe by credit card—when she had no idea who they were. "She doesn't have any luggage," Joanna returned. "But thanks. I appreciate it."

As Joanna climbed into the Civvie, her cell phone began to ring. She could see her caller was Chief Deputy Montoya. "Hello, Frank," she said.

Unfortunately Old Bisbee existed in a cleft in the Mule Mountains into which no cell phone signal could penetrate. The only sounds emanating from Joanna's receiver were unintelligible sputterings. Hanging up in frustration, she reached for the radio.

"Tica," she said to Dispatch. "Can you patch me through to Chief Deputy Montoya? He tried to call me on the cell phone a minute ago, but I'm up in Old Bisbee in a dead zone."

Putting the Civvie in gear, she began negotiating the series of one-way streets that would take her back down to Main Street. After several long minutes, Frank's voice came through the radio. "Where are you?" he demanded. "I could hear your voice, but you kept breaking up."

"I'm just now leaving Old Bisbee," she told him. "I'm on my way out to the ranch."

"How did the ID go?"

"About how you'd expect. I just dropped the victim's sister off at the Copper Queen Hotel for a medicinal Scotch to calm her nerves. I also rented her a room. I've got to go home to see Jenny. I told Maggie MacFerson that I'll drive her back to Phoenix in the morning. The idea that there aren't hourly Greyhounds running through Bisbee overnight was news to her."

"So the ID is positive, then?" Frank asked.

"Yes," Joanna said. "Constance Haskell is the victim all right. I trust the DMV information from that Encanto address has been broadcast to all units?"

"Absolutely—a Beemer and a Lincoln Town Car. Neither one of them were at the residence in Phoenix, right?"

"That's correct."

"Good. I listed them both as possibly stolen and the perp presumed armed and dangerous. That way, if someone spots either one of 'em, they'll be pulled over. Where are you headed?"

"Out to the ranch to see Jenny," Joanna replied.

"So you've heard about what happened to Dora then?" Frank asked.

"Some of it," Joanna returned grimly. "Doc Winfield told me. I think I'll stop by their house on my way home and wring my mother's neck."

"From what Jim Bob told me, I guess Jenny's really upset about what happened."

"Tell me," Joanna urged.

"When Dora figured out what was going on—that we knew what her mother had been up to and that a caseworker was there to put Dora back into foster care—she lit out the back door and tried to make a run for it. The caseworker must have seen it coming. She took off out the front door and caught Dora as she came racing around the house. I mean she literally tackled Dora. They both went down in a heap. Dora fought tooth and nail all the way to the car. She was yelling and crying and screaming that she didn't want to go, that she'd rather die. I'm sure it was traumatic for everybody concerned. If I'd been there, I'd be upset, too."

So am I, Joanna thought grimly. But right at that moment, powerless to change what had happened, she did the only thing that might help her forge through the emotional maelstrom—she changed the subject. "Anything else happening?"

"Well, I have one small piece of good news," Frank replied. "I managed to get through to the phone factory. It's possible the missing message on that answering machine really did say Connie Haskell should meet her husband in Paradise. The call to the house in Phoenix originated from a pay phone outside the general store in Portal, which happens to be only eight miles or so from Paradise—town of, that is. I told Ernie about the Portal connection. He and Detective Carbajal will head over there first thing in the morning and start asking questions."

Mentally Joanna made some quick geographical calculations. Portal was located on the eastern side of the Chiricahua Mountains at the far southern end of the range. Apache Pass was at the north end and on the western side. To get to Apache Pass from Portal, one would have to go around the Chiricahuas, traveling on either the Arizona or New Mexico side, or else cross over the range itself, using a twisting dirt-and-gravel track that crossed at a low spot called Onion Saddle.

"You're thinking that when Ron Haskell left his message, he was referring to having Connie meet him in the town of Paradise?"

"Makes sense to me, but we don't have a clue as to where in town he'd be meeting her. I checked with Directory Assistance. I asked for any business listings with a Paradise address. The operator came up with a couple that sounded like bed-and-breakfast-type places, and Ron Haskell might well be staying at one of those. The problem is, they all had phones, so I'm a little puzzled as to why he'd be using a pay phone at the general store. The operator hit on something else promising, a place called Pathway to Paradise. I just finished checking out Pathway to Paradise on the Internet. Their web site says it's a rehab facility that specializes in gambling problems."

"That fits," Joanna said. "A severe gambling problem could go a long way toward explaining how Connie Haskell's money left her bank accounts and disappeared into thin air. You've told Ernie and Jaime to check that out as well?"

"Right."

"Good job. So where are you right now?" Joanna asked.

"Standing across the street from Sally Matthews's place up in Old Bisbee," Frank said. "I've talked to a couple of the Haz-Mat guys. They said the house is a wreck inside. Aside from the chemical pollution, the house is so filthy that it's totally uninhabitable. He said he was surprised people were still trying to live there." Frank paused. "I feel sorry for Dora. She's been through a really rough time. And don't be too hard on your mother, either, Boss. The way I see it, compared to where she was living, foster care is probably the best thing that could happen to Dora Matthews."

"I'll try to remember that," Joanna said.

"You're staying overnight then?" Frank asked.

"That's my plan at the moment."

Signing off, Joanna headed for High Lonesome Ranch, seven miles east of town. On the way, she tried calling Butch once more. It was late enough that she hoped he might have returned from the dinner. This time, when she dialed, she had driven out from behind the signal-eating barrier of the Mule Mountains. But instead of reaching the Conquistador Hotel in Peoria, Joanna heard the recorded voice of a cell phone company operator from across the line in Old Mexico.

With the recent proliferation of cell phone sites across the border, cell phone use in the Bisbee area had become more and more problematic. People attempting to make wireless calls within the sight lines of newly built Mexican cell sites often found themselves sidetracked into the Mexican system. And once a call was answered by the Mexican operator, the hapless U.S. customer could count on being billed a minimum of four dollars for the call despite the fact that it had gone no farther than a less than helpful Spanish-language recorded message.

"Damn!" Joanna muttered, and gave up trying.

When she pulled into the yard at High Lonesome Ranch, Tigger and Sadie came racing out to dance around the car in a gleeful greeting that made it look as though Joanna had been gone for weeks rather than mere days. By the time Joanna finished calming the two ecstatic dogs, Jim Bob Brady was standing next to the Civvie.

"You heard, I guess," he said.

Nodding, Joanna let herself be drawn into her former father-in-law's welcoming embrace. She stayed there, imprisoned against Jim Bob Brady's massive chest, letting herself be comforted for the better part of a minute before she finally pulled away.

"Do you think Jenny's asleep?" she asked.

"Could be, but I doubt it," Jim Bob answered gravely. "She was mighty upset when she went to bed. Don't seem too likely that she'd drop right off."

Joanna hurried into the house through the back door and went directly to her daughter's room. She tapped lightly on the closed door. "Jenny," she said softly. "Are you still awake? May I come in?"

"It's open," Jenny answered. It wasn't exactly an engraved invitation, but Joanna opened the door and eased herself into the room. Guided by the shadowy glow of a night-light, Joanna crept over to the rocking chair that had once belonged to Butch's grandmother.

Joanna settled herself in the old rocker, which emitted a loud squeak as she put her weight on it. "Do you want to talk about it?" she asked softly.

"No." Jenny flopped over on the bed. Even in the dim light, Joanna could see tears glistening on her daughter's cheeks. "I hate Grandma Lathrop!" Jenny whispered fiercely. "I don't care if I ever see her again!"

Joanna was taken aback by the ferocity in her daughter's voice, by the burning anger tears hadn't begun to extinguish. "I'm mad at her, too," Joanna said quietly, "but I know Grandma Lathrop didn't mean any harm. I'm sure she had no idea your friend would be hurt."

Jenny sat up. "Dora Matthews is not my friend," she declared. "I don't even like her, but she doesn't deserve to be treated like that. That woman grabbed her and threw her into the car. It was like an animal control officer dragging a stray dog off to the pound."

It wasn't the time to point out to Jenny that animal control officers were only doing their thankless jobs the same way the CPS caseworker had been doing hers. For once, Joanna managed to keep quiet and let her daughter do the talking.

"Why couldn't Dora have stayed here with us?" Jenny demanded. "She wasn't bothering anybody or hurting anything. She did everything the Gs said, like clearing the table and emptying the dishwasher and even making her bed. All she wanted to do was go home and be with her mother, the same way I want to be with you. She said she's already done the foster-care thing and would rather be dead than go through that again."

"I don't doubt that foster care can be pretty miserable at times," Joanna agreed. "But surely Dora didn't mean she'd rather be dead. She'll be fine, Jenny. I promise. Girl Scout's honor."

Suddenly Jenny erupted out of her bed. In a single motion, she crossed the space between her bunk bed and the rocking chair. Jenny had shot up more than three inches in the last few months. There wasn't enough room for Joanna to hold her daughter on her lap. Instead, Jenny knelt in front of the rocker and buried her face in her mother's lap. For several minutes they stayed that way, with Jenny sobbing and with Joanna caressing her daughter's tangled hair.

Finally, Jenny drew a ragged breath. "Why did Grandma have to go and do that?" she asked with a shudder. "Why couldn't she leave well enough alone? We were doing all right. The Gs wouldn't have let anything bad happen to Dora."

Joanna had to wait a moment until her own voice steadied before she attempted an answer. "I don't like what happened either, but there's a good chance Grandma Lathrop was right," she said carefully. "Dora's mother has evidently been running a meth lab out of their house. Do you know what that means?"

Jenny shrugged. "Not really," she said.

"It means that the house had illegal drugs and potentially dangerous chemicals in it. The people who are up there now, cleaning it up—the DPS Haz-Mat team—are doing it in full hazardous-material protective gear. Those chemicals are dangerously explosive, Jenny. If the house had caught fire, for example, Dora and her mother both might have been killed. They shouldn't have been living in a place like that. It's irresponsible for a mother to raise a child in such circumstances.

"That's what society means when they say someone is an unfit mother. Considering what they found in Sally Matthews's house, I think there's a good chance that's exactly what will happen—she'll be declared an unfit mother. She may even go to jail. In other words, Dora Matthews would have ended up in foster care anyway, sooner or later. Grandma Lathrop fixed it so it happened sooner, is all. I'm sorry it had to be tonight, and I'm terribly sorry that you had to be here to see it happen."

"But even if Dora's mother is a bad mother, Dora still loves her."

"That's right," Joanna agreed. "And I understand exactly how she feels. When I first heard about Grandma Lathrop calling CPS, I was really upset, too—just like you are. But Eleanor's still my mother, Jenny, and I still love her."

"And I love you," Jenny said.

For the next few minutes, as they sat together, with Jenny resting her head in her mother's lap, Joanna was glad Jenny couldn't see her face. If she had, Jenny would have seen that her mother was crying, too.

7

Joanna and Jenny might have sat there much longer, but Eva Lou knocked on the door. "Could I interest anyone in some cocoa and toast?" she asked.

"How about it?" Joanna asked.

Jenny nodded. "Okay," she said.

On her way to the kitchen, Joanna stopped at the telephone long enough to try calling Butch one more time. Once again, rather than reaching her husband, she found herself connected to the voice-mail system. "Mother called CPS, and they came out to the house and hauled Dora away like she was a criminal being arrested," she told the machine. "Naturally, Jenny is in a state about it, and I don't blame her. I'm out at the house now and planning to spend the night. I'm way too tired to try driving back to Phoenix again tonight. I'll come first thing in the morning. And, oh yes, I almost forgot. The woman I brought down, Maggie MacFerson, did turn out to be the murdered woman's sister after all. So we have our positive ID. Sorry I missed you. Hope you had fun at the dinner. I love you. It's almost nine o'clock now. Call if you get this by ten or so. Any later, and you'll wake people up. If I don't hear from you tonight, I'll talk to you tomorrow."

Out in the kitchen, Jim Bob was spreading toast while Eva Lou carried mugs of steaming cocoa over to the breakfast nook. Jenny settled herself at the far corner of the table, and Joanna slipped onto the bench seat beside her.

"I'm sorry you had to come all the way down from Phoenix just because of what happened to Dora," Jenny said as she began using her spoon to target and sink the dozen or so miniature marshmallows Eva Lou had left floating on the surface of the cocoa.

Absorbed in her task, Jenny failed to notice the momentary hesitation on her mother's part. Jenny's unquestioning belief in Joanna's having responded in an entirely motherly fashion made Sheriff Brady feel more than slightly guilty. She had come to Bisbee on departmental business rather than in response to Jenny's crisis. It would have been easy to take credit where it wasn't due, but Joanna didn't work that way.

"I didn't find out about Dora until I was already in Bisbee," she admitted. "I brought a woman down from Phoenix with me. It was her sister, Connie Haskell, whose body you found in Apache Pass last night."

"You know who the victim is, then?" Jim Bob asked.

Joanna nodded, looking at Jenny and trying to judge if having brought up the topic of the murdered woman was having any negative effects. Jenny, meanwhile, continued to chase marshmallows. Her air of total detachment seemed to imply that the conversation had nothing at all to do with her.

"How are you doing on finding the killer, then?" Jim Bob asked. Joanna's former father-in-law had always taken a keen interest in Andy's ongoing cases. Now, with Andy dead, he was just as vitally concerned with whatever cases Joanna was working on.

"Not very well," Joanna responded. "The sister gave us a positive ID. She's staying overnight at the Copper Queen. I'll have to pick her up first thing in the morning and take her back to Phoenix."

"So you'll be there in time to see Butch be in the wedding?" Jenny asked. Having just been through her mother's wedding to Butch, Jenny had been intrigued by the idea of Butch being the bride's attendant and had teased him about whether he'd have to wear a dress.

"I had almost forgotten about the wedding," Joanna said. "With everything that's going on, maybe I should just turn around and come straight back home."

"You'll do no such thing!" Eva Lou exclaimed. "Jim Bob and I are here to look after things. Jenny's fine. There's no reason for you to miss it."

Joanna glanced at Jenny. "Are you fine?" she asked.

Jenny nodded and spooned what was left of one of the marshmallows into her mouth. "Yes," she said.

"You're sure?"

"I'm sure. I'm still mad at Grandma Lathrop, but I'm fine."

"See there?" Eva Lou said. "If you miss the wedding, you won't be able to use Jenny as an excuse. Now what time do you plan on leaving in the morning? And would you like us to go home, so you can sleep in your own bed? All you have to do is say the word. We can be back here tomorrow morning whenever you want us to be."

"You don't have to do that," Joanna said. "I'm perfectly capable of sleeping on the couch. And I want to be up and out early, by seven or so."

"Not the couch," Eva Lou objected. "I won't hear of it."

"Me, either," Jim Bob put in. "Those hide-a-bed things are never comfortable. There's always that danged metal bar that hits you right in the middle of your ribs."

Jenny gazed at her mother from under a fringe of long blond eyelashes. "If you want," she offered quietly, "you can sleep on the bottom bunk, and I'll sleep on top."

There was nothing Joanna Brady wanted more right then than to be near her daughter. "Thanks, Jen," she said. "What a nice offer. I'll be happy to take you up on it."

Half an hour later, still warmed by the hot cocoa, Joanna lay in Jenny's bed, peering up through the glow of the night-light at the dimly visible upper bunk. She was thinking about all that had happened. In a little over twenty-four hours, Jenny had been through a series of terribly traumatic experiences and yet she really did seem fine.

They had both been quiet for such a long time that Joanna assumed Jenny had drifted off.

"Mom? Are you still awake?"

"Yes."

"You never said anything to me about the cigarettes."

Butch's counsel came back to Joanna. What was it he had said? Something about not making a federal case of it. "Should I have?" Joanna asked.

"Well, I mean, you never bawled me out about them or anything."

"You already apologized to me about the cigarettes," Joanna said. "Remember last night on the phone? You told me then you were sorry about that. It's true, isn't it? You are sorry?"

"Yes."

"And you don't plan on trying another one anytime soon, right?"

"Right."

"Well then, I don't guess there's any reason to bawl you out."

"Oh," Jenny said. "Well, good night then."

"Good night."

Minutes later, Joanna was half asleep when Sadie crept onto the foot of the bed and flopped down between Joanna's feet and the wall. She had long suspected that Sadie sneaked up onto Jenny's bed once the bedroom door was safely closed behind them. Careful not to waken Jenny, Joanna shooed the dog off, only to have her clamber back on board just as Joanna herself was about to doze off. The third time it happened she gave up. The words *Let sleeping dogs lie* were drifting through her head as she finally fell asleep.

When Joanna awakened out of a deep sleep hours later, she was briefly disoriented by being in a strange bed and room. Then, gathering her faculties, she realized that what had roused her was the tantalizing smell of frying bacon and brewing coffee. The alarm clock on Jenny's bedside table said six forty-three.

Joanna stumbled out of bed and hurried to the kitchen, where she found both Eva Lou and Jim Bob up and dressed and busily engaged in fixing breakfast. "You two!" she said, shaking her head. "You didn't need to do this. I could have stopped off for breakfast somewhere along the way."

Eva Lou looked back at her and smiled. "Yes," she returned. "You could have, but you shouldn't have to. Now come sit down and eat something. There's no sense in waking Jenny this early."

While Jim Bob left to do one more outside chore, Joanna settled into the breakfast nook.

"Oh, my," Eva Lou said, as Joanna mowed through her very welcome bacon and eggs. "I forgot to tell you. Olga Ortiz called last night about Yolanda."

Yolanda Ortiz Cañedo was one of two female jailers employed by the Cochise County Jail. Only a month earlier, the young mother with two children in elementary school had been diagnosed with cervical cancer. She had undergone surgery at University Medical Center in Tucson and was now involved in chemotherapy.

"How is she?"

"Not well," Eva Lou said. "Her mother says Yolanda's back in the hospital. She's having a bad reaction to the chemo. Olga didn't come right out and say so, but I think she was hoping you might try to stop by the hospital."

University Hospital was where Andy had been taken after being shot. It was also where he had died. It was one of the places Joanna Brady would cheerfully never have set foot in again. "I'll try," she said. "Maybe Butch and I can stop by there on our way back down tonight."

"After the wedding? You're planning to come back home tonight?"

"The wedding is late in the afternoon. I was thinking if we left at seven, maybe . . ."

"Joanna," Eva Lou said kindly. "You didn't ask my advice, but I'm giving it too you all the same. Tomorrow's Memorial Day, a holiday. You've made arrangements for the department to be covered, haven't you?"

"Yes."

"And we're here to take care of Jenny and the ranch, right?"

"Right."

"Then give yourself and that new husband of yours a break. Spend the time with him."

Jim Bob returned to the kitchen just then. He looked from his wife's face to Joanna's. "What's up?" he asked. "Is something wrong?"

"Just girl talk," Eva Lou said with a smile as she handed him a cup of coffee. "Now sit down and eat before it gets cold."

An hour later, Joanna was standing at the front desk of the Copper Queen Hotel. "I'm sorry." The morning desk clerk was responding to Joanna's request that he ring room 19. "Ms. MacFerson has asked that she not be disturbed."

"But I'm here to take her back to Phoenix," Joanna objected.

"There must be some mistake then," he replied, riffling through the file of registration cards. "Ms. MacFerson has extended her stay for two and possibly three days."

"Really," Joanna said. "I believe I'll go check on that. Since I'm the one who's responsible for bringing her to town, I'm also the one who's responsible for getting her back home." With that, Joanna strode across the lobby and started up the carpeted stairway.

"Please, Sheriff Brady," the clerk pleaded. "You shouldn't . . ."

By the time he completed his sentence, Joanna was out of earshot. At the door to room 19, Joanna took one look at the DO NOT DISTURB sign hanging from the doorknob and then knocked anyway. "Housekeeping," she called.

"Housekeeping!" Maggie MacFerson croaked. "At this ungodly hour? What the hell kind of place is this, anyway?"

Remembering the bandages that had turned both of Maggie's hands into useless fists, Joanna guessed correctly that she wouldn't have locked the door.

"Oh, it's you," Maggie said, when Joanna let herself into the room. Maggie was still in bed, groaning and cradling her bandaged hands. "I told them I wasn't to be disturbed. I finally managed to get some sleep, but now my hands hurt like hell."

"Sorry to disturb you, but I thought I was taking you back to Phoenix this morning," Joanna said.

"I changed my mind. I'm a reporter, remember?" Maggie replied. "There's a story here, and the *Reporter's* sending a team to cover it. I'm part of that team. I'm an *investigative* reporter, Sheriff Brady, which means I'm used to asking tough questions and getting answers. Which reminds me. I happen to have one of those questions for you."

"Like what?" Joanna asked.

"Like why, all the time you were telling me about what happened to

Connie, you never happened to mention to me that one of the two people who found the body was none other than your own daughter?"

"It wasn't important," Joanna said. "There was no reason to tell you."

"There was no reason not to tell me," Maggie retorted. "I wouldn't know it even now if I hadn't been chatting up the bartender last night. Just like I wouldn't know that the local ME is a relative of yours. That strikes me as a little incestuous, Sheriff Brady. Taking all that into consideration, I've decided to hang around town for a while and ask a few more questions. No telling what I might turn up. Now go away!"

Without replying, Joanna started to leave the room. "One more thing," Maggie added before the door could close. "You might want to check out the first story. It'll be in late editions of the *Reporter*. I phoned it in last night, too late to make the statewide editions, but it'll be in the metropolitan ones."

"Great," Joanna muttered, after slamming the door shut behind her. "I can hardly wait."

Joanna left Bisbee seething with anger. Between there and Phoenix, she drove too hard and too fast. Twice she booted left-lane-hugging eighteen-wheelers out of the way by turning on the Civvie's under-grille lights. Several times along the way she tried phoning Butch, but now when he didn't answer she hung up before the voice-mail system ever picked up the call. She was tired of leaving messages in the room since he evidently wasn't bothering to pick them up. A call to Dispatch told her that Detectives Carpenter and Carbajal were on their way to Portal, where they hoped to locate and question Ron Haskell. She also learned that there was still no trace of Sally Matthews.

No surprises there, Joanna told herself.

A little past ten she pulled into the porte cochere at the Conquistador and handed her car keys over to the parking valet. Joanna let herself into their twelfth-floor room to find that the bed was made and the message light was flashing. She assumed that the room had been made up after Butch left that morning, but a check of the messages disabused her of that notion. The messages were all her messages to Butch. There were none from him for her.

She felt a sudden tightening in her stomach. *What if something's happened to him?* she wondered. *What if he's been in a car accident or was struck while crossing a street?*

Turning on her heel, she hurried out of the room and back down to the lobby, where she planned to buttonhole someone at the desk. By now it was verging on checkout time, so naturally she was stuck waiting in a long line. While there, she caught a glimpse of a copy of the Sunday edition of the *Arizona Reporter* held by a man two places in front of her.

"Murder Strikes Close to Home," the newspaper headline read. Beneath the headline was a black-and-white photo of two women, one of whom was unmistakably a much younger version of Maggie MacFerson.

Leaving her place in line, Joanna went to the hotel gift shop and purchased her own copy of the paper and then sat down on one of the couches in the lobby to read it. There were actually two separate articles. Keeping an eye on the line at the front desk, she skimmed through the staff-written piece with three different reporters' names listed in the byline. That one was a straightforward news article dealing with the murder of Constance Marie Haskell, daughter of a well-known Valley of the Sun developer, Stephen Richardson, and his wife, Claudia. Maggie MacFerson, a longtime *Arizona Reporter* columnist and investigative reporter, was listed in the article as a sister of the victim. The other article carried a Maggie MacFerson byline and was preceded by an editor's note.

For years *Arizona Reporter* prizewinning staff member Maggie MacFerson has distinguished herself as one of the foremost investigative reporters in the nation. Now, after years of being on the reporting side of the news, she finds herself in the opposite camp.

The discovery late Friday night of Ms. MacFerson's brutally slain younger sister and fellow heiress, Constance Marie Haskell, puts Maggie in the shoes of countless others who have suffered through the unimaginable horror of having a loved one murdered.

Ms. MacFerson's reputation as a trusted investigative reporter allows her a unique position from which to write about the other victims of homicide—the relatives and friends of the dead—who have few choices to make and even less control in the aftermath of a violent death.

She has agreed to write a series of articles recounting her terrible journey, which began with the discovery of her murdered sister's body two days ago in rural Cochise County. The first of those articles appears below.

Editor

Years ago I stood in a rainy, windblown cemetery in south Phoenix talking to a grieving mother whose sixteen-year-old son's bullet-riddled body had been found in the garbage-strewn sands of the Salt River four days earlier. Her son, a gang member, had been gunned down by two wannabe members of a rival gang as part of an initiation requirement. I'll never forget her words.

"Cops don't want to tell me nothin'," she said. "Just what they think I *need* to know. Don't they understand? I'm that boy's *mother*. I *need* to know it *all*."

That woman's words came back to me today with a whole new impact as I tried to come to grips with the horror that someone has murdered my forty-three-year-old sister, Constance Marie Haskell.

I didn't hear the news over the phone. The cops actually did that part right. Connie's body was found Friday night in Cochise County, near a place called Apache Pass. Cochise County Sheriff Joanna Brady herself came to see me Saturday to give me the terrible news. But somehow, in the process she neglected to tell me several things, including who it was who had found the body.

I suppose that oversight should be understandable since, in addition to being sheriff, Joanna Brady is also the mother of a twelve-year-old-daughter, and mothers—even mothers who aren't sheriffs—are known to be protective, sometimes overly so.

Jennifer Ann Brady and an equally headstrong friend, Dora Matthews, slipped away from a Girl Scout camp-out on Friday night to have a smoke. It was while they were AWOL from their tent that they discovered my sister's naked and bludgeoned body.

Most of the time juveniles who find bodies are interviewed and made much of in the media. After all, in reporting a crime they're thought to be doing the "right thing." Sheriff Brady told me none of this, but the information was easy enough for me to discover, along with a possible explanation for Ms. Brady's apparent reticence.

After all, what law enforcement officer wants to reveal to outsiders that his or her offspring is hanging out with the child of a known criminal? Because that's exactly what Dora Matthews is—the daughter of an alleged dealer in illegal drugs.

The fact that convicted drug dealer Sally Lorraine Matthews was reportedly running a meth lab out of her home in Old Bisbee may have been news to local law enforcement authorities who called for a Department of Public Safety Haz-Mat team to come clean up the mess last night, but it certainly wasn't news to some of Sally's paying customers, the drug consumers who hang out in city parks or wander dazedly up and down Bisbee's fabled Brewery Gulch.

With my sister's chilled body lying in the Cochise County Morgue, all I had to do was ask a few questions to find out what was really going on. I suspect that Sheriff Brady could have discovered that same information earlier than yesterday—if she'd bothered to ask, that is. But then, maybe she thought what she didn't know wouldn't hurt her, either.

Moving on to the Cochise County Morgue brings me to something else the sheriff failed to mention—the fact that Cochise County Medical Examiner Dr. George Winfield happens to be married to Sheriff Brady's mother. I'm sure if I had asked her why she didn't tell me that, her answer would have been the same—I didn't need to know.

Which brings me back to that heartbroken mother standing in that Phoenix cemetery. What all did police officers fail to tell her that she, too, didn't need to know?

At this moment, the only thing I know for sure is that Connie, my baby sister, is dead. I can't think about her the way she was as a sunny six-year-old, when I taught her how to ride a bike. I can't think about how she almost drowned when I tried to teach her to swim in our backyard pool. I can't think about how we sounded when our mother tried, unsuccessfully, to teach us to sing "Silent Night" in three-part harmony.

No, all I can think about is the way Connie looked tonight, lying on a gurney in the awful fluorescent lighting of the Cochise County Morgue. I am appalled by remembering her once beautiful face beaten almost beyond recognition.

There's much more that I need to know that I haven't yet been told—the why, the where, and the how of her death. Why, where, and how are the Holy Grails that keep all journalists and cops seeking and working and on their toes. But this time, I'm experiencing that search in an entirely different manner from the way it has been before both in my life and in my career. I'm seeing it through the eyes of that grieving mother, cloaked in her pain, standing in that lonely, desolate cemetery.

I'm not much of an expert on the grief process. I'm not sure which comes first, anger or denial. I can tell you that, right this moment, hours after learning about Connie's death, I am consumed with anger. Maybe I'm taking that anger out on Sheriff Brady when I should be taking it out on Connie's killer. The problem is, although I have my suspicions, I don't know who that person is yet. When I do, you'll hear about it.

When my editor asked if I would be willing to chronicle my experiences and share this painful journey with you, my readers, I said yes immediately. Why? Because I understand that, no matter how hurtful it may be for all concerned, we will all learn things from it—things we all *need* to know.

Maggie MacFerson

Astonished by what she had read, Joanna was in the process of reading through it a second time when she heard Butch's voice. "Why, look who's here. Why aren't you up in the room? Did you lose your key?"

Joanna looked up to see Butch walking across the spacious lobby accompanied by a tall, willowy blonde. Butch left the woman behind and hurried around a massive brass-and-glass coffee table. Reaching Joanna's side, he bent over and planted a kiss on her cheek.

"This is my wife, Joanna Brady," he said, turning back to the woman, who had paused uncertainly on the far side of the table. "I didn't make her change her name, and she didn't make me change mine," he added with a grin. "Joey, this is a good friend of mine, Lila Winters. She used to live here, but she's moving to Texas now. She came for the wedding, of course. We've been reminiscing about old times."

Caught unawares, Joanna took a moment to gather her wits, stand up, and offer her hand. "Glad to meet you," she said.

Blond, blue-eyed, and with palely luminescent skin, Lila Winters was beautiful in the same fragile, delicate way that expensive English porcelain is beautiful. She wore a blue denim pantsuit the top of which was decorated with a constellation of rhinestone-outlined stars.

"I've heard a lot about you," Lila said. "Including the fact that you'd been called out of town on some kind of official investigation."

Simultaneously, Joanna Brady made several quick calculations. If Lila Winters was such a good friend of Butch's, why hadn't he ever mentioned her name before? And why hadn't the name Lila Winters been on the guest list to Joanna and Butch's own wedding back in April? There could be only one answer to those two damning questions. Butch and Lila had to have been far more than just "good friends." And since Butch had evidently been away from his hotel room all night long, there could be little doubt that he had passed the time in the company of that selfsame "good friend" while Joanna had been stuck driving up and down freeways, doing her job, and looking after her daughter.

"Yes," she said levelly. "I've had my hands full. And I guess Butch has been pretty busy, too."

Lila gave Joanna an appraising look, then she nodded at Butch. "Thanks for breakfast, Butch," she said. "And for everything else, too," she added. "See you at the wedding."

With that, Lila Winters turned and walked slowly across the lobby. Meanwhile, Butch turned back to Joanna.

"What was that all about?" he asked.

She gazed at him in stony silence and didn't answer for several long seconds. "What do you *think* it was about?" she demanded finally. "I come in after being out working all night—after trying to call you time and again—and find you haven't slept in our room. And then I meet you with someone I don't know, someone who obviously knows you *very* well. 'Thanks for *breakfast,* Butch,'" Joanna mimicked sarcastically. "'Thanks for *everything.*'"

"Joanna . . ." Butch began.

Flinging the newspaper down on the table, Joanna stalked away, leaving Butch standing alone in the lobby. At the hotel entrance she handed her parking receipt over to the parking attendant. "I need my car right away," she said.

Butch picked up the newspaper from the table and hurried after her. "Joanna, what's going on? Where are you going?"

"Out," she snapped. "It's getting a little stuffy in there. I need some air."

"Joey, it's not what you think, really. I can explain everything."

"I'm not interested in your *explanations,*" she said. "Now go away and leave me alone!"

By then the parking attendant had returned, bringing the Crown Victoria to a stop under the portico and opening the door. As Joanna got in, she handed the attendant his tip. "Will you be needing directions this morning?" he asked.

Not trusting herself to speak, Joanna shook her head mutely. Then she drove off without a backward glance, leaving Butch standing alone on the curb. She made it only as far as the first stoplight before she burst into tears. Sobbing so hard she could hardly see, she finally turned into a nearby parking lot, one belonging to the Peoria Public Library. Looking around, she was grateful to see that late on a Sunday morning the lot was completely deserted.

She had put the car in neutral and set the parking brake when her cell phone began to crow. She picked it up and looked at it. The readout said UNAVAILABLE, which meant her caller might possibly be Butch calling from the hotel. It could also be someone else who needed to reach the sheriff of Cochise County. Sniffing to stifle her tears, she punched SEND, then sat there holding the phone in her hand but saying nothing.

"Joey?" Butch's voice sounded frantic. She winced when she heard him utter his pet name for her. "Joey," he repeated. "Are you there? Can you hear me? Where did you go?"

Still she said nothing. She couldn't.

"Joey," he pleaded. "Please talk to me. I can explain what happened."

Suddenly she could speak, but in that odd strangled way that was just above a whisper. It seemed as though the strength of her voice was somehow inversely proportional to whatever she felt. The stronger her emotions, the smaller her voice.

"I already told you," she croaked. "I don't want any of your damned explanations."

She heard Butch's sigh of relief, and that hurt her, too. The very sound of his voice—the voice she had come to love—made her whole body ache. "You are there, then," he said. "You've got to come back to the hotel, Joey. You've got to give me a chance to tell you what went on."

"I know what went on," she snapped back at him. "And I'm not coming back." With that, she punched the END button. Butch called back almost immediately. Eventually the ringing—that awful roosterlike crowing—stopped, only to begin again a moment later. He called five more times in as many minutes, but she didn't answer. Each time the phone rang, and each time she didn't answer it, Joanna Brady gathered a little more of her anger around her. Finally she switched the ringer to SILENT and flung the phone out of reach on the far side of the car.

Out of sight, out of mind, she thought. But that gave her pause, too. Wasn't that exactly what had happened with Butch? Evidently, the moment Joanna had been out of sight, *she* had been out of his mind as well, enough so that Lila Winters had been able to walk in and make her move.

Just then a group of skateboarders and in-line skaters—bronzed, bare-chested teenagers oblivious to the scorching, one-hundred-fifteen-degree sun—appeared at the far end of the parking lot. Not willing to let even strangers see her in such a state, Joanna put the Crown Victoria back in gear and drove away. For a while, she drove aimlessly through Peoria, Glendale, and North Phoenix. She could think of only one person who might be able to help her, only one who would understand her sense of betrayal and offer comfort—her best friend, pastor, and confidante, Marianne Maculyea. The problem was, Marianne was more than two hundred miles away, back home in Bisbee.

So distracted that she hardly noticed her surroundings, Joanna was brought up short by a blaring horn. To her dismay she discovered she'd gone through an amber light and had almost been broadsided by someone jumping the green. With her heart pounding in her throat, she turned right at the next intersection, a side street which led to the back entrance of one of Phoenix's major shopping malls, Metrocenter.

Realizing it wasn't safe for her to continue driving, she parked in the broiling parking lot. Her cell phone had slipped off the end of the seat. She had to walk around the car and open the passenger door in order to retrieve it. When she picked it up, the readout said she had missed fifteen calls, all of which were from UNAVAILABLE. *All from Butch, no doubt,* she told herself.

Slamming the car door shut, she made her way into the mall. Finding a bench near a noisy fountain, she glanced down at her watch. One o'clock was time enough for Jeff and Marianne to have finished up with both the church service and the coffee hour and to have returned home to the parsonage. Gripping the phone tightly, Joanna punched Marianne's number into the keypad.

"Maculyea/Daniels residence," Julie Erickson said. Julie was the live-in nanny who cared for Jeff and Marianne's two children—their almost-four-year-old adopted daughter, Ruth Rachel, and their miracle baby—the one doctors had assured the couple they would never have—one-and-a-half-month-old Jeffrey Andrew.

For years, Marianne Maculyea had been estranged from her parents. A partial thaw had occurred a year earlier, when Ruth's twin sister, Esther Elaine, had been hospitalized for heart-transplant surgery. Marianne's father, Tim Maculyea, had unbent enough then to come to the hospital in Tucson. Later, when Esther tragically had succumbed to pneumonia, he had come to the funeral as well. Marianne's mother, Evangeline Maculyea, had not. Only the birth of little Jeffy had finally effected a lasting truce. Julie Erickson, complete with six months' worth of paid wages, had been Evangeline's peace offering to her daughter. It was Julie's capable presence that had made possible Marianne's rapid post-childbirth return to her duties as pastor of Bisbee's Tombstone Canyon United Methodist Church.

"Marianne," Joanna gulped.

"Who's calling, please?"

"It's Joanna," she managed to mumble. With that, she dissolved into tears.

8

W hy, Joanna!" Marianne exclaimed, the moment she heard Joanna's voice. "What on earth is the matter?"

"It's Butch," Joanna whispered.

"What about him?" Mari demanded. "Is he hurt? Has there been an accident?"

Joanna shook her head. "No," she whispered. "No accident."

"What is it, then? You've got to get hold of yourself, Joanna. Tell me what's going on."

"Oh, Mari," Joanna sobbed. "What am I going to do? What am I going to tell Jenny? It'll break her heart."

"Tell her what? What's happened?"

Joanna drew a shuddering breath. "Butch stayed out all night. He was with another woman. I saw them together, just a little while ago."

Marianne was all business. "Where did this happen?" she asked.

"At a hotel up in Phoenix—Peoria, really. There's a wedding tonight . . ."

"I remember now," Marianne said. "Butch is the man of honor."

"Right," Joanna said. "The rehearsal dinner was last night. I was supposed to go, but I ended up having to work. I had to drive a homicide victim's sister down to Bisbee to identify the body. Then there was a huge flap with my mother calling CPS and upsetting everyone out at the ranch. By the time things settled down, it was too late to drive back, so I spent the night and came back to Phoenix this morning. I had tried calling Butch to let him know. I left several messages on voice mail in the room, and they were all still there because he never came back to the room. He was with another woman, Mari. When I saw them, they had just finished having breakfast together."

Like a wind-up toy running down, Joanna subsided into silence.

"Breakfast," Marianne interjected. "You said they had breakfast. What makes you think there's anything more to it than just that?"

"I *saw* them," Joanna said. "I saw them together. And he introduced me to her. He said she was an old friend, Mari. But if she was such a good friend, why haven't I ever heard her name before? Why wasn't she invited to our wedding? Believe me, they're more than good friends. And I can't stand it. We've been married less than two months, and already Butch may have been unfaithful to me. I can't believe it."

"Do you know that for sure?" Marianne asked. "Did he tell you he's been unfaithful?"

"No, but—"

"How do you know then?"

"I just know. I'm not stupid, Mari. I saw them together. I know what I saw." In the silence that followed, Joanna heard Lila Winters's voice once more. *"Thank you for everything."*

"What you *think* you saw," Marianne admonished. "Have you actually talked to Butch about this? Did you ask him?"

"No. Ever since I left the hotel, he's been trying to call me. He says he wants to explain. *Explain!* As if there could be any explanation. But I won't talk to him. He thinks all he has to do is give me some kind of lame excuse, and the whole thing will go away. It won't!"

"You still haven't spoken to him?" Marianne asked.

"No. What's the point? What's tearing me up is what am I going to tell Jenny, Mari? She loves Butch almost as much as she loved her dad. What will happen to her if she loses Butch, too? And how am I going to face all the people in town, the ones who came to our wedding—the ones who told me I was jumping in too soon? The ones who said I should have given myself more time? It turns out that they're right and I'm wrong. How will I ever be able to live this down?"

"Where are you right now?" Marianne asked.

"Metrocenter," Joanna answered. "When I left the hotel, I didn't know where to go. I thought about coming home, but I was crying so hard that it wasn't safe to drive. I stopped here at the mall because I was afraid I was going to kill someone."

"Good decision," Marianne said. "Nobody should try to drive when they're crying their eyes out. So what are you going to do now?"

"Come home," Joanna said in a small voice.

"Where's Butch?" Marianne asked.

"Back at the hotel," Joanna answered. "At the Conquistador, in Peoria. That's where the wedding's going to be held, the one where Butch is the man of honor. What a joke!"

"And how's he getting home?"

"How should I know?" Joanna asked.

"Does he have a car?"

"No. We took my county car up to the Sheriffs' Association Conference in Page. We stopped off in Phoenix for the wedding on the way back down."

"How's he getting back to Bisbee?"

"He can walk, for all I care."

"I see," Marianne said.

Around her, the mall was filling up with people while Joanna Brady had never felt so alone in her life. Families—mothers and fathers with young, boisterous children—walked through the mall. Some were just out shopping. Others, still dressed in their Sunday finery, were headed to the food court for an after-church lunch. There were throngs of teenagers, kids Jenny's age, laughing and joking as though they hadn't a care in the world. Everyone else seemed happy and glad to be alive while Joanna was simply desolate. She noted that a few of the passersby aimed wary, sidelong glances in her direction.

They probably think I'm crazy, she thought self-consciously. *Here I sit. Tears are dripping off my chin, and I'm holding on to my cell phone as though it's a damned life preserver!*

"I think you should go back," Marianne Maculyea was saying when Joanna's straying attention returned to the phone.

"I should do what?"

"When it's safe for you to drive, you should go back to the hotel and talk to Butch."

"Why? What's the point?"

Marianne sighed, sounding the way she did when dealing with Ruth, her recalcitrant three-year-old. "Before we go into that, I want you to tell me what's been going on. All of it, from the beginning."

And so Joanna found herself relating all the events of the past several days, including how Jenny and Dora Matthews had found Constance Haskell's body and how Joanna had ended up leaving Phoenix the previous afternoon in order to bring Maggie MacFerson to Bisbee to identify her sister's body. She explained how Eleanor had precipitated a crisis at home by dragging Child Protective Services into an already overwrought situation. It was harder to talk about coming back to the hotel that morning and discovering Butch hadn't been there. Finally she came to the part where Butch and Lila Winters had found her reading Maggie MacFerson's article in the hotel lobby. As she recounted that, Joanna was once again struggling to hold back tears.

"So that's it," she finished lamely. "I got in the car, drove away, and eventually ended up here."

"Tell me about the wedding," Marianne said. "Whose wedding is it again?"

"Tammy Lukins," Joanna answered. "She used to work for Butch. She was one of his waitresses at the Roundhouse Bar and Grill up in Peoria. She's marrying a guy named Roy Ford who used to be a customer at the Roundhouse. Since Butch is the one who introduced them, they both wanted him to be in the wedding. Tammy wanted Butch to be her . . ." She started to say, "man of honor," but the words stuck in her throat. "Her attendant," she said finally.

A short silence followed. Marianne was the one who spoke first. "You told me a few minutes ago that the dead woman's sister from Phoenix . . ."

"Maggie MacFerson," Joanna supplied.

"That Maggie MacFerson thought her brother-in-law . . ."

"Ron Haskell."

"That he was the one who had murdered his wife. That he had stolen her money and then murdered her."

Joanna nodded. "That's right," she said.

"So what will happen next?" Marianne asked.

Joanna shrugged. "Ernie Carpenter and Jaime Carbajal were supposed to go out to Portal this morning to see if they could find him."

"And what will happen when they do?"

"When they find him, they'll probably question him," Joanna replied. "They'll try to find out where he was around the time his wife died and whether or not he has a verifiable alibi."

"But they won't just arrest him on the spot, toss him in jail, and throw away the key?"

"Of course not," Joanna returned. "They're detectives. They have to find evidence. The fact that the money is gone and the fact that Connie Haskell died near where her husband was staying is most likely all circumstantial. Before Ernie and Jaime can arrest Ron Haskell, they'll have to have probable cause. To do that they'll need to have some kind of physical evidence that links him to the crime."

"What if they arrested him without having probable cause?"

"It would be wrong," Joanna answered. "Cops can't arrest someone simply because they feel like it. They have to have good reason to believe the person is guilty, and they can't simply jump to conclusions based on circumstantial evidence. It has to be something that will stand up in court, something strong enough to convince a judge and jury."

"That's true in your work life, Joanna," Marianne said quietly. "What about in your personal life? Is it wise to allow yourself to jump to conclusions there?"

A knot of anger pulsed in Joanna's temples. "You're saying I've jumped to conclusions?"

"Criminals have a right to defend themselves in a court of law," Marianne said. "You told me yourself that you didn't listen to anything Butch had to say. That when he tried to talk to you, you didn't listen—wouldn't even answer the phone."

"This is different," Joanna said.

"Is it? I don't think so. I believe you've tried and convicted the man of being unfaithful to you without giving him the benefit of a fair hearing. I'm not saying Butch didn't do what you think he did, and I'm certainly not defending him if he did. But I do think you owe him the courtesy of letting him tell you what happened, of letting him explain the circumstances, before you hire yourself a divorce attorney and throw him out of the house."

Joanna sat holding the phone in stunned silence.

"A few minutes ago you asked me what you should tell Jenny," Marianne continued. "How you should go about breaking the news to her and how you'd face up to the rest of the people in town. Have you talked to anyone else about this?"

"Only you," Joanna said.

"Good. You need to keep quiet about all this until you know more, until you have some idea of what you're up against. It could be nothing more than bachelor-party high jinks. I've seen you at work, Joanna. When your department is involved in a case, you don't let people go running to the newspapers or radio stations and leaking information so the public ends up knowing every single thing about what's going on in any given investigation. You keep it quiet until you have all your ducks in a row. Right?"

Joanna said nothing.

"And that's what I'm suggesting you do here, as well," Marianne said. "Keep it quiet. Don't tell anyone. Not Jenny, not your mother, not the people you work with—not until you have a better idea of what's really going on. You owe it to yourself, Joanna, and you certainly owe that much to Butch."

"But—"

"Let me finish," Marianne said. "Since Butch came to town, Jeff and I have come to care about him almost like a brother. We feel as close to him as we used to feel to Andy. I also know that he's made a huge difference in your life, and in Jenny's, too. I don't want you to throw all that away. I don't want you to lose this second chance at happiness over something that may not be that important."

Joanna was suddenly furious. "You're saying Butch can do anything he wants—that he can go out with another woman and it doesn't matter?"

"If something happened between him and this woman, this Lila, then of course it matters. But it's possible that absolutely nothing happened. Before you write him off, you need to know exactly what went on."

"You mean, I should ask him and then I should just take his word for it?" Joanna demanded. "If he tells me nothing happened, I'm supposed to *believe* him? He was out all night long, Mari. I don't think I can ever trust him again. I don't think I can believe a word he says."

"In my experience," Marianne said, "there are two sides to every story. Before you go blasting your point of view to the universe, maybe you should have some idea about what's going on on Butch's side of the fence. He's been used to running his own life, Joanna. Used to calling the shots. Now he's in a position where he often has to play second fiddle. That's not easy. Ask Jeff about it sometime. Things were rough that first year we were married, when I was trying to be both a new bride and a new minister all at the same time. If fact, there were times when I didn't think we'd make it."

Joanna was stunned. "You and Jeff?" she asked.

"Yes, Jeff and I," Marianne returned.

"But you never mentioned it. You never told me."

"Because we worked it out, Joanna," Marianne said. "We worked it out between us. Believe me, it would have been a whole lot harder if the whole world had known about it."

"What are you saying?" Joanna asked.

"I'm saying you have a choice," Marianne said. "It's one of those two paths diverging in the woods that Robert Frost talks about. You can go home and tell Jim Bob and Eva Lou and Jenny that something terrible has happened between you and Butch and that you're headed for divorce court. Do that, and you risk losing everything. Or, you can pull yourself together, drive your butt back to the hotel, go to that damned wedding with a smile on your face and your head held high, and see if you can fix things before they get any worse."

"Swallow my pride and go back to the hotel?" Joanna repeated.

"That's right."

"Go to the wedding?"

"Absolutely, and give Butch a chance to tell you what went on. What's going on. If he wants to bail out on the marriage and if you want to as well, then you're right. There's nothing left to fix and you'd better come home and be with Jenny when her heart gets broken again. But if there is something to be salvaged, you're a whole lot better off doing it sooner than later."

"I thought you were my friend, Mari. How can you turn on me like this?"

"I am your friend," Marianne replied. "A good enough friend that I'm prepared to risk telling you what you may not want to hear. A friend who cares enough to send the very worst. Some things are worth fighting for, Joanna. Your marriage is one of them."

Soon after, a spent Joanna ended the call. Butch had evidently given up trying to call, since the phone didn't ring again. Sitting in the mall, with the overheated but silent telephone still cradled in her hand, Joanna sat staring blindly at the carefree Sunday afternoon throng moving past her.

And then, sitting with her back to the noisy fountain, Joanna could almost hear her father's voice. "Never run away from a fight, Little Hank," D. H. Lathrop had told her.

Joanna was back in seventh grade. It was the morning after she had been suspended from school for two days for fighting with the boys who had been picking on her new friend, Marianne Maculyea.

"No matter what your mother says," her father had counseled in his slow, East Texas drawl, "no matter what anyone says, you're better off making a stand than you are running away."

"So other people won't think you're a coward?" Joanna had asked.

"No," he had answered. "So *you* won't think you're a coward."

The vivid memory left Joanna shaken. It was as though her father and Marianne were ganging up on her, with both of them telling her the exact same thing. They both wanted her to stop running and face whatever it was she was up against.

Standing up, Joanna stuffed the phone in her pocket and then headed for the mall entrance. Getting into the Crown Victoria was like climbing into an oven. The steering wheel scorched her fingertips, but she barely noticed. With both her father's and Marianne's words still ringing in her heart and head, she started the engine and went looking for the side road that would take her away from the mall.

As she drove, she felt like a modern-day Humpty Dumpty. She had no idea if what had been broken could be put back together, but D. H. Lathrop and Marianne were right. Joanna couldn't give up without a fight. Wouldn't give up without a fight. Maybe she didn't owe that much to Butch Dixon or even to Jenny, but Joanna Brady sure as hell owed it to herself.

It was almost two by the time Joanna returned to the hotel. She pulled up to the door, where a florist van was disgorging a mountain of flowers. Dodging through the lobby, Joanna held her breath for fear of meeting up with some of the other wedding guests. In her current woebegone state, she didn't want to see anyone she knew.

When she opened the door to their room, the blackout curtains were pulled. Butch, fully clothed, was lying on top of the covers, sound asleep. She tried to close the door silently, but the click of the lock awakened him. "Joey?" he asked, sitting up. "Is that you?"

She switched on a light. "Yes," she said.

"You're back. Where did you go?"

"Someplace where I could think," she told him.

Rather than going near the bed, Joanna walked over to the table on the far side of the room. Pulling out a chair, she sat down and folded her hands into her lap.

"What did you decide?" Butch asked.

"I talked to Marianne. She said I should come back and hear what you have to say."

"Nothing happened, Joey," Butch said. "Between Lila and me, I mean. Not now, anyway. Not last night."

"But you used to be an item?"

"Yes, but that was a long time ago, before I met you. Still," Butch added, "I'm sorry."

"For what?" Joanna asked the question even though she feared what the answer might be. "If nothing happened, what do you have to be sorry for?"

"I shouldn't have been with Lila in the first place," Butch admitted at once. "After the rehearsal dinner, she offered me a ride back to the hotel. I should have come back with someone else, but I didn't. I was pissed at you, and I'd had a few drinks. So I came back with Lila instead. At the time, it didn't seem like that bad an idea."

"I see," Joanna returned stiffly.

"No," Butch said. "I don't think you see at all."

"What I'm hearing is that your defense consists of your claiming that nothing happened, but even if it did happen, you're not responsible because you were drunk at the time."

"My defense is that nothing *did* happen," he replied. "But it could have. It might have, and I shouldn't have run that risk. She's dying, you see."

"Who's dying?"

"Lila."

"Of what?" Joanna scoffed derisively, remembering the willowy blonde who had accompanied Butch through the lobby. "She didn't look sick to me."

"But she is," Butch replied. "She has ALS. Do you know what that is?"

Joanna thought for a minute. "Lou Gehrig's disease?"

Butch nodded. "She just got the final diagnosis last week. She hasn't told anyone yet, including Tammy and Roy. She didn't want to spoil their wedding."

"But, assuming it's true, she went ahead and told you," Joanna said. "How come?"

"I told you. Lila and I used to be an item, Joey. We broke up long before you and I ever met. She married somebody else and moved to San Diego, but the guy she married walked out on her two months ago," Butch continued.

She got dumped and now she wants you back, Joanna thought. She felt as though she were listening to one of those interminable shaggy-dog stories with no hope of cutting straight to the punch line. "So this is a rebound thing for her?" Joanna asked. "Or is that what I was for you?" Her voice sounded brittle. There was a metallic taste in her mouth.

"Joey, please listen," Butch pleaded. "What do you know about ALS?"

Joanna shrugged. "Not much. It's incurable, I guess."

"Right. Lila went to see her doctor because her back was bothering her. She thought maybe she'd pulled a muscle or something. The doctor gave her the bad news on Thursday. Even though she's not that sick yet, she will be. It'll get worse and worse. The doctor told her that most ALS patients die within two to five years of diagnosis. She's putting her San Diego house on the market. She's going to Texas to be close to her parents.

"Lila needed to talk about all this, Joey," Butch continued. "She needed somebody to be there with her, to listen and sympathize. I happened to be handy. We talked all night long. I held her, and she cried on my shoulder."

"You held her," Joanna said.

"And listened," Butch said.

"And nothing else?"

"Nothing. I swear to God."

"And why should I believe you?" Joanna asked.

Butch got off the bed. He came across the room to the table, where he sat down opposite Joanna. As he did so, his lips curved into a tentative smile. "Because I wouldn't do something like that, Joey. I'm lucky enough to be married to the woman I love. She's also somebody who carries two loaded weapons at all times and who, I have it on good authority, knows exactly how to use them. What do you think I am, stupid?"

Joanna thought about that for a minute. Then she asked another question. "You said you were pissed at me. Why?"

"That's hard to explain."

"Try me."

"Tammy and Roy and the rest of the people at the wedding are all my friends," he said slowly. "I had just finished spending the last three days up at Page being sheriff's spouse-under-glass. Don't get me wrong. Antiquing aside, I was glad to do it. But turnabout's fair play, Joey. I really wanted you to be here with me last night at the rehearsal dinner. I wanted to show you off to my old buddies and be able to say, 'Hey, you guys, lucky me. Look what I found!' But then duty called and off you went.

"As soon as you said you were going, I knew you'd never make it back in time for the dinner, and I think you did, too. But did you say so? No. You did your best imitation of Arnold Schwarzenegger saying, 'I'll be back,' which, of course, you weren't. You left in the afternoon and didn't turn back up until sometime in the middle of the night. I know you weren't back earlier because I, too, was calling the room periodically all evening long in hopes you'd be back and able to join in the fun. Either you weren't in yet, or else you didn't bother answering the phone."

"You didn't leave a message," Joanna said accusingly. "And you could have tried calling my cell phone."

"Right, but that would have meant interrupting you while you were working."

Joanna thought about that for a moment. They had both made an effort to reduce the number of personal phone calls between them while she was working. Still, she wasn't entirely satisfied.

"That's why you were pissed then?" she asked. "Because I missed the rehearsal and the rehearsal dinner and wasn't around for you to show me off to your old pals?"

"Pretty much," Butch admitted. "I guess it sounds pretty lame, but that's the way it was."

A long silence followed. Joanna was thinking about her mother and father, about Eleanor and Big Hank Lathrop. How many times had Sheriff Lathrop used the call of duty to provide an excused absence for himself from one of Eleanor's numerous social functions? How often had he hidden behind his badge to avoid being part of some school program or church potluck or a meeting of the Bisbee Historical Society?

Joanna loved her mother, but she didn't much like her. And the last thing she ever wanted was to *be* like Eleanor Lathrop Winfield. Still, there were times now, when Joanna would be talking to Jenny or bawling her out for something, when it seemed as though Eleanor's words and voice were coming through Joanna's own lips. There were other times, too, when, glancing in a mirror, it seemed as though Eleanor's face were staring back at her. That was how genetics worked. But now, through some strange quirk in her DNA, Joanna found herself resembling her father rather than her mother. Here she was doing the same kind of unintentional harm to Butch that D. H. Lathrop had done to his wife, Eleanor.

And Joanna could see now that although she had been hurt by her belief in Butch's infidelity—his presumed infidelity—she wasn't the only one. Butch had been hurt, too.

"What are you thinking?" he asked.

"I called, too," she said contritely. "I left messages on the room's voice mail trying to let you know what was going on—that all hell had broken loose and I was going to have to go to Bisbee. You never got any of them. They were all still listed as new messages when I came in."

"This sounds serious," Butch said. "Tell me now."

And so Joanna went on to tell Butch about going to see Maggie MacFerson and finding the woman drunk in the unlocked house that belonged to her dead sister. Joanna told Butch about the loaded gun and the smashed glass and the bleeding cuts on Maggie's hands that had triggered a trip to the emergency room. She told him about Eleanor's blowing the whistle to Child Protective Services and how a zealous caseworker had wrested a screamingly unhappy Dora away from Jim and Eva Lou's care at High Lonesome Ranch.

"What a mess!" Butch said when she finished. "How's Jenny taking all this?"

"That's why I stayed over in Bisbee. To be with Jenny, but she's okay, I think. At least she *seemed* to be okay."

"I read the article on the front page of the *Reporter*," Butch said. "How can that woman—Maggie MacFerson—get away with putting Jenny's and Dora's names in an article like that? I didn't think newspapers were supposed to publish kids' names."

"They usually don't with juveniles who are victims of crimes or with juvenile offenders, either. In this case, Dora and Jenny weren't either. They were kids who found a body. That means their names go in the papers."

"It wasn't exactly a flattering portrait of either one of them—or of you, either," Butch added.

She gave Butch a half-smile. "I'm getting used to it."

"Is Marianne the only person you talked to?" he asked. "Today, I mean. After the little scene down in the lobby."

"She's the only one."

"That way, even though nothing happened, at least it won't be all over town that I'm the villain of the piece. Marianne is totally trustworthy. She also seems to be of the opinion that you're right and I'm wrong. She told me to get my butt in the car and head straight back here, to the hotel."

Butch shook his head. "I think we were both wrong, Joey," he said after a pause. "I'm a married man. No matter what, I shouldn't have been spending all night alone with an unmarried ex-girlfriend, sick or not. And I had no right to want you to take a pass on your job. Being sheriff is important, Joey—to you and to me as well as to the people who elected you. But that doesn't mean I can't be jealous on occasion." He grinned then. "And the same goes for you. I mean, if you want to be jealous of me, have a ball."

Which, of course, she had been, Joanna realized. More so than she ever would have thought possible.

"I still don't understand why Lila had to talk to you about all that," she said. "Doesn't she have any other friends she could have talked to?"

Butch shrugged. "Bartenders are the poor man's psychologists. We listen and nod and say uh-huh, and all we charge is the price of a drink or two."

And Joanna realized that was true as well. One of the things she had always appreciated about Butch was that he was a good listener. He heard not only the words, but paid attention to the subtext as well.

Just then, Butch glanced at his watch. "Yikes!" he said. "I'm due downstairs in five minutes for pictures. I'd better jump into that tux." He started toward the bathroom, then stopped. "You will come, won't you?" he asked. "To the wedding, I mean."

Joanna nodded. "I'll be there."

His face broke into a smile. "Good," he said, but then he turned serious again. "With everything that's going on back home, do you want to head for Bisbee after the reception is over? It probably won't be all that late. If you want to, we can."

That kind of offer, made in good faith, was exactly what made Butch Dixon so damned lovable, and it made Joanna remember her former mother-in-law's advice about spending time with her husband.

Joanna got up, went to over to Butch, and let him pull her into a bear hug. "Thanks," she said. "But I don't think we have to do that. Jenny's fine. Jim Bob and Eva Lou have everything under control. Besides," she added, smiling up at him, "it's too late to check out without being charged for another night. It would be a shame to waste an opportunity to be alone together, wouldn't it?"

He kissed her on the lips. "It would be a shame, all right. Now let loose of me, so I can get dressed."

9

Once Butch had left for the photo session, Joanna stripped off her clothes and took a shower. When she came out of the bathroom, the message light was blinking on the phone. "There's a package for Mr. Dixon waiting at the front desk," she was told. Dialing the front desk, Joanna asked to have the package sent up. When it arrived, the package showed a return address of a place called Copy Corner. Ripping off the wrapping, Joanna found an eight-and-a-half-by-eleven-inch-sized box that was about as thick as a ream of paper.

With trembling fingers, she lifted the cover. Inside was a computer disk. Lifting that, she then read what was typed on the top page. *"To Serve and Protect,"* it said. "By F. W. Dixon." Beneath the author's name were the words "To Joey." Seeing that simple dedication put a lump in Joanna's throat.

Taking the open box with her, Joanna settled onto the bed and began to read. *To Serve and Protect* was a murder mystery, set in a fictional Arizona town, with a lady police chief named Kimberly Charles in charge of a tiny police department. That much of the story bore a certain familiarity to Joanna's own life, but there the resemblance seemed to end. The story was told in a droll fashion that made what happened on the pages, complete with typical small-town politics, far more funny than serious.

Lost in the story, Joanna lost track of time. When she came up for air, it was twenty past four; there was just enough time to comb her hair, put on her makeup, dress, and make it to the wedding. She had brought along one of the outfits she had bought in Paris on her honeymoon. Next to her own wedding dress, the silk shirtwaist was the most expensive piece of clothing she had ever owned. She'd fallen in love with it on sight and had been forced to buy it because it came in her favorite color—the brilliant emerald-green hue of freshly sprouted cottonwood leaves, a color desert dwellers find hard to resist. It didn't hurt that, with her red hair and light skin, that particular shade of green was, in Butch's words, a "killer" combination.

The nuptials were scheduled to be held in one of the several ballrooms on the Conquistador's second floor. Joanna was already seated in one of the rows of chairs when Lila Winters entered the room. Blond and elegant, she wore a sapphire-blue suit. Watching her start down the aisle, Joanna couldn't quite stifle the stab of jealousy that shot through her whole body. Watching closely, however, Joanna did detect the smallest trace of a limp as Lila made her way to a chair. That limp caused Joanna's jealousy to change to compassion.

Only three people among the assembled guests—Butch, Joanna, and Lila Winters herself—knew that the strikingly elegant woman who looked so vibrantly alive was actually dying. *What must it be like,* Joanna wondered, *to be given that kind of devastating diagnosis? Whom would I tell if that happened to me?* In the end there was only one answer. *Butch,* she realized. *He'd help me figure out what to do.*

At that juncture the first strains of the "Wedding March" sounded. Joanna rose and turned with everyone else to watch the procession. Butch preceded the bride down the aisle, walking in the slow, halting manner dictated by the occasion. Catching Joanna's eye as he passed, Butch winked. Tammy Lukins walked down the aisle on the arm of her adult son, who also gave her away. During the brief and joyful ceremony Joanna couldn't help feeling a grudging respect for Lila Winters's decision to keep her bad news away from the happy bride and groom.

After the ceremony, the wedding entourage moved to a second ballroom for the reception. While Butch was occupied with his attendant duties, Joanna sat down at one of the tables which offered a panoramic view of the entire reception. She was sipping a glass of champagne when someone said, "Mind if I join you?"

Joanna looked up to see Lila Winters in her sapphire-blue suit. "Sure," Joanna said. "Help yourself."

As Lila took a seat, Joanna noted the fleeting wince that crossed the woman's face when her back came in contact with the chair. The expression passed so swiftly that only someone looking for it would have noticed.

"You seemed upset earlier," Lila began, once she was seated. "When Butch and I met up with you in the lobby, I mean. I didn't want you to think anything untoward had happened."

During that earlier encounter, Joanna Brady would willingly have scratched the woman's eyes out. Now she simply said, "I know. Butch told me."

They were interrupted by a roar of laughter from a group gathered across the room, where the groom had just tossed the bride's garter high into the air, and several of the guests, graybeards all of them, scrambled to retrieve it.

"He told you about me, then?" Lila asked, once the laughter subsided. "About what's going on?"

Joanna nodded. "I'm sorry," she said.

"Please," Lila said, cutting her off. "Let's not discuss it. I'm still feeling pretty sorry for myself, and I don't want to go into it here. Not now. Not yet. I just wanted to say that I think you're very lucky—to have Butch, that is."

"I know," Joanna said. "Thank you."

For the space of almost a minute they sat in silence while both sipped at their respective glasses of champagne. Across the room it was time for the bride to toss her bouquet.

"It doesn't seem real," Lila said quietly. "It wasn't all that long ago when I was the one tossing the bouquet, and now . . ."

Even though she had said she didn't want to discuss her looming illness, Joanna realized that's what they were doing nevertheless. "It must be very difficult," she replied.

Lila nodded. "These are my friends," she said, gazing around the room. "I've known these people for years. It was bad enough to have to come back and face them all at a wedding, of all things, after Jimmy walked out on me the way he did. But now that I know about—" She stopped short of naming her illness. "I don't want to tell them, but . . . I don't want to die alone, either."

Law enforcement circles are full of heroes and acts of derring-do—the kind that make for newspaper headlines and for riveting television newscasts. Lila Winters's courage was far quieter than that, and far more solitary. In her life-and-death struggle, she couldn't reach for a radio and call for backup.

"It was very kind of you not to upset the wedding plans," Joanna said. "If I had been in your place, I don't think I could have done it."

Lila gave Joanna a quick, self-deprecating smile. "Don't give me too much credit," she said. "I think it's really a case of denial. As long as nobody else knows about it—as long as I don't say the actual words out loud—maybe it's all a big mistake and it'll just go away. But that's not going to happen, and now that I've told Butch, I'm hoping I'll be able to work up courage enough to tell the others—in good time, that is. But talking to Butch helped a lot. Thanks for sharing him with me."

With that, Lila Winters excused herself and walked away. A few minutes later, Butch showed up at Joanna's table. "Is everything all right?" he asked, a concerned frown wrinkling his forehead. "I mean, I noticed the two of you were . . ."

Looking at him, the last vestiges of Joanna's earlier anger melted away. "We were talking," she said, smiling. "Comparing notes, actually."

Butch looked thunderstruck. His obvious consternation made Joanna laugh. "We both think you're a pretty good listener," she added. "For a boy."

"Whew," he said, mopping his brow in relief. "So I'm still alive then?"

"So far."

The reception included a buffet dinner followed by cake and dancing to a swing band that lasted far into the night. Joanna surprised herself by having a delightful time. Rather than rushing out early to drive back to Bisbee, she and Butch stayed until eleven, when the party finally began to wind down. When they at last went back upstairs to their room, Butch stopped short at the mound of manuscript pages scattered across the bed.

"It came," he said.

"And I opened it," Joanna said. "I also started reading it."

"How far did you get?" he asked.

"The first hundred pages or so," she said.

"And?" he asked. "What do you think?"

"It's funny."

"Yes."

"Why did you write it that way?"

He came across the room to her and gathered her into his arms. "I had to," he said. "Because, if I wrote it the way things really are, it would be too hard."

Joanna frowned and pushed him away. "What do you mean?"

"Because the truth of the matter is, the real job scares the hell out of me. Look at yesterday. You walked into a house to tell someone her sister died, and the woman at that kitchen table was sitting there drunk and with a fully loaded weapon within easy reach. If that isn't scary, I don't know what is. I decided to make it funny to preserve my own mental health."

"I don't mean to worry you," Joanna said, nestling against his chest and staying there.

"But you do."

Had Joanna had this same conversation with Deputy Andrew Brady before he was shot and killed? How many nights had she lain awake in her bed at High Lonesome Ranch worrying about whether or not he would make it home safely after his shift? And how often had Eleanor done exactly the same thing when Big Hank Lathrop had been sheriff?

Once again, she was struck by the sense of history repeating itself, but with the lines mysteriously crossed and with her somehow walking both sides of the street at the same time.

While Butch went to change out of his tux, Joanna retrieved the cell phone she had deliberately left upstairs when she went down to the wedding. There were five missed calls, two from the department and three from Frank Montoya's cell phone. When she listened to the three messages, they were all from Frank—all of them asking that she call him back regardless of what time she got in.

"What's up?" she asked when Frank came on the line.

"We've got a problem in Paradise," he said.

"That sounds like the title of a bad novel."

"I wish," he said. "That place I told you about, 'Pathway to,' could blow up in our faces."

"How so?"

"Ernie and Jaime went over there this morning and were met at the gate by an armed guard who wouldn't let them inside to see anybody. In other words, if Ron Haskell is inside—which we don't know for sure at this time—nobody's going to be talking to him anytime soon."

"Have them call up Cameron Moore and get a court order."

"We tried. Judge Moore and his family are down in Guaymas, fishing. It's Memorial Day Weekend, you know. He won't be back from Mexico until late Tuesday."

"Great," Joanna said. "Did you say armed guard?"

"That's right."

"Shades of Waco?"

"That's what I'm worried about," Frank said.

Joanna sighed. "Well, there's not much we can do about it tonight. Anything else happening that I should know about? There were a couple of other calls from the department."

"No. They called me after they called you. Everything is under control."

"Any word on Dora's mom?"

"Not so far."

"She's bound to surface eventually," Joanna said.

"Who?" Butch said, coming out of the bathroom.

"Dora Matthews's mother," Joanna said, covering the mouthpiece of the phone. "We still haven't found her." She uncovered the mouthpiece and spoke to Frank once more. "Tomorrow morning we'll have to stay in Peoria long enough to drop off Butch's tux, then we'll head home."

"Have you heard that Yolanda Cañedo is back in University Medical Center?" Frank asked.

"I did," Joanna told him. "Her mother called out to the house and left a message with Eva Lou. If we have time, Butch and I will stop by the hospital on the way down. Do you have any idea how bad it is?"

"Pretty bad, I think."

"That's what I was afraid of. Talk to you tomorrow." She signed off.

"What's pretty bad?" Butch asked.

"Yolanda Cañedo is back in the hospital in Tucson."

"She's the jail matron with cervical cancer?"

Joanna nodded. "Her mother wants us to stop by the hospital to see her if we can."

"I don't see why not," Butch said.

Joanna slipped out of her dress and took off her makeup. By the time she came to bed, Butch was sitting with the first pages of the manuscript on his lap. He was reading and making notations on the pages as he went. She slipped into bed and found her spot in the manuscript. She began reading with the best of intentions, but a combination of too much champagne and not enough sleep soon overwhelmed her. She fell asleep sitting up, with the lamp still on, and with the manuscript laid out across her lap. When she awakened, it was daylight. Butch was carefully retrieving pages of the manuscript, which had slipped off both her lap and the bed and lay in a scattered heap on the carpeted floor.

Joanna stirred and groaned. Her back was stiff. Her neck felt as though it had been held in a hammerlock all night long.

"It must have been exciting, all right," Butch said as he sorted through the jumbled pages. "It put you out like a light."

"Not until midnight," she said. "I loved every minute of it, right up until I fell asleep."

"Really?" he asked. "You really do like it?"

"I didn't say I liked it," she corrected. "I said I loved it. In my book, love is better than like."

"Oh," Butch said. "I see. Thanks."

"You're welcome."

After breakfast, Joanna and Butch had to hang around Peoria until the tux shop opened at ten, then they headed for Bisbee. With Joanna driving, Butch sat in the passenger seat and read his manuscript aloud, pausing now and then while he changed a word or scribbled a note. Joanna continued to be intrigued by the fact that the story was funny—really funny. There were some incidents that seemed vaguely familiar and no doubt had their origins in events in and around the Cochise County Sheriff's Department, but just when she would be ready to point out that something was too close to the mark, the story would veer off in some zany and totally unpredictable fashion that would leave her giggling.

"This is hilarious," Joanna said after one particularly laughable scene. "I can't get over how funny it is—how funny *you* are."

Butch looked thoughtful. "When I was a kid," he said, "I was usually the smallest boy in my class. So I had a choice. I could either get the crap beaten out of me on a regular basis or I could be a clown and make everybody laugh. I picked the latter. Once I grew up and went into business, it was the same thing, I could let things get to me or have fun. I don't like serious, Joey. I prefer off-the-wall."

Joanna looked at him and smiled. "So do I," she said.

Listening to him read the story made the miles of pavement speed by. Traffic was light because most Memorial Day travelers were not yet headed home. It was a hot, windy morning. The summer rains were still a good month away, so gusting winds kicked up layers of parched earth and churned them into dancing dust devils or clouds of billowing dust. Near Casa Grande Joanna watched in amusement as long highway curves made the towering presence of Picacho Peak seem to hop back and forth across the busy freeway. They had sped along at seventy-five, and just before noon they pulled into the parking garage at University Medical Center in Tucson.

"Are you coming up?" she asked before stepping out of the car.

Butch rolled down his window. "I don't think so," he said. "You go ahead. If you don't mind, I'd rather sit here and keep on proofreading."

With her emotions firmly in check and trying not to remember that awful time when Andy was in that very hospital, Joanna made her way into the main reception area.

"Yolanda Cañedo," she said.

The woman at the desk typed a few letters into her computer keyboard. Frowning, she looked up at Joanna. "Are you a relative?"

Joanna shook her head. "Ms. Cañedo works for me," she said.

"She's been moved into the ICU. You can go up to the waiting room, but only relatives are allowed into the unit itself."

"I know the drill," Joanna said.

"The ICU is—"

"I know how to get there," Joanna said.

She made her way to the bank of elevators and up to the ICU waiting room, which hadn't changed at all from the way she remembered it. Two people sat in the far corner of the room, and Joanna recognized both of them. One was Olga Ortiz, Yolanda's mother. The other was Ted Chapman, executive director of the newly formed Cochise County Jail Ministry.

Ted stood up and held out a bony hand as Joanna approached. He was a tall scarecrow of a man who towered over her. After retiring as a Congregational minister, he had seen a need at the jail and had gone to work to fill it. His new voluntary job was, as he had told Joanna, a way to keep himself from wasting away in retirement.

"How are things?" Joanna asked.

"Not good," he said. "Leon's in with her right now." Leon Cañedo was Yolanda's husband.

Joanna sat down next to Mrs. Ortiz, who sat with a three-ring note-book clutched in her arms. "I'm so sorry to hear Yolanda's back in here," Joanna said. "I thought she was doing better."

Olga nodded. "We all did," she said. "But she's having a terrible reac-tion to the chemo—lots worse than anyone expected. And it's very nice of you to stop by, Sheriff Brady. When I called to ask you to come, Yolanda wasn't in the ICU. I thought seeing you might cheer her up, but then . . ." Olga Ortiz shrugged and fell silent.

"They moved her into the ICU about ten this morning," Ted Chap-man supplied.

"Is there anything I can do?" Joanna asked. "Anything my department can do?"

Olga Ortiz's eyes filled with tears. She looked down at the notebook she was still hugging to her body. "Mr. Chapman brought me this," she said. "I haven't had a chance to show it to Yolanda yet. She's too sick to read it now, but it'll mean so much to her when she can." Olga offered the notebook to Joanna, holding it carefully as though it were something pre-cious and infinitely breakable.

Joanna opened it to find it was a homemade group get-well card. Made of construction paper and decorated with bits of glued-on greeting cards, it expressed best wishes and hopes for a speedy recovery. Each page was from one particular individual—either a fellow jail employee or an inmate. All of the pages were signed, although some of the signatures, marked by an X, had names supplied in someone else's handwriting, Ted Chapman's, most likely.

Joanna looked at the man and smiled. "What a nice thing to do," she said.

"We try," he returned.

Joanna closed the notebook and handed it back to Olga, who once again clutched it to her breast. "What about Yolanda's boys?" Joanna asked. "Are they all right? If you and Leon are both up here, who's look-ing after them?"

"Arturo," Olga said. "My husband. The problem is, his heart's not too good, and those boys can be too much for him at times."

"Let me see if there's anything we can do to help out with the kids,"

Joanna offered. "We might be able to take a little of the pressure off the rest of you."

"That would be very nice," Olga said. "I'd really appreciate it."

Just then Joanna's cell phone rang. Knowing cell phones were frowned on in hospitals, she excused herself and hurried back to the elevator lobby. She could see that her caller was Frank Montoya, but she let the phone go to messages and didn't bother calling back until she was outside the main door.

"Good afternoon, Frank," Joanna said. "Sorry I couldn't answer a few minutes ago when you called. What's happening?"

"We found Dora Matthews," Frank replied.

"What do you mean, you found her?" Joanna repeated. "I thought Dora Matthews was in foster care. How could she be missing?"

"She let herself out through a window last night and took off. Once the foster parents realized she had skipped, they didn't rush to call for help because they figured she'd come back on her own. No such luck."

The finality in Frank Montoya's voice caused a clutch of concern in Joanna's stomach. "You're not saying she's dead, are you?"

Frank sighed. "I'm afraid so," he said.

Joanna could barely get her mind around the appalling idea. "Where?" she demanded. "And when?"

"In a culvert out along Highway 90, just west of the turnoff to Kartchner Caverns. A guy out working one of those 4-H highway cleanup crews found her. Ernie Carpenter and Jaime Carbajal are on the scene here with me right now. We're expecting Doc Winfield any minute."

"You're sure it's Dora?" Joanna asked. "There's no possibility it could be someone else?"

"No way," Frank replied. "Don't forget, I saw Dora Matthews myself the other night out at Apache Pass. I know what she looks like. There's no mistake, Joanna. It's her."

Joanna sighed. "I forgot you had met her. What happened?"

"Looks like maybe she was hit by a car and then dragged or thrown into the ditch."

"What about skid marks or footprints? Anything like that?"

"None that we've been able to find so far."

"What about Sally Matthews? Any sign of her yet?" Joanna asked.

"Negative on that. We're looking, but we still don't have a line on her."

"Great," Joanna said grimly. "When we finally get around to arresting her for running a meth lab out of her mother's house, we can also let her know that the daughter we took into custody the other night is dead. 'Sorry about that. It's just one of those unfortunate things.'"

"Dora Matthews wasn't in our custody, Joanna," Frank reminded her. "CPS took over. They're the ones who picked her up from High Lonesome Ranch, and they're the ones who put her in foster care."

"You're right. Dora Matthews may not have been our problem *legally,*" Joanna countered. "When all the legal buzzards get around to searching for a place to put blame for a wrongful-death lawsuit, Child Protective Services is probably going to take the hit. But that's called splitting hairs for liability's sake, Frank. Morally speaking, Dora *was* our problem. You know that as well as I do."

Frank's dead silence on the other end of the phone told Joanna he knew she was right. "Butch and I are just now leaving University Medical Center," she added. "Thanks for letting me know. I'll be there as soon as I can."

She sprinted from the front door to the garage. "What's wrong?" Butch demanded as she threw herself into the car.

"Dora Matthews is dead."

"No."

"Yes. I just talked to Frank. Someone ran over her with a car. A Four-H litter patrol found her out on Highway 90 by the turnoff to Kartchner Caverns."

"But I thought she was in a foster home," Butch said. "How can this be?"

"That's what I want to know," Joanna returned grimly.

They drove through Tucson with lights flashing and with the siren wailing. They were passing Houghton Road before Butch spoke again.

"What if they're related?" he asked.

Turning to look at Butch's face, Joanna ran over the warning strip of rough pavement that bordered the shoulder of the freeway. Only when she had hauled the car back into its proper lane did she reply. "What if what's related?" she asked.

"Dora's death and the murder of the woman Dora and Jenny found in Apache Pass. What if whoever killed Connie Haskell thinks Dora and Jenny know something that could identify him? What if Dora's dead because the killer wanted to keep her quiet?"

Without another word, Joanna picked up the phone and dialed High Lonesome Ranch. Eva Lou answered.

Joanna willed her voice to be calm. "Hi, Eva Lou," she said casually. "Could I speak to Jenny, please?" she asked.

"She's not here right now," Eva Lou answered.

Joanna's heart fell to the pit of her stomach. "Where is she?"

"Out riding Kiddo," Eva Lou replied. "She was still really upset about Dora this morning. When she asked if she could go riding, I thought it would do her a world of good. Why? Is something the matter?"

"How long has she been gone?"

"I'm not sure. An hour or so, I suppose."

"Do you have any idea where she was going?"

"Just up in the hills. Both dogs went with her. I understand she some-times rides down toward Double Adobe to see . . . What's that girl's name again?"

"Cassie," Joanna supplied. "Cassie Parks."

"That's right. Cassie. But as far as I know, Cassie's still away on the camp-out. Joanna, are you all right? You sound funny."

"Something's happened to Dora Matthews," Joanna said carefully.

"Not her again," Eva Lou said. "What's wrong now?"

"She's dead."

"Dead! My goodness! How can that be? What happened?"

"She evidently ran away from the foster home sometime overnight," Joanna said. "She was hit by a car out on Highway 90, over near the turnoff to Kartchner Caverns."

"Jim Bob's outside messing with the pump," Eva Lou said. "I'll go tell him. We'll take your Eagle and go out looking for Jenny right away to let her know what's happened."

"Go ahead," Joanna said. "Butch and I will be there as soon as we can."

She ended that call and then dialed Frank Montoya again. "I'm not coming," she said. "I'm going home instead. What if whoever killed Con-nie Haskell also killed Dora Matthews? What if they're coming after Jenny next?"

There was a pause. "I can see why you'd be worried about that," Frank replied at last. "If I were in your position, I'd be worried, too. But remember, this could be just a hit-and-run. It wouldn't be the first time a hitchhiker got run over in the dark."

"If Jenny were your child, would you settle for believing Dora's death was nothing but a coincidence?" Joanna demanded.

"No," Frank agreed. "I don't suppose I would. You go on home and check on her. We'll handle things here and keep you posted about what's going on at the scene."

"Thanks, Frank," she said. "I really appreciate it."

Joanna put down the phone. She drove for another five miles without saying a word. Once again it was Butch who broke the silence.

"I'm sure she's fine," he said.

Joanna gripped the steering wheel. "I am, too," she said.

"And what happened to Dora Matthews isn't your fault."

"I know it isn't my fault," Joanna said, "but just wait till I have a chance to talk to Eleanor."

At two-fifteen they pulled into the yard at High Lonesome Ranch. Joanna's Eagle was nowhere to be seen, which meant Jim Bob and Eva Lou were probably still out searching. As Joanna and Butch stepped out of the car, Jenny came strolling out of the barn, with Sadie and Tigger following at her heels.

Joanna went running toward her and pulled Jenny into a smothering hug. "Mom!" Jenny said indignantly, pulling back. "Let go. I'm all dusty and sweaty. You'll dirty your clothes." Then, catching sight of her mother's face, Jenny's whole demeanor changed. "Mom, what's the matter? Is something wrong?"

"Dora's dead," Joanna blurted out.

"Dead," Jenny repeated as all color drained from her face. "She's dead? How come? Why?"

"She must have run away from the foster home," Joanna said. "Someone hit her with a car. When Grandma Brady said you were out riding Kiddo, I was so afraid . . . That's where the Gs are now—out looking for you."

"But, Mom, I was just out riding, why should you . . ." Jenny drew back. "Wait a minute. You think the guy who killed Dora might come looking for me next, don't you!"

Joanna and Jenny were mother and daughter. It wasn't surprising that the thoughts of one should be so readily shared by the other, although, in that moment, Joanna wished it weren't true. Saying nothing, she merely nodded.

"Why?" Jenny asked.

"Because of what happened in Apache Pass," Butch said, stepping into the fray. "Your mother and I are afraid that whoever killed Connie Haskell may have targeted you and Dora."

"But why?" Jenny repeated. "Dora and me didn't see who did it or anything. All we did was find the body."

For once Joanna resisted the temptation to correct her daughter's grammar. "You know that," she said quietly. "And so do we. The problem is, the killer may believe you saw something even though you didn't."

Just then Joanna's Eagle came wheeling into the yard, with Jim Bob Brady at the wheel. The car had barely come to a stop before Eva Lou was out of it. With her apron billowing around her, Eva Lou raced toward Jenny.

"There you are, Jenny," she said. "I'm so glad to see you! When we couldn't find you, I was afraid—"

"She's fine, Eva Lou," Joanna interjected. "Jenny's just fine."

That's what she said, but with Dora Matthews dead, Joanna wasn't sure she believed her own reassuring words. Neither did anybody else.

10

It was a grim family gathering that convened around the dining room table at High Lonesome Ranch. Joanna began by briefly summarizing what Frank Montoya had told her about Dora Matthews's death.

"Supposing what happened to Dora and what went on in the Apache Pass case are connected," Jim Bob began. "How would the killer go about learning the first thing about Jenny and Dora?"

In response, Butch retrieved a copy of Sunday morning's *Arizona Reporter* from the car and handed it to Jim Bob Brady. Once he finished reading, Jim Bob sighed and shook his head. "That still doesn't say for sure that the cases are connected."

"That's right," Joanna agreed. "But we can't afford to take any chances. As of now, Jenny, consider yourself grounded. You don't go anywhere at all unless one of us is with you. No more riding off on Kiddo by yourself. Understand?"

A subdued Jenny nodded and voiced no objection.

"What about us?" Eva Lou asked. "Do you want us to stay on?"

Joanna glanced at Butch, who gave his head an almost imperceptible shake. "No," Joanna said. "That's not necessary. We've disrupted your lives enough as it is. You go on home. We'll be fine."

"All right," Jim Bob said, "just so long as you all know you can count on us if you need to."

"Has anybody found Dora's mother?" Jenny asked.

Joanna shook her head. "Not yet."

"Are you going to?"

"I'm sure we will."

Jenny stood up and pushed her chair away from the table. "Then maybe you should go back to work," she said, and left the room. At a loss, and not knowing what else to do, Joanna got up and followed her daughter into her bedroom, where she found Jenny lying facedown on the bed.

"Jen?" Joanna said. "Are you all right?"

"You said she'd be safe," Jenny said accusingly. "You gave me Scout's honor."

"Jenny, please. I had no idea this would happen."

"And now you're saying that if I stay home, I'll be safe?"

"Jenny, Butch and I—"

"Just go," Jenny interrupted. "Go away and leave me alone. You let someone kill Dora. You'd better find out who did it before I'm dead, too."

Stung by the anger and betrayal in Jenny's voice, Joanna retreated. A few minutes later she was outside by the Crown Victoria, struggling to fasten her Kevlar vest, when Butch came out of the house.

"Jenny will be all right," he assured her, once he had unloaded the luggage. "You go do what you have to. Don't worry about her."

Tears welled in Joanna's eyes. "Jenny blames me for what happened. I told her last night that I was sure Dora would be safe, but I was wrong. She wasn't safe at all, goddamn it! She's dead."

"No matter what Jenny said, Joey, and no matter what you may think, what happened to Dora Matthews isn't your fault," Butch said.

"I think you're wrong there," Joanna told him. "I'm not first in line for that; I'm second—right behind my mother."

As soon as Joanna was back on the highway, she looked at her watch. Almost two hours had passed since she had last spoken to Frank Montoya. In the world of crime scene investigation, two hours was little more than a blip on the screen.

Picking up her radio microphone, she called in to Dispatch. "Is Chief Deputy Montoya still out at the crime scene on Highway 90?" she asked.

"He sure is, Sheriff Brady," Larry Kendrick told her.

"Good. Let him know I've left High Lonesome Ranch, and I'm on my way."

As she drove, Joanna battled to control her churning emotions. Under most circumstances, where someone else's crisis was concerned, Sheriff Brady could be calm and completely unflappable. To her dismay she was now learning that her law enforcement training counted for little when her own family was threatened.

It still shamed Joanna to recall how completely she had fallen apart in those first awful minutes when she had come home to High Lonesome Ranch to find her dogs poisoned and her own home virtually destroyed by the frenzied anger of a drug-crazed woman. Joanna had surveyed Reba Singleton's rampage of destruction with her knees knocking, her heart pounding, and with her breath coming in short harsh gasps. It had taken time for her to separate the personal from the professional before she could gather her resources and go out and deal with the troubled woman herself.

Driving from the ranch to the crime scene, Joanna once again had to make that tough transition. She had to put her own worries about Jenny aside and focus instead on finding Dora Matthews's killer and Connie Haskell's killer, knowing that once the perpetrator—or perpetrators—were found, Jenny—her precious Jenny—would no longer be in danger.

An hour later, as she approached the clot of emergency vehicles parked along Highway 90, she felt more in control. Slowing down, she noted a road sign announcing that Sierra Vista was twenty-three miles away. As she made her way through the traffic backup, Joanna found herself wondering how it was that Dora Matthews—a thirteen-year-old with no driver's license—had made it more than twenty miles from her foster home in Sierra Vista to here. *She sure as hell didn't walk,* Joanna told herself.

Minutes later, she parked behind Frank Montoya's vehicle, a Crown Victoria that was a twin to hers. Deputies had coned the roadway down to one lane and were directing traffic through on that single lane while investigators clustered in the other lane and on the shoulder. Walking in the traffic-free left-hand lane, Joanna stopped beside Detective Ernie Carpenter, who stood staring off the edge of the highway.

"Hello, Sheriff," Ernie said.

"What's going on?"

"The victim's still down there," he said. "Jaime's just finishing taking the crime scene photos. Want to take a look before they haul her out?"

The last thing Joanna wanted to see was a young girl's lifeless body. "I'd better," she said.

Had she tried, Joanna probably could have seen enough without ever leaving the roadway. Rather than taking the easy way out, though, she picked her way down the rocky embankment. At the bottom, standing with her back to the yawning opening of a culvert that ran under the highway, Joanna looked down at the sad, crumpled remains of Dora Matthews.

Totally exposed to the weather, the sun-scorched child lay faceup in the sandy bed of a dry wash. Her lifeless eyes stared into the burning afternoon sun. Her long brown hair formed a dark halo against the golden sand. She wore a pair of shorts and a ragged tank top along with a single tennis shoe and no socks. A knapsack, its contents scattered loose upon the ground, lay just beyond her outstretched fingertips. The ungainly positions of Dora's limbs sickened Joanna and made her swallow hard to keep from gagging. Her twisted arms and legs lay at odd angles that spoke of multiple broken bones inside a savagely mangled body.

Breathing deeply to steady herself, Joanna turned away and joined Frank Montoya and George Winfield, who stood just inside the opening of the culvert, taking advantage of that small patch of cooling shade. "What do you think?" she asked.

"Looks like a hit-and-run to me," Frank said. "I've had deputies looking up and down the highway in either direction. So far we've found no skid marks, no broken grille or headlight debris, and, oddly enough, no tennis shoe. Whoever hit her made no effort to stop. I wouldn't be surprised to find we're dealing with a drunk driver who is totally unaware of hitting, much less killing, someone."

Like a drowning victim, Joanna wanted to clutch at the drunk-driver theory, one that would mean Dora's death was an awful accident. That would mean Jenny wasn't really in danger. But Joanna didn't dare allow herself that luxury. Instead, she turned to George Winfield.

"What about you?" she asked.

"You know me," George Winfield said. "Until I have a chance to examine the body, I'm not even going to speculate." He looked at his watch and sighed impatiently. "Jaime Carbajal drives me crazy. He's slower than Christmas. Even I could take those damn crime scene pictures faster than he does."

It was Sunday. Joanna suddenly realized that George's impatience with Jaime was probably due to the fact that this crime scene call was keeping Eleanor Lathrop's husband from attending one of his wife's numerous social engagements. Joanna's simmering anger toward her mother, held in check for a while, returned at once to a full boil. Rather than lighting into George about it, Joanna simply turned and walked back up to the roadway. Frank Montoya, reading the expression on her face, followed.

"Something wrong, Boss?" he asked.

"My mother's what's wrong," she said heatedly. "That little girl wouldn't be dead right now if Eleanor Lathrop Winfield hadn't opened her big mouth and gone blabbing around when she shouldn't have."

"You don't know that for sure."

"I don't *know* it, but it's a pretty fair guess. There are times when private citizens should mind their own damned business. Now, please bring me up to speed."

"Don't be too hard on private citizens," Frank counseled. "One of them may have just saved our bacon."

"What do you mean?"

"Someone found Connie Haskell's car. The call came in from Tucson a few minutes ago."

"Where was it?"

"At the airport in Tucson. Some little old lady, on her way to Duluth to see her daughter, made a 911 call on Saturday morning. She reported what she thought to be blood on the door of the car parked next to hers in the airport lot. The call got mishandled, and nobody bothered to investigate it until a little while ago. The woman's right. It *is* blood, and it's also Connie Haskell's Lincoln Town Car. It's being towed to the City of Tucson impound lot. I tried to get them to bring it down to Bisbee, but that didn't fly. Casey Ledford is on her way to Tucson to be on hand when they open the trunk. She'll be processing the vehicle for us. Not that I don't trust the Tucson crime scene techs," Frank added. "But they don't have quite the same vested interest in that Town Car that we do."

"Well, at least we're making progress somewhere," Joanna said. "Is it possible Connie Haskell's killer could be the carjacker after all?"

Frank shook his head. "I doubt it. The UDAs who were picked up in the other hijacked cars sure weren't heading for any airport."

Joanna considered his answer for a moment. "All right then," she said. "Let's assume for the moment that whoever's doing the carjackings isn't involved with this. What do we know about Connie Haskell's husband? Are we sure Ron Haskell is actually in residence at Pathway to Heaven? Or, if he was there, do we know if he still is?"

"It's called Pathway to Paradise," Frank corrected. "And we *think* he's there. The guy who runs the general store in Portal says one of the residents came in on Thursday morning and hit him up for some telephone change."

"That could have been Haskell, all right," Joanna said.

Frank nodded. "But when Jaime and Ernie tried to gain admittance to Pathway, there was an armed guard who wouldn't let them inside. He also refused to verify whether or not Haskell was there. He said all patient records are confidential and that only authorized visitors are allowed on the grounds. In the process he made it abundantly clear that police officers aren't authorized under any circumstances."

"Unless they have a court order," Joanna added.

"Right."

"What about checking with the airlines to see if somebody named Ron Haskell flew out of Tucson between Thursday night and the time the car was found?"

"I'm sure we can check on that tomorrow," Frank said.

Joanna thought for a minute, then made up her mind. "Let's go then," she said. "You're with me, Frank. There's no sense in our standing around second-guessing Jaime and Ernie. They both know what they're doing."

"What about the press?" Frank asked. "They're going to want a statement." Frank Montoya's duties included serving as the department's media-relations officer.

"For right now, forget them," Joanna told him. "Until we locate Sally Matthews and notify her of her daughter's death, you've got nothing to tell the media. Besides, the longer we keep Dora's death quiet, the better."

"Where are we going then?" Frank asked.

"To Paradise," Joanna said.

"But why?" Frank asked. "We still don't have a court order. Judge Moore won't be back until tomorrow."

"We don't need a court order," Joanna said. "We're not going there to question Ron Haskell. This is a humanitarian gesture—a matter of courtesy. We're going there to notify the poor man of his wife's death—assuming, of course, that he isn't already well aware of it."

"What makes you think we'll be able to get inside Pathway to Paradise when Ernie and Jaime couldn't?" Frank asked.

"For one thing, they weren't wearing heels and hose," Joanna said.

Frank Montoya glanced dubiously at Joanna's grubby crime scene tennis shoes. "You aren't either," he ventured.

"No," Joanna Brady agreed. "I may not be right now, but my good shoes are in the car. By the time we get to Paradise, I will be. Now how do we get there?"

Pointing at the map, Frank showed her the three possibilities. Portal and Paradise were located on the eastern side and near the southern end of the Chiricahua Mountains. One route meant taking their Arizona law enforcement vehicles over the border and into New Mexico before crossing back into Arizona's Cochise County in the far southeastern corner of the state. Potential jurisdictional conflicts made that a less than attractive alternative. Two choices allowed them to stay inside both Arizona and Cochise County for the entire distance. One meant traveling all the way to the southern end of the mountain range before making a long U-turn and heading back north. The other called for crossing directly through the Chiricahua Mountains at Onion Saddle.

"It's getting late," Joanna said. "Which way is shorter?"

Frank shrugged. "Onion Saddle's closer, but maybe not any faster. It's a dirt road most of the way, although, since there's been no rain, we shouldn't have to deal with any washouts."

"We can make it over that even in the Civvies?" Joanna asked.

"Probably," Frank replied.

Joanna nodded. "I choose shorter," she said. "We'll go up and over Onion Saddle. Did Ernie or Jaime mention who's in charge at Pathway to Paradise?"

Frank consulted a small spiral notebook. "Someone named Amos Parker. I don't know anything more about him than his name and that he wasn't interested in allowing Ernie and Jaime on the premises."

"Let's see if we have any better luck," Joanna told him.

More than an hour later, with the afternoon sun slipping behind the mountains, Joanna stopped beside the guard shack at the gated entrance to Pathway to Paradise. The shack came complete with an armed guard dressed in a khaki uniform who pulled on an unnecessary pair of wrap-around mirrored sunglasses before strolling outside. Joanna rolled down the window, letting in the hot, dusty smells of summer in the desert.

"Like I've told everyone else today," he said. "We're posted no hunting, no hiking, no trespassing. Just turn right around and go back the way you came."

Joanna noted that the guard was middle-aged, tall, and lanky. A slight paunch protruded over the top of his belt. As he leaned toward Joanna's open window, he kept one hand on the holstered pistol at his side. A black-and-white plastic name tag identified him as Rob Whipple.

"Good afternoon, Mr. Whipple," Joanna said carefully, opening her identification wallet and holding it for him to see. "I'm Sheriff Joanna Brady," she said. "Frank Montoya, my chief deputy, is in the next car. We're here to see Mr. Parker."

"Is Mr. Parker expecting you?" Rob Whipple asked. "Don't recall seeing your names on this afternoon's list of invited guests."

Rob Whipple's thinning reddish hair was combed into a sparse up-and-over style. A hot breeze blew past, causing the long strands to stand on end. The effect would have been comical if the man's hand hadn't been poised over his weapon.

"Chief Deputy Montoya and I don't have an appointment," Joanna said easily. "We're here on urgent business. I'm sure Mr. Parker will be more than willing to see us once he knows what it is."

Whipple's eyes may have been invisible behind the reflective glasses, but Joanna felt them narrow. A frown wrinkled across the man's sunburned forehead. "Does this have anything to do with those two detectives who were by here yesterday?" he asked "Like I already told them. This here's private property. No one's allowed inside unless Mr. Parker or his daughter gives the word. Mr. Parker's last order to me was that no cops were to enter unless they had themselves a bona-fide court order."

"We're here to speak to Mr. Parker," Joanna insisted. "And since he's not a suspect of any kind, we don't need a court order for that. Would you call him, please, and let him know we're here? You can assure him in advance that we won't take up much of his valuable time."

"If you don't mind, ma'am, you'd best tell me what this is in regard to," Whipple countered.

"I do mind," Joanna replied with an uncompromising smile. "My business with Mr. Parker is entirely confidential."

Shaking his head, Rob Whipple sidled back into his guard shack. Joanna saw him pick up a small two-way radio and speak into it. What followed were several of what appeared to be increasingly heated exchanges. Finally, shaking his head in disgust, Rob Whipple slammed down the radio and then emerged from the shack, carrying a clipboard.

"Miss Parker says you can go in," he growled. "Sign here."

Taking the clipboard, Joanna quickly scanned the paper. Blanks on the sheet called for date, time of entrance, time of departure, name, and firm, along with a space for a signature. Joanna noted that the first date mentioned on that sheet was May 22. Several of the listed firms were companies that delivered foodstuffs and other supplies to her department back in Bisbee, but of the names of the eighteen delivery people listed, Joanna recognized no one. Nowhere on the sheet was there any listing for Constance Marie Haskell. Ernie Carpenter's and Jaime Carbajal's names were also conspicuous by their absence.

"Are you going to sign in or not?" Whipple demanded. He was clearly angered by being countermanded. Joanna filled in the required information, signed her name, and handed Whipple his clipboard. As soon as she did so, the guard slapped a VISITOR sticker under her windshield wiper. "Wait right here," he ordered. "Someone's coming down to take you up." Still brandishing his clipboard, he stomped back to have Frank Montoya sign in as well.

It was several long minutes before a sturdy Jeep appeared, making its way down a well-graded road. The vehicle was totally enclosed in dark, tinted-glass windows that allowed no glimpse inside. When the door opened, Joanna expected another uniformed guard to emerge. Instead, the woman who stepped out wore a bright yellow sundress and matching hat. The ladylike attire stood in stark contrast to the rest of her outfit, which consisted of thick socks and heavy-duty hiking boots. Punching the button on an electronic gizmo, she opened the gate. Then, returning to her vehicle, she waved for Joanna and Frank to follow in theirs. They drove up and over a steep, scrub-oak-dotted rise and then down into a basin lined with a series of long narrow pink-stuccoed buildings complete with bright red-tiled roofs.

The Jeep stopped near the largest of the several buildings, one that was fronted by a wooden-railed veranda. The wood may have been old, but it was well-maintained with multiple layers of bright blue paint. Joanna's first impression was that they had strayed into some high-priced desert resort rather than a treatment center. On either side of the front entrance stood two gigantic clumps of prickly pear, both of them at least eight feet high. Joanna may not have heard of Pathway to Paradise until very recently, but it certainly wasn't a new establishment. Those two amazing cacti had been there for decades.

The woman in the yellow dress led Joanna and Frank up onto the veranda. Once in the shade, she removed her hat. Without the hat brim concealing her face and hair, Joanna realized the woman was probably well into her fifties, but she was tan and fit with a face whose fine lines and wrinkles revealed a history of too much time in the sun. The smile she turned on her visitors, however, was surprisingly genuine and welcoming.

"I'm Caroline Parker," she said, holding out her hand in greeting. "Amos Parker is my father. It's before dinner siesta time, so he's taking a nap at the moment, as are most of our clients. Is there something I can help you with?"

"I'm Sheriff Joanna Brady," Joanna told her. "This is my chief deputy, Frank Montoya. We're hoping to speak to a man named Ron Haskell who is thought to be staying here. Do you know if that's the case?"

Caroline Parker frowned. "Didn't someone come by yesterday looking for him as well?"

Joanna nodded. "That would have been my two homicide detectives, Ernie Carpenter and Jaime Carbajal. They were turned away at the gate and told not to come back without a court order."

Caroline nodded. "I heard about that," she said. "I was away at the time, and it did cause something of a flap. My father tends to be overprotective when it comes to our clients. He doesn't like to have them disturbed, you see. It gets in the way of the work they're here to do, which is, of course, paramount. Won't you step inside?"

She opened an old-fashioned spindle-wood screen door and beckoned Joanna and Frank inside. They entered a long room that was so dark and so pleasantly cool that it almost resembled a cave. Once her eyes adjusted to the dim light, Joanna saw that the flagstone floor was scattered with a collection of fraying but genuine Navajo rugs. The furnishings were massive and old-fashioned. The set of indestructible leather chairs and couches might once have graced the lobby of a national park hotel. At the far end of the room was a huge fireplace with its face covered by a beautifully crafted brass screen. The walls were lined with bookshelves whose boards sagged beneath their weighty loads. The room smelled strongly of wood smoke and furniture wax.

Caroline Parker walked across the room and switched on a lamp that cast a pool of golden light on the highly polished surface of a mahogany desk. Then she seated herself in a low, permanently dented leather chair and waved Joanna and Frank onto a matching leather couch.

"What kind of work do your clients do?" Joanna asked.

"As you may have surmised, Pathway to Paradise is a recovery center," Caroline explained. "A Bible-based recovery center."

"Recovery from what?" Joanna asked.

"Not alcohol or drugs, if that's what you're thinking," Caroline responded. "We have a doctor on staff, but we're not a medical facility. We specialize in treating addictions of the soul. In the past we've worked mostly with folks who have sexual and gambling difficulties. Now we're seeing people who are addicted to things like the Internet or day-trading. Whatever the problem, we approach it with the underlying belief that people suffering from such disorders have handed their lives over to Satan. Pathway to Paradise helps them find their way back."

"I've been sheriff here for several years," Joanna said. "Until the last few days, I didn't know you existed."

"That's exactly how we like it," Caroline Parker returned. "We've been here for almost thirty years. We prefer to maintain a low profile, although the people in need of our services have an uncanny way of finding us."

"Only thirty years?" Joanna questioned. "This room looks older than that."

Caroline nodded. "Oh, the buildings are, certainly. In the thirties, the place was a dude ranch. It fell on hard times and was pretty much a wreck when Daddy and I bought it."

"Why the armed guard?" Joanna asked.

"To keep out troublemakers. We set up shop here because we wanted privacy and affordability. The same holds true for any number of our neighbors who are looking for privacy and cheap land, too. The problem is, some of them aren't necessarily nice people. We had a few unfortunate incidents early on. We found we were too far off the beaten path to ask for or receive timely help, so we created our own police force. That's also part of our creed here: God helps those who help themselves."

"That doesn't explain what happened to my officers," Joanna said. "They had a legitimate reason for coming here, and they were turned away."

Caroline shook her head. "Over the years we've heard all kinds of stories," she said. "You'd be surprised at the number of off-duty police officers who turn out to be moonlighting process servers trying to get to our clients because a disgruntled spouse is trying to file for a divorce, for example. We've had to become very proactive in the area of looking out for our clients. They're often in extremely vulnerable states, especially when they first arrive. We have an obligation to see to it that they're not trampled on by anyone, be it angry ex-spouses or parents or even officers of the law. If our clients have legal difficulties, it's our belief that they'll be better able to deal with those problems *after* they've gotten themselves square with God."

"Does that include withholding the timely notification that a client's wife has died?" Joanna asked.

Caroline Parker's eyes widened in alarm. "Are you telling me Ron Haskell's wife is dead?"

"Yes," Joanna answered. "I certainly am. Constance Marie Haskell was murdered over the weekend. She was last seen alive in Phoenix on Thursday. Our understanding, from her sister, is that Mrs. Haskell was on her way here to meet with her husband. Her body was found in Apache Pass Friday evening. Detectives Carbajal and Carpenter were here to notify Ron Haskell of what had happened."

"Was my father aware of that?" Caroline asked.

"Was I aware of what?" a stern voice asked behind them.

Joanna turned in time to see a tall, stoop-shouldered man enter the room. In the dim light his wispy white hair formed a silvery halo around his head. Even in the gloom of that darkened room he wore a pair of sunglasses, and he made his way around the furniture by tapping lightly with a cane. Amos Parker was blind.

"Daddy," Caroline said, "we have visitors."

"So I gathered," Amos Parker said, stopping just beyond the couch where Joanna and Frank were sitting. "And they are?"

Joanna stood up and went forward to meet him. "My name is Joanna Brady," she said. "I'm sheriff of Cochise County. Frank Montoya is my chief deputy."

Joanna held out her hand, but Amos Parker didn't extend his. Instead, he addressed his daughter. "What are they doing here, Caroline?" he demanded. "You know my position when it comes to police officers."

"I'm the one who let them in," Caroline said. "They came to tell Ron Haskell that his wife is dead—that she's been murdered. That's why those two officers were here yesterday."

"You know very well that Ron Haskell broke the rules and that he's in isolation. Until his isolation period is over, he's not to see anyone, including you, Miss Brady."

"It's Mrs.," Joanna corrected.

"So you're married, are you?" Amos Parker asked, easing himself into a chair that was off to the side from where the others had been sitting. "I should have thought a woman who would take on a man's job and become sheriff wouldn't have much use for men. I'd expect her to be one of those fire-breathing, cigar-smoking feminists who insists on wearing the pants in her family."

"She's wearing a dress, Daddy," Caroline put in.

The fact that Caroline Parker felt constrained to defend Joanna's manner of dress to this unpleasantly rude man was disturbing. Even so, whatever Sheriff Joanna Brady was or wasn't wearing had nothing to do with the business at hand.

"The only part of my wardrobe that should matter to you, Mr. Parker, is the sheriff's badge pinned to my jacket. Is Mr. Haskell still here?"

Amos Parker crossed his arms. "I have nothing to say," he said.

"Oh, Daddy," Caroline interceded. "Don't be ridiculous. The man's wife has been murdered. He needs to be told."

Parker shook his shaggy head. "You know the rules," he said. "Ron Haskell broke his contract. He's in isolation until I say he's ready to come out."

"And I think you're wrong." Caroline blurted out the words and then looked stricken—as though she wished she could take them back.

Amos Parker turned his sightless eyes toward his daughter's voice. "Caroline, are you questioning my authority?"

There was a moment of stark silence. As the brooding quiet lengthened, Joanna fully expected Caroline to cave. She didn't.

"In this instance, yes," Caroline said softly. "I believe you're wrong."

Another long silence followed. Finally, Amos Parker was the one who blinked. "Very well," he conceded. "We'll probably lose him now anyway. You could just as well bring him down."

"From where?" Joanna asked.

"The isolation cabin is about a mile away," Caroline said. "I'll go get him and bring him here."

Interviewing Ron Haskell in a room where Amos Parker sat enthroned as an interested observer seemed like a bad idea. Joanna glanced at Frank Montoya, who nodded in unspoken agreement.

"Why don't we go with you?" Joanna suggested.

Caroline looked to her father for direction, but he sat with his arms folded saying nothing. "All right," Caroline said, plucking her hat off a table near the door. "Come on then. Someone will have to ride in the back."

"I will," Frank volunteered.

Once they had piled into the Jeep, Caroline started it and drove through a haphazard collection of several buildings all of whose blinds were still closed. No one stirred, inside or out. Beyond the buildings, Caroline turned onto a rocky track that wound up and over an adjoining hillside.

"How did Ron Haskell break his contract?" Joanna asked.

"He was seen making an unauthorized phone call," Caroline replied. "Clients aren't allowed to contact their families until their treatment has progressed far enough for them to be able to handle it."

"When was this phone call?" Joanna prodded.

"Thursday morning," Caroline answered. "One of the kitchen help had gone to the store to pick up something. She saw him there and reported it to my father. Since Ron hadn't asked for a pass, that meant two breaches of contract rather than one: leaving without permission and making an unauthorized phone call."

The Jeep topped a steep rise. Halfway down the slope a tiny cabin sat tucked in among the scrub oak. "That's it?" Joanna asked. Caroline Parker nodded. "And how how long has he been here?"

"Since Thursday afternoon. When people are in isolation, we bring them up here and drop them off along with plenty of food and water. It's our form of sending someone into the wilderness to commune with God. Even at Pathway, there's so much going on that it's hard for someone to find enough quiet in which to concentrate and listen."

"No one has seen Ron Haskell since he was brought here last Thursday?"

"That's what isolation is all about," Caroline said. "You're left completely alone—you and God."

As the Jeep rumbled down the hill, Joanna fully expected that they would find the cabin empty, but she was wrong. As the Jeep rounded the side of the cabin, the door flew open and a stocky man hurried out, buttoning his shirt as he came. Ron Haskell was anything but the handsome Lothario that Maggie MacFerson's acid descriptions had led Joanna to expect. He waited until the Jeep stopped, then he rushed around to the passenger side of the vehicle. As he flung open the door, his face was alight with anticipation. As soon as his eyes came to rest on Joanna's face, the eager expression disappeared.

"Sorry," he muttered, backing away. "I was hoping you were my wife."

It was long after dark when Joanna finally rolled back into the yard at High Lonesome Ranch to the sound of raucous greetings from Sadie and Tigger. She was relieved to find that Jim Bob and Eva Lou's Honda was no longer there. Lights behind curtains glowed invitingly from all the windows.

Weary beyond bearing, Joanna was frustrated as well. The meeting with Ron Haskell had left her doubting that he had been involved in his wife's death. And if that was true, they were no closer to finding out who had killed either Connie Haskell or Dora Matthews, which meant that Jenny, too, was possibly still in grave danger.

As she got out of the car, Joanna heard the back door slam. Butch came walking toward her.

"How's Jenny?" she asked over an aching catch in her throat.

Butch shook his head. "About how you'd expect," he said.

"Not good?"

"Not good. She's barely ventured out of her room since you left this afternoon. I tried cajoling her into coming out for dinner. No dice. Said she wasn't hungry. Maybe you'll have better luck."

Remembering that last difficult conversation with her daughter, Joanna shook her head. "Don't count on it," she said.

"Hungry?" he said. Joanna nodded. "I don't think Eva Lou trusts my cooking abilities," Butch continued. "She left the refrigerator full of leftovers and the freezer stocked with a bunch of Ziploc containers loaded with precooked, heat-and-serve meals. What's your pleasure?"

"How about a Butch Dixon omelette?"

"Good choice."

Inside the kitchen, Joanna noticed that the table was covered with blueprints for the new house they were planning to build on the property left to Joanna by her former handyman, Clayton Rhodes. "Don't forget," Butch said as he began rolling up the plans and securing them with rubber bands, "tomorrow night we have a mandatory meeting scheduled with the contractor."

"I'll do my best," she said. "Right now, I'm going to change clothes and see if Jenny's awake. I just talked to Ernie Carpenter. Jenny will have to come to the department with me tomorrow morning so the Double Cs can interview her." Since both detectives had last names beginning with the letter C, that's how people in the department often referred to Joanna's homicide detective division.

"Because of Connie Haskell, because of Dora, or because Jenny herself may be in danger?" Butch asked.

Joanna sighed. "All of the above," she said.

She went into the bedroom, removed her weapons, and locked them away. Thinking about the threat to Jenny, she briefly considered keeping one of the Glocks in the drawer of her nightstand, but in the end she didn't. As she stripped off her panty hose, she was amazed to discover that they had survived her crime scene foray. *That hardly ever happens,* she thought, tossing them into the dirty-clothes hamper.

Dressed in a nightgown and robe, she went to Jenny's bedroom and knocked on the door. Her questioning knock was answered by a muffled "Go away."

"I can't," Joanna said, opening the door anyway. "I need to talk to you."

The room was dark, with the curtains drawn and the shades pulled down. Even the night-light had been extinguished. Joanna walked over and switched on the bedside lamp. At her approach, Jenny turned her face to the wall in her cavelike bottom bunk and pulled a pillow over her head.

"Why?" Jenny demanded. "Dora's dead. What good will talking do?"

"We're not going to talk about that," Joanna told her daughter. "We can't. You're a witness in this case. Tomorrow morning you'll have to go to work with me so Ernie Carpenter and Jaime Carbajal can talk to you. They'll want to go over everything that happened this weekend, from the time you went camping on Friday. They'll question you in order to see if you can help them learn what happened to Dora and who's responsible."

"Grandma Lathrop is responsible," Jenny insisted bitterly. "Why couldn't she just mind her own business?"

"I'm sure Grandma Lathrop thought she was doing the right thing—what she thought was best for Dora."

"It wasn't," Jenny said.

They sat in silence for a few moments. "I didn't really like Dora very much," Jenny admitted finally in a small voice. "I mean, we weren't friends or anything. I didn't even want to sleep in the same tent with her. I was only with her because Mrs. Lambert said I had to be. But then, after Dora was here at the ranch that day with Grandpa and Grandma, she acted different—not as smart-alecky. I could see Dora just wanted to be a regular kid, like anybody else."

Just like you, Joanna thought.

"Dora cried like crazy when that woman came to take her away, Mom," Jenny continued. "She cried and cried and didn't want to go. Is that why she's dead, because Grandma and Grandpa Brady let that woman take her away?"

"Grandpa and Grandma didn't have a choice about that, Jenny," Joanna said gently. "When somebody from CPS shows up to take charge of a child, that's the way it is. It's the law, and the child goes."

"You mean if Grandpa and Grandma had tried to keep her they would have been breaking the law?"

"That's right."

"Well, I wish they had," Jenny said quietly.

"So do I," Joanna told her. "God knows, so do I."

There was another long silence. Again Jenny was the first to speak. "But even if I didn't *like* Dora Matthews, I didn't want her dead. And why do there have to be so many dead people, Mom?" Jenny asked, turning at last to face her mother. "How come? First Dad, then Esther Daniels, then Clayton Rhodes, and now Dora. Are we a curse or something? All people have to do is know us, and that means they're going to die."

Jenny lay on her back on the bottom bunk, absently tracing the outlines of the upper bunk's springs with her finger. Meanwhile Joanna searched her heart, hoping to find the connection that had existed only two nights earlier between herself and her daughter, when Joanna had been the one lying on the bottom bunk and Jenny had been in the one on top. The problem was that connection had been forged before Dora was dead; before Sheriff Joanna Brady—who had sworn to serve and protect people like Dora Matthews—had failed to do either one.

"It seems like that to me sometimes, too." With her heart breaking, that was the best Joanna could manage. "But dying's part of living, Jen," she added. "It's something that happens to everyone sooner or later."

"Thirteen's too young to die," Jenny objected. "That's all Dora was, thirteen—a year older than me."

A momentary chill passed through Joanna's body as she saw in her mind's eye the still and crumpled figure of a child lying lifeless in a sandy wash out along Highway 90. "You're right," she agreed. "Thirteen is much too young. That's why we have to do everything in our power to find out who killed her."

"You said she was hit by a car and that maybe it was just an accident," Jenny said. "Was it?"

"That's how it looks so far," Joanna said, although that answer wasn't entirely truthful. Hours of searching the highway had failed to turn up any sign of where the collision might have occurred as well as any trace of Dora Matthews's missing tennis shoe.

"When's the autopsy?" Jenny asked.

Jennifer Ann Brady had lived in a house centered on law enforcement from the day she was born. As in most homes, dinnertime conversation had revolved around what was happening in those two vitally important areas of their lives—school and work. In the Brady household, those work-related conversations had featured confrontations with real-life criminals and killers. There were discussions of prosecutions won and lost, of bad guys put away or sometimes let go. Young as she was, Jenny knew far too much about crime and punishment. And, with Eleanor's fairly recent marriage to George Winfield, discussions of autopsies were now equally commonplace. In that moment, Joanna wished it were otherwise.

"I believe he's doing it tonight."

Jenny absorbed that information without comment. "What about Dora's mother?" she asked after a pause. "Does she know yet?"

Every question as well as every answer drove home Joanna's sense of failure. "No," she said. "And I can't imagine having to tell her any more than I can imagine what I'd do if something terrible happened to you."

"Will Mrs. Matthews have to go to jail even if Dora is dead?"

"If she's convicted of running a meth lab," Joanna conceded.

Heaving a sigh, Jenny flopped back over on her side, signaling that the conversation was over. "Come on, Jenny. We probably shouldn't talk about this anymore tonight. Let's go out to the kitchen. Butch is making omelettes."

"I'm not hungry," Jenny said.

I'm not now, either, Joanna thought. "Well, good night then."

"Night."

Joanna returned to the kitchen. Butch looked up from the stove where he was about to flip an omelette. "No luck?" he said.

"None."

"You look pretty down."

Joanna nodded. "I talked to Connie Haskell's husband. I don't think he did it."

"Why not?"

"I can't be absolutely sure because he doesn't have a real alibi. He was off away from everyone else in an isolation cabin that's Pathway to Paradise's version of solitary confinement. He was there from Thursday morning on. Still, Butch, you should have seen how he looked when we drove up. He was expecting his wife to get out of the car. He wasn't expecting me. He'd have had to be an Academy Award–winning actor to fake the disappointment I saw on his face."

"I see what you mean," Butch agreed. "If he'd killed her, he wouldn't have been expecting her to show up."

"My point exactly."

"But what if he *is* that good an actor?" Butch said after a moment of reflection. "It's possible, you know."

Joanna nodded. "You're right. It is possible, but he also volunteered to come into the department tomorrow and let us take DNA samples. Innocent people volunteer samples. Guilty ones demand lawyers and court orders."

Butch set Joanna's plate in front of her and then sat down across the table from her. "What you're really saying is, you don't have the foggiest idea who the killer is and you're afraid Jenny may still be a target."

"Exactly," Joanna said.

The omelette was good, but Joanna didn't do much justice to it. The table was cleared and they were on their way to bed when the blinking light on the caller ID screen caught Joanna's eye. Without taking messages off the machine, she scrolled through the listed numbers. Marianne Maculyea had called several times, as had Joanna's mother, Eleanor. There were also several calls from Jenny's friend Cassie Parks. The contractor who was working with Butch on plans for the new house had called once, as had Arturo Ortiz, Yolanda Cañedo's father. Two of the calls were designated caller ID–blocked. The only remaining listed name and number were totally unknown to Joanna—a Richard Bernard. He had called on Saturday morning at ten-fifteen.

Wondering if Richard Bernard had left a message, Joanna skimmed through the spiral-ringed message log that was kept next to the phone. In Eva's neat handwriting was a note saying that Marianne Maculyea had called to remind Joanna that she and Butch were scheduled to be greeters at church the following Sunday morning. There was a written message for Butch to call Quentin Branch, the contractor on their new house. A separate note told Jenny to call Cassie, but there was nothing at all from a Richard Bernard.

Shrugging, Joanna picked up the phone. The broken beeping of the dial tone told her there were messages waiting in the voice-mail system—another one from Cassie to Jenny and one from Eleanor Lathrop Winfield. Again there was nothing at all from Richard Bernard. By then it was too late for Jenny to return Cassie's call, and Joanna wasn't particularly eager to call Eleanor back. Like Jenny, Joanna remained convinced that Grandma Lathrop's actions had contributed to Dora Matthews's death. Talking to Eleanor was something Joanna was willing to postpone indefinitely.

Putting down the phone, Joanna was halfway to the door when the telephone rang. Joanna checked caller ID before answering. When she saw her mother's number listed, Joanna almost didn't pick up the receiver, but then she thought better of it. *Might as well get it over with,* she told herself.

To her relief, she heard George Winfield's voice on the phone rather than her mother's. "So you are home!" he said.

"Yes," Joanna told him.

"How's Jenny?" George asked.

"She's taking Dora's death pretty hard," Joanna said.

"So's Ellie," George said. "She's under the impression that it's all her fault Dora Matthews is dead—that if she hadn't interfered by calling Child Protective Services, Dora would still be alive."

This was news. For as long as Joanna could remember, Eleanor Lathrop had made a career of dishing out blame without ever accepting any of it herself. It was one thing for Joanna and Jenny to think Eleanor had overstepped the bounds as far as Dora Matthews was concerned. It was unheard of for Eleanor herself to say so.

"I tried telling her that wasn't true," George continued, "but it was like talking to a wall. She wasn't having any of it. In fact, she took a sleeping pill a little while ago and went to bed. Her going to bed this early is worrisome. I don't think I've ever seen her so upset. That's why I'm calling, Joanna. At least it's one of the reasons. I'm hoping you'll find time tomorrow to talk to Ellie. Maybe you'll be able to make her see reason."

Fat chance, Joanna thought. *For once in our lives, it sounds as though Eleanor and I are in total agreement.* "I'll talk to her" was all she said.

"Good."

Joanna expected George Winfield to sign off. Instead, he launched into another topic. "I know it's late, and this information will be at your office tomorrow morning in my official autopsy report. But I thought, because of Jenny's involvement, you'd want to know some of this now. Dora Matthews was pregnant when she died, Joanna. And all those broken bones you saw, were broken postmortem."

"You're saying she was dead before she was hit by the car?"

"That's right. I'm calling the actual cause of death asphyxiation by means of suffocation."

"And she was pregnant?"

"At least three months along," George replied.

"But she was only thirteen years old, for God's sake," Joanna objected. "Still a child! How could such a thing happen?"

George sighed. "The usual way, I'm sure," he said. "And that's what's happening these days—children having children. Only, in this case, neither child lived."

"Will we be able to tell who the father is?"

"Sure, if we find him," George replied. "I saved enough DNA material from the embryo so we can get a match if we need to. Sorry to drop it on you like this, Joanna, but under the circumstances I thought you'd want some time to think this over before tomorrow morning when you're reading the autopsy report."

Joanna closed her eyes as she tried to assimilate the information. "So whoever killed Dora just left her body lying in the middle of the road for someone else to hit?"

"I didn't say she was run over," George corrected. "And she wasn't. She was hit by a moving vehicle while she was fully upright. But she wasn't standing upright under her own power. There were some bits of glass and plastic found on her clothing. There was also a whole collection of black, orange, yellow, and white paint chips on her body and what looks like traces of polypropylene fiber embedded in the flesh of both wrists. I believe her body was tied to something—a Department of Transportation sawhorse, maybe—while the vehicle crashed into her. The lack of bleeding and bruising from those impact wounds would indicate that she was already dead at that point."

"Whoever did it wanted us to believe Dora Matthews was the victim of an accidental hit-and-run," Joanna surmised.

"Correct. And since there's no evidence of a struggle or any defensive wounds, Dora may even have been sedated at the time of suffocation. I'm doing toxicology tests."

"But toxicology tests take time—weeks, even," Joanna objected.

"Sorry," George said. "You'll just have to live with it. In the meantime, on the chance that there may be some addititional microscopic paint flecks, I've preserved all of Dora's clothing. I sent them back to your department with Jaime Carbajal so your AFIS tech—what's her name again?"

"Casey Ledford."

"Right. So Casey can take a look at them. Whoever killed Dora obviously doesn't know much about forensic science, so I'm guessing he or she wouldn't have been all that sharp about not leaving fingerprints behind, either."

"Thanks, George," she told him. "I think."

"And you'll be sure to give your mother a call tomorrow?"

"I promise."

"Who was that on the phone?" Butch asked once Joanna walked into the bedroom. He was already in bed. Manuscript pages were stacked on top of the sheet while he alternately read and scribbled penciled notes in the margins.

"It was George," Joanna answered dully. "Calling to give me the news that Dora Matthews was dead before the car hit her. Somebody suffocated her, most likely after drugging her first, and then tried to fake a hit-and-run. George also said that she was three months pregnant when she died."

"Yikes," Butch said. "Do you think Jenny knows who the father is?"

The question startled Joanna. "I doubt it," she said.

"He's probably some little smart-mouthed twerp from school," Butch theorized.

That was another disturbing thought, that someone in Jenny's sixth-grade class at Bisbee's Lowell School—some boy who might very well be sitting next to Jenny in math or science—might also be the father of Dora Matthews's unborn child.

"I don't even want to think about it," Joanna said.

"You'd better," Butch returned grimly. "We'd all better think about it. If there's some little shit in the sixth grade who can't keep his pants zipped, somebody at the school had better wise up and do something about it—before an irate father does it for them."

As upset as she was, Joanna couldn't help smiling. "You sound like an irate father yourself," she said.

"I *am,*" Butch returned.

Joanna went into the bathroom. When she emerged, the manuscript and pencil were both gone. It was only then, as she crossed the room to turn out the light, that she noticed the baseball bat leaning against the wall between Butch's nightstand and the head of the bed.

"What's that?" she asked, pointing.

"It's a baseball bat."

"I can see that. What's it doing here?"

Butch shrugged. "I ran a bar, remember? Some people believe in Glocks. I believe in baseball bats, and, believe me, I know how to use them. If somebody turns up here looking for Jenny, I'll be ready."

"You'd go after someone with a baseball bat?" Joanna asked.

"Wouldn't you?"

Shaking her head, Joanna switched off the light and climbed into bed beside him. He threw one arm over her shoulder and pulled her close. Joanna lay snuggled next to him, grateful to feel his solid bulk against her, for the sturdiness of his chest against her back, and for the strength in the arm that encircled her.

"Who's Richard Bernard?" she asked a little later.

"Who?" Butch asked, and Joanna felt guilty when she realized he already must have dozed off.

"Richard Bernard. He called Saturday morning, but he didn't leave a message. I saw his name on caller ID and figured he was someone you knew."

"I have no idea," Butch told her. "Never heard of him."

"Neither have I," Joanna said.

"Eva Lou and Jim Bob were here then. Maybe he's a friend of theirs."

"Could be," Joanna said.

Within minutes, Butch was snoring lightly. Tired as she was, Joanna lay awake for what seemed like hours. She tossed from side to side, trying to find a comfortable position and hoping to quiet the paralyzing fear in her mind, the suspicion that a crazed killer was lurking somewhere outside in the dark, hiding and waiting and looking for an opportunity to make Jennifer Ann Brady his next victim.

Operating on a minimum of sleep, it was an edgy Joanna Brady who took her daughter to the Cochise County Justice Center at eight o'clock the next morning. They entered the department using the keypad-operated private entrance that led directly from the parking lot into Joanna's office.

After having been gone for several days, Joanna knew she'd have mountains of paperwork to attend to. A day like this wasn't the best time to bring her daughter to work, or to have to deal with the added complication of being present during the course of Jenny's homicide investigation interview.

"Should I go get you a cup of coffee?" Jenny asked as Joanna dropped her purse onto her desk and eyed the stacks of correspondence awaiting her there.

Jenny had been so quiet on the ride in from High Lonesome Ranch that Joanna's spirits rose at this hint of normalcy. "Sure," Joanna said. "That would be great."

Jenny darted out of the room while Joanna settled in behind her desk. Before she could reach for the first stack of correspondence, the door opened and Kristin Gregovich came into the office. The blond, blue-eyed Kristin greeted her returning boss with a cheerful smile.

"Welcome back," she said. "Did you have a good trip?"

Kristin was newly married to Joanna's K-nine officer, Terry Gregovich. She was also pregnant and due to deliver their first baby—a boy—in November. She had survived the first few months of fierce morning sickness and now was far enough along in her pregnancy that she no longer had to keep soda crackers and a glass of Sprite on her desk at all times. She glowed with a happiness and sense of well-being that Joanna usually found endearing. This morning, though, knowing what had happened to Dora Matthews and her unborn baby, Joanna felt a clutch in her gut at the sight of Kristin's new but still relatively unnecessary maternity smock.

"It was fine," Joanna told her. "Right up until people down here started dying left and right."

"How did the poker game go?" Kristin asked.

"I won," Joanna answered.

"Enough so Sheriff Forsythe noticed, I hope," Kristin said.

That late-night poker game seemed aeons ago rather than mere days. "He noticed, all right," Joanna said. "Now bring me up-to-date. Is there anything in particular I need to know before I go into the morning briefing?"

Over the next few minutes Joanna listened while Kristin gave her a rundown of the phone calls that had come in during the past several days. At eight-thirty, leaving Jenny in her office and deeply engrossed in the latest Harry Potter book, Joanna hurried into the conference room. Frank Montoya was already there. So were Detectives Carpenter and Carbajal.

Joanna nodded in their direction. "I brought Jenny along," she told them. "I'll be sitting in on the interview."

Both detectives nodded in unison. "Sure thing, Boss," Ernie said. "I'd be surprised if you weren't."

There was a knock on the door and Casey Ledford, the fingerprint technician, poked her head inside. "You wanted to see me?" she asked uncertainly.

"Yes," Frank said hurriedly. "I asked Casey to stop by. She has some information that I think will be of interest to everybody concerned. We'll take care of that before we start on routine matters."

Joanna nodded. "All right," she said. "Go ahead, Casey. You're on."

Slipping into a chair, Casey Ledford smoothed her very short skirt and then placed a file folder in her lap. "As you know, I went up to Tucson yesterday to examine Connie Haskell's vehicle, the blood-stained Lincoln Town Car that was left in the parking lot at Tucson International. The thing that surprised me was the minimal amount of blood showing on the outside of the car—not enough that an ordinary passerby was likely to notice it. Most of the blood was inside the trunk. And there's a big difference between the two—between the blood on the Town Car's exterior and that inside the trunk."

"What difference?" Joanna asked.

"They're two different types," Casey responded. "Which means they came from two different people."

"So maybe some of it is from the killer and some from the victim?" Joanna suggested.

Casey Ledford nodded. "Possibly," she said. "The evidence we found in the trunk is consistent with a body having been transported in it. The DPS crime lab is going over that for trace evidence."

"Good," Joanna agreed with a nod.

"I picked up a whole bunch of fingerprints," Casey continued, "some of which belong to the deceased and some that don't. I'm in the process of enhancing the ones I've found. So far I have no way of knowing whether or not AFIS will come up with a match, but I did find something odd."

"What's that?" Joanna asked.

Casey opened the folder and handed around pieces of paper. Each contained a typed transcript of the 911 call reporting the location of Connie Haskell's vehicle. It seemed straightforward enough. A woman, giving her name as Alice Miller and her address as 2472 East Grant Road, had reported that on her way to Minnesota to visit her daughter in Duluth she had parked next to a vehicle at the Tucson airport, a Lincoln Town Car with what looked like bloodstains on the car door.

Joanna read through the transcript. "So?" she inquired.

"Don't you see anything that doesn't fit?" Casey Ledford asked.

Joanna reread the transcript. "I still don't see anything," she said. "What's the deal?"

"If, as Mrs. Miller claimed, she was on her way to Duluth, Minnesota, at ten o'clock on Saturday morning, why did her 911 call originate from a pay phone on North First Avenue?" Casey asked. "Look at the address for the phone. When I saw it, I smelled a rat. If the woman who called really was on her way out of town by plane, wouldn't she have called in the report either from the airport or from her daughter's home in Minnesota once she got there? That struck me as odd, so just to be on the safe side, I drove past the address of the phone booth. It turns out to be inside a Target store on North First. Then I checked out the address she gave as her home address, the one on East Grant Road. It's a vacant lot. Alice Miller doesn't live there, and neither does anybody else."

"Way to go," Joanna breathed. "You wouldn't be interested in putting in for detective, would you?"

"No, thanks," Casey Ledford replied with a grin. "I'm perfectly happy being an AFIS tech. I have zero interest in watching autopsies. But there is one more thing."

"What's that?"

"Doc Winfield sent over Dora Matthews's clothes. I found something interesting in the pocket of her shorts, something the Doc evidently missed."

"What's that?"

"A cash receipt from Walgreens in Sierra Vista. It was dated Sunday and contains two items—a Snickers bar and one Know Now Kit."

"So?" Ernie Carpenter asked with a frown.

"Ever heard of Know Now?" she asked.

"Never," he replied.

"It's a home pregnancy test," she said. "Gives you results in three minutes."

"In our day, Rose had to go to the doctor to find out whether or not she was pregnant," Ernie said.

Casey Ledford shook her head. "That may have been true in the good old days," she told him with a laugh, "but not anymore."

"Doc Winfield already told us she was pregnant," Ernie said. "All that receipt means is Dora must have known, too."

"It was dated Sunday?" Joanna asked.

Casey nodded.

"It gives us something else," Joanna says. "It gives us one more bit of information about what happened *after* she left High Lonesome Ranch."

Ernie nodded. "We'll check into it," he said.

12

S o this Alice Miller must know something," Joanna said to the others after Casey Ledford had returned to her lab and the group's attention had veered away from pregnancy testing kits in favor of the mysterious 911 call.

"If that's even the woman's real name," Ernie Carpenter grumbled. "After all, if she gave a phony address in making the report, what makes you think she'd give the 911 operator her real name?"

"Point taken. So how do we flush her out?"

"How about checking with the phone company and seeing if any other phone calls were made from that same pay phone about the same time?" Jaime Carbajal suggested. "Maybe she made more than just that single call. If we find any other numbers dialed right around then, they might give us a lead as to who she is."

"Good thinking," Joanna said.

She glanced in her chief deputy's direction. Frank Montoya was the department's designated hitter when it came to dealing with telephone company inquiries. Joanna was grateful to see that he was already making a note to follow up on it.

"What about this cabin at Pathway to Paradise where you say Ron Haskell was in isolation from Thursday afternoon on?" Ernie added. "Just how remote is it?"

"Pretty," Joanna replied.

"But you said no one saw him from Thursday on. Isn't there a chance he could have slipped away from the cabin, done one murder or maybe even two, and then come back again to his cozy little isolation booth without anyone at Pathway being the wiser?" the detective asked. "There may be an armed guard posted at the gate, but who's to say someone coming and going on foot would have had to go anywhere near the gate?"

Joanna could tell Ernie was reluctant to drop Ron Haskell from his position as prime suspect in his wife's murder investigation. Joanna didn't blame Detective Carpenter for his reluctance. She didn't want to drop Ron Haskell from prime suspect status, either. Without him, the investigation into who had killed Connie Haskell was still stuck at the starting gate.

"I suppose you're right," Joanna conceded. "It is possible that Haskell could have come and gone without being noticed, but don't forget—he's due in here this morning to allow us to collect DNA samples."

"If he actually shows up, that is," Ernie returned. "I wouldn't bet money on it."

"All right. Let's go back to the Dora Matthews situation for a moment," Joanna suggested. "What's happening there?"

"I talked to the foster mother in Sierra Vista a few minutes ago," Jaime Carbajal said. "She called to say one of the kids in the neighborhood reported seeing a girl in shorts getting into a car around midnight Sunday night. I have the kid's name. We'll interview him ASAP and see if he can give us a description of the car. I'll also make it a point to check out that Walgreens store to see if anybody remembers seeing Dora Matthews there, either alone or with someone. If I were a drugstore clerk, I'd remember if a thirteen-year-old kid stopped by to pick up a pregnancy test kit."

"While I'm dealing with the phone factory," Frank Montoya said, "I'll check incoming and outgoing calls from the foster home as well."

"Good call," Joanna said. "Now, what about Dora's mother?"

"Still no trace of her," Jaime answered. "None at all."

Joanna aimed her next question at her chief deputy. "What's happening on the media front?"

"Because we can't locate and notify Sally Matthews, we're still not releasing Dora's name to the press," Frank replied. "The problem is, I don't know how long that line will hold. Word of Dora's death has already spread all over town. Sooner or later some reporter is going to pick up on it and publish it. As you know, Jenny's and Dora's names have already been in the papers in connection with finding Connie Haskell's body. Once the reporters find out Dora is dead as well, they're going to go to press without giving a damn as to whether or not Sally gets news of her daughter's death from us or from the media."

Joanna nodded. "Let's continue delaying the official release of Dora's name for as long as possible," she said. "But, bearing in mind that most people are murdered by people they know, what are the chances that Sally Matthews is somehow involved in her daughter's death?"

"There's nothing much on Sally Matthews's sheet," Frank said with a shrug. "My guess is she's been slipping by the criminal justice system for a long time, doing drugs and probably manufacturing and selling, too, but without getting caught. The first time she really got busted was last summer. She got six months for possession and sale. It should have been more, but her public defender came through like a champ. Her current boyfriend, Mr. Leon 'B. B.' Ardmore, has a couple of drug-violation convictions as well. From what I've learned so far, I'd say he's the mastermind behind the meth lab.

"But going back to Dora, it was while her mother was in the slammer that she ended up in foster care the first time—up in Tucson. From her reaction to the CPS caseworker out at High Lonesome Ranch the other night, I'd say she didn't like it much. Maybe foster care made her feel like she was in jail, too."

"What about Dora's clothing?" Joanna asked. "Has Casey Ledford started processing them for possible fingerprints?"

"Not yet," Frank Montoya said. "She agrees with Doc Winfield about the paint flecks, and there may be a whole lot more trace evidence on that clothing than just fingerprints and paint. Her suggestion is that we deliver all the clothing to the Department of Public Safety Satellite Crime Lab in Tucson and have their guys go over everything. The state has better equipment than we do, and a whole lot more of it, too. Needless to say, the sooner we get the clothing into the DPS pipeline, the better."

"I'll take care of that," Jaime Carbajal offered. "Once we finish with Jenny's interview, Ernie and I will take the clothing to Tucson."

"Speaking of which," Ernie said, peering at his watch, "Shouldn't we get started?"

Joanna glanced questioningly at Frank. "Anything else of earth-shattering importance for the morning briefing?" she asked.

"All pretty standard," Frank said, closing his folder. "Nothing that can't wait until after the interview or even later." He stood up. "Want me to send Jenny in on my way out?"

"Please," Joanna murmured. She had dreaded bringing Jenny into the conference room for the interview, and she was more than happy to let Frank do the summoning. Jennifer entered the conference room clutching Harry Potter to her chest, as though having the book with her might somehow ward off the evil wizards. She paused in the doorway and surveyed the room. Joanna sensed that the conference room—a place Jenny knew well and where she often did her homework—had suddenly been transformed into alien territory. When Jenny's eyes finally encountered her mother's, Joanna responded with her most reassuring smile.

"You know both Detective Carbajal and Detective Carpenter, don't you?" she asked.

Jenny nodded gravely.

"They'll be the ones asking you questions and taping your answers. It'll be important for you to tell them everything you know, down to the smallest detail. Sometimes it's those tiny bits of information that provide investigators with their most helpful leads. Understand?"

Jenny nodded again.

"And you have to remember not to nod or shake your head," Joanna added. "We may know what you mean, but your answer won't show up on the tape."

At that point, Ernie Carpenter stood up and took control of the proceedings. "Thanks for coming, Jenny," he said, leading her to a chair. "Make yourself comfortable."

For Joanna, the next hour and a half lasted an eternity. The process was excruciating for her. Motherly instinct made her want to prompt her daughter and encourage her, but the rules of interview procedure required her to keep still. There was too much likelihood that she might end up putting words in Jenny's mouth. On the other hand, knowing how the game was played, it was difficult for Joanna to sit silently on the sidelines while Ernie Carpenter and Jaime Carbajal volleyed questions at Jenny. The process was designed to tell them which of the two had established a better rapport with the witness—which had succeeded in gaining her trust. As a police officer Joanna recognized and applauded the way the detectives manipulated her daughter; as a mother she hated it.

Ernie Carpenter's children were grown and gone. Jaime Carbajal still had young children of his own at home. Whether or not that made the difference, soon after the interview began, it was clear the younger detective would be doing most of the questioning.

"So tell me about your friend Dora, Jenny," Detective Carbajal said, settling back into his chair and crossing his arms.

Jenny stuck out her lower lip. Joanna's heart constricted at that familiar and visible sign of her daughter's steadfast stubbornness.

"I knew Dora," Jenny answered. "But she wasn't my friend."

"But you were tentmates on the camp-out."

"That's because Mrs. Lambert made us," Jenny said. "She had us draw buttons—sort of like drawing straws. If two people got the same color button, they were partners for the whole camp-out. That's how I got stuck with Dora."

"Tell me about her."

"What do you want to know?"

Jaime Carbajal shrugged. "Everything," he said.

"She wasn't very smart," Jenny began.

"Why do you say that?"

"Because she had been held back—at least one grade and maybe even two. She was thirteen. Everybody else in our class is only twelve. Dora always looked dirty, and she smelled bad. She smoked, and she acted like she knew everything, but she didn't. And she wasn't very nice."

"I can understand why Dora smelled funny and looked dirty," Jaime Carbajal said quietly. "The place where she lived with her mother was filthy. The bathroom had been turned into a meth lab and the kitchen sink was full of dirty dishes and rotten food. There was no place for Dora to shower or bathe."

Jenny looked questioningly at Joanna. The idea of living with a mother who preferred manufacturing drugs to allowing her child to be clean must have seemed incomprehensible to her, just as it did to Joanna.

"There was some food in the house, but not much, and most of that wasn't fit to eat," Jaime Carbajal continued. "All in all, I don't think Dora Matthews's mother knew much about being a good mother. There's a reason I'm telling you all this, Jenny. I understand why you may not have wanted to be Dora's friend while she was alive, but I'm asking you to be her friend now. You can do that by helping us find out who killed her."

"I don't know how," Jenny said in a subdued voice.

"Tell us whatever you remember," Jaime urged. "Everything. Let's start with Friday afternoon, when you went on the camping trip. What happened there?"

"Well," Jenny began, "first we drove to Apache Pass. After we put up our tents, we ate dinner and had a campfire that wasn't really a campfire—because of the fire danger. Mrs. Lambert had us use a battery-powered lantern instead of a regular fire. It was after that—after we all went to our tents—that Dora said we should go for a walk and . . ."

Jenny paused and looked at Joanna. Sitting across the conference table from her daughter, Joanna forced her expression to remain unchanged and neutral.

"And what?" Jaime prodded.

". . . and have a cigarette." Jenny finished the sentence in a rush. "I tried smoking one, only the taste of it made me sick—so sick that I threw up. It was after I barfed that we found that woman's body—Mrs. Haskell's body."

"Did you see or hear anyone nearby when you found the body?" Jaime asked.

Jenny shook her head. "No. There wasn't anyone. She was lying there by the road, naked and all by herself."

"Did you see a vehicle, perhaps?" Jaime asked. "Maybe there was one parked somewhere along the road."

"No," Jenny said. "There wasn't, at least not that I saw."

Next to Joanna, Ernie Carpenter stirred, like a great bear waking from a long winter's sleep. His thick black brows knit together into a frown. "You said a minute ago that Dora Matthews wasn't nice. What did you mean by that, Jenny? Did she cuss, for instance, or beat people up?"

This time, instead of pouting, Jenny bit her lip before answering. Lowering her eyes, she shook her head.

"By shaking your head, you mean she didn't do those things, or do you mean you don't want to answer?" Ernie prodded.

Jenny looked beseechingly at her mother. "Mom, do I have to answer?"

Joanna nodded and said nothing. Jenny turned back to Ernie and squared her shoulders. "Dora told lies," she declared.

"About what?"

Jenny squirmed in her seat. "About stuff," she said.

"What stuff?" he asked.

"She said she had a boyfriend and that they like . . . you know." Jenny ducked her head. A curtain of blond hair fell across her face, shielding her blue eyes from her mother's gaze. "She said that they did it," Jenny finished lamely.

"You're saying that Dora and her boyfriend had sex?" Ernie asked.

"That's what Dora *said*," Jenny replied. "She said they did and that he wanted to marry her, but how could he? She was only thirteen. Isn't that against the law or something?"

"Dora wasn't lying, Jenny," Jaime Carbajal said softly. "Maybe the part about getting married was a lie, but Dora Matthews did have a boyfriend and they were having sex. And that *is* against the law. Even if Dora was a willing participant, having sex with a juvenile is called statutory rape." He paused. "What would you think if I told you Dora Matthews was pregnant when she died?" he asked a moment later.

Jenny's eyes widened in disbelief. She turned to her mother for confirmation. Again Joanna nodded. "It's true," she said.

"So what I'm asking you now is this," Jaime continued quietly. "Do you have any idea who the father of Dora's baby might be?"

To Joanna's amazement, Jenny nodded. "Yes," she said at once. "His name is Chris."

"Chris what?" Jaime asked.

"I don't know his last name. Dora never told me. Just Chris. I tried to tell her not to do it, but Dora went ahead and called him—called Chris—from our house."

"When was that?"

"Friday night, after Mrs. Lambert sent us home from the camp-out. It was while we were at home and when Grandpa and Grandma Brady were taking care of us. Dora called Chris that night, after the Gs fell asleep. Then, the next morning, Chris called her back. I was afraid Grandma would pick up the phone in the other room and hear them talking. I knew she'd be mad about it if she did, but she must have been outside with Grandpa. I don't think she even heard the phone ring."

"What time was that?" Jaime asked.

"I don't know," Jenny replied with a shrug. "Sometime Saturday morning, I guess."

"Could it have been about ten-fifteen?" Joanna blurted out the question despite having given herself strict orders to keep silent. Jenny looked quizzically in her mother's direction. So did the two detectives.

"It may have been right around then," Jenny said. "But I don't know for sure."

"I do," Joanna said. "And I would guess that Chris's last name will turn out to be Bernard," she added, addressing the two detectives. "That name and a Tucson phone number showed up on our caller ID last night when I got home. Since neither Butch nor I know anyone by that name, I thought it had to be someone Jim Bob or Eva Lou Brady knew. Now I'm guessing it must have been Chris calling Dora."

Jaime swung his attention from Joanna back to Jenny. "Did you happen to overhear any of that conversation?"

"A little," Jenny admitted. "But not that much. Part of the time I was out of the room."

"What was said?"

"Chris was supposed to come get her."

"When?"

"That night," Jenny murmured. "Saturday night. She said she'd be back at her own house by then, and that he should come by there—by her house up in Old Bisbee to pick her up. She gave him the address and everything. She told me later that they were going to run away and live together. She said Chris told her that in Mexico thirteen was old enough to get married."

"Did you mention any of this to your grandparents?"

Jenny shook her head. "No," she said softly.

"Why not?"

Jenny looked at Joanna with an expression on her face that begged for understanding. "Because I didn't want to be a tattletale," she said at last. "The other kids all think that just because my mother is sheriff that I'm some kind of a goody-goody freak or perfect or something. But I'm not. I'm just a regular kid like everyone else."

For Joanna Brady it was like seeing her own life in instant replay, a return to her own teenage years, when, with a father who was first sheriff and then dead, she too had struggled desperately to fit in. To be a regular kid. To be normal. It distressed her to think Jenny was having to wrestle the same demons. As a mother she may have been wrong about a lot of things, but she had called that shot—from the cigarettes on to this: Jenny's stubborn determination to keep her mouth shut and not be a squealer.

"I see," Jaime Carbajal said. "You already said you didn't know Dora was pregnant. Do you think Chris knew?"

Jenny shrugged. "Maybe," she said.

"What kind of arrangement was made for him to come get her?"

"I don't know that exactly, either. Like I said, I heard Dora give him her address and directions so he could get here. She said she'd sneak out to meet him just like she used to do up in Tucson. She said her mother wouldn't even notice she was gone. But then Grandma Lathrop called CPS. The next thing I knew, that awful woman was there at the house to take Dora away, and all the while Dora was yelling, 'No, no, no. I don't want to go. Don't make me go!'"

Jenny paused then. A pair of fat tears dribbled down her cheeks and dripped onto the surface of the table. "I should have told, shouldn't I? If I had, would it have made any difference or would Dora still be dead anyway?"

Joanna wanted to jump up, rush around the table, take Jenny in her arms and comfort her. She wanted to tell Ernie and Jaime, "Enough! No more questions." But she didn't. Even though it killed her to do so, she sat still and kept her mouth shut. It was Detective Carbajal who reached over and laid a comforting hand on Jenny's trembling shoulder.

"I don't know the answer to that," he said gruffly. "Child Protective Services took Dora Matthews into their custody. They're the ones who were ultimately responsible for safeguarding her once she left your grandparents' care."

There was a knock on the door. Ernie lumbered up from his chair. "I'll tell whoever it is to get lost," he said.

Just then the door opened. Kristin poked her head inside and beckoned to Joanna. "I have a phone call for you, Sheriff Brady," she said. "It's urgent."

Joanna looked at Jenny. "Will you be all right? I can ask Detectives Carpenter and Carbajal to not ask any more questions until I get back."

Jenny shook her head. "It's all right," she said. "I don't mind."

Joanna followed Kristin into the lobby. "Who is it?" she asked.

"Burton Kimball," Kristin replied.

Burton Kimball was Bisbee's premier attorney. He did a fair amount of local defense work. He had also handled Clayton Rhodes's will, the one in which Joanna's former handyman had left his neighboring ranch to

Joanna and Butch. Surely there was no lingering problem from that trans-action that necessitated Joanna's being yanked from Jenny's interview.

"What does he want?" Joanna demanded. "I thought I told you we weren't to be interrupted."

"I'm sorry," Kristin apologized. "Mr. Kimball insisted that it was vitally important that he speak to you. I offered to put him through to Chief Deputy Montoya, but he said you were the only one who would do."

"All right then," Joanna sighed. Shaking her head in frustration, she stomped into her office and unearthed her telephone from the mounds of papers that covered her desk. Then she sat down and took several deep breaths to compose herself. Finally she picked up the receiver and punched the "hold" button.

"Good morning, Burton," she said as cordially as she could manage. "What can I do for you?"

"Well, sir," Burton said in his mannerly drawl. "I'm sitting here in my office with my newest client, a lady by the name of Sally Matthews. I han-dled her parents' estate, so she came to see me. Ms. Matthews is interested in turning herself in, Sheriff Brady. The City of Bisbee has passed this case along to the Multi-Jurisdiction Force, so in actual fact, she'll be turning herself in to them. But, given what all has happened, she wants to talk to you first. Before Sally turns herself in to them, she wants to hear the straight scoop about what happened to Dora and what's being done to find whoever's responsible. That seems to me like a reasonable enough request."

"She knows her daughter is dead?" Joanna asked.

"Yes, she does," Burton replied. "She came back to town and heard it from an acquaintance—someone she ran into when she stopped to get gas. She took it hard, Sheriff Brady, real hard, but she's had a chance to pull herself together now. If it wouldn't be too inconvenient, I'd like to bring her out to see you as soon as possible. What do you think?"

There wasn't much Joanna could say. "Sure," she agreed. "Bring her right down."

"I'm concerned that there might be reporters out front at your office due to that murder out in Apache Pass," Burton Kimball continued. "Considering Dora's previously publicized connection to that case, I'm afraid Sally's appearance will cause quite a stir. Is there possibly a more dis-creet way of bringing her down to your place rather than just driving up to the front door and marching in through the main lobby?"

Joanna sighed. "Sure," she said. "Come around to the back. There's a door close to the west end of the building. That opens directly into my office. Knock on that, and I'll let you in."

"Thank you so much, Sheriff Brady," Burton said. "You're most kind. We'll be there in a matter of minutes."

As soon as Burton Kimball hung up, Joanna dialed Frank Montoya's office. "What's up?" her chief deputy asked. "Is the interview over already?"

"It's about to be," she said. "Burton Kimball just called. He has Sally Matthews in his office. She's ready to turn herself in, and he's bringing her here."

"Why here?" Frank asked. "That meth lab was inside the city limits. It should be the City of Bisbee's problem, not ours."

"The city has passed the case off to MJF," Joanna told him. "She'll turn herself in to them, but Burton Kimball is bringing Sally Matthews here first so we can brief her about what happened to Dora. I'm calling to let you know that Sally Matthews now knows about her daughter's death. That being the case, you can go ahead and officially release Dora's name to the press. We shouldn't put it off any longer."

"Will do," Frank said.

Before returning to the conference room, Joanna stopped long enough to call Butch at home. "Scroll through the caller ID screen," she asked him. "I need the number of the guy named Richard Bernard who called on Saturday morning. I think we may have found the father of Dora Matthews's baby."

"The name is listed here as Richard Bernard, MD," Butch said, once he'd read Joanna the number. "What is this, a doctor who's some kind of pervert child molester?"

"I doubt it," Joanna told him. "According to Jenny, Chris was the name of Dora's boyfriend. They're kids, so naturally there was no last name. I'm guessing Chris Bernard is a teenaged son or maybe even a grandson. Jenny also said that Dora talked to Chris a couple of times while she was staying out there at the house with The Gs. That means Ernie or Jaime will need to interview him in case she told Chris anything on the phone that could shed light on what happened later."

"I wonder if Chris knew he was going to be a father," Butch said.

"Maybe," Joanna said. "On Sunday Dora bought one of those home pregnancy test kits. I'm guessing that once she knew the results, she probably told him as well. I need to have Frank check their phone records as well."

"Whose?" Butch asked.

"The Bernards'," she said. "Never mind. I'm just thinking aloud."

"So Jenny's interview is over then?" Butch asked, switching gears. "Do you want me to come pick her up?"

"It's not over, although they're probably close to finishing up. I got called out of the conference room to take the phone call from Burton Kimball about Sally Matthews turning herself in. They're on their way here from Bisbee right now."

"In that case, I'll definitely come pick up Jenny," Butch declared. "That'll be one less thing for you to worry about."

"Thanks," Joanna said. "Once they're done, I'm sure Jenny will be more than ready to go."

"It was pretty tough then?"

"Yes, it was," she replied. "For both of us."

"Sorry about that, Joey. I'll be there in a few minutes."

"If you come too soon, Jenny might not be ready."

"That's all right. I'll wait."

Without touching any of the papers waiting on her desk, Joanna headed back to the conference room. She met Jenny and Ernie Carpenter in the lobby.

"Finished?" Joanna asked.

Ernie nodded. "For the time being."

Joanna handed him the piece of paper on which she'd jotted down Dr. Richard Bernard's name and number. "Good enough," Ernie said. "I guess Jaime and I had better head up to Tucson. We'll deliver the clothing to the crime lab so they can get started processing it. After that, we'll track down Chris and talk to him."

"Before you go, you need to know that Sally Matthews is about to turn herself in to MJF. Burton Kimball is bringing her in. They'll be here in a few minutes. I told them to use the back door. She wants to know what's going on with Dora's case, and I'm going to tell her."

"So she knows?"

Joanna nodded. "How much she knows remains to be seen."

Ernie Carpenter left to find his partner. With a subdued Jenny following behind, Joanna returned to her office and made a futile attempt to straighten the mess on her desk. Meanwhile, Jenny slouched in one of the captain's chairs. For several minutes, neither mother nor daughter said a word.

Joanna finally broke the lingering silence. "What's wrong?" she asked.

"Are you mad at me?" Jenny returned.

"Why would I be mad at you?"

Jenny bit her lip. She had chewed on it so much during the course of the interview that morning that it looked chapped and swollen. "For not telling Grandma and Grandpa about Dora talking to Chris on the phone. I didn't think she was serious about running away. I thought she was just talking big again, you know, like bragging. But maybe, if I had told . . ."

Joanna went over to Jenny's chair and knelt in front of her. "Jenny, honey, you're going to have to decide that what happened wasn't your fault. And now that we know a little more about what went on, it probably isn't Grandma Lathrop's fault, either. From what you said, it's clear Dora Matthews was determined to run away. She would have done it anyway, whether she was at our house or at her own home up in Bisbee or in foster care."

"You really think so?" Jenny asked.

"Yes, I do."

"What about Chris? Do you think he's the one who killed her?"

"It could be," Joanna said. "At this point in the investigation, anything is possible."

There was a knock on Joanna's private entrance. "Is that them?" Jenny asked. "Mr. Kimball and Dora's mother?"

"Probably."

"I don't want to see them," Jenny said urgently.

"Of course you don't," Joanna said. "Come on. You can wait outside in the lobby with Kristin. Butch will be here in a few minutes to pick you up."

Still clutching her book, Jenny retreated, closing the lobby door behind her, while Joanna went to open the outside door. Through the security peephole Joanna saw Burton Kimball, overdressed as usual in his customary suit and tie. With him was a desperately thin woman who must have been about Joanna's age but who looked much older. Sally Matthews was gaunt and looked worn in her bottom-of-the-barrel thrift-store clothing. A loose-fitting baggy dress two sizes too large covered her bony, emaciated frame. On her feet was a pair of old flipflops. Bedraggled, ill-cut brown hair dangled around a thin face that was mostly obscured by a huge pair of sunglasses. In one knotted fist she clutched a soggy hanky.

"Good morning, Sheriff Brady," Burton Kimball said when Joanna opened the door. "May we come in?"

Joanna held the door open and beckoned them inside. By the time she returned to her desk, she found that Sally Matthews had shed her sunglasses to reveal a haggard, homely, and entirely makeup-free face.

"You can go ahead and put me under arrest if you want," Sally said, in a harsh voice that trembled with suppressed emotion. "I don't give a damn what happens to me. All I know is, your department took charge of my daughter, and now Dora is dead. Who's responsible for that, Joanna Brady? Are you the one?"

As she spoke, the agitated Sally Matthews had leaned so far forward in her chair that, for a moment. Joanna was afraid she was going to clamber across the expanse of desk that separated them. It must have seemed that way to Burton Kimball as well. He laid a restraining hand on his client's arm. "Easy," he said. "Take it easy."

"I won't take it easy," Sally Matthews hissed, shrugging away his hand. "I want to know who killed my daughter."

"So do I," Joanna breathed. "Believe me, so do I."

She punched the intercom button. "Kristin," she said when her secretary answered. "Would you please have Chief Deputy Montoya come to my office?"

When she looked back at Sally Matthews, the woman had dissolved into tears, sobbing into a large men's handkerchief that had most likely come from Burton Kimball's pocket. From the way Jaime Carbajal had described the Matthews's home, Joanna knew Sally wouldn't have won any Mother of the Year awards. Still, there was no denying that the woman was overwhelmed by grief at the loss of her only daughter.

Before Joanna could say anything to comfort Sally, there was a sharp knock at her door. Turning, Joanna expected to see Frank Montoya. Instead, Kristin stood in the doorway, beckoning frantically to Joanna.

"If you'll excuse me for a moment," Joanna said. She got up and walked over to the door. Kristin drew her into the lobby and then closed the door after them.

"What's the matter?" Joanna said.

"You'd better go out front," Kristin said, speaking in an urgent whisper. "All hell's broken loose out there."

"Why? What's happened?"

"From what I can tell, right after Frank's news conference, one of those photographers from the *Arizona Reporter* tried to jump in and get a picture of Jenny as Butch was leading her out of the building. I think Butch grabbed the camera out of the guy's hands and lobbed it into the parking lot. He and Jenny are both in Frank's office."

Joanna could barely believe her ears. "They're not hurt, are they?" she demanded.

"No, they're fine," Kristin answered quickly. "But the photographer is out in the public lobby raising hell. He wants somebody to arrest Butch for assault and battery. And then there's Ron Haskell. He's here waiting . . ."

Joanna looked across the room and saw Ron Haskell sitting forlornly on the lobby loveseat. Stifling her own roiling emotions, she walked across the room to him and shook hands. "Thank you for coming, Mr. Haskell. As you can see, there's a bit of an emergency going on right now. If you don't mind, I'll have my secretary here take you back to speak to one of our evidence technicians."

Joanna turned back to Kristin. "Take him to see Casey Ledford," she said, struggling to keep her voice steady. "She'll need to take fingerprints from him. We'll need to collect DNA samples as well."

With that, Joanna Brady headed for her chief deputy's office, where, with the public brawl now over, her husband and daughter were waiting.

13

By early afternoon, Joanna was in her office and elbow-deep in paperwork. Kristin Gregovich had gone out for an early lunch and had returned with a tuna sandwich for Joanna, the half-eaten remains of which lingered on her correspondence-littered desk. With two separate murder investigations under way, it was difficult for Joanna to stay focused on the routine administrative matters that had to be handled—duty rosters to approve and vacation schedules to be juggled, as well as making shift-coverage arrangements around Yolanda Cañedo's extended sick leave.

Looking over the schedule, Joanna was reminded of her stop at University Medical Center. Picking up her phone, Joanna dialed Frank's number. "All the inmates and all the jail employees made and signed get-well cards for Yolanda Cañedo," she said. "Have the deputies done anything similar?"

"Not that I know of," Frank replied.

"Is Deputy Galloway on duty?"

"He should be. Why?"

"If you can track him down, let him know I need to see him."

Deputy Kenneth W. Galloway was one of Joanna's problem children. He was the nephew and namesake of another Cochise County deputy, Ken Galloway. Ken Galloway the elder had been part of the corrupt administration that had preceded Joanna's. He had died as a result of injuries suffered in a car accident during a high-speed car chase. A coroner's inquest had ruled his death accidental, but years later, many members of the Galloway clan still held Joanna Brady personally responsible for his death.

At the time of his uncle's death, Ken W., as he was called, was fresh out of the academy. He was still far too young and naive to have been involved in any of his uncle's underhanded dealings. After her election, Joanna had allowed Ken W. to stay on with the department. He had been a capable enough deputy, but he had never made any pretense of loyalty to Joanna or her administration. His obvious antipathy to Joanna made him a natural for membership in and eventual leadership of Local 83 of the National Federation of Deputy Sheriffs, where he had recently been elected president.

Months earlier, one of Joanna's decisions had resulted in saving Deputy Galloway's life, but if she had thought that would make her relationship with the union leader any smoother, she had soon been disabused of the notion. More than half hoping Frank wouldn't find the man, Joanna returned to the morass on her desk.

One whole stack was devoted to requests for civic appearances: Rotary and Kiwanis meetings where she was asked to be the guest speaker; a call-in talk show on a radio station in Sierra Vista, where she would be joined on the air by a group of Latino activists who were concerned about racial profiling by various members of the law enforcement community, the Cochise County Sheriff's Department included; and Elfrida High School, which wanted to know if she would be the main speaker at its career-day program.

As Joanna penciled one obligation after another into her rapidly filling calendar, she realized that even without having officially announced her candidacy, as far as the people of Cochise County were concerned, she was already running for reelection. Every appearance put her in front of voters. Eventually she would have to make an official announcement one way or the other. Right that minute she wasn't sure what she would do. The morning's confrontation between Butch and photographer Owen Faulk of the *Arizona Reporter* had left her feeling as though the most important pieces of her world were at war with one another.

Butch Dixon had yet to come to terms with the idea that being married to Arizona's only sitting female sheriff meant giving up all claim to anonymity. The incident with Owen Faulk wasn't the first time Butch had bridled at the unaccustomed and unwelcome intrusion of the press in their lives, but it was certainly the most serious. The fact that Butch had been protecting Jenny made it easy for Joanna to forgive his overreaction, but she doubted that the rest of the world would be equally understanding.

Dealing with that volatile situation had required Joanna's personal intervention and all her diplomatic skill. First Joanna had had to persuade Butch to cool it. Then she'd had to soothe Jenny, who, after her grueling interview with the Double Cs, was even more traumatized. And, after all that, she'd had to smooth Owen Faulk's ruffled feathers, managing to dodge a potential liability suit in the process. She had offered assurances that Faulk's expensive equipment, if broken, would be repaired or replaced. Since the photographer had accepted her offer without any argument, Joanna surmised that Owen Faulk realized that he, too, had been out of line.

So that thorny problem was solved for the time being, but dealing with it had taken Joanna's attention away from her job and away from the conference room, where Sally Matthews, with Burton Kimball present, was still being interviewed by Raul Encinas, a detective with the City of Bisbee Police Department, and Frank Bonham, one of the officers from the Multi-Jurisdiction Force, along with a representative from the county attorney's office. By the time Joanna had finished handling the photographer uproar, the interview with Sally Matthews had been in process for well over an hour. Joanna had known better than to walk in and interrupt, and it bothered her that, all this time later, it was still going on without her.

Realizing she'd have to content herself with reading the transcript, Joanna had gone into her office and tackled her logjam of waiting correspondence, only to be interrupted shortly thereafter by Casey Ledford poking her head into her office.

"Mr. Haskell is outside," Casey told Joanna. "Kristin suggested I bring him back by here so one of the detectives could interview him."

"That would be great except for one small glitch," Joanna replied. "At the moment we're fresh out of detectives."

"What should I do with him then?"

"Let me talk to him."

Ron Haskell looked up when Joanna entered the lobby. "Both my detectives are busy this afternoon," she told him. "Are you planning on going back out to Pathway to Paradise?"

Haskell shook his head. "Amos Parker gave me the boot. He said that since I had violated Pathway rules and was insisting on leaving again without completing my course of treatment, that he's keeping my money, but I'm not welcome to return. He had me pack up my stuff before I left this morning. I drove into Bisbee on my own."

"Will you be staying here then?"

Again Ron Haskell shook his head. "I just heard that Connie's sister, Maggie, is still in town. She's saying all kinds of wild things about me and making lots of unfounded allegations. I think it's a bad idea for me to be here when she is. Not only that," he added, as his eyes filled with tears, "I guess I need to plan Connie's funeral."

Knowing Maggie MacFerson's penchant for carrying loaded weapons, Joanna Brady heartily concurred with Ron Haskell's decision to leave town. "That's probably wise," she said. "Your going home, that is."

"From what I've heard, Maggie seems to think I'm responsible for what happened to Connie," Ron added. "And she's right there, you know. I *am* responsible even if I didn't kill her myself. I'm the one who made the phone call and asked her to come down to Paradise to see me. If it hadn't been for that, she'd most likely still be at home—safe and alive. But Connie was my wife, Sheriff Brady. I loved her." His voice cracked with emotion.

While Ron Haskell struggled with his ragged emotions, Joanna thought about how difficult it would be for her already overworked detectives to schedule an interview with him once he had returned to Phoenix, two hundred miles away.

Time to make like the Little Red Hen and do it myself, she thought.

"I expected my homicide investigators to be here this afternoon, but they were called to Tucson this morning," she said. "If you don't mind, I'd like to go ahead and ask you a few questions myself."

"Sure," Haskell said. "I guess that would be fine. I've got nothing to hide."

"Do you want an attorney to be present?"

"I don't really need one. I didn't kill my wife, if that's what you mean."

"All right, but I'll need to record our interview and have another officer present when I do it," Joanna told him.

"Fine," Ron Haskell said.

Joanna went out of her office and knocked on Frank Montoya's door. "Care to join me playing detective?" she asked. "Ron Haskell is here and ready to be questioned, except Ernie and Jaime are both in Tucson."

"Where should we do it?" Frank asked.

"The interview room is still busy with the Sally Matthews bunch. I guess it'll have to be in my office."

When Joanna reentered the room, Ron Haskell was standing by the large open window and staring up at the expanse of ocotillo-dotted limestone cliffs that formed the background to the Cochise County Justice Center.

"I really did love Connie, you know," he said softly, as Joanna returned to her desk. "I never intended to do that—love her, you see. And I didn't at first. Maggie must have figured that out. She didn't like me the moment she first laid eyes on me. She said right off the bat that all I was after was Connie's money, and to begin with, money *was* all I wanted. Why not? I'd had to struggle all my life. I went to school on scholarships and had to fight and work for everything I got while Connie was born with a silver spoon in her mouth. Other than taking care of her folks when they got old and sick, she never had to work a day in her life. When we got married, she had money—enough, I suppose, so the two of us would have been comfortable as long as we didn't do anything too wild or crazy.

"But then she made it too easy for me. She gave me free rein with running the finances—turned them over to me completely. About that time is when I came up with the bright idea that I could turn that tidy little sum of hers into a real fortune for both of us."

"I take it that didn't work?" Joanna asked dryly.

Ron nodded miserably in agreement. "I got hooked into day-trading—tech stocks and IPOs mostly. I figured it was just a matter of time before I'd hit it big, but I ended up taking a bath. Connie's money slipped through my fingers like melted butter. And that only made me try harder and lose more. It turned into a kind of sickness."

"Which is how you ended up at Pathway?"

"Yes."

Frank came in then, carrying a tape recorder which he set up on Joanna's desk. "Tell us about last Thursday," Joanna said to Ron Haskell, after Mirandizing him and going through the drill of starting the recording and identifying the participants.

"I called Connie," Ron Haskell said. "I went down to the general store in Portal a little before noon. I called her at home without having Amos Parker's express permission to do so. Clients at Pathway aren't allowed to have any contact with their families until Amos gives the go-ahead, but I wanted to talk to her right then. I needed to tell her what had happened and explain what was going on. By then I was sure she had to know the money was gone, but I wanted to see her in person."

"What money?" Joanna asked.

"Her money," Ron Haskell said. "The money her parents left her. I had lost it all playing the stock market, and I wanted to tell her about it face-to-face."

"Did you talk to her?"

"No. She wasn't home. I left a message on her machine," Haskell said. "I asked her to come down to Pathway that evening so I could see her. I planned to slip out to the road and meet her there—to catch her and flag her down before she ever made it to the guard shack. That was my plan."

"But then you got put in isolation," Joanna offered.

Haskell shook his head. "No," he said. "That was what I intended. I *counted* on being put in isolation. Otherwise there are chores for clients to do and work sessions to attend. When you're in isolation, you're left totally alone. I figured that once it was dark, I'd be able to slip off and meet her without anyone being the wiser."

"You're telling us that when you went to make your illicit phone call, you actually planned on being caught?" Joanna asked.

"Absolutely."

"What happened?"

"It worked out just the way I wanted it to. As soon as it was dark, I made my way out of the isolation cabin and back to the road. I stationed myself in a ditch just the other side of Portal—between Portal and the entrance to Pathway. I waited all night, but Connie never showed up. When she didn't, I was hurt. I figured that she'd decided not to bother; that she'd found out about the money and had just written me off. When you told me she'd tried to come see me after all, I . . ."

Ron Haskell's voice broke and he lapsed into silence. Joanna's mind was racing. She had thought his being in isolation had given Haskell an airtight alibi, but she had been wrong. In fact, just as Ernie Carpenter had suggested, it had actually been the opposite. Caroline Parker had told them Haskell had been left alone from Thursday on. That meant he could have been AWOL from Pathway to Paradise for the better part of four days without anyone being the wiser. That would have given him plenty of time to murder his wife and dispose of her body. It also meant that he had no alibi for the night Dora Matthews was murdered, either.

"How long did you stay away from the cabin?" Joanna asked.

"I came back just before sunrise Friday morning. I had sat on the ground all night long, so my back was killing me, and I was heartsick that Connie hadn't shown up. I was sure she loved me enough that she'd come talk to me and at least give me a chance to explain, but by the time I came back to the cabin that morning, I finally had to come face-to-face with the fact that I'd really lost her. That's why it hurt so much when I found out she had tried to come see me after all. She really did try, after everything I had done."

"While you were waiting by the road," Frank said, "did you see any other vehicles?"

"A couple, I guess."

"Anything distinctive about them? Anything that stands out in your mind?"

"Not really. The cars I saw go by were most likely going on up to Paradise—the village of Paradise, I mean. I've been told there are a few cabins up there and one or two B and Bs. One of them did stop at the guard shack for a few minutes, but then whoever it was left again almost right away. I figured whoever it was must have been lost and that they had stopped to ask directions."

"What about insurance?" Joanna asked.

"Insurance?" Ron Haskell repeated. "We had health insurance, and long-term care—"

"What about life insurance?"

"There isn't much of that," he said. "Stephen Richardson, Connie's old man, was the old-fashioned type, not somebody you'd find out pushing for equal rights for women or equal insurance, either. There was a sizable insurance policy on him when he died, but all he carried on Claudia, his wife, was a small five-thousand-dollar paid-up whole-life policy. Connie told me one time that her father had started ten-thousand-dollar policies on each of his daughters, but Maggie cashed hers in as soon as he turned ownership of the policy over to her. Connie still had hers."

"For ten thousand dollars?" Joanna asked.

Ron Haskell nodded. "Not very much, is it?" he returned.

"But you're the sole beneficiary?"

"Yes," he said. "At least I think I am. That policy was paid up, so it's not like we were getting bills for premiums right and left. I know Connie talked about changing the beneficiary designation from her sister over to me right after we got married, but I'm not sure whether or not she ever got around to doing it."

"And that's all the insurance there is—just that one policy?" Joanna asked.

Ron Haskell met Joanna's gaze and held it without wavering. "As far as I know, there was only that one. There's one on me for Connie's benefit but not the other way around. I know you're thinking I killed her for her money," he said accusingly. "But I didn't. I didn't *have* to. When it came to money, Connie had already given me everything, Sheriff Brady. What was hers was mine. I was doing day-trades and looking for a way to give back what she'd already given me. By the time it was over, I sure as hell wasn't looking for a way to get more."

"Did your wife have any enemies?"

"How would she? Connie hardly ever left the house."

"Do you have any enemies, Mr. Haskell?" Joanna asked. "Someone who might think that by getting to her they could get to you?"

He shook his head. "Not that I know of—other than Maggie MacFerson, if you want to count her."

The room was silent for some time before Ron Haskell once again met Joanna's gaze. "If you're asking me all these questions," he said, "it must mean you still don't have any idea who killed her."

Joanna nodded. "It's true," she said.

"But last night, when I talked to you out at Pathway, you said something about a series of carjackings. What about those?"

"Nobody died in any of those incidents," Joanna replied. "In fact, with all of the previous cases there weren't even any serious injuries."

"And nobody was raped," Haskell added bleakly.

"That's right," Joanna said. "Nobody else was raped."

"Anything else then?" Ron asked. "Any other questions?"

Joanna glanced in Frank's direction. He shook his head. "Not that I can think of at the moment," Joanna said. "But this is just a preliminary session. I'm sure my detectives will have more questions later. When you get back to Phoenix, you'll be staying at your house?"

"If I can get in," he said. "There's always a chance that Connie or Maggie changed the locks, but yes, that's where I expect to be."

"If you're not, you'll let us know?"

"Right," he said, but he made no effort to rise.

"Is there anything else, Mr. Haskell?"

Ron nodded. "When I came in this morning, I had to fight my way through a whole bunch of reporters, including some that I'm sure were from Maggie's paper." He looked longingly at Joanna's private entrance. "Is there any way you could get me back to my car out in the parking lot without my having to walk through them again?"

"Sure," Joanna said. "You can go out this way. Chief Deputy Montoya here will give you a ride directly to your car."

"Thanks," he said, breathing a sigh of relief. "I'd really appreciate it."

After Frank left with Ron Haskell in tow, Joanna sat at her desk, rewinding the tape and mulling over the interview. On the one hand, Connie Haskell's widowed husband seemed genuinely grief-stricken that his wife was dead, and it didn't look as though he stood to profit from her death. Ron Haskell may not have said so directly, but he had certainly implied that, considering the amounts of money he had squandered playing the stock market, a ten-thousand-dollar life insurance policy was a mere drop in the bucket and certainly not worth the risk of committing a murder. It also struck Joanna that he obviously held himself responsible for Connie Haskell's death though all the while claiming that he himself had not been directly involved.

Those items were all on the plus side of the ledger. On the other side was the possibility that Ron Haskell could have had some other motivation besides money for wanting his wife out of the way, like maybe an as yet undiscovered girlfriend who might be impatient and well-heeled besides. Someone like that might make someone like Ron Haskell eager to be rid of a now impoverished wife. Haskell's once seemingly airtight alibi now leaked like a sieve. He had chosen a course of action—a premeditated course of action—that had placed him in an isolated cabin from which he knew he would be able to sneak away at will and without being detected.

Forced to acknowledge that her original assumption about the isolation cabin had been blown out of the water, Joanna now wondered if some of her other ideas about Ron Haskell were equally erroneous. He had volunteered to come in for DNA testing. Joanna had thought of that as an indicator of his innocence—that it showed confidence that Ron Haskell knew his genetic markers would have nothing in common with the rape-kit material collected during Doc Winfield's autopsy of Connie Haskell. However, what if Ron Haskell had decided to divest himself of his wife by hiring someone else to do his dirty work? In that case, somebody else's DNA would show up on the body. Ron Haskell wouldn't be implicated.

Joanna picked up her phone and dialed Casey Ledford. "What do you think about Ron Haskell?" she asked.

"He seemed nice enough," Casey replied. "Upset that his wife is dead, but eager to cooperate and wanting to find out who killed her. I took his prints, by the way," she added. "For elimination purposes. Just looking at them visually, I can see they do match some of the partial prints I found in Connie Haskell's Lincoln, but the ones I saw were mostly old and overlaid by far more recent ones. Based on that alone, I'd have to say that, unless he was wearing gloves, Ron Haskell hasn't been in his wife's car for weeks or even months."

"Too bad," Joanna said with a sigh. "I was hoping we were getting someplace."

"Sorry about that," Casey Ledford said.

Joanna had put down the phone and was still sitting and thinking about what Casey had said when it rang again. "Hi, George," she said when she heard the medical examiner's voice on the line. "What's up?"

"Have you had a chance to talk to your mother yet?" he asked.

When George called Eleanor Lathrop "your mother" rather than his pet name, Ellie, Joanna recognized it as a storm warning. "Not so far," Joanna answered guiltily. "It's been pretty busy around here today. I haven't had a chance."

"She left the house this morning before I woke up and she didn't bother starting the coffee before she left. She was supposed to join me for lunch, but she didn't show up," George said. "I checked a few minutes ago, and she still isn't home. Or, if she is, she isn't answering the phone. I thought maybe the two of you had gotten together, and that's why she ended up forgetting our lunch date."

Who has time for lunch? Joanna thought. She said, "Sorry, George. I haven't heard from her at all."

"Well, if you do," Doc Winfield said, "have her give me a call. I'm worried about her, Joanna. She was really agitated about this Dora Matthews thing. I've never seen her quite so upset."

"Don't worry," Joanna reassured her stepfather. "I'm sure mother will be just fine."

"I suppose you're right," he agreed. "I'll let you go."

"No, wait. I have a question for you, too. Do you think Dora Matthews and Connie Haskell were killed by the same person?"

"No," George Winfield said at once.

His abrupt, no-nonsense answer flooded Joanna with relief. It opened the door to the possibility that perhaps the two homicides—Connie's and Dora's—weren't related after all. If that was the case, maybe Jenny wasn't a target, either.

"Why do you say that?" she asked.

"For one thing, because the two deaths were so dissimilar," George Winfield replied. "The person who killed Connie Haskell wasn't afraid of getting down and dirty about it. He was more than just brutal, and most of it was done while she was still alive. Her killer wasn't the least bit worried about being bloodied in the process. In fact, I'd go so far as to say he enjoyed it.

"On the other hand, Dora Matthews's killer went about doing the job in an almost fastidious fashion. That death wasn't messy. I'd bet money that Dora's killer was an inexperienced first-timer who is downright squeamish about even seeing blood, to say nothing of wearing it. The other guy isn't, Joanna. Once you identify Connie Haskell's killer, I'm convinced you'll discover that he's done this before, maybe even more than once."

"And he'll do it again if we don't catch him first," Joanna returned.

"You've got that right," George said. "Sorry, there's another call. It may be Ellie. But please, Joanna. I need you to talk to her."

"I'll call her," Joanna said. "I promise."

She punched down the button and was getting ready to dial her mother when Frank came rushing back into her office. "We just hit pay dirt," he said, waving a piece of paper over her head. "I finally got a call back from the phone company about that pay phone in Tucson. It belongs to some little private company that operates a small network of pay phones only in the Tucson area. That's why it took longer to track down the calls than it would have otherwise. But there is some good news. Another call was made from that pay phone within thirty seconds of the end of Alice Miller's 911 call."

"Really," Joanna breathed. "Where to?"

"A place called Quartzite East."

"Isn't that a new RV park off I-10 in Bowie?"

Frank nodded. "Relatively new," he corrected. "It opened last year. It's a joke, named after the real Quartzite, that mostly migratory motor-home town on the other side of the state. That's where the next phone call went—to the office at Quartzite East."

"Good work, Frank," Joanna said. "Our mysterious Alice Miller may not live at Quartzite East, but she sure as hell knows someone who does. What say you and I head out there ourselves?"

"My car or yours?" Frank asked.

"Let's take yours," Joanna said.

"I'll have to go down to the Motor Pool and fill it with gas."

"You do that," Joanna told him. "I'll be right there."

Going back for her purse, Joanna found Deputy Galloway standing by Kristin's desk. "You wanted to see me?" he asked.

Joanna nodded and ushered him into her office. "I wanted to talk to you about Yolanda Cañedo," she said as Galloway took a seat.

"What about her?"

"You know she's back in the hospital?"

"I guess," he said in a nonchalant tone that said he wasn't particularly concerned one way or the other.

"Are the deputies as a group going to do anything about it?"

"Like what?"

"Like sending a group card or flowers. Or like offering to look after the kids during off-hours to give Leon and the grandparents a break. Or like showing up at one of the boys' Little League games to cheer them on."

Deputy Galloway shrugged. "Why should we?" he asked. "Yolanda doesn't even belong to the local. Besides, she's a . . ."

"She's a what?" Joanna asked.

"She's just a matron in the jail."

"Yes," Joanna replied evenly but her green eyes were shedding sparks. "She is, and it turns out all the jail inmates and the people who work there got together to send her get-well wishes. It seems to me the deputies shouldn't do any less."

"You can't order us to do anything." Galloway bristled.

"Who said anything about ordering?" Joanna said. "It's merely a suggestion, Deputy Galloway. A strong suggestion. In case you haven't noticed, we're a team here. Yes, Yolanda Cañedo is a jail matron. In your book that may make her somehow less worthy, but let me tell you something. If it weren't for the people running our jail, you'd only be able to do half your job, and the same would hold true for every other deputy out on a patrol. You wouldn't be able to arrest anyone, because there wouldn't be anyplace to put them. So what I'm strongly suggesting, as opposed to ordering, is that some of the deputies may want to make it their business to see that some cards and letters go wending their way to Yolanda in care of University Medical Center in Tucson."

"Yes, ma'am," Ken Galloway said, standing up. His face was flushed with anger. "Will there be anything else?"

"No," Joanna said quietly. "I think that just about covers it."

Galloway strode out of her office. With her hands still trembling with anger, Joanna cleared her desk by swiping the remaining paperwork into her briefcase, then she took a stack of correspondence due for mailing and/or filing out to Kristin.

"Frank and I are leaving for Bowie," she told her secretary. "If either Jaime Carbajal or Ernie Carpenter calls in, tell them to try reaching me by cell phone."

"When will you be back?"

"That remains to be seen," Joanna said. "How about that bunch of reporters? Are they still parked outside?"

Kristin nodded. "I thought the heat would have driven them away by now, but so far they haven't budged."

"Call over to Motor Pool and have Frank pick me up at the back door," Joanna said. "When we take off, I'd rather not have a swarm of reporters breathing down our necks."

Back at her desk, she paused long enough to marshal her thoughts before dialing her mother's number. Three rings later, the answering machine came on. It seemed unlikely that leaving a recorded message would qualify for keeping her promise to George Winfield. She certainly wasn't about to launch into any detailed discussion of the Dora Matthews situation.

"Hi, Mom," Joanna said in her most noncommittal and cheerful voice. "Just calling to talk for a minute. I'm on my way to Bowie with Frank Montoya. Give me a call on my cell phone if you get a chance. Bye."

She was waiting in the shaded parking area a few minutes later when Frank came around the building.

"I was thinking," he said, once she was inside with her seat belt fastened. "We may be making too much of this telephone thing. We don't know for sure that Alice Miller or whatever her name is really made that second call."

"Who was it billed to?" Joanna asked.

"It wasn't. The call to Quartzite East was paid for in cash. The problem is, Alice Miller could very well have put the phone down and someone else was standing next to the phone waiting to pick it up."

"You could be right," Joanna said a moment later. "I guess we'll see when we get there."

They drove past the collection of air-conditioned press vehicles that were parked in front of the building and from there out through the front gate and onto the highway. Watching in the passenger-side mirror, Joanna was happy to see that no one followed them. "It's like a feeding frenzy, isn't it," she said.

Frank nodded. "Since the *Arizona Reporter* thinks it's an important story, everybody else thinks it's an important story, too."

"Maybe it *is* an important story," Joanna allowed. "Doc Winfield is of the opinion that the guy who killed Connie Haskell wasn't a novice."

"Point taken," Frank said. "In other words, if he's done it before, we'd better nail the bastard quick before he does it again."

"Exactly," Joanna said, trying to keep the discouragement and dread out of her voice, because she was sure both George Winfield and Frank Montoya were right. If she and her people didn't catch Connie Haskell's killer soon enough, he would certainly strike again.

14

Half an hour later they were nearing Elfrida when Joanna's cell phone rang. "Hello, Jaime," she answered. "What's up?"

"I've spent the last two hours of my life with a bitch on wheels named Mrs. Richard Bernard—Amy for short."

"Chris's mother?"

"Affirmative on that."

"What about Chris himself? Did you talk to him?" Joanna asked.

"According to Mama Bernard, she has no idea where her son Christopher is at the moment and no idea when he's expected home, either. He's evidently out for the afternoon with some pals of his. In addition, she says nobody's talking to him without both his father and his attorney being present. Ernie and I have made a tentative appointment with the Bernards for tomorrow morning at ten o'clock. But we did manage to ferret out the connection between Chris Bernard and Dora Matthews."

"Really. What's that?"

"When Dora was placed in foster care here in Tucson last summer, the foster family she lived with happened to be the Bernards' next-door neighbors, some people named Dugan. I can tell you for sure that Mrs. Bernard is still ripped about that. The Bernards live in a very nice, ritzy neighborhood up in the foothills off Tanque Verde. In that neighborhood, they're the new kids on the block. They happen to have more money than anybody, and they don't mind flaunting it. When they moved in, they were dismayed to learn that the Dugans—Mr. and Mrs. Edward Dugan, who are the Bernards' nearest neighbors—happen to be state-approved foster parents with a long history of taking in troubled kids and helping them get a fresh start.

"The Bernards were unhappy about the foster-parent bit and went before the homeowners' association to complain. They asked the association to keep the Dugans from accepting any more foster children. As Amy Bernard told us, she didn't like the idea of her son being exposed to *those* kinds of kids.

"But it turns out the Dugans are nice people who have been doing foster-care work for years. Most of the kids they've taken in have gone on to have excellent track records. When the Bernards' complaint came before the homeowners' association, the board ruled against them. Caring for foster children may have been against the neighborhood's official CC and Rs, but that rule had gone unenforced for so long that the board just let it slide."

"So much for neighborly relations," Joanna said.

"Let me add," Jaime continued, "that when it comes to plain old ordinary obnoxiousness, Amy Bernard is a piece of work. She doesn't approve of the Dugans' foster-care work, and from the way she acted, she didn't much like having to talk to a Latino detective, either. If I had been on the homeowners' board, I probably would have voted against the woman on principle alone. I'm sure she has lots of money—her hubby's a radiologist—but she's not exactly Mrs. Congeniality. When we told her Dora Matthews was dead, she said, and I quote, 'Good riddance. She was nothing but a piece of trash.'"

"Not a nice way to talk about the person who was carrying your grandchild," Joanna said. "And how old is Christopher Bernard?"

"Sixteen," Jaime answered. "Just turned. According to his mother, he got his driver's license in April."

"That makes him three years older than Dora. So my question is, who was being exposed to whom?"

"Exactly," Jaime Carbajal said.

"What are you doing now?"

"First we have an appointment to go back and talk to the Dugans half an hour from now, when the husband gets home from work. After that, we'll drop by Sierra Vista on the way home, talk to the kid who claims to have seen Dora Matthews getting into a car on Sunday night. We'll also go by Walgreens to see what we can find out there."

For the next several minutes, she briefed Jaime Carbajal on everything that had happened while the two detectives had been otherwise engaged. Once the call ended, Frank turned to her. "Sounds to me as though we may have found ourselves a brand-new prime suspect in the Matthews murder," he said.

Joanna nodded. "It could be. A sixteen-year-old prime suspect, at that," she added grimly. "Let me ask you something, Frank. What would you do if you were sixteen and your thirteen-year-old girlfriend turned up pregnant?"

"I sure as hell wouldn't kill her," Frank said.

"No," Joanna agreed. "I know you wouldn't, and neither would I. But from the way Jaime talked about them, I have a feeling Christopher Bernard and his parents live in an entirely different universe from the one you and I inhabit. I suspect they don't believe the rules apply to them."

"In other words, you think Chris found out Dora was pregnant and decided to get rid of her."

Joanna nodded.

"Well," Frank said thoughtfully. "He does have a point."

"What do you mean?"

"Think about it. Christopher Bernard is sixteen—a juvenile. Supposing he gets sent up for murder. What's the worst that'll happen to him?"

Joanna shrugged. "He gets cut loose at twenty-one."

"Right. And the same thing goes if he's convicted of statutory rape. He's out and free as a bird in five years. He'll probably have his record expunged besides. But think about what happens if his girlfriend has a baby and she can prove paternity. Then little Christopher Bernard and/or his family is stuck for eighteen years of child support, minimum. No time off for good behavior. No hiding behind the rules that apply to juvenile justice. Based on that, a murder that unloads both mother and child might sound like the best possible alternative."

The very thought of it sickened Joanna. "Please, Frank," she said. "Just drive. I can't stand to talk about this anymore. The whole thing is driving me crazy."

For the next twenty minutes Frank drove while Joanna rode in utter silence. As appalling as it was to consider, what Frank had said sounded all too plausible. A juvenile offender could dodge any kind of criminal behavior far more easily than he could escape being ordered to pay child support. Joanna knew there were plenty of deadbeat dads out there who didn't pay their court-ordered support money, but it was disturbing to think that the justice system was more eager to order teenagers to pay uncollectible child support than it was to hold them accountable for other far more serious offenses.

Whatever happened to motherhood, apple pie, and the American way? she wondered. One case at a time Joanna Brady was learning that what her father had always told her was true. In the criminal justice system, there was always far more gray than there was either black or white.

They hit I-10 just north of Cochise and turned east. They exited at Bowie and followed the directions on a billboard advertising Quartzite East that said: TURN SOUTH ON APACHE PASS ROAD.

Seeing that sign sent a shiver of apprehension down the back of Joanna's neck. In some way she didn't as yet understand, the dots between the mysterious Alice Miller and the location of Connie Haskell's body seemed somehow to be connected.

"I didn't realize Apache Pass Road came all the way into Bowie" was all she said.

"Oh, sure," Frank agreed. "I knew that, but then I grew up in Willcox. You didn't."

When they reached the entrance to Quartzite East, it had the look of a family farm turned RV park. The building marked OFFICE was actually an old tin-roofed house that looked as though it dated from the 1880s. Around it grew stately old cottonwoods. A checkerboard of orchards surrounded the house. Laid out among the carefully tended orchards were fifty or so concrete slabs complete with utility hookups. This was early June, so while the trees were laden with green fruit, most of the slabs were empty. By March or April at the latest, most Arizona snowbirds had usually returned home for the summer. As far as Quartzite East was concerned, however, several had evidently decided to summer over, since a number of spaces were still occupied.

Frank pulled up next to the farmhouse and parked in a place that was designated REGISTRATION ONLY. Just to the right of the house was a clubhouse and swimming pool area surrounded by a tall adobe wall. As soon as Joanna stepped out of the car and closed the door, a man appeared on the far side of the fence. He was wearing overalls and carrying a paintbrush.

"Just a second," he called. "I'll be right there as soon as I finish cleaning my brush. You might want to go up on the porch and wait for me there."

Nodding, Joanna and Frank did as directed. A screened-in porch covered the front of the house. Outside the screen, swags of wisteria dripped clusters of dead and dying blooms. Inside the screen sat a line of wooden rocking chairs.

"Take a load off," Frank said, pushing one of the chairs in Joanna's direction. They both sat and waited. Several minutes passed before the man from the swimming pool reappeared. He was tall and good-looking, tanned and fit. His paint-spattered clothing had been replaced by a monogrammed golf shirt, a pair of well-worn Dockers, and scuffed loafers. He held out a work-callused hand. "The name's Brent Hardy," he said.

"Sheriff Joanna Brady," she responded. "This is Frank Montoya, my chief deputy."

"You've found her, haven't you?" Brent said, easing into a rocking chair of his own.

"Found who?" Joanna asked.

"Irma," he said. "Irma Sorenson. Tom and I have been arguing about it ever since Saturday—about whether or not we should call and report her missing. When I saw the cop car pull up, I thought maybe he'd finally come to his senses and called in the cavalry."

"Who's Tom?" Frank asked.

"Tom Lowrey's my partner," Brent replied. "We run this place together. Irma is one of our guests."

"And she's missing?"

"*I* happen to think she's missing," Brent replied. "Tommy's of the opinion that I'm pushing panic buttons, but then Tom didn't talk to her on Saturday, and I did. She didn't sound right on the phone. Something about it was off. Of course, Tom does have a point. Some of our guests are a bit elderly, and a few of them get somewhat confused now and then. Tom thinks Irma called to tell us where she was going, but once she got on the phone, she forgot what she meant to say—that she was going off to visit friends or relatives or something. I say that if she was that confused, maybe she was sick and landed in a hospital. I thought we should report her missing and let the cops find her. Have you?" he asked. "Found her, that is?"

"Tell me about Irma Sorenson," Joanna said. "When was it you talked to her on the phone?"

"Saturday morning. Sometime around mid-morning, I suppose," Brent replied. "And her voice sounded funny to me. Shaky. Just not herself. But if you haven't found her, what's all this about?"

"We're actually looking for a woman named Alice Miller," Joanna said. "She placed a 911 call in Tucson from the same pay phone that was used to call here a few minutes later. We were wondering if there's a chance Alice Miller and Irma Sorenson are one and the same."

Brent Hardy shrugged. "I wouldn't know about that," he said.

"When Irma called, what exactly did she say?" Joanna asked.

"That's the thing. She didn't say much. She said, 'Oh, Brent, I'm so glad to hear your voice. I just wanted to tell you . . .' And then she just stopped. Then, after a moment or two, I heard her say, 'Oh, never mind.' Then she mumbled something about a wrong number, but I couldn't quite make it out. She hung up. That's all there was to it. As I told you, I tried to convince Tom that it wasn't right, but he said not to worry. He said she'd turn up sooner or later. She always does."

"So you haven't reported her missing."

"We really don't have any right," Brent said. "She isn't a relative, and this is an RV park, not a jail. Our guests come and go. So many of them have two vehicles—their motor home and then something smaller so they can get around more easily and take short trips without having to move their big rigs. Not that Irma would move hers. Her husband parked it. Once he died, Irma said she wasn't driving that thing another foot."

"Her husband died?"

Brent Hardy nodded. "Last December. About three weeks after they arrived. They turned up the last week in November. Originally they planned to stay through the middle of March. But then, when Kurt—that's Irma's husband—died of a massive heart attack, Irma asked Tom and me if she could stay on permanently. She said Kurt had sold their farm in South Dakota to buy that 'damned motor home,' as she put it. She said he was the one who was supposed to drive it and she didn't have anyplace else she wanted to go. I guess their son lives somewhere around here, but I'm not sure where."

"This son," Joanna said. "Have you ever met him? Do you know his name?"

Brent Hardy shook his head. "I've never seen him. She talked about going to see him a time or two, but I don't know if she did or not. As far as I know, he never came here."

Brent paused and looked from Joanna to Frank. "It's hot as blue blazes today," he said. "I need something to drink after working on that pool. Could I get you something?" he asked. "Iced tea, lemonade, sodas?"

"Iced tea would be wonderful," Joanna said. "No sugar, but lemon if you have it."

"I'll have the same," Frank said.

Brent disappeared into the house. "I think we've found our Alice Miller," Frank said.

Joanna nodded, but before she could say anything more, a late-model Cadillac drove into the yard and stopped next to Frank Montoya's Crown Victoria. A silver-haired man in his early to mid-sixties stepped out of the car. He hurried up the walkway and onto the porch.

"That's a police car out there," he announced. "Is something wrong? Has something happened to Brent?"

"Brent's fine," Joanna said, standing up. "He went inside to get something to drink. I'm Sheriff Joanna Brady, and this is my chief deputy, Frank Montoya. We're here asking some questions about a woman who may be a guest here. Who are you?"

"Tom Lowrey," the man returned. "My partner and I own this place. What guest?" he added. "And what's going on?"

Just then Brent came out through the front door carrying a wooden tray on which was a hastily assembled collection of glasses and spoons, a plateful of lemon slices, and a full pitcher of iced tea.

"Tom," he said upon seeing the new arrival. "I'm glad you're back. These officers are here asking about Irma. Do you know her son's name?"

Tom Lowrey shook his head. "All I know is that whenever she talked about him she called him Bobby."

"Bobby Sorenson?"

"No. I think Sorenson was Irma's name, but not his," Tom Lowrey replied. "As I understand it, Bobby was from her first marriage. In talking to her, I've gathered Kurt and the son didn't get along very well. In fact, after the funeral, I remember Irma's feelings were hurt because her son didn't bother to come to the service."

"That was held here in Bowie?" Joanna asked.

Lowrey shook his head. "Oh, no. The funeral was in South Dakota. I forget the name of the town. We took Irma into Tucson so she could fly home for the funeral. When she came back, we picked her up and brought her home. That's when she asked if she could stay on permanently. That's not as uncommon as you might think. The men buy the big RVs so they can see the USA. Then, when they croak out, the women are left with three hundred thousand dollars' worth of something they're scared to death to drive, but they can't get their money back, either. That's hers over there, by the way," he added, pointing. "The big bronze-and-black Marathon jobby. I didn't blame Irma in the least for not wanting to drive it herself, so we told her she could stay."

"What about the other rigs?" Joanna asked. "Are they occupied, too?"

Brent Hardy shook his head. "The owners decided to leave them parked rather than drive them back and forth. Irma's our only guest in residence at the moment."

"And you have no idea where her son lives or works?"

Both men shook their heads.

"So she has the motor home. Is that her only vehicle?" Joanna asked.

"No, she also drives a Nissan Sentra," Tom said. "Light pink. Irma told us she won it as a prize for selling Mary Kay cosmetics."

"A pink Nissan Sentra," Joanna said, writing it down. "With South Dakota plates?"

"No," Tom answered. He pulled a cigarette pack out of his pocket, extracted one, lit it, and blew a plume of smoke into the air. "Her plates expired sometime in the last month or two. Since she was staying on here, she got Arizona plates."

"I know exactly when it was," Brent offered. "April fifteenth, remember? She was bent out of shape because everything came due at the same time. She had to get new plates, get her new driver's license, and pay off Uncle Sam all on the same day."

Tom Lowrey laughed. "If I was her, I would have kept the South Dakota plates and license. That way, at least, she wouldn't have to pay Arizona income tax. But she said, no, she was starting her new life. She wanted all the t's crossed and i's dotted. There's just no fixing some people."

Frank Montoya got to his feet. "If you'll excuse me, I'll go check with the Department of Motor Vehicles and see if the son is listed on the licensing records as her next of kin."

Joanna nodded, and he hurried off the porch. "You said Irma's husband died?"

"Kurt. It was totally unexpected," Brent Hardy offered. "The guy looked like he was in fine shape. He wasn't overweight or anything like that. He'd been a farmer and had worked hard all his life. One night they were sitting watching TV—they have one of those little satellite dishes. He fell asleep in front of the set. When the news was over, Irma tried waking him up and couldn't. She came running up here, screaming for help. We called the volunteer fire department, and we tried CPR until the EMTs got here, but there was nothing they could do. She wanted them to airlift him into Tucson, but they told her it was no use—that she should save her money."

"You said he died in December, but you still haven't seen her son?"

Brent shook his head. "Not much of a son, right? But Tom and I are looking after her. We make sure her water and propane tanks get filled regularly, and we make sure her waste-water tanks get emptied as well." He grinned. "And then there was the skunk that took up residence under her RV. We had to hire a guy to come in and trap him and take him away. I guess we're a little more full-service than we planned to be, but Irma's a nice lady and I don't mind keeping an eye on her."

There was a pause in the conversation, and Joanna wasn't sure what to ask next. "This is a nice place you've got here," she said, changing the subject slightly. "And I'm sure Irma Sorenson appreciates your full-service service. How long have you had it, by the way—Quartzite East, that is?"

Brent Hardy shrugged. "The farm itself has been in my family for years. My mother left it to me when she died three years ago. Tom and I sold our place in Santa Cruz and came here to retire, but we didn't much like being retired, and neither one of us was any good at farming, either. So we decided to do something else. This is the end of our second year. Some of our clients are straight, of course, like Kurt and Irma. But a lot of them aren't. We keep the welcome mat out for both."

Joanna nodded. She had already surmised that Brent Hardy and Tom Lowrey were a couple, but she was a little taken aback to find them living and running a business in redneck Bowie. "So how are the locals treating you?" she asked.

"It's not as though I'm an outlander," Brent replied with yet another grin. "My mother, Henrietta, taught at Bowie High School for thirty-five years, just as her mother, Geraldine Howard, my grandmother, did before that. Between them, they pretty well fixed it so I can do no wrong. At least, forty years later, I can do no wrong. When I was in high school here, that was another matter. Now I'm back and I'm plugging money into the local economy. That makes me all right. And, since Tommy's with me, he's all right, too. Not that people say much of anything about us. It's pretty much don't ask/don't tell, which, for Bowie, is progress."

A car door slammed and Joanna caught sight of Frank Montoya sprinting back up the walkway. "I've got it," he announced as he stepped onto the porch. "Irma's son's name is Whipple, Robert Whipple."

Joanna frowned. "Wait a minute. Wasn't that the name of the guard at Pathway to Paradise?"

Frank nodded. "That's the one."

"Pathway to Paradise," Brent said. "Now that you mention it, I do remember Irma saying something about that once, only she just called it Pathway, I think. I got the distinct feeling she thought it was some kind of cult. Is it?"

"Not exactly," Joanna replied. "But close enough." She stood up and joined Frank on the steps. "We should be going then," she added. "Thanks so much for the tea and the information. And if you should happen to hear anything from Irma Sorenson, please contact me or my department right away." Taking a business card out of her pocket, she handed it over to Brent Hardy.

He looked at it and frowned. "Do you think something's happened to her or not?" he asked.

That was precisely what Joanna was thinking—that something terrible had happened to Irma Sorenson—but she didn't want to say so. "Not necessarily," she hedged, but Brent Hardy wasn't so easily put off.

"When you first got here, you said Irma's phone call was placed right after a 911 call. What was that all about?"

"There was a call to Tucson's emergency communications center about a bloodied vehicle found at Tucson International Airport. That vehicle, a Lincoln Town Car, belonged to a woman named Connie Haskell, who was found murdered in Apache Pass last Friday night."

"What color Lincoln Town Car?" Tom Lowrey asked suddenly. "And what year?"

"A 1994," Frank Montoya answered before Joanna had a chance to. "A dark metallic blue."

"I saw that car," Tom Lowrey said. "Or at least one like it. I never noticed when it drove up. All I know is there was a dark blue Lincoln

Town Car parked right behind Irma's Nissan early Saturday morning when I headed into Tucson to get groceries. I didn't think all that much about it. I saw it and figured Irma must have been entertaining overnight guests. When I came back home around noon, it was gone, of course. So was the Nissan."

"Are you saying Irma Sorenson is somehow mixed up in this murder thing?" Brent asked. "That's ridiculous. Preposterous."

The pieces were tumbling into place in Joanna's head. It didn't seem at all preposterous to her. Irma Sorenson was mixed up in it all right, and so was her son. Had Rob Whipple been on guard when Connie Haskell tried to gain admittance to Pathway to Paradise to see her husband? Had that been Connie's fatal mistake—speaking to the armed guard stationed in the shack outside the gates of Amos Parker's treatment center?

"She *may* be involved," Joanna said carefully after a momentary pause. "It's also possible that she may be either an unwitting or an unwilling participant. The woman who called herself Alice Miller—the one who made that 911 call—obviously wanted the car to be found. From what Mr. Hardy has told us about his abortive conversation with Irma a few minutes later, I believe she may have been interrupted and wasn't able to finish saying whatever it was she had intended to say when she called here."

"So she's most likely in danger," Tom Lowrey concluded.

If she's not already dead, Joanna thought. "Possibly," Joanna said with a sigh.

"Is there anything we can do to help?" Brent asked.

"You've already helped more than you know," Joanna told them. "Whether Connie Haskell's killer turns out to be Irma's son or someone else altogether, there's obviously some connection between your Irma Sorenson and the dead woman's car. So if you hear anything from her or her son or if she turns up, please call us immediately. I don't suppose I need to add that these people should be considered dangerous. Whatever you do, make no attempt to detain either of them on your own."

The two men nodded in unison as Joanna left the porch and followed Frank Montoya out to the car. He headed for the driver's seat, but Joanna stopped him. "I'll drive," she said. "You run the mobile communications equipment."

For months, and in spite of unstinting derision from his fellow officers, Frank Montoya had tinkered with his Crown Victoria, taking it beyond the normal patrol-car computing technology and adding additional state-of-the-art equipment whenever the opportunity presented itself. The chief deputy's Civvie now boasted a complete mobile office with the latest in wireless Internet and fax connections powered by the department's newest and most expensive laptop. And the investment of both time and money had paid off. In the last several months, Frank Montoya's high-tech wizardry had saved the day on more than one occasion. Around the Cochise County Sheriff's Department, joking references to Frank's "electronic baby" had been replaced by grudging admiration.

"To do what?" Frank asked.

Joanna got behind the wheel and held out her hand for Frank to pass the keys. "Do you have a cell phone signal?" she asked.

"I get it. You want me to run Rob Whipple's name through the NCIC database? What makes you think he'll be there?"

"It's a long shot, but Doc Winfield says our guy wasn't a first-timer. I'm thinking maybe he's been caught before." With that, Joanna shifted the Crown Victoria into gear and backed out of the parking place.

"And where are we going in the meantime?" Frank asked as he picked up the laptop and turned it on.

"Paradise," she returned. "We're going to pay a call on our friend Mr. Rob Whipple. You did get his driver's license info, didn't you?"

"Yes."

"And his address."

"That too, but do you think going to see him is such a good idea?" Frank asked. "After all, we don't really have probable cause to arrest the man, and we sure as hell don't have a search warrant."

"We're not going to arrest him," Joanna returned. "If he's our man, he may already have taken off for parts unknown. Or, if he *is* the killer and he's still hanging around, showing up for work, and acting as if nothing out of the ordinary has happened, he may be thinking he's getting away clean. All I want to do is shake him up a little. Put the fear of God in him. Give him a shove in the right direction and see if we can get him to give himself away."

Frank shook his head. "I still don't like it," he said. "How about calling Jaime and Ernie and letting them know what's up? They ought to be in on this, you know, Joanna. You and I shouldn't be off doing this all by ourselves."

"Jaime and Ernie are in Tucson," she reminded him. "You can call them, but we're here—a good hour and a half earlier than they can be. We're going anyway."

"But why the big hurry?"

"Because I happen to agree with Mr. Hardy back there. He thinks Irma Sorenson is in danger, and so do I, and I'd a whole lot rather look stupid than hang around doing nothing but wringing my hands until it's too late."

Joanna paused uncertainly at the entrance to Quartzite East. "Which way's faster?" she asked. "Right or left?"

"From here, I'd say down the New Mexico side," Frank told her.

Joanna nodded. "Time for a little mutual aid," she said, switching on the flashing light. "Before you start dialing up that database, you'd better call somebody over in New Mexico and let them know we're coming through."

15

With the Civvie's warning lights flashing, Joanna tore east on I-10 and across the state line into New Mexico. By then Frank had alerted the Hidalgo County Sheriff's Department and let them know what was happening. Once off the interstate and onto an almost deserted Highway 80, Joanna shoved the gas pedal down and let the speedometer hover around ninety.

"Damn," Frank muttered finally.

"What's the matter?"

"I finally managed to dial into the NCIC database, but now I've lost the signal. That's the problem out here in the sticks. Cell-site coverage is still too spotty. I'll have to try again when we get a stronger signal."

"You could always radio in and have Dispatch run it," Joanna suggested.

Frank was quiet for a moment but reluctant to give up. "I'll wait for a better signal," he said.

Joanna understood completely. He didn't want someone else to run the computer check any more than she had been eager to call Ernie and Jaime in to contact Rob Whipple.

"What's the plan in the meantime?" Frank asked.

"We'll go straight to Pathway," Joanna said. "Whipple may be there, but I'm guessing he's taken off. Mostly, I want to talk to Caroline and Amos Parker. I want to know how long Rob Whipple has worked for them and where he came from before that. What's his address again?"

Frank consulted his notes. "Box 78, San Simon/Paradise Star Route, Paradise, Arizona."

"Get on the radio to Dispatch about that, then. Have them give us an exact location on that address, complete with detailed directions," Joanna said. "When it's time to go there, I don't want to be fumbling around in the dark getting lost. And while you're at it," she added, "find out where Ernie and Jaime are. If they're not on their way, see if there are any other available units who could back us up on this. Better safe than sorry."

Nodding, Frank picked up the radio microphone. Meanwhile, Joanna drove on with the heightened sense of awareness left behind by all the extra energy flooding her body. The arch of sky overhead took on a deeper shade of blue while the steep green flanks of the Chiricahua Mountains stood out against the sky with a three-dimensional clarity that mimicked one of her old View Master photos.

In her time as sheriff, Joanna Brady had seen enough action to understand what was happening to both her body and her senses. They were gearing up for whatever was to come, switching into a state of preparedness—a sustained red alert. Although Joanna welcomed the sudden burst of energy, she also recognized how long periods of that kind of tension could sometimes backfire. That was how endorphin-fueled hot pursuits sometimes exploded into incidents of police violence. In hopes of holding herself in check, she deliberately slowed the Civvie and switched off both siren and lights.

On the passenger side of the car, Frank had relented, swallowed his high-tech pride, and asked Dispatch to check on Rob Whipple's criminal past. Now he was busily jotting down directions to Whipple's house located off San Simon/Paradise Road. When the Crown Victoria slowed for no apparent reason, he glanced in Joanna's direction and nodded approvingly.

"Ask Larry what else is happening," Joanna said.

Frank relayed the question. "There's been another carjacking," Larry Kendrick answered over the radio speaker.

"Where?" Joanna demanded. This time no relay was necessary because she had wrenched the radio microphone out of Frank's hand and was using it herself.

"The rest area in Texas Canyon."

"When did it happen, and was anybody hurt?"

"About forty minutes ago," Kendrick replied. "No one was hurt, but it sounds like the perpetrator was the same guy who did the old guy from El Paso last week. This time it was a couple from Alabama. The husband went in to use the rest room, leaving his wife sitting in the car with both the motor and the air-conditioning running. A guy came running up, opened the door, pulled her out, and threw her on the ground. Then he jumped in and drove off. She had a couple of bruises and abrasions, but that's about it. Her husband's upset about losing the car. She's upset about losing her purse."

"Okay," Joanna said, shaking her head. "That's it. I'm tired of nickel-and-diming around with this thing. We're going to put a stop to it once and for all! Get hold of Debbie Howell and one of the other younger deputies. I know: team her up with Terry Gregovich and Spike. Have them dress in plain clothes and drive one of the late-model cars we have locked up in the impound yard. I want them to cruise the freeway and stop at every damn rest area for the remainder of their shifts today. In fact, I want them to do the same thing every day until I tell them otherwise. And if they feel like working longer than that, tell them overtime is authorized—as much as they can handle. Have Debbie stay in the car with Spike while Terry uses the phone or the rest room or whatever. If somebody tries to pull a carjacking then, he'll be in for a rude surprise when a trained police dog comes roaring out of the backseat."

By then the Civvie had reached the turnoff to Portal. Needing both hands to keep the speeding Crown Victoria on the washboarded surface of the road, Joanna relinquished the microphone to Frank.

"Sounds like a plan," he said mildly, even though Joanna knew that when it came time to cut checks for the next pay period, Frank would be griping about having to pay the extra overtime. "You still haven't heard anything from Detectives Carpenter and Carbajal?" Frank asked into the radio.

"I have now. They're just leaving Tucson on their way to Sierra Vista," Larry Kendrick replied. "Anything you want me to tell them, or would you like me to patch you through?"

Frank glanced questioningly in Joanna's direction. "Tell them to go on to Sierra Vista as planned," Joanna said. "See who else can work backup for us."

After doing so, Frank put the mike back into its clip. "It could be days, you know," he said.

"What do you mean?"

"If the carjacker got away with a vehicle today, it could be days before he comes back looking for another one. How much overtime are you planning on paying?"

"As much as it takes," Joanna answered grimly.

It was only four-thirty in the afternoon, but as they drove toward Portal, the sun slid behind the mountains, sending the eastern side of the Chiricahuas into a shadowy, premature version of dusk. Fifteen minutes later Joanna drove up to the guard shack at Pathway to Paradise. With her shoulders aching from suppressed tension, she waited to see if Rob Whipple would emerge from the shack. She was disappointed when a young, buck-toothed man in his early thirties approached the Crown Victoria instead. His name tag identified him as Andrew Simms and his cheerful, easygoing manner made him far less menacing than Rob Whipple had been.

"May I help you?" he asked, leaning down to peer in the window.

"I'm Sheriff Brady," Joanna said, presenting her ID. "We're here to see Caroline Parker."

"If I could tell her what this is concerning—" Simms began spouting the party line, but Joanna cut him off.

"It concerns urgent police business," she told him. "I'm not at liberty to disclose anything more."

She expected an additional argument. Instead, without further objection, Andrew Simms retreated to the guard shack and returned with both the sign-in clipboard and a visitor's pass for the windshield.

"Just fill this out, if you will," he said. "Do you know the way, or do you want me to have someone come down to guide you up?"

"We know the way," Joanna said.

A few minutes later, when the Crown Victoria entered the Pathway to Paradise compound, Caroline Parker was waiting for them on the front veranda.

"What is it now?" she demanded with a frown. "Ron Haskell's gone, if that's who you're looking for."

"We want to talk to you about Rob Whipple," Joanna said.

Caroline's face grew wary. "What about him?" she asked.

"When is he due to work again?" Joanna asked.

Caroline glanced at her watch. "He was supposed to work today, but he traded with Andrew Simms. They're not permitted to do that without getting prior approval, but since the shift was covered . . ."

Joanna felt a hard knot of concern form in her gut. She was right. Rob Whipple had missed work. That meant there was a strong likelihood that he had also fled Joanna's jurisdiction. "Do you know when he made those arrangements, the ones to cover his shift?" she asked.

Caroline Parker shook her head. "No," she said. "I have no idea."

"How long has Rob Whipple worked for you?" Joanna asked.

Caroline shrugged. "A long time. Five or six years. He came as a client to begin with. After he finished his course of treatment, he ended up hiring on to work here. He did grounds maintenance for a year or two. After that he transferred to security. He's been doing that ever since."

"What was he treated for?"

Caroline Parker smiled and shook her head. "Come on, Sheriff Brady. Don't be naive. You know I won't tell you that."

"What about his mother?" Joanna asked. "Did you ever meet her? Her name's Irma Sorenson."

"Irma, oh yes," Caroline Parker replied. "I believe I did meet her once, only her name was still Whipple back then. She came to Rob's family-week program. Unless I'm mistaken, she's also the one who paid for him to come here in the first place—as a client, that is."

"You haven't seen Irma Sorenson since then?"

"No."

"How many patients do you have here at Pathway to Paradise, Ms. Parker?"

"Clients, not patients," she corrected. "And not more than thirty at a time. That's when we're running at full capacity."

"Generally speaking, how long do they stay?" Joanna asked.

"Two months. Sometimes longer than that, depending on what's needed and the kind of progress they're making."

"That means that, in the course of a year, you see several hundred different 'clients'?"

"Yes. That's true."

"You said Rob Whipple was a patient—excuse me—a 'client' here five or six years ago, but you still remember exactly who paid for his course of treatment. Do you remember the details of every client's bill-paying arrangements so clearly?"

Caroline Parker looked uncomfortable. "Well, no," she admitted. "I don't suppose I do."

"And yet, after all this time, you still remember clearly that Irma Sorenson paid for Rob Whipple's stay here. Why is that, Ms. Parker?"

"The circumstances were unusual, but I'm not at liberty to disclose what they were since that would be a breach of Mr. Whipple's presumption of confidentiality."

"What would you say if I told you that someone's life was at stake?" Joanna asked.

"My answer would still have to be the same, Sheriff Brady," Caroline answered primly. "We don't do situational ethics here at Pathway to Paradise. Ethics are ethics."

"And murder is murder," Joanna returned. She swung back to her chief deputy. "Come on, Frank. Let's go."

But Caroline stopped them. "Wait a minute. Are you implying that Rob Whipple had something to do with the murder of Ron Haskell's wife?"

"I didn't say that; you did," Joanna told her. "How come?"

Realizing her error, Caroline Parker shook her head. "I can't say," she declared.

"But I can guess," Joanna said. "What was the sickness that infected Rob Whipple's soul, Ms. Parker, the one he came here to be cured of? It wasn't day-trading or lotto fever, was it. I'd guess he liked to hurt women—hurt them first and kill them later. You and your father may be under the happy delusion that your ethical counseling program cured the man of his ailment, but I'm here to tell you it didn't. I think Rob Whipple has just suffered a major relapse."

The sharp corners of Caroline's angular face seemed to blur and soften. She stepped over to the Crown Victoria and leaned against the roof, burying her head in her arms. "Dad fired him," she said at last in a subdued voice, one that had had all the authority wrung out of it.

"When?" Joanna demanded.

"Last night. Right after you left here, Dad called Rob into the office. He asked Rob point-blank if he was involved in what had happened to Ron Haskell's wife. Rob denied it, of course, and my father called him a liar. Dad may be blind, but he can see through people when they're not telling him the truth. And so Dad fired him, just like that. He had me take away Rob's name badge and weapon—"

"Those didn't belong to him?"

"No. They're ours—company-owned, that is. After that, Dad sent him packing; told Rob to go away and never come back."

"Why?" Joanna asked.

"Why what?"

"Why did your father want Rob Whipple to leave?"

"We run a very profitable and well-thought-of program here, Sheriff Brady," Caroline said proudly. "When people come here, they're looking for results. They don't want to know about our failures."

"You told us earlier that Rob had gotten Andrew Simms to cover his shift. Now you're saying your father fired him. Why the discrepancy, and which is the truth? I thought you people didn't deal in situational ethics."

Caroline shrugged. "Father wanted to buy some time. He said sending Rob packing would give things a chance to simmer down a little."

"In other words, to keep from damaging Pathway to Paradise's reputation and cure rate, you and your father would stoop to anything, including knowingly turning a murderer loose on the world. Why didn't you call and tell us what was going on?" Joanna demanded.

"We couldn't," Caroline wailed tearfully. "You've got to understand. If we had called, it would have been a breach of confidentiality."

"You can call it whatever you like," Joanna hissed back at her. "But once we find out Rob Whipple has killed again, I hope your conscience is clear, Ms. Parker. I hope you and your father will both be able to sleep at night."

"You just said 'again,'" Caroline whispered. "Does that mean someone else is dead, someone other than Ron Haskell's wife?"

"That's right," Joanna said. "Remember Irma Whipple Sorenson, the lady who wrote that check to pay for her son's treatment? She's missing and has been ever since Saturday morning, moments after she made an anonymous call, nervously reporting the whereabouts of Connie Haskell's bloodied vehicle. I'm assuming that she's already dead, but you and your father had better hope like hell that she died prior to last night and not after, because if Irma was killed after you and your father sent Rob Whipple merrily on his way without calling us, I'm going to see about charging the two of you with being accessories."

"Accessories?" Caroline Parker repeated weakly. "Us? You can't do that, can you?"

"I can sure as hell try," Joanna said grimly.

"But you have no idea what that kind of trauma would do to my father. It would kill him. It would be the end of everything he's done; everything he's worked for—everything we've both worked for."

"That may well be," Joanna returned. "But at least you'll both be alive, which is more than can be said for Connie Haskell and most likely for Irma Sorenson as well. And if you know what's good for you, you won't lose Rob Whipple's badge or weapon, because if we end up needing them, they'd better be here! Come on, Frank. We're done."

"You can't do that, can you?" Frank asked once they were out of earshot inside the Civvie and buckling their seat belts. Once again, Joanna was driving.

"Do what?"

"Charge Amos and Caroline Parker with being accessories."

"No, probably not," Joanna conceded. "But it did my heart a world of good to tell her that we could. I loved seeing that look of sheer astonishment wash across her face, and I'm proud to be the one who put it there. Caroline Parker lied to us, Frank, and I lied right back. Maybe that makes us even."

"Maybe so," Frank agreed. "Where to now?"

"Rob Whipple's house, but I'm guessing he's not there. Notify Dispatch about where we're going and find out where those damned backup units are. Then call the DMV and get whatever information they may have on all vehicles belonging to either Rob Whipple or Irma Sorenson. That way, when it comes time to post the APBs, we'll have the information we need to do it."

Before Frank could thumb the radio's talk button, Larry Kendrick's voice boomed through the car. "We got a hit on Rob Whipple," he said. "I tried faxing it to you, but it didn't go through."

"We're out of range," Frank told him. "What does it say?"

"Robert Henry Whipple served twenty-one years in prison in South

Dakota. He was convicted of two counts of rape and one count of attempted murder. He was paroled in 1994. One of the conditions of his release was that he seek treatment as a convicted sex offender."

"So much for treatment," Joanna muttered.

While Frank handled the radio, Joanna dealt with the road. From the highway to Portal the washboarded surface had been bad enough, but the five miles from Portal to Paradise were even worse. Several times the winding dirt track climbed in and out of the same dry wash and around bluffs of cliff that made for treacherous blind curves on a road that was little more than one car width wide. At last a brown-and-gold Forest Service sign announced that they had arrived in Paradise. Despite the sign, there were no houses or people in sight, only a long line of twenty or so mailboxes that stood at attention on the far side of the road. It was just after five o'clock in the afternoon, but the false dusk created by being in the shadow of the mountains made it difficult to read the numbers on the boxes. Naturally, Box 78 was the last one in the row.

From that T-shaped intersection, San Simon/Paradise Road veered off to the north. Following the directions Frank had obtained from Dispatch, Joanna followed a new stretch of road that was only slightly worse than the previous one had been. Both of them made her long to be driving her sturdy Blazer rather than picking her way around rocks and boulders in Frank's relatively low-slung Civvie.

"There," Frank said, pointing. "Turn left here. From what I was told, the house is just beyond that ridgeline."

"How about if we stop here and get out and walk?" Joanna suggested. "I'd rather our arrival be a surprise. If we drive, we'll show up trailing a cloud of dust. He'll see us coming a mile away."

"It's okay by me," Frank said. "But before we leave the car, let me radio our position one last time."

Joanna drove up the rutted two-track road until she reached a point where a grove of trees crowded in on the roadway. By parking in that natural bottleneck, she effectively barricaded the road, making it impossible for anyone else to drive around. Setting the parking brake, Joanna stepped out of the car and pulled her cell phone from her pocket. She wasn't at all surprised to find that once again there was no signal. For the third time in as many hours, the high-tech world had let her department down. Sighing with disgust, she turned off the useless device and shoved it back in her pocket.

When Frank finished with the radio and got out, Joanna locked the doors and passed him the keys. "From here on out, you're driving," she said.

"The DMV says Whipple drives a '97 Dodge Ram pickup," Frank

told her. "I've got the plate number. I told Larry to go ahead and post that APB."

"Good," Joanna said. "What about your phone?"

Frank checked his. "Still no signal," he said.

"I know that," Joanna told him. "All the same, turn the useless thing off. We may not be able to talk on them, but you can bet they'll still be able to ring just when we don't want them to."

Frank complied, and the two of them set off up the road. As she walked, Joanna was grateful that on this particular day she had chosen to wear a uniform complete with khaki trousers and lace-up shoes rather than office attire, which most likely would have included heels and hose, neither of which would have cut it for this rocky, weed-lined hike.

It turned out that Rob Whipple's house was set much farther back from San Simon/Paradise Road than Dispatch had led them to believe. Joanna and Frank hiked the better part of a mile, crossing two ridges rather than one. Between the two ridges lay another sandy creek bed. This one showed signs of numerous tire tracks, but there was no way to tell which ones were coming and which were going. Signaling silently for Frank to follow, Joanna skirted the tracks, leaving them intact for later in case the need should arise to take plaster casts.

At last, panting and sweating, they topped the second steep rise and saw a house—little more than a shabby cabin—nestled in a small clearing below. No vehicle was parked outside, but for safety's sake they took cover and watched silently for several minutes before moving forward again. There was no sign of life. Even so, when Joanna set out again, she did so by dodging carefully from tree to tree.

Moving and consciously maintaining cover, Joanna was all too aware of the danger and of their vulnerability. Her breathing quickened and she heard the dull thud of her own heart pulsing in her ears. Once again she found herself utterly aware of everything around her—a dove cooing in the trees just ahead of her; the abrasive cawing of a crow; the white-noise buzz of cicadas that was noticeable only when, for some reason unknown to her, the racket stopped and then resumed once more. A small puff of cooling breeze caressed the overheated skin of her face.

At any moment, an armed and dangerous Rob Whipple could have materialized out of the house or from between trees in front of her. Given that, it was with some surprise Joanna realized that although she was being careful, she wasn't necessarily scared. She was doing her job—what she was supposed to do; what others expected of her and what she expected of herself. It was during that silent and stealthy approach to Rob Whipple's isolated cabin that she realized, for the first time, that she was doing the one thing she had always been meant to do.

Struck by that electrifying thought, Joanna sidled up to the gnarled trunk of a scrub oak and leaned her full weight against it. Standing in the deepening twilight, she suddenly felt closer to both her dead husband and her dead father than she had at any time since their deaths. It was as if she were standing in the presence of both Sheriff D. H. Lathrop and Deputy Andrew Roy Brady and hearing once again what both of them had tried to tell her from time to time—how once they set out on the path to "serve and protect," it had been impossible for either one of them to do anything else.

Joanna's father had spoken time and again about the importance of "making a contribution" and "doing one's part." Andy had insisted that he was in law enforcement because he wanted to make the world "a better place for Jenny to live." And now Joanna Brady was amazed to realize that she had been bitten by the same idealistic bug. She, too, wanted to make a contribution. There were far too many Connie Haskells and Irma Sorensons who needed to be saved from the many Rob Whipples that were loose in the world.

Still leaning against the tree, Joanna wiped away a trickle of tears that suddenly blurred her vision. She had never been someone who believed in ghosts, yet she sensed ghosts were with her right then, watching and listening.

All right, you two, she vowed silently to her father and Andy. *I'll run for reelection. In the meantime, let me do my job.*

Ahead of her and off to the left, Frank Montoya was waving frantically, trying to attract her attention. He had moved forward far enough that he was almost at the edge of the clearing. Now, with broad gestures, he pantomimed that he would creep around to the side of the cabin and try looking in through the window. Nodding for him to go ahead, Joanna looked around her own position while she waited.

She and Frank had moved forward on either side of the road. Eventually he sidled up to the cabin and peered inside. Then he turned back to her. "It's okay," he called. "There's nobody here."

Looking down, Joanna noticed a faint pair of tire tracks branching from the road and winding off through the trees, leaving behind only the slightest trace in the dense ground-covering layer of dead oak leaves. Curious, she traced the dusty trail of crushed leaves. The snapping and crackling underfoot told her she was leaving a trail of her own. In the deepening twilight she threaded her way between trees and bushes and around freestanding chunks of boulders the size of dishwashers. A quarter of a mile from where she had started, the tracks stopped abruptly at the edge of a rockbound cliff.

For a moment, Joanna thought the vehicle had simply reversed directions and returned the way it had come. But then, studying the terrain on her hands and knees, Joanna realized the vehicle had gone over the edge and down the other side. Easing her way to the precipice, Joanna peered down. Immediately she was aware of two things: the form of a vehicle, lying with its still wheels pointed skyward, and, rising from the crippled wreck, like a plume of evil smoke, the unmistakable odor of carrion.

"Damn!" Joanna exclaimed. With a heavy heart, she drew back and out of the awful stench which, caught in an updraft, eddied away from the cliff. "Poor Irma," she whispered softly. "I'm so sorry."

It was then she heard Frank calling, "Joanna, where did you go? I can't see you."

"I'm over here," she called back. "I found a car. And you're wrong, Frank. There is somebody here—somebody who's dead."

Frank trotted up a few moments later. For the better part of a minute the two of them stood on the edge of the cliff trying to ascertain the best way to climb down. Joanna found herself feeling sick to her stomach.

"I don't want to look," she said. "Seeing Irma's body is likely to make me puke."

"I'll go then," Frank offered. "You stay here."

But as soon as Joanna said the words, she realized they were wrong—a cop-out. It was her job to look; her sworn duty. "We'll both go," she said.

Twenty minutes later Joanna Brady and Frank Montoya finally managed to reach the crumpled remains of Irma Sorenson's pale pink Nissan. By then it was mostly dark. When they were finally able to approach the driver's side together, Joanna found it necessary to switch on the tiny flashlight she kept clipped to her key ring. Steeling herself for what lay inside, Joanna was astonished to see that the driver's seat was empty. The passenger seat wasn't. There, a lone figure, still secured by a seat belt, dangled upside down.

When the beam of light from her flashlight finally settled on the figure's face, Joanna could barely believe her eyes. "I'll be damned!" she exclaimed. "I don't believe it!"

"What?" Frank demanded.

"See for yourself," she said.

Joanna handed him the flashlight and then let her body slip down beside the crumpled doorframe. The person hanging in Irma Sorenson's Nissan wasn't Irma at all. It was her son, Rob Whipple, with what looked like a single bullet hole marring the middle of his forehead.

"How the hell do you think that happened?" Frank Montoya asked.

"The usual way," Joanna returned. "We'd better go back to the car and change that APB. So much for saving the Irma Sorensons of the world."

16

By the time Joanna and Frank had climbed back up the cliff and hiked back to the Civvie, they were both beat. Fortunately, by then their requested backup had arrived in the person of Deputy Dave Hollicker. While Frank set about making the necessary notifications, Joanna brought Hollicker up to speed on what had happened.

"I want you to go up to the wash and make plaster casts of the tire tracks you'll find there," she told him. "If nothing else, the tracks can tell us which was the last vehicle to drive out this way. The sooner the casting is done, the sooner we'll be able to get other vehicles in and out to the crime scene. If we're all on foot, it's a hell of a long walk."

Hollicker retrieved his casting kit and set off for the wash just as Frank finished up on the radio. "I talked to Doc Winfield," he said. "He's on his way. So are Jaime and Ernie. And I revised the APB. I gave them Irma Sorenson's name and driver's license number so they can post her picture. I also said she could be armed and dangerous."

"Good," Joanna returned.

Frank went to the trunk and returned with two bottles of water, one of which he handed over to Joanna. "Better have some of this," he said.

The water was warm, but as soon as Joanna tasted it, she realized how dehydrated she was. "Thanks," she said. "I needed that."

They both drank silently until the bottles were empty. "Do you really think Irma did it?" Frank asked at last. "Rob Whipple was her son, for God's sake."

Joanna nodded.

"How come?"

"How come she did it or how come I think so?"

"Both," Frank replied.

"The reason Caroline Parker talked to us as much as she did is that both she and her father are grappling with the fact that their supposedly 'cured' killer has killed again. I'm guessing Irma reached the same conclusion. She must feel responsible for what her son did. I think I'd feel the same way if I were in her position."

"Enough to kill your own child?" Frank returned.

Joanna sighed. "Probably not," she said.

"But aren't we jumping to conclusions here? We don't *know* Irma Sorenson has done anything wrong. For that matter, who's to say that Ron Haskell didn't set the whole thing up? Maybe he hired Whipple to unload Connie for him. We still don't know for sure that Ron Haskell's in the clear. Maybe he stopped by and took care of Rob Whipple *before* he came into town to deliver those DNA samples. If there was a conspiracy between them, it'll be a whole lot more difficult to prove with Whipple out of the way."

"I still think Ron Haskell had nothing to do with it," Joanna insisted.

"Why?" Frank countered. "Because he sounded innocent when we talked to him? He sure as hell isn't innocent of relieving his wife of her money."

"That may be true," Joanna agreed. "But that doesn't make him a killer."

"And as for Irma, just because she may have discovered her son had killed again doesn't mean she'd put him out of his misery like a rabid dog. Not only that, her driver's license says she's seventy-four years old. How the hell would she get the drop on him?"

"If we ever catch up with her, I guess we'll have to ask her."

"But I still can't understand it," Frank said. "How does a parent do something like that to her own child?"

"I don't know," Joanna said wearily. "Maybe it was self-defense. Or maybe she shot her rabid-dog son to save others."

"Sheriff Brady?" Tica Romero's radio voice reached them through the open window.

Finishing the last of her water, Joanna got into the Civvie and unclipped the mike. "Sheriff Brady here," she said. "What's up?"

"I'm in for Larry now. Doc Winfield says to ask you if you ever had a chance to speak to your mother."

Joanna sighed. Wasn't it enough that she was out in the desert climbing up and down cliffs and finding dead bodies? Expecting her to find time to be a dutiful daughter was asking too much.

"Tell him no," Joanna said. "I tried calling her, but she wasn't home."

"He says she *still* isn't home," Tica relayed a moment later. "He says he's really worried about her."

"Tell him I'm worried too, but I'm on the far side of the Chiricahuas at a crime scene right now, and there isn't a whole lot I can do about it at the moment. But Tica, once you let him know, you might also radio the cars that are out on patrol right now and ask the deputies to keep an eye out for my mother. Eleanor Lathrop Winfield drives a light blue 1999 Buick sedan. I can't remember the license plate number right off, and don't ask Doc Winfield for it. Get it from the DMV and put it out to everyone who's currently on duty."

"Will do, Sheriff Brady."

"And when you finish with that, would you mind calling out to the ranch and letting Butch know that I won't be home until later."

"Sure thing."

Shaking her head, Joanna went back to where Frank was standing with the heel of one boot hooked on the Civvie's rear bumper. "What was that all about?" he asked.

"My mother," Joanna grumbled. "She and Doc Winfield must be having some kind of row. George called me this afternoon and wanted me to talk to her. I tried calling, but she wasn't home. According to George, Eleanor was upset last night when she heard about what had happened to Dora Matthews. And that's understandable. I'm upset about what happened to Dora, too, but my best guess is that Eleanor is pissed at George about something else altogether. She's decided to teach him a lesson, so she left the house early this morning without making his coffee, and she hasn't been seen or heard from since."

"Do you think something's happened to her?" Frank asked.

Joanna shook her head. "It's not the first time Eleanor's pulled a stunt like this. She did it to my dad on occasion. It used to drive him nuts. What drives *me* crazy is the fact that I have to be caught in the middle of it."

"You're the daughter," Frank pointed out. "Sons get off light in that department. Daughters don't. If you don't believe me, ask my sisters."

The better part of an hour passed before the first additional vehicles arrived. George Winfield was still enough of a newcomer to Cochise County that he had caravanned out to Paradise behind a van driven by one of the crime scene techs.

"So where's the body?" he demanded as soon as he caught sight of Joanna.

She pointed. "About a mile and a little bit that way and at the bottom of a cliff."

"Who's driving?" George asked.

"Nobody's driving."

"You mean we have to walk?"

Joanna nodded. "Until Deputy Hollicker has finished taking plaster casts, nobody's driving in or out."

"Great," George Winfield said with a sigh. "When I signed on to be medical examiner around here, I never realized how many bodies we'd have to haul in from out in the boonies. And I sure didn't understand about the hours. Couldn't you get your murderers to do their deeds in places that are a little more on the beaten path, Joanna? And it would be nice if it wasn't almost always the middle of the night when it happens. How about instituting a rule that says all bodies are to be found and investigated during normal office hours only?"

Despite her own weariness, Joanna couldn't restrain a chuckle. "Stop griping, George," she said. "Come on. I'll show you where the body is. Frank, didn't I see Dave Hollicker again just a minute ago?"

"Yeah. He came back for more plaster."

"As long as he's here, ask him to help carry the Doc's equipment."

Using a battery-powered lantern to light the way, Joanna retraced the path she and Frank had followed earlier. George Winfield trudged along behind her. He was a good thirty years older than Joanna, but he had no apparent difficulty in keeping up with her.

"I can't imagine what's happened to your mother," he groused as they walked. "Maybe she's been in an accident."

Joanna chose not to go into the details of Eleanor and D. H. Lathrop's history of marital discord. "I'm sure Mother's fine, George," Joanna said reassuringly. "Did the two of you have a fight?"

"Not really."

"Look, George," she said. "If anyone's an expert on fighting with my mother, I'm it. How not really did you fight?"

"I told her about Dora last night after I came home. I do that—talk to her about my cases. Most of the time it's okay, but this time, she just went off the deep end about it. I've never seen her upset like that before, Joanna. Your mother isn't what I'd call an hysterical woman, but she was hysterical last night. I did my best to calm her down. I told her she was overreacting, that she was being far more emotional than the situation warranted. I told her she shouldn't blame herself for what happened. That there was no way anyone could possibly think that Dora Matthews's death was her fault. That's when she really lit into me, Joanna. She told me I didn't understand anything about her. That's when she took that sleeping pill and went to bed, without even staying up to watch the news, which she usually does every night.

"Maybe Ellie was right," George Winfield added miserably. "Maybe I don't understand her." He paused for a moment before continuing. "Ellie was never particularly good friends with Dora's grandmother, was she?"

"No," Joanna answered. "She wasn't."

"When she found Dora was at your place," George continued, "she was just livid about that—about the camp-out and the cigarettes and the girls' being sent home. It sounded to me as though she thought everything that had happened out there was Dora's fault. So why should she fall apart the moment she hears Dora Matthews is dead? It's more than I can understand.

"But still, that's no excuse for her disappearing without saying a word to me about where she was going or when she'd be back. This morning I checked the house to see if she had left me a note. She hadn't. All day long, I kept calling in for messages. She never called. The whole thing beats me all to hell. And now, just when she might finally show up at home, where am I? Out here hiking to God knows where trying to track down another body. So if Ellie finally gets over being mad at me because of the business with Dora Matthews, by the time I get home she'll be mad all over again because I've been out late one more time."

He stopped walking and talking both. When Joanna turned to look at him, he shook his head. "Oh, hell, Joanna. I'm just rambling on and on. Why don't you tell me to shut up?"

"Because I thought you needed to talk."

He sighed. "I suppose you're right there. But tell me about this case now, and how much farther do we have to walk?"

They had already passed the clearing containing the deserted house. "It's only another quarter of a mile or so, but then we have to climb down a cliff. The car's at the bottom of that."

"And what's this all about?"

"The victim is a guy named Rob Whipple. Just this afternoon, he turned into a suspect in the Connie Haskell homicide. Frank and I were on our way to talk to him when we found him dead."

"Any idea who killed him?"

"It was probably his mother," Joanna said. "A woman by the name of Irma Sorenson."

"I was told this was a car accident. Something about it going over a cliff."

"The victim is in a car that went over a cliff, but since there's a bullet in the middle of his forehead, and since he wasn't in the driver's seat, I have a feeling he was dead long before the car went over the edge."

"And you think his own mother did it?" George asked wonderingly. "I guess I'm not the only one who doesn't understand women. But at least I'm still alive—so far."

"Eleanor's not going to kill you, George," Joanna told him. "Even if she's mad, she'll get over it."

George Winfield shook his head. "That's easy for you to say. You don't have to live with her."

"No, but I've done it, and I've got the T-shirt!"

About then they reached the edge of the cliff. By the time Dave Hollicker and the two crime scene techs had strung a rope and helped lower George Winfield and his equipment to the ground, Jaime Carbajal and Ernie Carpenter had both shown up, accompanied by Frank Montoya.

Ernie peered down over the edge of the cliff and shook his head. "Looks like it's time for more of Jaime's crime scene photography. Doc Winfield may have gotten down there, but I'm not climbing down that cliff on a bet."

"Give me the camera then," Jaime said. As he headed for the rope, Joanna turned to Ernie.

"Did you guys do any good today?" she asked.

"That depends on what you call good," he groused. "We talked to Buddy Morris, the kid in Sierra Vista who supposedly saw Dora Matthews get into a car sometime Sunday night. Buddy's fifteen years old. When I was his age, I knew every make and model of car on the road. When it comes to cars, Buddy Morris is practically useless. He doesn't know shit from Shinola, if you'll pardon the expression. He *thinks* maybe it was a white Lexus he saw, but he's not sure. Not only that, he couldn't tell us for certain if it was Dora Matthews he saw getting into the car because he doesn't really know her, which is hardly surprising since she'd only been in the neighborhood for a little over twenty-four hours.

"Still, Buddy tells us, he thinks the girl was one of the kids from the foster home because they've got a special window at the back of the house that they use to sneak in and out of the house at all hours of the night. Why people volunteer to become foster parents in the first place is more than I can understand.

"Anyway, Buddy claims he saw a girl getting in the unknown car with a driver he couldn't see and the two of them took off in a spray of gravel."

"What about Walgreens?" Joanna asked.

"Didn't have time," Ernie said. "We got the call and came straight here, but we do have the phone company checking the line at the foster parents' house to see if Dora may have made any unauthorized phone calls from there. I've also asked for them to check the Bernards' number for any calls going from there to Sierra Vista. Without Frank the phone wizard doing the checking, we probably won't have results until tomorrow morning, hopefully *before* our appointment with Christopher Bernard and his father and his lawyer, and not *after*. Which reminds me of something else. We were supposed to see them at ten A.M but there's a conflict with the doctor. The appointment has now been moved to two o'clock in the afternoon. So that's all I know, and Frank's pretty much told me what's going on here, so why don't I shut up, go back to the cabin, and get to work."

With that, Ernie turned and stomped away from them, leaving Joanna and Frank staring at one another in astonishment. "I think that's more words than I've ever heard Ernie Carpenter string together at one time," Joanna said.

"I didn't even know he *knew* that many words," Frank Montoya agreed.

It was the beginning of another long night. As people showed up and began doing the jobs they were trained to do, it was clear there was little reason for Joanna and Frank to hang around. At nine they finally left the scene for the long drive back to Bisbee.

"I can take you straight home if you want," Frank offered. "It's on the way."

"No, thanks," Joanna told him. "I'd rather go by the department and pick up my car."

"Suit yourself," Frank said.

When they reached the department, Joanna knew that if she even set foot inside her office she'd be trapped, and it would be hours before she got back out again. Instead, she simply exited Frank Montoya's Civvie and climbed into her own.

As Joanna drove from the justice center toward High Lonesome Ranch, she felt a sense of letdown and disappointment wash over her, draining the last of the waning energy out of her body. In a matter of days, three different homicides had occurred within the boundaries of Cochise County.

Three! Joanna lectured herself. *Connie Haskell, Dora Matthews, and now Rob Whipple. If my department is supposed to be serving and protecting, we're not doing a very good job of it.*

She turned off onto High Lonesome Road and drove through the series of three steep arroyos that made the approach to the ranch feel more like a roller coaster than a road. As she crested the final rise, the Civvie's headlights bounced off the headlights of a car parked next to Joanna's mailbox.

A sudden bolt of fear set Joanna's fingertips tingling and her heart racing. This was the same deserted stretch of roadway where a drug dealer's hit man had lain in wait to slaughter Andy. Easing her Glock out of its holster, Joanna laid it on the seat beside her. Then, knowing that whoever was waiting in the darkness would be blinded by the sudden light, she switched on her high beams and roared forward. Only as she drew even with the parked car did she recognize her mother's Buick and slam on the brakes. The speeding Crown Victoria fishtailed back and forth on the rough gravel surface before she finally managed to wrestle it under control and bring it to a stop fifty feet beyond where she had intended.

With her hands shaking and her heart still pounding in her throat, Joanna threw the car into reverse. By the time she reached the mailbox, Eleanor Lathrop Winfield was already out of her car and standing beside the roadway.

"Why on earth were you driving so fast?" she demanded when Joanna rolled down her window. "Do you always speed that way when you're coming home late at night? You could have been killed, you know."

Having Eleanor go on the attack was so amazingly normal—so incredibly usual—that it was all Joanna could do to keep from laughing aloud.

"What are you doing here, Mother?" she asked.

"Waiting for you. What do you think? And why are you so late?"

"I just left George at a crime scene over by Paradise, Mom," Joanna said. "He's upset because he hasn't heard from you. He says you've been among the missing all day, and he's worried. He's afraid you're mad at him. Are you?"

To Joanna's surprise, Eleanor's strong facial features suddenly crumpled as she dissolved into tears. Astonished, Joanna flung open the door. Clambering out of the car, she pulled the weeping woman into her arms. She held her mother close and rocked her back and forth as though she were a child. Eleanor had always been taller than her daughter, but Joanna realized with a shock that Eleanor had somehow shrunk and now they were almost the same size. Through their mutual layers of clothing, Eleanor's body felt surprisingly bony and fragile.

"What's wrong, Mom?" Joanna begged. "Please tell me what's the matter."

"I tried to tell George," Eleanor croaked through her tears. "I tried to tell him, but he just didn't understand. I couldn't *make* him understand."

"Tell *me*, Mom."

Coming from across the desert, Joanna heard the joyous yips from Sadie and Tigger, who had no doubt heard the sound of the familiar engine and were coming to welcome their mistress home.

"Let's get back in my car before the dogs get here," Joanna urged. "Then I want you to tell me what's going on."

To Joanna's surprise, Eleanor didn't object. Instead, she leaned against her daughter and allowed herself to be led. Joanna opened the door. Before letting her mother in, she reached over and brushed her unholstered Glock under the seat of the car. After helping Eleanor inside, Joanna stopped at the trunk long enough to retrieve two bottles of water. She regained the inside of the car just as Sadie and Tigger burst through the mesquite and came racing toward them. The dogs circled the car madly, three times each. Then, finding it immovable, they gave up and went bounding off through the underbrush after some other, more interesting, prey.

Joanna passed the bottled water to her mother. "This should probably be something stronger, Mom, but it's the best I can do at the moment."

Eleanor took the bottle, opened it, and downed a long grateful swallow.

"So what is it?" Joanna asked after a moment. "Tell me."

Eleanor sighed and closed her eyes. "It was bad enough to know Dora was dead," she began shakily. "As soon as George told me that, I knew that was all my fault. I mean it's obvious that Dora was perfectly content to be out here at the ranch with Eva Lou and Jim Bob. If I had only let things be . . ."

"That's not true," Joanna said. "Dora wasn't happy at all. Have you talked to Jenny today? Have you spoken to Butch?"

Eleanor shook her head. "No," she said. "I haven't spoken to anyone. I was too ashamed."

"You shouldn't be," Joanna told her. "The reason Dora didn't want to go with the woman from Child Protective Services was that she had already made arrangements for her boyfriend to come pick her up later that same night at her mother's house up in Old Bisbee."

"He was?" Eleanor asked. "Her boyfriend really was going to come get her?"

"Yes. At least that's what we were told. His name is Christopher Bernard. He's sixteen years old and lives up in Tucson. Ernie Carpenter and Jaime Carbajal will be interviewing him tomorrow afternoon."

"Do they think he may have had something to do with Dora's death?"

"Possibly," Joanna said. "Although, at this point, no one knows anything for sure."

"Oh, dear," Eleanor said. "That poor girl, that poor, poor girl." With that, Eleanor once again burst into uncontrollable sobs.

Joanna was baffled. She had thought that what she had said would make her mother feel better, but it was clearly having the opposite effect. For several minutes, she let her mother cry without making any effort to stop her. Finally Eleanor took a deep shuddering breath and the sobs let up.

"Mother," Joanna said. "I don't understand. What's wrong?"

"Don't you see?" Eleanor pleaded. "George told me Dora was pregnant. Thirteen and pregnant. Unfortunately, I know exactly how that felt. Of course, I was a little older than that when it happened to me, but not all that much older, and every bit as alone. Your father loved me and would have married me then, if my parents would have stood for it and given permission, but they wouldn't. I've never felt so lost, Joanna. Never in my whole life. And knowing that's what was going on with poor Dora Matthews brought it all back to me, that whole awful feeling of not knowing where to go or what to do or whom to turn to for help.

"I've spent the rest of my life blocking out that terrible time, but when George told me about Dora, a floodgate opened and it all came rushing back. Like it was yesterday. No, that's not true. Like it was today, like it was happening to me all over again. I know George didn't mean to upset me when he told me about Dora. He couldn't have seen how I'd react, but I just had to get away for a while, and not just from him, either. I had to get away from everyone. I had to be off by myself so I could think things through. You do understand, don't you, Joanna? Please tell me you do."

Joanna shut her eyes momentarily to squeeze back her own tears. She had once been through the exact same anguish when she, too, had found herself pregnant and unmarried. She had been old enough that she and Andy had been able to marry without parental consent, but at the time and for years afterward, it had never occurred to Joanna that her mother might possibly have lived through a similar ordeal. She had needed her mother's help and had been no more able to ask for it than Eleanor had been to give it.

Joanna and Eleanor had battled over all kinds of things in the years after Joanna's overly hasty marriage to Andy Brady, but the underlying foundation for most of those hostilities had been Joanna's feeling of betrayal, Joanna's belief that Eleanor hadn't been there for her when she had needed her most. For years she had endured Eleanor's constant criticism without realizing that her mother's finger-pointing had been a ruse to conceal her own long-held secret—the baby Eleanor had borne and given up for adoption prior to her marriage to Big Hank Lathrop. It wasn't until that long-lost child, a grown-up and nearly middle-aged Bob Brundage, had come searching for his birth parents that Joanna had finally learned the truth as well as the depth of her mother's hypocrisy.

Instead of forming a bond between mother and daughter, Bob Brundage's appearance had made things worse. For Joanna, learning of her brother's existence and her mother's youthful indiscretion constituted yet another betrayal on Eleanor's part. And now, after years of continual warfare, Eleanor Lathrop Winfield had come suing for peace and pleading for understanding, asking for the kind of absolution she herself had never been able to grant.

Joanna's first instinct was to say, "No way!" But then she thought about Marianne Maculyea. For years her friend had been estranged from her own mother. Only now, after years of separation, Evangeline Maculyea had finally come around. It had taken the death of one grandchild and the birth of another, but Marianne's mother had finally opened the door to a reconciliation. It was, as Marianne had told Joanna, "the right thing to do." And so was this.

"I do understand," Joanna said quietly.

"Would that boy have married Dora, do you think?" Eleanor whispered, making Joanna wonder if she had even heard. "Not right now, of course," Eleanor added. "Dora was only thirteen, so she would have been too young. But maybe later, when she was older, this Chris could have married her the same way your father married me." She paused before saying what before would have been unthinkable. "The same way Andy married you."

Joanna wanted to answer, but her voice caught in her throat. She thought about what Jaime had said on the phone about Christopher Bernard and his family. Much as she would have liked to believe in the fairy tale, it didn't seem likely that Chris Bernard was cut from the same cloth as either D. H. Lathrop or Andrew Roy Brady.

"I don't know, Mom," Joanna finally managed. "I honestly don't know."

"I hope so," Eleanor returned, wiping new tears from her eyes. "I hope he cared about her that much. I suppose that's a stupid thing to say, isn't it. George said something about my being overly emotional about this, and it's true. But I hope Christopher really did care. I hope Dora found someone to love her even for a little while because it doesn't sound as though that mother of hers has sense enough to come in out of the rain."

Joanna sighed. This was far more like the Eleanor Lathrop Winfield she knew. "I hope so, too," she said.

Eleanor straightened now, as though everything was settled. The emotional laundry had been washed and dried and could now be safely folded and put away.

"Well," she added, "I suppose I ought to head home now. You said George had been called out to a crime scene? How late do you think he'll be?"

"Most likely not that much later. Because of where the body is, they probably won't be able to retrieve it before morning."

"Had he eaten any dinner before he left?" Eleanor asked.

"I don't know."

"Probably not. The man's smart as a whip, but when it comes to sensible things like eating at reasonable hours, he's utterly hopeless. So I'd better be going then," Eleanor continued. "That way I can have a little something ready for him when he gets home."

She turned to Joanna, took her daughter's hand, and squeezed it. "Thank you so much," she said. "I'm glad we had this little talk. I'm feeling ever so much better."

Joanna reached over and gave her mother a hug. "I'm glad we had this talk, too. Now go on home. George was worried sick about you. He'll be delighted to find you at home. Just don't tell him I told you so."

Eleanor frowned. "Do you think I should try explaining any of this to him? I'm afraid he'll think I've lost my marbles."

"Try him," Joanna Brady urged gently. "As you said, George is a very smart man. He might just surprise you."

Without another word, Eleanor got out of the car. She marched back to her Buick, got in, started it and drove off without a second glance. Shaking her head in wonder, Joanna turned and watched her drive away. Then, starting the Civvie, Joanna headed up the dirt road that led into the ranch. Before she made it all the way into the yard, Sadie and Tigger reappeared to reprise their earlier greeting. By the time Joanna had parked the car, Butch was standing on the back porch waiting for her.

"It's about time you got here," he said. "The dogs went rushing off a little while ago. I thought it was you coming, but then the dogs came back without you."

"It was me," Joanna said.

"But that must have been fifteen or twenty minutes ago," Butch said. "What did you do, stop to read the mail?"

"Eleanor was there waiting for me."

"What for?"

"She needed to talk."

"What about?"

"Dora Matthews."

"I suppose she still thinks it's all her fault."

Joanna thought about that. Butch was a good man and, in his own way, every bit as smart as George Winfield. And yet, Joanna wasn't the least bit sure he would understand what had happened that night between Joanna Brady and Eleanor Lathrop Winfield any more than George had understood what was going on with his own wife.

"Something like that," Joanna said, peering around the kitchen. "Now is there anything around here to eat? I'm starved."

That's when she saw the blueprints unrolled all over the kitchen table. It was also when she belatedly remembered that evening's scheduled appointment with Quentin Branch. "Oh, Butch," she said. "I'm so sorry. I forgot all about it."

"I noticed," he said. "But the way things are going, I guess I'd better get used to being stood up."

17

It was a quarter past seven when Butch shook Joanna awake the next morning. "Time to rise and shine," he said. "Coffee's on the nightstand, and breakfast is in five."

Grateful that he wasn't holding a grudge over last night's missed appointment, she gave him a warm smile. "Thanks," she said.

Struggling out of bed, Joanna staggered into the bathroom. She felt as though she had tied one on the night before, although she'd had nothing at all to drink. But between the forced-march hike and climbing up and down the cliff face, there was no part of her body that didn't hurt. Not only that; tired as she'd been, once she went to bed, she hadn't slept. Instead, she'd once again tossed and turned for a long time before finally drifting into a fitful sleep.

She showered hurriedly and then, with her hair still wet, went into the kitchen where a bowl of steaming Malt-o-Meal was already on the table. "I really don't have time to eat . . ." she began, looking at the clock.

"Yes, you do," Butch insisted. "This way you'll have at least one decent meal today."

Knowing he was right, Joanna sat and ate. She was in her office by ten after eight and pressing the intercom button. "Good morning, Kristin. Would you let Chief Deputy Montoya know that I'm here?"

"He's not," Kristin said. "He called a little while ago and said to tell you he'll be a few minutes late."

"Good," Joanna said. "Maybe you could come in and help me make some sense of all this new paper." She said nothing at all about the previous batch, which was still stowed in her unopened briefcase.

When Kristin entered the office, Joanna was shocked by her secretary's appearance. Her nose and eyes were red. She looked almost as bad as Joanna felt, and she walked as though she had aged twenty years overnight.

"Kristin," Joanna demanded, "what's wrong?" as the younger woman deposited a new stack of papers on one corner of Joanna's desk.

"Nothing," Kristin mumbled, turning away.

"Come on," Joanna urged. "Something's not right. Tell me."

"It's Terry," her secretary replied with a tearful sniffle.

"What about him?"

"He didn't come in until four o'clock this morning. He tried to tell me he was working overtime, but I looked on the schedule after I got here. He wasn't cleared for any overtime. He tried to tell me he was teamed up for some special operation with Deputy Howell. It was a special op, all right. I think he's sneaking around with her behind my back and—"

"They *were* on a special operation," Joanna interrupted. "I personally authorized the overtime last night. From now until we catch that I-10 carjacker, I want them cruising the freeway rest areas for as many hours a day as they can stand."

Kristin's face brightened. "Really?" she said.

Joanna sighed. "Really."

Kristin shook her head. "I don't know what's gotten into me. Terry tried telling me the same thing, but I didn't believe him."

"It's hormones, Kristin," Joanna said patiently. "They're all out of whack when you're pregnant." As she spoke, Joanna couldn't help realizing that she had made the exact same kinds of accusations with Butch on Sunday—and without the benefit of hormonal imbalance to use as an excuse. "You'd better call Terry and apologize," she added.

"I can't. He's asleep right now."

"Well, when he wakes up later, call and apologize."

"I will," Kristin promised. "I'll call as soon as I can."

It was almost nine o'clock before Frank came dragging into Joanna's office carrying yet another sheaf of papers, this one containing the stack of incident reports that would constitute the morning briefing.

"Sorry I'm late, Boss. With both of us out of the office all afternoon and half the night, there were a lot of pieces to pull together."

"Don't worry about being late," she assured him. "If you think your desk is a disaster, look at mine. So what's on today's agenda—other than Rob Whipple's murder and the Texas Canyon carjacking?"

"Burton Kimball cut a deal for Sally Matthews."

"What kind of deal?"

"He played the sympathy card big-time—as in, officials of the State of Arizona have already cost Sally Matthews the life of her only daughter. Consequently, she shouldn't be punished further, et cetera, et cetera.

Phoenix PD busted Sally's boyfriend, B. B. Ardmore, while he was making a drug sale in downtown Phoenix yesterday afternoon. If Sally agrees to turn state's evidence and if she tells investigators everything she knows about B. B.'s organization and his associates, she's off the hook. She also has to agree to enter rehab as soon as possible after Dora's funeral, which is currently scheduled for Friday afternoon at two o'clock."

"Are you telling me Sally Matthews has been cut loose?" Joanna demanded. "Sally Matthews was running a meth lab—an illegal and dangerous meth lab inside the city limits. She broke any number of laws, one of which should be child neglect. Nonetheless, she gets to turn Dora's death into a get-out-of-jail-free card. That's not right."

"Talk to Arlee Jones about that," Frank Montoya suggested. "Until the voters decide to replace him with a county attorney with brains, that's what we can expect. In the meantime, the charges are open, so that if she doesn't carry through on her promises, they can be refiled."

Joanna shook her head in disgust. "What else?" she asked.

"A single car, non-injury rollover, just outside of Hereford. Then there was a bunch of drunk Harley riders who left one of the bars in Tombstone and then went out to the municipal airport for a late-night fistfight session. When a pair of Border Patrol agents broke it up, everybody else jumped on their bikes and took off. The only one left was the one who was too busted up to leave. He's in the county hospital down in Douglas with a broken jaw and three broken knuckles. Then there're two DWIs and a domestic violence down in Pirtleville. Oh, and I almost forgot, yesterday's carjacking's car—the Pontiac Grand Am that was taken from over in Texas Canyon—was stopped at the crossing in Naco early this morning with a full load of illegals. The car's in the Border Patrol's impound lot down on Naco Highway. The lady's purse isn't."

"What's the word from the crime scene in Paradise?"

"I talked to Ernie. He and Jaime stayed there until three this morning. According to him, somebody did a half-assed job of trying to clean up Rob Whipple's house, but there are still plenty of traces of blood there. The crime scene team and Casey Ledford will be working that today, as well as Irma Sorenson's Nissan once we get it dragged out of where it landed and back here to the justice center. Since Rob Whipple was shot in Irma Sorenson's car, presumably the blood in his cabin will be from someone else."

"Like Connie Haskell, for instance," Joanna said. Frank nodded. "But there's still no trace of Irma or Rob Whipple's Dodge Ram?" she asked.

"Not so far."

Joanna shook her head. "Nothing like being under the gun," she said.

"It's more than that, Joanna," Frank returned. "Think about it. We've had three homicides in four days, and here the department sits with only two detectives to its name. We're understaffed and underfunded, and—"

Joanna held up her hand and stopped him. "Please, Frank. Let's not go into this right now. I know you're right. What do you think kept me awake half the night? I was worrying about the same thing, but before we go off trying to deal with all the political and financial ramifications, let's handle what's on our plates right now. What are Ernie and Jaime doing at the moment?"

"I told them to take the morning off. They have to sleep sometime. At noon they'll head up to Tucson to talk with Chris Bernard and his lawyer. As a result, Rob Whipple's autopsy will most likely have to be put off until tomorrow."

"Which shouldn't hurt Doc Winfield's feelings any," Joanna added.

"Since the Grand Am's been found," Frank resumed, "it may mean our carjacker will be back on the prowl again. Deputies Gregovich and Howell are also taking the morning off, but I've scheduled them to hit I-10 again today. By the way, did you know Kristin thought there was some hanky-panky going on?"

"I hope you told her otherwise," Joanna said.

Frank nodded. Before he could say anything more, Joanna's intercom buzzed. "What is it, Kristin?"

"There's someone on the phone who insists on talking to you."

"Who is it?"

"His name is Hardy. Brian Hardy."

"Brent, maybe?" Joanna asked.

"Sorry. Yes, that's it. Brent. He says it's urgent."

"Put him through, then," Joanna told her. "Good morning, Mr. Hardy. What can I do for you?"

"It's about Irma. She just left."

"Left from where?" Joanna demanded.

"From here, from Quartzite East," Hardy said. "Tommy and I had a big argument about whether or not we should call you. He said we ought to mind our own business, but I told him, 'No way. I'm calling.'"

Joanna switched her phone to speaker. "What exactly happened?"

"Irma must have shown up late last night, after we were asleep. When we woke up this morning, there was a strange car—a big blue Dodge pickup—parked next to her RV. I went over to check, because I was afraid whoever was there was someone who wasn't supposed to be. I knocked, and Irma herself came to the door. After what you told us about her son, I was really relieved to see her. She told us that the pickup belongs to her son, but that didn't exactly set my mind at ease, especially since Irma's been hurt."

"Hurt?" Joanna asked. "How so?"

"She's got a gash on her hand. It's bad enough that it probably should have had stitches. I told her it looked infected to me and suggested she see a doctor. She said she's been putting Neosporin on it, and she's sure it'll be just fine. She told me she'd had an accident in her Nissan and that was how she hurt her hand. Anyway, she said the car was totaled and that Rob, her son, had lent her his pickup. She also said that she's decided to sell the RV. She's found an RV dealer—in Tucson, I think—who's willing to pay her for it in cash rather than selling it on consignment. With that kind of hurried sale, she's probably being taken to the cleaners over it, but it's not my place to say. Anyway, she asked Tommy and me to help hitch up the pickup to the back of the RV and off she went."

"How long ago?" Joanna asked.

"Fifteen, maybe twenty minutes. Just long enough for Tommy and me to get into a pissing match over it. Like I said, she came sneaking back into the park late last night, after we had gone to bed. We didn't even know she was here until this morning. Since neither Tommy nor I actually set foot inside Irma's RV, I'm thinking it's possible that her son may be in there—that she drove it out of the park herself so we wouldn't see her son and know that she was hiding him."

"Irma Sorenson's son isn't in her RV," Joanna said. "He's dead."

"Dead!" Brent exclaimed. "How did that happen?"

"The incident is currently under investigation. Now, Mr. Hardy, thank you so much for calling, but if you'll excuse me, I have some other matters to attend to. If Irma Sorenson should happen to return, please call us immediately. Dial 911 and have the operator locate me."

"You sound as though you think she's dangerous," Brent Hardy said hesitantly.

"I suspect she is," Joanna returned. "Possibly to herself more than anyone else, but I don't think you and Mr. Lowrey should take any more chances."

"We won't."

"I'll go get a car," Frank said as Joanna ended the call.

Joanna nodded and dialed Dispatch. "Larry," she said. "The subject of our APB, Irma Sorenson, is believed to be heading west on I-10. She left Bowie about twenty minutes to half an hour ago, driving a bronze-and-black Marathon motor home and towing a blue '97 Dodge Ram pickup. I want her pulled over and stopped in as deserted a place as possible. Not in town, and not, for God's sake, at one of the rest areas. Maybe it would be a good idea to put down some spike strips on that long grade coming up from the San Pedro River in Benson. It's a long way out of town, so there shouldn't be lots of people around. She'll already have lost speed by then, and it's less likely she'll lose control when the tires go."

"Got it," Larry Kendrick said.

"This woman is armed and dangerous," Joanna continued. "As soon as she's spotted, I want you to set up roadblocks and stop all westbound traffic immediately behind her. Eastbound freeway traffic coming into Cochise County should be stopped at J-6 Road. Frank and I are on our way. Once you alert all units, get back to us. We'll try to deploy manpower in a way that blocks off as many freeway exits and entrances as possible. The fewer innocent people we have caught up in this action, the better."

By the time Joanna put down the phone and grabbed her purse, Frank Montoya was parked beside her private entrance with his Crown Victoria's engine fired up and running.

"Did you tell Kristin we're leaving?" Frank asked as he wheeled away from the door and through the parking lot.

"I didn't have time." As soon as she was settled in with her seat belt fastened, Frank handed her an atlas. After opening it to the proper page, Joanna unclipped the radio. "Okay, Larry. Where do we stand?"

"I've notified DPS and let them know what's happening. They're sending units as well. Currently I've got a long-haul trucker named Molly who says the subject just passed her at Exit 344," Larry returned. "Molly is convoying with another trucker. They're going to turn on their hazard lights and stop on the freeway. That should bottle up all the traffic behind them, and it takes care of the westbound roadblock. If I can find someone else to do the same thing at J-6 Road, our people will all be free to deal with the stop itself. City of Benson is closing all exits and entrances to the freeway there. The chief of police in Benson wants to know if we're putting down the spike strips, or are they?"

"Do we have anyone on the scene yet?"

"Not so far," Kendrick said. "Where are you and Chief Deputy Montoya?"

Joanna looked up and was amazed to see that they were already out on the broad, flat plain between the Mule Mountains and the hills leading into Tombstone. "Not quite halfway," she told him.

"I tried Deputy Rojas from Pomerene. He's up at Hooker Hot Springs investigating some dead livestock. It'll take him a while to get back down from there. Matt Raymond and Tim Lindsey are on their way from Elfrida and Sierra Vista respectively. Tim should be there first."

"Okay," Joanna said. "Have Matt try to catch up with the subject from behind and keep her in visual contact. Put Matt and Tim in touch directly, so Tim can lay down the strips with just enough time to get back in his car and take cover. And then, in your spare time, call the Double Cs.

Tell Detectives Carpenter and Carbajal that we need them both in Benson ASAP."

Joanna settled back in the seat and listened to the squawking radio as Larry Kendrick relayed her orders to various officers. Meanwhile Frank's Civvie flew through Tombstone and out onto the straight stretch of newly repaved highway between Tombstone and St. David.

"Sounds like you've got things under control," Frank said.

Joanna shook her head. There were too many variables; too many jurisdictions and people involved; too much opportunity for ordinary citizens to be injured or killed. "We'll see," she said.

They were halfway between St. David and Benson when Larry Kendrick's voice addressed her once again. "Sheriff Brady?"

"Yes."

"We've got a problem. Deputy Raymond reports that the subject is pulling off on the shoulder just west of Exit 318."

Joanna studied the map. "The Dragoon Exit?" she asked.

"That's right."

That meant Irma Sorenson was stopping far short of Tim Lindsey and his tire strips. "Why's she stopping?" Joanna asked.

"Matt's not sure. No, wait. He says a lone woman has stepped out of the vehicle and is walking back toward the rear. He says it looks like maybe she's got a flat."

Joanna took a deep breath. It could be a trap. Irma Sorenson might have noticed the sudden reduction in traffic volume traveling in both directions on the freeway. She might also have noticed the presence of a marked patrol car following her even though Deputy Raymond had been directed to keep his distance. There was no question in Joanna's mind that Irma Sorenson was capable of murder. What were the chances that she was faking the flat for some reason? On the other hand, it was possible that since the RV had been parked in one place for more than six months, it really did have a ruined tire.

"All right, Larry," Joanna said, steadying her voice and trying not to think about Matt Raymond's wife and the five-year-old twin girls who were the light of his life. "Here's what I want you to do. Tell Matt to drive past the vehicle and see if he can tell if the woman is carrying any kind of weapon. If none is visible, have him put on his lights—the orange ones, not the red—and back up on the shoulder. Have him—"

"Deputy Raymond's on the radio now," Larry reported. "He says the subject is attempting to flag him down. He doesn't see any weapon. I've directed Deputy Lindsey to leave his position in Benson and back up Deputy Raymond."

Holding the radio mike clenched tightly in her white-knuckled fist,

Joanna looked entreatingly at Frank Montoya. "Can't you drive any faster than this?" she begged.

Frank merely shook his head. "Not if you want us to get there in one piece," he said.

Now they heard Deputy Raymond's static-distorted voice coming through the speaker, broadcasting into his shoulder-mounted radio. "Ma'am, is something the matter?" That transmission was followed by something garbled that Joanna was unable to decipher, followed by Raymond again, "Well, let me take a look."

Holding her breath, Joanna gripped the microphone even harder and wondered why the hard plastic didn't simply crumble to pieces in her hand. Suddenly she heard the sound of a scuffle. "Get down! Get down! Hands behind your back. *Behind your back!*"

Then, after what seemed an eternity, Joanna heard Deputy Raymond's voice once more. "Got her." He panted jubilantly. "Subject is secured. Repeat: Subject secure. She wasn't carrying a weapon, and she really does have a flat. Lost the whole tread on her right rear tire. I just finished checking out the RV. It's full of packing boxes, but there's no one else inside."

In the background of Deputy Raymond's transmission Joanna heard the screeching of a siren announcing the arrival of Tim Lindsey's patrol car. It was all under control and her officers were safe. Joanna's voice shook with gratitude and relief when she spoke into the microphone again.

"Okay, Larry. Tell Deputy Raymond good work. Have him put the subject in the back of his patrol car and wait for Frank's and my arrival. Under no circumstances is he to ask her anything until we arrive, understand?"

"Got it."

"And tell our trucker friends who've been stopping traffic that they can let things start moving again. If possible, I'd like their names, company names, and addresses. I want to be able to write to their bosses and express my appreciation."

"Will do."

Joanna put down the microphone, leaned back in the seat, closed her eyes, and let out her breath.

"Way to go, Boss," Frank said. "Running an operation like that by radio is a little like giving somebody a haircut over the phone, but you made it work. Congrats."

A few minutes later, Frank turned the Crown Victoria onto I-10 east of Benson. With the emergency over, he had now slowed to the posted legal limit, and the Civvie dawdled along at a mere seventy-five. By the time they made a U-turn across the median, they could see that backed-up traffic from both sides of the freeway was now approaching the scene. Frank and Joanna's Civvie was the third police vehicle in a clot of shoulder-parked vehicles lined up behind the massive RV.

As soon as Joanna stepped out of the car, she went straight to her two deputies. "Good job," she told them.

Matt Raymond still seemed a little shaken by the experience. "It could have been a whole lot worse," he said.

Joanna nodded. "I know," she said. "Believe me, I know."

"I haven't talked to the woman much, but she's begging us to change her tire and let her drive on into Tucson," Matt Raymond said. "She claims she's got a deal to sell the Marathon, but she has to deliver it to the dealer by one o'clock this afternoon. Otherwise, he rescinds his offer to buy."

"I'll talk to her," Joanna said. "She's under arrest for murder. She's not in any position to be selling a motor home."

"I tried to tell her that myself," Matt said. "I don't think she was listening."

Joanna looked up as a speeding eighteen-wheeler blew past in a burst of hot air, followed by a long, unbroken line of other vehicles. "We need to get this mess off the road. It's not safe for any of us. Is this thing drivable, or are we going to need a tow truck?" she asked, looking down at the mangled flat.

"All we have to do is change the tire," Matt Raymond replied.

Joanna walked over to the idling Bronco that was Matt Raymond's marked patrol car. There Irma Sorenson, a white-haired unassuming lady with a pair of thick glasses perched on her nose, sat handcuffed in the backseat. She looked like somebody's grandmother, not a cold-blooded killer.

"Mrs. Sorenson?" Joanna said. "I'm Sheriff Brady. Having all these vehicles parked on the shoulder of the freeway is causing a hazard. We need to move them. Would it be all right if one of my deputies changed that tire?"

"Please," Irma said. "I don't know where the jack and spare are. I'm sure they're in one of those locked compartments. The keys are still in the ignition."

"So you don't mind if my officers enter your vehicle? We don't have a search warrant."

"You don't need a search warrant," Irma said. "I'm giving you permission to enter. If you need me to sign something, give it to me and I'll sign. And if you'll just let me take it on up to Tucson, I'll tell you whatever you need to know. But I have to sell this thing, and I have to sell it today."

"Because it contains evidence?" Joanna asked.

"No. Because I need the money. I'm going to need a lawyer."

Joanna closed the car door and walked back to where her deputies stood waiting. "She says the keys are in the ignition. You have permission to get the keys and change the flat tire, but whatever you do, don't touch anything else. You got that?"

Raymond and Lindsey nodded. Together they set about finding the keys, locating the jack and spare, and changing the tire.

"Frank, do you happen to have that miniature tape recorder of yours in your pocket?"

"Sure do, why?"

"Bring it," Joanna said. "I want you to Mirandize Mrs. Sorenson. And I want that recorded as well."

"You don't think she's going to confess, do you?"

"Yes, I do." Feeling half-guilty about what she was about to do, Joanna led the way back to the car. "Mrs. Sorenson, you told me a minute ago that if we let you keep your appointment with the RV dealer in Tucson, that you would tell us everything we want to know. Is that true?"

Irma Sorenson nodded.

"We'll have to record your answers."

"That's all right. It doesn't matter."

"This is my chief deputy, Frank Montoya. I'd like him to switch on his recorder and read you your rights."

"Sure," Irma said. "Go ahead."

Frank and Joanna sat in the front seat of the Bronco. Irma remained in the back.

"So what happened?" Joanna asked, once the legal formalities had been handled.

"I killed him," Irma said simply and without blinking. "I shot my son in the middle of the forehead."

"Why?"

"Because he was going to kill me," Irma replied. "I know he was. I knew too much about what he had done. He just didn't know I had the gun."

"What gun?" Joanna asked sharply. "Where did you get it?"

"From the car," Irma said. "From that blue Lincoln Rob had me drive to the airport for him. I knew something dead had been in that car. I could smell it, and given Robby's past . . ." Irma paused then and gulped to suppress a sob. "Given that, I knew what it had to be. I knew it had started all over again, with him doing what he used to do. The only thing I could think of was to let someone know about the car."

"But what about the gun?" Joanna prodded.

"That's what I'm telling you. I knew I had to have a reason for some-one to look at it—at the car, I mean. I couldn't just call up and say, 'Oh, by the way, I need someone to go check out a car that's sitting in the lot at Tucson International because I think maybe someone's been killed in it.' No, if an old lady calls in and says that, they'll probably think she's a complete wacko and pay no attention. But I thought if I said, 'Hey, there's a car at the airport with blood on it. Somebody needs to go check it out,' maybe they would. But for that I needed some real blood, so I cut my hand. And it was when I was looking around on the floor of the car for something to use to cut my hand with that I found the gun. It must have belonged to the person Robby killed, the one whose car it was. Anyway, I found the gun on the floor along with an old Bible that was full of hundred-dollar bills. I put them both in my purse. I know it was wrong to take the money. It didn't belong to me, and I should have left it where it was. But I took the gun just in case I needed it, you see. When you're dealing with someone like Robby—someone that unpredictable—you just never can tell."

"And where is it right now?"

"The gun? It's still in my purse," Irma said. "Inside the RV."

"Getting back to your son," Joanna said. "You're saying you wanted him to be caught?" Irma nodded. "Then why didn't you go ahead and call the Tucson Police Department? You could have turned him in right then instead of going through the ruse of making a phony phone call and pretending to be someone you weren't."

"He was my son," Irma said as though that explained everything. "I couldn't just turn him in. My heart wouldn't let me do that."

"But if you shot him, your heart evidently let you kill him."

"That was self-defense," Irma declared.

"You mean Rob Whipple had a weapon, too? He was holding a knife on you or a gun?"

"No. But he was going to kill me all the same. I knew too much. I had driven that car to the airport for him, and I had spent two days cleaning up the blood that was spattered all over that filthy cabin of his. I pretended to believe him when he told me he had hit a deer with his pickup and killed it. He claimed he had cleaned it inside the cabin so the forest rangers wouldn't see it and nail him for hunting out of season. That's the thing that really galls me. That he thought I was that stupid. But I knew it was no deer that had died there—it was a woman. It had to be."

"Why do you say that?" Joanna asked.

Irma shrugged. "That's who he always went after—women."

"Did you talk about her with your son?" Joanna asked. "Did you talk about the dead woman?"

"Are you kidding?" Irma asked. "We were both too busy pretending she didn't exist. Of course we didn't talk about her. But I knew that as soon as the mess in the cabin was cleaned up and as soon as I had collected the money from selling the RV, Robby would have to get rid of me, too."

"So he was the one who wanted you to sell the RV?" Joanna asked.

Irma nodded. "It was his idea, and he's the one who made the deal. We spent all day Sunday and a big part of Sunday evening looking for a dealer who would make me a good enough offer."

"Wait a minute," Joanna said, thinking of Dora Matthews. "You and Robby were together on Sunday?"

"All day, and all night, too. I stayed with him out at the cabin."

"And he was with you the whole time?"

"The whole time. Until he had to go back to work on Monday. Yesterday, I went back to Tucson and rented a locker at one of those self-storage places where I can store my stuff for the time being. They sell boxes there, too. I brought some of those home and spent most of last night taping them together and throwing junk into them. All we have to do is drop them off at the storage unit on the way to the dealer—they're both on Twenty-second Street—and they'll all be there waiting when I get out."

"Out of where?"

"Jail, of course," Irma replied. "What else would I be talking about? I knew once Robby had me sign over the title, that would be it. Once I had the money in my hand, he wouldn't need me anymore. So I got to Robby before he had a chance to get to me," Irma continued without even pausing for breath. "He came home from work that night all upset, saying he'd been fired. I was scared of him. I told him I was going to go back to my place for the evening, back to the RV. He got in the car with me. I think he was going to try to stop me. When I pulled the gun out of my purse, you should have seen the surprised look on his face. He just couldn't believe it. He laughed at me and said, 'Come on, Mom. Put that thing away. You're never going to use it.' But I did. Then I belted him into the car—that's the law, you know. Passengers have to have their seat belts fastened. Then I drove him off the cliff. In the movies, cars always burst into flame when they go over cliffs. That was what I was hoping this one would do, but it didn't. It just made a big whanging sound and then a huge cloud of dust rose in the air. That's all there was to it."

"And this was when?"

"Night before yesterday. Monday, it must have been. Monday evening."

Joanna wanted to ask more questions, but right at that moment she could no longer think of any. Shooting her son in cold blood hadn't bothered Irma Sorenson, but she had been sure to have his seat belt buckled when she sent the Nissan over the cliff.

Shaking her head, Joanna clicked off the recorder. The criminal mind was more or less understandable; motherhood unfathomable. In sending her son to Pathway to Paradise, Irma Sorenson had hoped to save him. Instead she had lost everything.

18

W e're going to do what?" Detective Ernie Carpenter demanded.
By the time the Double Cs arrived, the whole circus of
Irma's RV, her son's pickup, and the collected entourage of
police vehicles had moved to the parking lot of a defunct motel east
of Benson.

"You heard me," Joanna told him. "We're going to drive Mrs. Sorenson into Tucson. First we're going to drop off her personal possessions at a
storage unit and then have her at the dealer's lot prior to that one o'clock
deadline so she can unload her RV. After that, there'll be plenty of time to
take her back to Bisbee and book her."

"That's crazy." Ernie scowled in objection. "The woman has just
confessed to the murder of her own son. You're going to let her unload
her stuff at a storage unit and sell off her RV without even bothering to
search it?"

"Do you happen to have a search warrant on you at the moment?"
Joanna asked.

"Well, no," he admitted.

"Who's to say we can't serve the search warrants later, at the RV
dealer's or even at the storage unit, for that matter?"

"But still . . ."

"But nothing, Ernie," Joanna said. "I gave Irma Sorenson my word,
and I fully intend to keep it. In exchange for letting her sell her RV, what
do we get? A signed confession that clears not one but two of the three
murders that have happened in Cochise County in the last week. That
sounds like a good deal to me."

Ernie Carpenter recognized there was no changing Joanna's mind.
"All right," he conceded. "What do you want me to do?"

"Can you drive this thing?" Joanna asked, indicating the motor home.
"Sure."

"Okay, here's the address of the storage unit, and the ignition key. You drive it there, and I'll send along a contingent of deputies to do the unpacking. Once the boxes are out of there, come to the dealer—Tex's RV Corral in the 5700 block of East Twenty-second Street. Frank and I will bring Irma with us and meet you there."

Grumbling under his breath, Ernie Carpenter stalked off. Joanna went looking for Frank. Two hours later, and a good fifteen minutes before the one o'clock witching hour, a small parade consisting of Irma Sorenson's RV, the towed Dodge Ram, and two police cars pulled into the parking lot at Tex's RV Corral. A bow-legged man in boots, jeans, Western shirt, and ten-gallon hat sauntered out of the office. He looked as though he would have been far more at home riding the range than running an RV dealership.

He held out his hand as Ernie Carpenter stepped down from the RV. "Howdy. Tex Mathers is the name," he said with an easygoing grin. "And you are?"

"It doesn't matter who I am," Ernie muttered. "The owner's the person you need to talk to. She's back there."

Tex Mathers's grin faded when he saw Irma Sorenson climbing out of the backseat of Deputy Raymond's Bronco. As Joanna had directed, Matt Raymond had removed Irma's handcuffs prior to letting her out of the vehicle.

"This is Mr. Mathers," Ernie said, as Joanna came forward, bringing Irma along. "He evidently owns the place. And this is Cochise County Sheriff Joanna Brady."

Tex Mathers sized Joanna up and down, then he glanced in the direction of the other uniformed officers. "What's this all about?" he asked. "And why the cops? Mrs. Sorenson didn't tell you I'm doing anything illegal, did she? Because I'm not. Assuming the rig is in the kind of condition her son said it was in, I'm paying her a fair price. Low blue book, of course, because she wants her money up front, but it's a good deal."

"And you're still prepared to go through with it?" Joanna asked.

"Well, sure," he said. "I suppose I am, as long as it's in good shape and all that. Her son told me it was low mileage and in excellent condition."

"Help yourself, Mr. Mathers," Joanna said. "Go have a look."

Joanna had been astonished at the luxury of the motor home when she had first stepped inside, from the flat-screen entertainment center and full-sized appliances to the etched-glass walls between the bathroom and the hallway. She could see why Tex Mathers was itching to get his grubby hands on it. Although the deal he had struck with Rob Whipple wasn't strictly illegal, Joanna had a hunch it wasn't in Irma's best interests, either. When it came to protecting widows and orphans, she doubted RV dealers would be very high on the trustworthy list.

"How much more would Irma get if you sold this on consignment?" Joanna asked.

Tex Mathers shrugged his narrow shoulders. "I dunno," he said. "Maybe forty or fifty grand more. It's a top-of-the-line and very desirable model, but the lady's son said his mother needed her money right away."

"Supposing she didn't need it instantly," Joanna said. "What then?"

"I pro'ly wouldn't have much trouble selling it," Tex admitted. "Might take a couple of months—until the first snowbirds show up this fall."

Without another word, Joanna left Tex Mathers to finish exploring the motor home and went outside to where a petite Irma Sorenson stood dwarfed by a circle of towering uniformed deputies.

"Irma, who said you needed an all-cash deal?" Joanna asked.

"Robby. He said it would be worth taking the lower price now just to have the cash in hand."

"It may not be worth it," Joanna said. "If it were mine, I wouldn't sell it for cash. I'd write it up as a consignment deal."

"But I told you. I need the money to hire an attorney."

"You'll have more money to work with if you don't take it now," Joanna said. "There are probably several attorneys in Bisbee who'd be willing to take you on without having the money up front."

"Are you sure?" Irma asked uncertainly.

"I'm pretty sure. Once you have an attorney, though, you might ask him about the deal as well."

Tex Mathers reappeared, looking abashed. "It's a sweet rig," he said. "Just like your son told me it was. And I'm still prepared to write out a check to you for the full agreed-upon amount today, but if you'd rather put it on consignment . . ." He gave Joanna a sidelong glance, as if checking to see whether or not she approved.

"And then Mrs. Sorenson receives what?" Joanna asked.

"The sales price less my commission."

"From what you said to me inside, that would be substantially more than what you offered to pay her today?"

Tex Mathers scuffed the toe of his boot in the gravel. "Well, yeah," he said. "I s'pose it would."

"All right," Irma Sorenson said after a moment. "We'll do it that way, then. Let's get the paperwork done. I don't want to keep these people standing around waiting all day."

"Frank," Joanna suggested. "Why don't you go along to keep an eye on things?" Tex Mathers took Irma's arm and led her inside. Frank, shaking his head, dutifully followed. Once they were gone, Joanna turned to her officers. "Okay, Matt, maybe you and Jaime could get the pickup unhitched from the RV."

"What do you want me to do?" Ernie asked.

"As soon as the pickup is loose, you drive it back to Bisbee. Get the taped confession transcribed onto paper, so Irma can sign it and get the gun in to Ballistics. Deputy Raymond will bring Irma back to Bisbee. If you need to ask her any more questions, have Frank sit in with you, since he was in on the other interview."

"What are you going to do?"

"Jaime and I are going to go do that interview with Christopher Bernard."

"Look, Sheriff Brady," Ernie began, "with all due respect . . ."

"Ernie, with the caseload we've got going, the department is at least two detectives short. For right now, until we can hire or train more, Frank Montoya and I are going to fill in as needed. Do you have any objections to that?"

"No ma'am," Ernie said. "I guess not."

"Good."

By one twenty-five, Ernie Carpenter was on his way back to Bisbee, but Frank and Irma had yet to emerge from Tex Mathers's office. "What time did you say that appointment was?" Joanna asked Jaime Carbajal.

The detective glanced at his watch. "Two," he said, "and their house is a ways from here."

"We'd best get going," Joanna told him.

Thirty minutes later, Jaime stopped the Econoline van in front of a closed wrought-iron gate. Beyond the gate sat an enormous white stucco house with a red tile roof. The house looked like a Mediterranean villa that had been transported whole and dropped off in the middle of the Arizona desert.

"Quite a place," Joanna commented. "Whereabouts do Dora's former foster parents live?"

Jaime pointed at a much more modest, natural adobe-style house that was right next door. "That's the Dugans' place right there," he said.

In addition to size, the other major difference between the two residences was in the landscaping. The Bernards' place was newly planted with baby trees, shrubs, and cacti. The mature shrubbery around the Dugans' house showed that it had been there far longer.

"There was evidently another house on the Bernards' lot originally," Jaime Carbajal explained. "They bought it as a tear-down and had their own custom design built in its place."

A phone was attached to the gatepost. Jaime picked up the handset and announced who they were. Moments later the iron gate swung open, allowing them admittance. The garage doors were open, revealing two cars parked inside. Scattered around the circular driveway were several more vehicles, including an obviously new silver Porsche Carrera.

"Get a load of the rolling stock," Jaime said. "The Porsche, a BMW-Z3 Roadster, a Mercedes S-600, and a . . . I'll be damned. Look at that—a Lexus 430. That's what the kid in Sierra Vista told us. Buddy Morris said he thought he saw Dora Matthews getting into a white Lexus. But I don't remember seeing one when we were here yesterday. By the time Ernie and I finished up in Sierra Vista, all hell had broken loose in Portal. We never had time to check with the DMV."

"It's all right, Jaime," Joanna said. "Just keep cool."

The blue-eyed, blond-haired woman who answered the door was only a few years older than Joanna, but she was so polished and cool-looking that she made Joanna feel dowdy in comparison. Amy Bernard was pencil-thin. Her navy-blue pantsuit and white silk shell accentuated her slender figure and made Joanna wish she had been wearing something other than a khaki uniform.

"I'm Amy Bernard," she said. Then, without giving Joanna a second glance, she added, "Come in. This way."

The woman of the house led Jaime Carbajal and Joanna through a spacious foyer and into a formal dining room. Under an ornate crystal chandelier stood a long, elegantly carved table surrounded by twelve matching chairs. Three people were seated at the far end of the table in front of a huge breakfront. Two were serious-looking men, both of them wearing the expensive but casual dressed-down attire that had long since replaced suits and ties among members of Tucson's upper crust.

Next to the man at the head of the table slouched the only incongruity in the room, a homely gangly young man with braces and spiked purple hair. A series of gold studs lined the edges of both ears. What looked like a diamond protruded from one side of his nose.

"Here they are," Amy said, before gliding down the far side of the table, where she slid gracefully onto a chair next to her son.

Both men rose. After some prodding from his father, Christopher rose as well. "I'm Dr. Richard Bernard," the man at the head of the table said. "This is my son Christopher, and this is our attorney, Alan Stouffer. I was led to believe there would be two detectives coming this afternoon, Detective Ernie Carpenter and Detective Jaime Carbajal. So you would be?" he asked.

"I'm Sheriff Joanna Brady," she replied. "Detective Carpenter is otherwise engaged at the moment, so I'm accompanying Detective Carbajal. I hope you don't mind."

"Have a seat," Dr. Bernard said. "What we do mind is having this unfortunate situation intrude on us. I'm sure Dora Matthews's life wasn't all it should have been, and I'm certainly sorry the poor girl is dead, but I can't see how you can possibly think our son Christopher had anything at all to do with what happened to her."

"I'm sure my officers didn't mean to imply that Christopher was involved in Dora's death," Joanna said soothingly. "But we do know that he spoke to her on both Friday and Saturday, prior to her death on Sunday. In situations like this it's our policy to interview all the victim's friends. We're here to learn if Christopher has any information that might help us track down Dora's killer."

"I don't know anything," Christopher Bernard blurted. "All I know is she's dead, and I'm sorry."

To Joanna's surprise, he turned sideways on his chair then and sat staring at the breakfront with its display of perfectly arranged and costly china. It was only when he brushed his cheek with the back of his hand that Joanna realized he was crying.

"As you can see, Chris and Dora Matthews were friends," Dr. Bernard said. "They met a few months ago when she was staying here in the neighborhood. Naturally he's grieved by her death, but—"

"Christopher," Joanna said. "Were you aware Dora Matthews was three months pregnant when she died?"

Chris Bernard swung back around on his chair. He faced Joanna with his eyes wide. "You're sure then?"

Joanna nodded. "Are you the father of Dora's baby?" she asked.

Chris looked at his father before he answered. Then he lifted his chin defiantly and straightened both his shoulders. "Yes," he answered, meeting and holding Joanna's questioning gaze. "I am."

"Christopher," Amy Bernard objected in dismay. "How can you say such a thing?"

"Because it's true."

"Excuse me," Alan Stouffer said, leaping into the fray. "I'm sure Chris has no way of knowing for sure if he was the father of that baby, and I must advise him—"

"I was too the father," Chris insisted. "Dora told me on the phone Friday night that she thought she was pregnant. I told her she needed to go to the drugstore and get one of those test kit things so she could find out for sure. I told her if she was, we'd run away to Mexico together and get married. Dad says I'll never amount to anything, but I do know how to be a man. If you have a kid, you're supposed to take care of it. That's the way it works. I have my trust money from Grandpa. We would have been all right."

The dining room was suddenly deathly quiet. From another room came the steady ticking of a noisy but invisible grandfather clock.

"Really, Chris," Alan Stouffer said. "You mustn't say anything more."

"But I want to," Chris argued, his face hot and alive with emotion. "Dora's dead, and I want to find out who did it. I want to know who killed her. I want that person to go to jail."

With that, Chris buried his head in his arms and began to sob. Meanwhile Joanna grappled with a whole new sense of respect for this homely and seemingly disaffected kid whom she had been prepared to write off as a privileged, uncaring jerk. She could see now that her own and Eleanor Lathrop's hopes had indeed been granted. The boy who had impregnated Dora Matthews had cared for her after all. Somehow, against all odds and against all rules of law and propriety, the two of them had met and fallen in love. And even though Dora was dead, Christopher Bernard loved her still.

Amy Bernard reached out and patted his shoulder. "There, there, Chris, darling. It's all right. Shh."

"Sheriff Brady," the attorney said, "I really must object to this whole situation. You haven't read Christopher his rights. Anything he has said so far would be automatically excluded from use in court."

"No one has said that Christopher Bernard is suspected of killing Dora Matthews," Joanna said quietly. "I'm just trying to get some information."

"It's all right, Alan," Dr. Bernard said. "It's my understanding that Dora Matthews died sometime Sunday night. Is that correct?"

Joanna nodded.

"Well, that's it then, isn't it? Amy went to see a play at the Convention Center that night, and Chris was with me and some of our friends. Two of the other doctors at the hospital—at TMC—have sons Christopher's age. The six of us spent Sunday night at a cabin up on Mount Lemmon. We went up Sunday before noon and didn't come home again until Monday morning."

"What play?" Joanna asked.

"*Annie Get Your Gun*—one of those traveling shows," Amy said. "Richard doesn't care for musicals all that much."

Joanna turned to Dr. Bernard. "You can provide us with the names, telephone numbers, and addresses of all these friends?"

"Certainly," he returned easily. "Amy, go get my Palm Pilot, would you? I think it's on the desk in my study."

"They're not *my* friends," Chris put in bitterly. "In case you haven't noticed, Dad. Those guys were jocks. I'm not. If it was supposed to be a 'bonding experience,' it sucked."

Amy Bernard returned from her errand. After placing her husband's electronic organizer within easy reach, she once again patted her son on the shoulder. He shrugged her hand away. "Would anyone care for something to drink? Iced tea? Coffee?"

"Oh, sit down, Amy. This isn't a social visit. We're not serving these people hors d'oeuvres."

With bright spots of anger showing in both of her smoothly made-up cheeks, Amy Bernard resumed her seat. With the plastic stylus, Richard Bernard searched through his database and then read off names, addresses, and telephone numbers for Drs. Dan Howard and Andrew Kingsley and their two sons, Rick and Lonnie. While Jaime jotted down the information, Joanna turned her attention back to Christopher.

"When's the last time you spoke to Dora?" she asked gently.

The boy blinked back tears and took a deep breath before he answered. "Saturday," he said. "Saturday morning. Dora was staying at someone's house, a friend of hers, I guess. She gave me the number Friday night. When I talked to her on Saturday, she said that she couldn't go to a drugstore in Bisbee because all the people there would know her. So I told her we'd get the test kit after I picked her up that night."

"In Bisbee?"

"Yes."

"Did you go?"

Chris nodded. "I tried to. Dora had given me directions, and I went there, only there was this huge mess on her street, with all kinds of emergency vehicles and everything. I parked the car and walked back up the street. At least, I tried to. It turned out that the problem was at Dora's house. I couldn't tell what had happened—if someone had been hurt or if the place had caught fire or what. I tried to get close enough to see if I could find Dora, but the cops chased me away, told me to get lost. I waited and waited, but she never showed up. Finally I gave up and came back home. I thought she would call me again, but she never did. And then Sunday, Dad made me go on that stupid trip to Mount Lemmon. He probably thought if I hung around with jocks long enough, maybe I'd turn into one, like it was catching or something."

"It sounds as though we're finished here," Alan Stouffer began. "Chris has been entirely cooperative. I don't see how he can—"

"Do you know when Dora's funeral is?" Chris asked Joanna.

"Christopher," Amy said, "I know you were friends, but that isn't—"

"Do you?" he insisted.

Joanna nodded. "I believe it's sometime on Friday afternoon. I don't know the time exactly, but if you call Norm Higgins at Higgins Funeral Chapel and Mortuary in Bisbee, I'm sure he'll be able to tell you."

"What's his name again?"

Joanna pulled out one of her cards and jotted down Norm Higgins's name on the back of it. "I'm sorry I don't know the number," she said, handing the card to Christopher.

"That's all right," he sniffed. "I can get it from information."

"Chris," Amy said. "You really shouldn't go. It just wouldn't be right."

"I'm going," Christopher Bernard said fiercely. "And you can't stop me!"

"And we should be going, too," Joanna said, rising to her feet. "You've all been most helpful. And, Chris," she added, offering him her hand, "please accept my sympathy for your loss. I know you cared deeply about Dora Matthews. She was lucky to have had you in her life."

Out in the car, Jaime Carbajal slammed the car door and turned on Joanna in exasperation. "Why did you just quit like that?" he demanded. "I have a feeling there was a whole lot more Chris could have told us."

"Yes," Joanna said. "But I want it to be admissible."

"You still think he did it?"

"No, I don't," Joanna replied. "When you turn around to drive out, I want you to stop as close as you can to the front of that Lexus. I want to get a peek at the front grille and see if there's any damage."

"But . . ." Jaime began.

"Humor me on this one, Jaime. All I want is a peek. And we're not violating anybody's rights here. The car isn't locked up in the garage. It's parked right out here in front of God and everybody."

Hopping out of the van, Joanna made a quick pass by the vehicle. And there it was: a slight depression in both the front bumper and the hood of the LS 430; the left front headlight cover had been shattered. The Lexus had hit something and had hit it hard. Seeing the damage took Joanna's breath away. In that moment, she knew Jenny wasn't the target—never had been. Uttering a prayer of thanksgiving, Joanna darted back to the open door of the van.

"Anybody see me?" she asked.

Jaime was staring into the rearview mirror. "Not that I could tell," he said. "So what's the deal?"

"Let's get out of here," she said. "It's damaged, all right. It hit something hard enough to dent in the front end and shatter the headlight cover."

"Where to now?" Jaime asked.

"Drive out of the yard, pull over into that next cul-de-sac, and stop there."

Having said that, Joanna took her cell phone out of her purse and switched it on. She dialed Frank's number and breathed a relieved sigh when he answered on the second ring.

"Irma's not booked yet, but she will be," he told her. "I suggested she call Burton Kimball."

"Good," Joanna said. "If anybody needs Burton Kimball's services, it's Irma Sorenson. Now I have a job for you, Frank. Did Ernie ever get any response on those telephone-company inquiries he made yesterday? If not, maybe you can hurry them up. We're looking for calls going back and forth between the Bernards' number in Tucson and Sierra Vista."

"I'll have to check with Ernie. Between him and Ma Bell, that may take a while. Can I get back to you?"

"Sure. If the line's busy, leave a message. I have a couple of other calls to make."

By then, Jaime had parked in a neighboring cul-de-sac as directed. He had put the vehicle in neutral but left the engine running. "What now?" he asked.

"We wait," Joanna answered. "If anyone comes through the Bernards' front gate driving that damaged Lexus, I want you to follow them. But first, give me your notebook with the names and numbers you wrote down. I'm going to check out Dr. Bernard's alibi."

It took several minutes for Joanna to get through to Dr. Daniel Howard. Since it was Wednesday afternoon, she ended up reaching him at home.

"Who's this again?" he asked, after Joanna had explained what she wanted.

"I'm Sheriff Joanna Brady," she said. "From Cochise County."

"Maybe I should check with Dick before I answer," Dr. Howard hedged.

"It would really be better if you answered my question without checking with anybody," she told him.

"Well, it's true then," he said after a pause. "We were up at the cabin—Andy Kingsley's cabin. There were six of us—my son, Rick, and me; Dick Bernard and his son, Chris; and Andy Kingsley and his son, Lonnie. We got there up about noon on Sunday. Barbecued some hamburgers, played some cards, drank a few beers. The kids played games and watched videos. We all came back early Monday afternoon. How come? What's this all about?"

"Never mind," Joanna told him. "It's nothing. Thanks for your help."

Next she tried the number for Andrew Kingsley. A young male voice answered. "Dad's not home," he said. "Wanna leave a message?"

"Is this Lonnie, by any chance?" Joanna asked.

"Yeah. That's me."

"My name's Joanna Brady. I was just wondering—did you go camping with Christopher Bernard last weekend?"

"That weirdo? Yeah, why?"

"And he was with you all Sunday night?"

"Yeah, but don't tell anyone," Lonnie said. "It was my dad's bright idea. It's not something I'm proud of."

"Right," Joanna said. "I know just what you mean."

She ended the call. As soon as she did, the phone rang again. "Hello, Frank. That was quick."

"You were right. Ernie's request had gone nowhere, but I know the right person to call," he said. "Her name's Denise, and she's a jewel. She told me there's a collect call from a pay phone in Sierra Vista at four twenty-seven in the afternoon. It's a pay phone located in a Walgreens store. The call lasted for more than ten minutes. What does it mean?"

"It means probable cause," Joanna said.

"So Chris Bernard did kill her then?"

"No, surprisingly enough, I believe Chris Bernard is a stand-up guy. He was out of the house when that call came in from the Walgreens pay phone. So was Dr. Bernard. It sounds to me as though both the father and the son could be in the clear on this. I'm beginning to believe that the mother did this job all by her little lonesome. Somehow Amy must have convinced Dora that she was on the kids' side and that she was coming to help her. I want a search warrant for the Bernards' house and for all their vehicles as well."

"You're saying the kid's mother is our killer?"

"*May* be," Joanna corrected. "Setting out to save her precious son from a fate worse than death. According to my scorecard, Frank, it's been a bad day for mothers all around."

"Oops, Sheriff Brady," Jaime Carbajal said. "Trouble. That Lexus is just now coming through the gate. It looks like the mother's alone in the vehicle. Want me to pull her over?"

"No," Joanna said. "Let her go, Jaime. Just follow her. Let's see where she's going. Gotta hang up, Frank. We're on the move here. Get cracking on that search warrant, will you? We may need it sooner than you think."

19

It was anything but a high-speed chase. With Amy Bernard obeying every posted speed limit, Jaime and Joanna followed at a distance of several car lengths. The van was so much taller than the surrounding vehicles that it was possible for Jaime to let other traffic merge in front of them and yet still maintain visual contact with the gleaming white Lexus.

"If anyone saw you looking at that vehicle in the yard, it could cause problems," Jaime said.

"We'll just have to hope they didn't. In the meantime, don't let that woman out of our sight."

"Where do you think she's going?" Jaime asked as Amy Bernard turned off Tanque Verde onto Grant Road.

"I don't know," Joanna said. "But the fact that she left right after we did makes me think we'd better find out. Our showing up at the house might have spooked her." Joanna was quiet for several seconds. "You're the one who dropped off Dora Matthews's clothing at the crime lab, aren't you?"

"Yes."

"Do you happen to have the name and number of the criminalist here in Tucson who's handling it?"

Jaime reached in his pocket, took out his small spiral notebook, and tossed it to her. "The guy's name is Tom Burgess," he said. "His phone number is in there somewhere."

Joanna thumbed through the pages until she found the one that contained Tom Burgess's name and number. As soon as she located it, she phoned him. "This is Sheriff Joanna Brady," she said, once he was on the line. "I'm calling about the clothing my investigators brought in yesterday—clothing from a homicide victim named Dora Matthews. Have you had a chance to start on it yet?"

"No, why?"

"We're currently following a damaged vehicle that may be implicated in that homicide. The medical examiner saw what he thought were flakes of paint on the victim's clothing. We're hoping you'll be able to give us a match."

"I'll try to move it up on the list," Tom Burgess said without much enthusiasm, "but I doubt if I'll be able to get to it before the first of next week. We're underbudgeted and understaffed."

Join the club, Joanna thought. She said, "Please try, Mr. Burgess. I'd be most grateful."

Joanna hung up and sighed. "Burgess didn't strike me as much of a go-getter," Jaime said.

Joanna allowed herself a hollow chuckle. "That makes two of us," she said.

They continued to follow Amy Bernard, mile after mile, all the way down Grant to Oracle and then north on Oracle until she turned left into Auto Row.

"Now I know what she's doing," Joanna groaned. "She's going to the dealer to have her car fixed."

Grabbing up her phone, she dialed Frank's number. "How's it going on that search warrant? The one we need right this minute is for the Bernards' Lexus."

"I'm working on it," Frank said. "What do you think I am, a miracle worker?"

"You'd better be," Joanna said. "When you get it, fax a copy of it to me in care of the Lexus dealer in Tucson."

"What's the number?"

"I have no idea," Joanna said, "but I can see the sign from here. It's called Omega Lexus."

As Joanna watched, Amy Bernard wheeled the white sedan off the street and up to the entrance to the service bays. Within moments a uniformed service representative came out to speak to her, clipboard in hand. "What do we do now, Boss?" Jaime asked.

"Pull up right behind her," Joanna directed. "We wait until she gives the guy her car keys. Once they're out of her hands and into his, we go up to her and have a little chat. You go one way, I'll go the other, just in case she decides to make a run for it."

As soon as the service rep took Amy Bernard's keys, Joanna and Jaime climbed down out of the van. Amy stood with her back turned to the approaching officers, her blond hair ruffling in the wind. She had no idea they were there until Joanna spoke.

"How nice to see you again, Mrs. Bernard. Having some car trouble?"

The woman spun around. "What are you doing here?" she demanded.

Ignoring her, Joanna walked past both Amy Bernard and the service guy. She stopped in front of the car and made a show of studying the dent in the grille and the broken headlight. "Looks as though you've had a little fender bender here," she said. "Have you reported it?"

"Of course I have," Amy returned indignantly. "I was out driving alone the other night and hit a deer out on the highway between here and Oracle. I reported the accident to both the police and to my insurance company yesterday morning. But you still haven't said why you're here."

"Do you happen to have a cell phone with you?" Joanna asked.

Amy Bernard's blue eyes narrowed ominously. "Yes. Why?"

"Because I thought you might want to have Mr. Stouffer present, Mrs. Bernard. Detective Carbajal here and I would like to ask you a few questions."

"You can't do that."

"You'd be surprised at what I can do, Mrs. Bernard," Joanna said quietly. "I'm placing you under arrest for the murder of Dora Matthews. And as for the car," she added, turning to the astonished service rep who stood frozen in place, "I've requested a search warrant for that vehicle. The actual search warrant won't be here until later, but as soon as it's available, I'm having it faxed to me here. Until it arrives, no one is to touch that vehicle."

"Wait just a minute!" Amy Bernard's smoothly made-up face screwed itself into a knot of fury. "I brought my car in here to have it fixed, and it's going to be fixed."

"No," Joanna said simply. "It's not. I believe this vehicle contains evidence of a homicide," she said to the service rep, who now had the presence of mind to step away from the two women and their heated exchange of words. "It's to be left alone. Understand?"

"Yes, ma'am," he said. The name on his uniform was Nick. He looked to be about twelve years old and scared to death.

Apparently, even then, Amy Bernard didn't believe the rules applied to her. Springing forward like a cat, she wrested the clipboard out of the service rep's hands and tore off the identification tag with the keys still attached. Stuffing the keys into her pocket, she put one hand deep inside the shiny leather bag that dangled from one shoulder.

Before either Joanna or Jaime could stop her, she stepped behind the hapless Nick. "I've got a gun," she announced ominously. "If you don't want this guy to get hurt, you'll let us drive out of here."

"Where to?" Joanna asked. "How far do you think you'll get? Do you want to add kidnapping charges to everything else?"

"You're never going to prove anything," Amy said, shoving the reluctant Nick ahead of her toward the driver's side of the Lexus.

"You have the right to remain silent," Joanna said. "Anything you say may be held against you. You have the right to an attorney. If you can't afford one, an—"

"Shut up!" Amy screamed. "Just shut up."

"Please, lady," Nick stammered. "I don't know what this is about, but—"

"Get in the car," she ordered. "Now!"

Prodding Nick forward with her purse, she pushed him as far as the front door of the Lexus. Then she slipped into the car ahead of him. She scrambled over the center console while pulling him behind her. Once they were both inside, she locked the doors.

"Get in the van, Jaime," Joanna ordered. "If she tries to drive out of here, stop her."

A man in a white shirt and tie emerged from the service office. "What's going on here?" he demanded.

"Get on the loudspeaker and clear this area," Joanna told him, waving her badge in front of him. "Everyone inside and under cover. Now!"

For a second or two the man blinked at her in stricken amazement, then he turned and sprinted back into the office. Within seconds, Joanna heard his frantic announcement to clear the area. In the meantime, Nick turned the key in the ignition and started the Lexus. Ducking behind the door of the van, Joanna pulled the Glock out of her small-of-the-back holster. Taking careful aim, she shot out first one rear tire and then the other.

To her amazement, the passenger-side door of the Lexus flew open and Amy Bernard shot out of it into the lot. "What the hell are you doing?" she railed. "You can't just stand there and shoot the hell out of my car. I'll have your badge."

Joanna noticed two things at once. For one, the driver's door opened. Nick sprang out of the car and sprinted into the relative safety of the office. For another, both of Amy Bernard's hands were empty. She had left her purse inside the Lexus. There was no weapon in either hand.

Seeing that, Joanna launched herself into the air. Her flying tackle caught Amy Bernard right in the midriff. The force of the blow knocked the wind out of both of them. They went down in a tangle of legs and arms. They rolled across the burning blacktop until they came to rest next to the wheel of the Econoline van. By the time they stopped rolling, Jaime Carbajal had entered the fray as well. As he reached for one of Amy's flailing arms, she nailed him in the eye with her elbow and sent him careening backward.

Joanna, too, was trying to grab on to Amy and hold her. She felt a sharp pain on her face as Amy's doorknob-sized diamond raked across her cheek. As Joanna's hand went reflexively to her face, Amy Bernard scuttled away. Before she made it to the open door of the Lexus, Joanna tackled her again. Jaime came charging back as well. By then, most of Amy's initial fury had been spent, and with two against one, it wasn't much of a contest. Between them, Joanna and Jaime shoved the struggling woman to the ground long enough to fasten a pair of handcuffs around her wrists. Once they were secure, Jaime hauled the still-screeching woman to her feet.

"You can't do this," Amy wailed. "It's police brutality. I have witnesses."

"Why?" Joanna managed, still gasping for breath.

It was almost as though she had thrown a glass of cold water in the woman's face. Amy Bernard stopped yelling and grew strangely still. "Why what?" she asked.

"Why did you kill Dora Matthews?" Joanna asked.

"She was a little piece of shit," Amy snarled. "She was going to ruin my son's life."

"I don't think so," Joanna said, shaking her head. "If anyone's going to ruin Christopher Bernard's life, it's you."

Jaime Carbajal was still holding on to Amy Bernard with one hand. Using his other hand, he reached into his pocket and pulled out a clean hanky, which he passed to Joanna.

"What's this for?" she asked.

"You're bleeding, Boss," he said. "Didn't think you'd want to wreck that brand-new uniform."

That night, when Joanna finally came home to High Lonesome Ranch, she had three ugly stitches in the jagged gash on her cheek and a sore butt from the tetanus shot.

"What in the world were you thinking?" Butch Dixon demanded once she told him what had happened. "Tackling her like that when you thought she had a gun; God knows what might have happened."

"She didn't have a gun in her hand," Joanna explained patiently. "And there wasn't one in her purse, either. We looked. She was bluffing the whole time."

"I don't care; you still could have been killed."

"I had to do something," Joanna said. "There were innocent bystanders everywhere. Someone else could have been hurt."

"*You* could have been hurt," Butch growled at her. "And it could have been a whole lot worse than just that cut on your cheek. What about Jenny and me?" he added. "Did you give a single thought to what the two of us would do without you?"

"I did, actually," Joanna admitted. "The whole time I was in the emergency room waiting to have my face stitched up and the whole way home from Tucson. Did you know," she added in a blatant bid for sympathy, "that when they're stitching up a facial wound, they can't deaden it because they might damage one of the nerves?"

Butch sighed. "I'm sorry," he relented. "I'll bet those stitches hurt like hell."

He took her in his arms then, and all the while he held her, Joanna felt more than a little guilty. It was bad enough that Butch had fallen for his wife's unconscionable womanly wiles. What was worse, Joanna Brady liked it. She doubted D. H. Lathrop would have been very proud of her just then, but somehow Joanna knew that Eleanor Lathrop Winfield would have been.

"By the way," Butch said. "You had a phone call a few minutes ago. Deputy Galloway."

Joanna's green eyes darkened. Considering everything that had happened since morning, her conversation with Ken Galloway could have been days ago rather than hours. "What did he want?" she asked.

"He asked me to give you a message," Butch replied. "He said, 'It's handled,' whatever that means. It was almost like he was talking in code and didn't want to give me too much information."

"It was code," Joanna said with a laugh. "I strong-armed him this morning into doing something nice. He's still pissed about it, but he did it. Good. That's all that counts."

"Did what?"

"Remember Yolanda Cañedo?"

"The jail matron with cancer, the one in the hospital in Tucson?"

Joanna nodded. "Right," she said. "Ted Chapman, the chaplain with the jail ministry, got all the inmates to join together and do something for Yolanda and her family. It seemed to me that the deputies ought to shape up and do as much, if not more. Ken Galloway wasn't exactly overjoyed at the prospect, but it looks as though he's come through."

"But his nose is still slightly out of joint," Butch said with a laugh.

"Too bad," Joanna replied.

That evening it was as though someone had posted an OPEN HOUSE sign at the end of the road that led to High Lonesome Ranch. Half a dozen cars showed up for a celebratory but impromptu potluck. As the kitchen and dining room filled up with guests and while Butch, Jeff Daniels, and Eva Lou Brady organized the food, Joanna and Marianne Maculyea sat in a quiet corner of the living room while Marianne nursed little Jeffy.

"I embarrassed myself in the emergency room this afternoon," Joanna admitted. That quiet confession, made to her best friend, was something she had yet to mention to her husband.

"What happened?" Marianne asked.

"I burst into tears."

"So what?" Marianne returned. "From the looks of those stitches, I would have done the same thing. That cut must hurt."

Joanna shook her head. "It's not that bad," she said. "And the cut isn't what made me cry. I was sitting there in the ER lobby, bleeding and waiting to see the doctor, when the full force of it finally hit me. That woman was after Dora. Poor Dora Matthews was the only target; Jenny wasn't. She wasn't in danger and never was. That's when I burst into tears. One of the nurses stopped by to see what was wrong; what I needed. She thought I was in pain. There were other people in the room who were in a lot worse physical shape than I was, Mari. I couldn't very well tell her it was just the opposite—that I was so relieved I could barely contain myself."

Marianne hefted little Jeffy to her shoulder and patted his back until he let loose with a satisfied burp.

"I know," Marianne said thoughtfully. "I felt the same way—that incredibly giddy sense of relief—right after Esther had her heart transplant. And then, when we lost her anyway . . ." Marianne paused, shook her head, and didn't continue.

Just then Jenny bounded into the living room with Marianne's daughter Ruth hot on her heels. Sensing the prospect of a possible game, both dogs trotted behind the girls. As Joanna looked at the two children, her heart swelled once more with love and pride and another spasm of enormous relief.

"Time to eat!" Jenny announced, standing with both hands on her hips.

"Time to eat!" Ruth mimicked, imitating Jenny's every gesture.

"Come and get it before we throw it out," Jenny added.

"Throw it out," was all Ruth could manage before dissolving into a gale of giggles.

Joanna reached out and took the sweet-smelling baby while Marianne set about fastening her bra and buttoning her blouse. Looking down at Andy's namesake, Jeffrey Andrew Daniels, with his fuzz of bright red hair,

Joanna felt fiercely protective about the little grinning lump of toothless humanity.

She looked up to find Marianne smiling at them both. "He's cute as a button," Joanna said.

"But do you think motherhood is worth it?" Marianne asked.

Joanna thought about Irma Sorenson and Amy Bernard. "I don't know," she said. "Ask me again in another twenty years."

"It's a deal," Marianne said. "Now let's go eat. I'm starved."

20

Christopher Bernard came alone to Dora Matthews's funeral on Friday afternoon. Joanna saw him sitting stiffly on a folding chair in the back row of Norm Higgins's funeral chapel. His navy sport coat, white shirt, and tie seemed totally at odds with his spiky purple hair, his braces, and his multiply pierced ears. Joanna smiled at him. He nodded briefly, but he left as soon as the service was over, and Joanna didn't see him again—not at the graveside service at Evergreen Cemetery and not during the coffee hour later at the Presbyterian Church's reception hall.

The second pew was occupied by Faye Lambert's Girl Scout troop, all of them wearing their uniforms and sitting at respectful attention. At the coffee hour after the service, while Jenny and the other girls milled around the refreshment table, Joanna sought out Faye.

"Oh, Joanna," Faye Lambert said. "I feel so awful about all this. I never should have sent the girls home. I guess I overreacted. It's just that I had tried so hard to help Dora fit in. I knew things weren't good at home, but it was stupid of me not to realize how bad they really were. Then, when I found out what Dora and Jenny had been up to that night—that they'd been off hiking around alone in the dark and smoking cigarettes— I was so terribly disappointed. I shouldn't have taken it personally, but I did. If only—"

"Stop it, Faye," Joanna told her. "What happened to Dora would have happened regardless. It's not your fault."

"But I can't keep from blaming myself."

"And my mother thinks it's her fault for calling CPS. And I think it's my fault for being out of town. It's nobody's fault, Faye. Nobody's except the killer's."

"I heard someone had been arrested," Faye said. "Some doctor's wife from up in Tucson? I can't imagine what the connection is."

Joanna sighed. "And I can't tell you, although I suppose the whole state will be reading about it soon enough. In the meantime, though, I almost forgot. I have something I need to give you."

"For me?" Faye Lambert asked.

"For the troop, really," Joanna said, digging in her purse for the envelope in which she had stored her poker-playing winnings. "When I was at the Arizona Sheriffs' Association meeting last weekend, some of my fellow sheriffs were kind enough to take up a collection for your troop—to help out with that planned trip to Disneyland at the end of the summer."

Faye opened the envelope and peered inside. Her eyes widened. "Why there must be close to seven hundred dollars here."

"Six ninety-nine, to be exact," Joanna said.

"How wonderful of them. I'll need to have the names of the people who made the donations," Faye said. "The girls will certainly want to send thank-you notes."

Joanna shook her head. "Don't bother," she said. "In this case, I believe they'd all prefer to remain anonymous."

Faye was called away just then. Joanna looked around the room for Butch and found him chatting with his mother-in-law. "Was that him?" Eleanor asked, when Joanna came up to join them. "That boy in the back row, the one with the purple hair?"

Joanna nodded. "That was Christopher Bernard," she said.

Eleanor's eyes filled with tears. She dabbed at them daintily with a lace-edged hanky. "Under the circumstances, it was very good of him to come, wasn't it? Very brave."

Joanna leaned over and gave her mother a hug. "Yes, Mom," Joanna said. "It was."

"That cut still looks awful. I wouldn't be surprised if it leaves a terrible scar."

"It probably will," Joanna agreed. "And if it does, I deserve it. That's the price of stupidity."

EPILOGUE

That night, when Joanna and Butch finally climbed into bed, Joanna scooted over and snuggled under his arm.

"Tough day?" he asked.

"Tough week."

"Was it only a week?" Butch asked, pulling her close while at the same time being careful not to touch her stitches. "It feels like more than a year since we got back home on Monday afternoon. I've barely seen you. You're working too hard, Joey. You'll wear yourself out."

"Sorry," Joanna said. She was so tired that she was almost falling asleep, but for a change Butch wasn't sleepy at all. He went right on talking.

"Whoever would have thought they'd do all that in the name of motherhood. I've always thought my mother was a couple of bubbles out of plumb, but Irma Sorenson and Amy Bernard put Mom to shame. And speaking of mothers, yours was certainly teary-eyed at the funeral this afternoon. It's nice that so many people came to the funeral and acted like they cared about Dora, but wouldn't it have been better if they had cared about her more when she was alive?"

"Amen to that," Joanna said.

"And would a male sheriff have sorted it all out the way you did?" Butch asked. "That yahoo from Pima County, what's his name?"

"Bill Forsythe."

"I can't imagine him seeing through Amy Bernard the way you did, or charming that confession out of Irma Sorenson, either. And even if I was upset with you for tackling Amy and getting hurt, it was still good work, Joey. I'm really proud of you, stitches and all."

Joanna was awake now. She sat up, turned on the bedside lamp, and looked Butch in the eye. "How proud?" she asked.

"What do you mean?"

"How proud are you?" Joanna asked. "Proud enough that you wouldn't mind if I ran for office again? I've been thinking about it, and I've decided I want to."

"Oh, oh. When do we start campaigning?"

"Soon," Joanna said. "Not right away, but soon."

"All right," Butch replied. "I'm new at this, so you'll have to tell me what I'm supposed to do."

"You have to smile a lot," she told him. "You have to go on the rubber-chicken circuit and nod your head attentively while I make speeches."

"Well, Scarface," he said, "I think I can manage that much. I can probably even do a fairly good job of it, but is there anything in it for me?"

She leaned over and kissed him. "I think so," she said. "I believe I know one or two things you happen to like. The good news is, you won't have to wait until after the election to get them."

Butch kissed her back. "Show me," he said.

And she did.